More praise for
Dying to Please

"Stalking takes on a fresh and creepy edge in bestselling author Linda Howard's newest thriller. Taut, electrifying, and oozing with sexual tension, *Dying to Please* is the latest in Ms. Howard's unbroken string of unforgettable books."
—*Romantic Times*

"*Dying to Please* is vintage Linda Howard. The unique storytelling elevates her to a special orbit."
—*Rendezvous*

By Linda Howard

DYING
TO PLEASE

LINDA HOWARD

BALLANTINE BOOKS • NEW YORK

This book contains an excerpt from the forthcoming *Cry No More* by Linda Howard. This excerpt has been set for this edition only and may not reflect the final content of the forthcoming edition.

A Ballantine Book
Published by The Random House Publishing Group
Copyright © 2002 by Linda Howington
Excerpt from *Cry No More* by Linda Howard copyright © 2003 by Linda Howington

www.ballantinebooks.com

ISBN 0-345-45340-9

Manufactured in the United States of America

First Edition: May 2002
First Mass Market Edition: November 2003

OPM   10 9 8 7 6 5 4 3 2 1

To two wonderful people and dear friends,
Phyllis and Basil Bacon.
Your friendship is a treasure.

ACKNOWLEDGMENTS
AND AUTHOR'S NOTE

Many thanks to Detective Jay Williams of the Mountain Brook Police Department, who took a big chunk of time out of his day to answer more questions than he anticipated and give me a guided tour of the town. Everyone in the department was wonderful whenever I called to check a detail. If I've missed anything or got it wrong, it's totally my error.

All of the addresses in this book are fictitious, as are the characters.

To Susan Bailey, George Edwards, Chad Jordan, Glenda Barker, Jim Robbins, Tom Comer—the character of Trevor Densmore is in *no way* based on *any* of you. Honest. An honorable mention to Linda Jones, who invented WMS.

If any reader is ever in the Birmingham area, you might want to check out Milo's Hamburgers. Any local can direct you to the nearest Milo's restaurant. And you might want to drive through Mountain Brook, where they really haven't had any murders in about five years now—and where the town clock is a Rolex.

—LINDA HOWARD

CHAPTER 1

THE CEILING FAN STOPPED.

Sarah Stevens was so accustomed to the slight whirring noise of the fan that the lack of it immediately awakened her. She cracked open one eye and peered at her digital clock, but there weren't any bright red numerals shining back at her. She blinked in sleepy confusion, then realized what was wrong.

The electricity had gone off. Oh, great.

She rolled over onto her back, listening. The night was quiet; there was no rumble of thunder to signal a violent spring storm in the vicinity, which would have explained the loss of power. She didn't close the curtains at night, since her rooms faced the back where the grounds had privacy fencing, and through her bedroom windows she could see the faint gleam of starlight. Not only was it not raining, the sky wasn't even cloudy.

Maybe a transformer had blown. Or an auto accident might have taken down a utility pole. Any number of things could have caused the power outage.

Sighing, she sat up and reached for the flashlight she kept on the bedside table. Regardless of why the electricity was off, her job was to minimize the effect it would have on Judge Roberts, make certain he wouldn't be inconvenienced more than necessary. He didn't have any appointments in the morning, but the old dear was fussy about what time he had breakfast. Not that he'd be cranky about it, but any change in his routine upset him more now than it had even a year before. He was eighty-five; he deserved to have breakfast when he wanted it.

She picked up the receiver of the telephone; it was a land line, so the loss of power wouldn't affect it. Cordless phones were great, until the electricity went off. In addition to this one, Sarah had made certain a few strategically placed phones in the main house were land lines.

No dial tone buzzed in her ear.

Puzzled, and growing slightly worried, she got out of bed. Her two rooms were over the garage, with her combined living room and kitchen area facing the front, while her bedroom and bath faced the back. She didn't switch on the flashlight; this was her home, and she didn't need guidance to make her way to the other room. She parted the curtains covering the front windows and looked out.

None of the strategically placed lights on the Judge's manicured lawn were lit, but to the right, the soft glow of the neighbor's security lights threw long, dense shadows across the lawn.

The electricity wasn't off, then. A breaker could have kicked, but that would have affected only part of the house, or the grounds, but not both. She stood very still, logic and intuition combining: (A) The electricity was off. (B) The phone lines were out. (C) The next-door neighbor had electricity. The conclusion she reached didn't require much of a leap: someone had cut the lines, and the only reason for doing so would be to break into the house.

Cat-silent in her bare feet, she ran back to the bedroom and got her nine-millimeter automatic from the bedside table. Her cell phone, damn it, was in her SUV, which was parked under the portico in back. She raced for the door, only briefly considering detouring to get the phone from her vehicle; her first priority was to protect the Judge. She had to get to him, make certain he was safe. He'd had a couple of credible death threats made against him during his last year on the bench, and though he had always passed them off as nothing, Sarah couldn't afford to be so cavalier.

Her quarters connected to the house via a staircase, with doors at both top and bottom; she had to switch on the flashlight as she went down the stairs so she wouldn't miss a step and fall, but as soon as she reached the bottom, she turned off the light. She paused for a moment to let her eyes readjust to the darkness, and as she did she listened, straining her ears for any sound that didn't belong. Nothing. Silently she turned the knob and opened the door in increments, an inch at the time, every nerve in her body alert. No strange sounds greeted her, so she stepped forward.

She was standing in a short hall; to her left was the door to the garage. Silently she tried the knob, and found it still locked. One door down was the laundry room; then directly across the hall was the kitchen. The battery-operated wall clock in the kitchen ticked monotonously, very loud now without the hum of the refrigerator to mask the sound.

She eased into the kitchen, the glazed ceramic tile cold beneath her feet. Skirting the huge cooking island, she paused again before entering the breakfast room. There was more light here, because of the big bay window that looked out into the rose garden, but that meant she was more likely to be seen if any intruder was watching. Her pajamas were a pale blue cotton, as visible as white. She would be an easy target.

That was a chance she'd have to take.

Her heart slammed against her rib cage, and she took a slow, deep breath to calm herself, trying to control the adrenaline rushing through her system. She couldn't let herself get sucked under by the whirlpool of excitement; she had to ride it, keep her mind cool and disengaged, remember her training. She took another deep breath and eased forward, minimizing her exposure by hugging the wall as closely as she could get without actually brushing against it. *Slow and easy,* she thought. One step at a time, placing her bare feet carefully so she was always balanced, she worked her way around the room and to the door that opened into the back hall. She paused again, listening.

Silence.

No. A muffled sound, so slight she wasn't sure she'd heard anything at all. She waited, breathing halted, eyes deliberately unfocused so her peripheral vision could detect any movement. The hall was empty, but after a moment the sound came again, slightly louder, from . . . the sunroom?

Two formal parlors, and the dining room, were on the front side of the house; the kitchen, breakfast room, library, and sunroom were all on the back. The sunroom was a corner room, with two walls composed mostly of windows, and two pairs of sliding French doors opened onto the patio. If she had been planning to break into the house, Sarah thought, she would have picked the sunroom as the best entry point. Evidently someone else had, too.

She sidled into the hall, paused half a heartbeat, then took two swift steps that carried her to the side of the huge, hundred-year-old buffet that was now used to store table linens. She went to one knee on the thick carpet, concealed by the bulk of the buffet, just as someone came out of the library.

He was dressed in dark clothes and carrying something big and bulky. The computer terminal, she thought, but the hall was too dark to be certain. He carried his burden into the sunroom, and she heard more of those muffled sounds, rather like the scuff of shoes on carpet.

Her heart was thudding, but all the same she felt a little relieved. The intruder was obviously a thief, rather than a criminal bent on revenge against the Judge. That wasn't to say they weren't in danger; the thief might be violent, but his movements so far were those of someone bent on stealing what he could and sneaking away. He was organized and methodical, witness the disabled electrical and phone lines. He had probably cut the power in order to disarm the alarm system, then cut the phone lines as an added precaution.

The question was, what should she do?

She was very aware of the weapon in her hand, but the situation didn't call for lethal force. She would shoot if necessary to save the Judge's life, or her own, but she wasn't about to shoot someone over some electronic equipment. That did not, however, mean she was inclined to let him get away.

It was also possible he was armed. Burglars as a rule *didn't* carry weapons, because if luck wasn't with them, the jail sentence for armed robbery was so much stiffer than for a simple robbery. Just because most burglars weren't armed, though, didn't mean she could afford to assume this one wasn't.

He was big; from what she'd been able to tell in the dark hall, he was around six feet tall, and burly. She could probably handle him in a face-to-face situation—unless he was armed, and then all the training in the world wouldn't stop a bullet. There was a big difference, her father had told her, between being confident and being cocky; cocky would get you killed. The best thing to do would be take him by surprise, from behind, rather than risk getting shot.

A whisper of sound warned her, and she held still as he moved into the hallway, reversing his path from the sunroom to the library. Now would be a good time to make her move, catch him when he came back out with his arms full of stolen goods. She placed her flashlight on the floor, then transferred the pistol to her left hand and silently began rising from her crouch.

Another man came out of the sunroom.

Sarah froze, her head exposed above the edge of the buffet. Her heart kicked sickeningly hard, almost taking her breath. All the guy had to do was look in her direction; her face, pale and distinct in the darkness, would be clearly visible.

He didn't pause as he stealthily followed the first man into the library.

She sank back against the wall, shaking with relief. She took several deep, quiet breaths, holding
each a few seconds to calm her racing heart. That
had been entirely too close; another second and
she would have been standing, fully revealed.

There being two men instead of just one definitely put a different spin on things. Her risk was
now doubled, and her chance of success halved.
Slipping outside to her SUV and calling 911 on the
cell phone was beginning to look like the best option, assuming she could get there undetected. The
biggest problem for her was leaving the Judge un-
protected. He didn't hear well; they could be in his
room before he knew it; he wouldn't have a chance
to hide. The old dear was valiant enough to fight
any intruder, which would at the least get him
hurt, and at the worst, killed.

Her job was to prevent that from happening.
She couldn't if she was outside talking on the
phone.

Her nerves gave one quiver, then settled down.
She'd made her decision; now she had to forget
everything else but her training.

There were scuffing sounds from the library and
a faint grunt. Despite her tension, she began smiling. If they were trying to hoist the fifty-five-inch
television, both of them would have more than
they could handle and their hands would be occupied. Maybe there wouldn't be a better time to
take them than right now.

She stood and stepped silently to the library, putting her back against the wall beside the door and
daring a lightning-fast peek inside. One of the
thieves had a penlight clamped in his teeth, allowing her to see that they were indeed wrestling with

the behemoth television. Bless their hearts, they had also ruined their own night vision, making it difficult for them to see her.

She waited, and after a few more grunts and a whispered curse, one of the thieves began backing out of the library, using both hands to grip one side of the television while the other man held the opposite side. She could almost hear their bones creaking under the weight, and thanks to the thin beam of the penlight as it shone straight into the first man's sweaty face, she could see the strain in his expression.

Piece of cake.

Sarah smiled. As soon as the first thief was clear of the doorway, she stuck out her bare foot and caught his left ankle, flipping it upward. He gave a startled yelp and crashed to his back in the hallway. The huge television slammed sideways against the doorframe, then toppled forward. The man on the floor yelled in alarm, the sound changing abruptly to a high-pitched scream as the television crashed down on his pelvis and legs.

His partner tried to catch his balance, his arms flailing. The penlight dropped out of his mouth, and in the abrupt darkness he said, "Fuck!" as he pitched forward. Sarah helped him along, pivoting and landing a punch to his temple. The punch lacked her full force, as he was already going down, but it was enough to sting her knuckles and send him sprawling bonelessly across the bulk of the television, which elicited even more screams from underneath. The unconscious man slowly slid to one side, crumpled and limp; a blow to the temple usually had that effect.

"Sarah? What's going on? Why is the power

off?" The Judge's voice came from the top of the back stairs, rising over the yells of the man pinned under the television.

Accurately judging that neither man was going anywhere in the next few minutes, Sarah went to the bottom of the steps. "Two men broke into the house," she said; between the Judge's partial deafness and the yowls of pain, she had to yell to make certain he heard her. "I have it handled. Stay there until I get the flashlight." The last thing she needed was to have him tumble down the stairs in the darkness, trying to come to her aid.

She retrieved the flashlight from the floor beside the buffet, then returned to the stairs to light the Judge's journey down, which he made with a speed that belied his eighty-five years. "Burglars? Have you called the police?"

"Not yet. They cut the phone lines, and I haven't had a chance to get my cell phone from my truck."

He reached the bottom of the steps and peered to the right, in the direction of all the racket. Obligingly, Sarah turned her flashlight on the scene, and after a second he chuckled. "If you'll give me that pistol, I believe I can keep these two under control while you make that call."

She handed him the pistol, butt first, then stripped the phone cord from the hall phone and bent over the unconscious thief. He was the big one, and she grunted with the effort it took to roll him over. Quickly she pulled his arms behind him, wrapped the phone cord around his wrists, then bent one leg backward and secured his wrists to his ankle. Unless he was extremely agile hopping on one foot—and with a concussion, no less—he wasn't going anywhere, regardless of whether or not there was a pistol trained on him; neither was the guy pinned under the television.

"I'll be right back," she said to the Judge, and handed him the flashlight.

Gentleman to the core, he tried to return it to her. "No, you'll need the light."

"The truck lights will come on when I hit the remote to unlock it; that's all the light I'll need." She looked around. "One of them had a penlight, but he dropped it and I don't know where it went." She paused. "I don't think I'd want to touch it, anyway; he was holding it in his mouth."

He chuckled again. "I wouldn't, either." In the reflected glow of the flashlight, she could see the sparkle of his eyes, even through his eyeglasses. Why, he was enjoying this! Come to think of it, retirement couldn't be nearly as interesting as sitting on a federal bench. He must have been thirsting for adventure, or at least a little drama, and here it had landed neatly in his lap. He'd be relating the details of this to his cronies for the next month.

She left him to the job of guarding the two thieves and retraced her steps through the breakfast room and kitchen. Her keys were in her bag, so she held carefully to the stair rail as she made her way upstairs in almost total darkness. Thank goodness she had left the door at the top open; the pale rectangle gave her a sense of orientation. Once in her quarters, she detoured to the tiny kitchen area and retrieved another flashlight from a cabinet drawer, then hurried to her bedroom and got the keys.

Thanks to the flashlight, her trip down the stairs was much faster than going up. She unlocked the back door and hit the "unlock" button on her remote even as she stepped outside. The front and rear lights on her four-wheel-drive TrailBlazer came on, as did the interior lights. She crossed swiftly to it, the flagstones cold and rough on her bare feet; darn it, she hadn't thought to put on a pair of shoes while she was upstairs.

Sliding into the driver's seat, she grabbed the tiny cell phone from the cup holder where she kept it and pressed the "on" button, waiting impatiently as it cycled through its program, then pressing the numbers with her thumb as she gingerly retraced her steps over the flagstones and went back into the house.

"Nine-one-one." The answering voice was female, calm, and almost bored.

"There's a robbery at Twenty-seven-thirteen Briarwood Road," she said, and started to explain the situation, but the 911 operator interrupted.

"Where are you calling from?"

"At the same address. I'm on the cell phone because they cut the phone lines." She skirted the kitchen island and entered the breakfast room.

"You're in the house?"

"Yes. There are two men—"

"Are they still in the house?"

"Yes."

"Are they armed?"

"I don't know. I didn't see any weapons, but they cut the power line to the house, too, so I couldn't really tell in the dark if they were armed or not."

"Ma'am, if you can, get out of the house. I have patrol units en route to the location and they should arrive in a few minutes, but you should get out of the house now."

"Send an ambulance, too," Sarah said, ignoring the operator's advice as she entered the hall and added the beam of her flashlight to that of the Judge's, playing it over the two men on the floor. She doubted either of them was capable of leaving under his own steam. The cries of the one under the television had subsided into mingled moans and curses. The one she'd punched in the temple hadn't moved at all.

"An ambulance?"

"A big television fell on one of the men, and may have broken his legs. The other man is unconscious."

"A television fell on them?"

"Just one of them," Sarah said, strictly honest. She was beginning to enjoy the phone call. "It's a fifty-five-incher, so it's really heavy. Both of them were trying to carry it out when one guy tripped and the television fell on him. The other guy landed on top."

"And the man the television fell on is unconscious?"

"No, he's conscious. The other one is the one who's out of it."

"Why is he unconscious?"

"I hit him on the head."

Judge Roberts glanced around and grinned at her, and managed to give her a thumbs-up with the hand holding the flashlight.

"So both men are incapacitated?"

"Yes." As she spoke, the unconscious one moved his head a little and groaned. "I think he's coming around. He just moved."

"Ma'am—"

"I have him tied up with phone cord," she said.

There was a tiny pause. "I'm going to repeat what you said to make sure I have it straight. One man was unconscious, but now he's coming around, and you have him tied up with phone cord."

"That's correct."

"The other man is pinned by a fifty-five-inch television, and may have broken legs."

"Correct."

"Cool," Sarah heard someone in the background say.

The 911 operator remained professional. "I have medics and two ambulances en route. Is anyone else injured?"

"No."

"Do you have any weapons?"

"One, a pistol."

"You have a pistol?"

"Judge Roberts has the pistol."

"Please tell him to put the pistol away, ma'am."

"Yes, of course." No sane police officer wanted to walk into a dark house when someone inside was holding a pistol. She relayed the message to Judge Roberts, who briefly looked mutinous, then sighed and put the pistol in a drawer of the buffet. Considering the condition of the two thieves, holding a gun on them wasn't necessary, even if it did appeal to his macho instinct.

"The pistol has been put away in a drawer," Sarah reported.

"Thank you, ma'am. The patrol units will be

there momentarily. They will want to secure the weapon, so please cooperate."

"No problem. I'm going to the door now to wait for them." Leaving Judge Roberts to watch their captives, she went into the front hallway and opened one of the nine-foot-tall double doors as two Mountain Brook black-and-whites with flashing roof lights pulled into the curving drive and stopped in front of the wide steps. "They're here," she reported to the emergency operator, stepping out so the officers could see her. Powerful flashlight beams played over her, and she held up one hand to shield her eyes from the glare. "Thank you."

"Glad to be of service, ma'am."

Sarah terminated the call as two uniformed officers approached her, hands on their weapons. From their car radios came a stream of static and staccato messages that she couldn't understand, and the rotating car lights made the manicured lawn look like a weird, deserted disco. To the right, the Cheatwoods' outside floodlights came on as the neighbors checked out the action. Before long, she figured, the entire neighborhood would be awake, though only a few would be crass enough to personally investigate. The rest would use the telephone to garner information.

"There's a pistol in the buffet in the hall," she said, giving the two officers that information up front. They were edgy enough as it was; their weapons weren't out, but each of them had his hand on his gun just in case. "It belongs to me. I don't know whether or not the thieves are armed, but they're both incapacitated. Judge Roberts is watching them."

"What's your name, ma'am?" the stockier of the

two asked as he edged inside the open front door, flashlight sweeping from side to side.

"Sarah Stevens. I'm Judge Roberts's butler."

She saw the glance they exchanged—*a woman butler?* She was used to that reaction, but all the stocky officer asked was, "Judge?"

"Lowell Roberts, retired federal judge."

He muttered something into the radio on his shoulder as Sarah led them through the dark entry, past the sweeping front staircase, and into the back hallway. Their flashlight beams played over the two men on the floor and the tall, thin, white-haired man standing watch at a safe distance.

The thief she had punched was conscious now, but definitely not with the program. He blinked several times and managed to mumble, "Wha' happened?" but no one bothered to answer. The one under the television was alternately sobbing and cursing, pushing at the weight on his legs, but he didn't have any leverage and he'd have been better off wiping his streaming nose; at least that would have accomplished something.

"What happened to that one?" the taller officer asked, shining his flashlight on the face of the one tied up.

"I hit him in the head."

"What with?" he asked, squatting beside the man and conducting a swift but thorough search.

"My fist."

He looked up in surprise, and she shrugged. "Caught him in the temple," she explained, and he nodded. A blow to the temple would addle King Kong. She didn't add that she had trained countless hours to be able to make that blow. If necessary she would elaborate, but until and unless a law enforcement officer asked her specifically about her skills, both she and her employer preferred to keep the bodyguard portion of her duties private.

The search produced a knife with a six-inch blade, secured in a sheath strapped to the man's ankle.

"They were carrying things out through there," she said, pointing to the sunroom door. "There are sliding glass doors and a patio outside."

In the distance came the shriek of sirens—many sirens—signaling the arrival of an entire fleet of policemen and medical personnel. Very shortly the house was going to be swarming with people, and she still had work to do.

"I'm going to sit over there out of the way," she said, pointing to the stairs.

The cop nodded, and Sarah took a seat on the fourth step, her bare feet tucked safely under her. First and foremost she needed to get power restored to the house, then phone service, though they could make do with cellular service. The burglar alarm had a battery reserve, so she had to assume the thieves had also done some damage there, or at least been smart enough to bypass it. Either way, the security people needed to check out everything. Probably the sliding glass doors would need to be replaced, too, but that could wait until morning.

With her list prioritized and firmly in mind and cell phone in hand, Sarah dialed Alabama Power to report a disruption in service. A good butler memorized all such pertinent numbers, and Sarah was a very good butler.

CHAPTER 2

IT WAS AFTER TWO IN THE MORNING WHEN THE RADIO ALERTED him to the call on Briarwood. Thompson Cahill was on his way home, but the call sounded a lot more interesting than anything he had waiting for him there, so he turned his pickup truck around and headed back up Highway 280. The patrol officers hadn't called for an investigator, but what the hell, the call sounded like fun and he could use a little amusement in his life.

He left 280 and got on Cherokee Road; at this time of morning there wasn't any traffic to speak of as he snaked his way through the quiet streets, so in just a few minutes he was on Briarwood. The address wasn't hard to find: it was the house with all the vehicles with flashing lights parked in front of it. That's why he was an investigator; he could figure out things like that. Duh.

He clipped his badge to his belt and got his sport jacket from the hook behind the seat, slipping it on over his faded black T-shirt. There was a tie in the pocket of the jacket; he left it there, since he didn't have a dress shirt to pull on over the T-shirt. He'd have to go for the *Miami Vice* look this time.

The usual assortment of uniforms were milling

around: cops, firemen, medics, ambulance atten-
dants. The windows in all the neighboring houses
were ablaze with lights, and occupied by onlookers, but only a few had been curious enough to
leave their houses and gather in the street. After
all, this was Briarwood Road, and Briarwood
meant *old money.*

The shift supervisor, George Plenty, greeted him.
"What are you doing here, Doc?"

"Good morning to you, too. I was on my way
home and heard the call. It sounded like fun, so
here I am. What happened?"

George hid a grin. The general public had no
idea how much fun police work was. Parts of it,
the parts that could drive a cop to drink, were grim
and dangerous, but a lot of it was just damn funny.
Plain and simple, people were nuts.

"The two guys were smart; cut the power and
phone lines, and disabled the alarm system. Seems
they thought only one old man lived here, so they
figured he'd never even wake up. Turns out,
though, he has a butler. The smart guys were busy
carrying out a big-screen television when she
tripped the one in the lead. He fell, the television
fell on him, and for good measure she sucker
punched the other one in the head as he was going
down and knocked him cold. Then she tied him up
with telephone cord." George chuckled. "He's
come around, but he still isn't making a lot of
sense."

"'She'?" Cahill asked, not certain George had
his pronouns straight.

"She."

"A female butler?"

"So they say."

Cahill snorted. "Yeah, right." The old guy might have a woman living with him, but he doubted she was his butler.

"That's their story and they're sticking to it." George looked around. "Since you're here, why don't you give the guys a hand with the statements, get this thing wrapped up."

"Sure."

He ambled into the huge house. Battery-powered lights had been set up in the hallway ahead, the spill of light—and the congestion of people—leading him to the scene. Automatically he sniffed the air; it was habit, a cop checking for alcohol or weed. What was it about the houses of rich people? They smelled different, as if the wood that framed the walls was different from the ordinary wood used to build ordinary houses. He detected fresh flowers, furniture polish, a faint, lingering odor of dinner— something Italian—but neither alcohol nor smoke of any kind, legal or illegal.

He reached the hallway and stood to the side for a minute, studying the scene. A team of medics was crouched around a guy on the floor; the carcass of a huge, broken television lay nearby. The guy on the floor was moaning and carrying on as they im-mobilized his left leg. Another man, a big dude, was sitting on the floor with his hands cuffed be-hind him. He was answering questions asked by a medic shining a light in his eyes, but it was evident the little birdies were still circling his head.

A tall, skinny old man with a shock of disor-dered white hair was standing to the left, out of the way, calmly giving a statement to an officer. He wore his dignity like a cloak, despite the fact that he was in a robe and pajamas, with slippers on his feet. He kept an eye on the proceedings even while he was answering questions, as if he wanted to make certain everything was handled correctly.

To the right was a flight of stairs, and on the fourth step from the bottom sat a woman in light cotton pajamas, talking on a cell phone. Her feet were bare and pressed closely together, perfectly aligned; her thick dark hair was tousled, as if she had just gotten out of bed. Well, she probably had. In another example of astute detective work, he deduced that she was the live-in, otherwise why would she be in pajamas? Damn, he was sharp tonight.

Even in pajamas, no makeup, hair a mess, she was a good-looking woman. No, better than just good-looking. She was downright fine—from what he could see maybe an eight, and that was without makeup. Money might not buy happiness, but it sure did buy old geezers some prime pussy, assuming he could still do anything other than reminisce.

The familiar anger bit at Cahill; he had lived, slept, and eaten with that anger for over two years now, and he was well aware he wasn't being fair to this woman. Finding out his wife was a lying, cheating bitch, then being dragged through a long, bitter divorce was enough to sour any man. He pushed the anger aside, though, to concentrate on the job. That was one thing he'd managed to do: the job.

He approached one of the patrol officers— Wilkins, fairly young, fairly new, and damn good, but then he had to be good to land a job with the Mountain Brook P.D. Wilkins was standing guard over the burly guy with the handcuffs and the concussion, watching as the medic checked him.

"Need a hand taking statements?"

Wilkins looked around, a little surprised to see him. In that split second of inattention the guy on the floor lunged forward, knocking down the medic and surging to his feet with surprising agility. Wilkins whirled, quick as a cat, but Cahill was quicker. Out of the corner of his eye he saw the woman on the stairs kind of flow to her feet as he pivoted on the ball of his left foot and planted his size eleven right boot square in the guy's solar plexus. He put just enough power in it to double the big guy over, gagging and gasping for breath. Wilkins was on the perp before he could hit the floor, and two other officers came up to help. Seeing they had him controlled—after all, he couldn't breathe yet—Cahill stepped back and glanced at the medic, who was wiping a bloody nose as he climbed to his feet. "Guess he wasn't hurt as bad as he acted."

"Guess not." Taking a pad of gauze from his supplies, the medic held it over his nose, then caught a deep breath. "Do you think he might be now?"

"He's just winded. I didn't kick him that hard." A full-power kick to the chest could stop the heart, crush the sternum, do all sorts of internal damage. He'd been careful not to even crack the guy's ribs.

Wilkins stood up, panting. "Do you still want to do some paperwork, Cahill?"

Paperwork was the bane of a cop's life; it was a measure of how bored Cahill was that he said, "Sure."

Wilkins nodded to the woman, who had resumed her seat on the stairs and her conversation on the cell phone. "Take her statement while we get Rambo here into a unit."

"Be glad to," Cahill murmured, and he meant it. The way she had moved when the robber tried to get away had piqued his interest. She hadn't screamed, hadn't scrambled to get out of the way; instead she had moved smoothly, totally balanced, her attention focused on the robber. If he himself hadn't stopped the guy, Cahill thought, she would have—or at least tried—which brought up a lot of questions he wanted to ask.

He approached the stairs, the glare of the battery-operated lights behind him and the stark light full on her face. She continued talking on the cell phone, her expression calm and focused, though she held up one finger at his approach to tell him she'd be finished in a moment.

He was a cop; he wasn't used to people telling him to wait. Faint irritation flashed through him, then instantly morphed into amusement. God, maybe he *was* an arrogant shithead, as his ex-wife had been fond of telling him. Besides, even if this woman was an old man's arm decoration, she was definitely easy on the eyes.

Because looking at her was so easy, he did, automatically cataloging the details: dark hair, not quite shoulder length, and dark eyes. If he were taking down a description of her, he'd have to say "brown" and "brown," but that didn't come close to the actual color. The lights glinted on her hair, making it look like dark, rich chocolate—and her eyes were darker.

He pegged her age at late twenties, early thirties. Height . . . five-five, maybe five-six. He was tempted to give her another couple of inches but realized it was her almost military posture that gave the impression of her being taller than she actually was. Weight between one-twenty and one-thirty. Her skin was smooth and flawless, with a creamy texture that made him think of licking an ice-cream cone.

She ended the call and extended her hand to him. "Thank you for waiting. I had waded through the phone company's computerized multiple-choice menu and didn't want to start over. I'm Sarah Stevens."

"Detective Cahill." Her hand felt small and cool in his, but her grip was surprisingly strong. "Could you walk me through what happened here tonight?" Her accent wasn't southern; it wasn't anything that he could nail down. Yeah, that was it: it wasn't anything. She didn't have any kind of accent.

"I'd be glad to." She indicated the stairs. "Would you like to sit down?"

He sure would, but then he'd be rubbing shoulders with her, and that wasn't a good idea while he was on the job. His thoughts since first seeing her had been way out of line, and that wasn't good. His mental brakes went on, and he pulled back from the edge, forcing himself to concentrate on the job. "No, thanks, I'll stand." He took his notebook from the pocket of his jacket and flipped to an empty page. "How do you spell your name?"

"*Sarah* with an *h, Stevens* with a *v.*"

"Are you the one who discovered the break-in?"

"Yes, I am."

"Do you know approximately what time it was?"

"No, my bedside clock is electric, but I estimate it has been about thirty minutes since I woke."

"What woke you? Did you hear a noise?"

"No. My quarters are over the garage; I can't hear anything from there. When they cut the power line, my ceiling fan stopped. That's what woke me."

"Then what happened?"

Sarah related the course of events as concisely as possible, though she was acutely aware of her thin pajamas and bare feet. She wished she had taken the time to put on a robe and slippers, or pull a brush through her hair. Or maybe even do a full makeup job and slip into a negligee, spray herself with perfume, and hang an "I'm available" sign around her neck. Then she could take Detective Cahill to her quarters and sit on the side of the bed while she gave him her statement.

She smiled inwardly at her own silliness, but her heartbeat had started racing at the sight of him and was still tripping along at too fast a pace. Through whatever quirk of chemistry or biology, or maybe a combination of the two, she felt an instant physical attraction to him. It happened occasionally— this sudden little buzz that made her remember what made the world go 'round—though not for a while, and never before this strongly. She enjoyed the private thrill; it was like riding a roller coaster without having to leave the ground.

She glanced at his left hand. It was bare, though that didn't necessarily mean he was single, or uninvolved. Men who looked like he did were seldom totally unattached. Not that he was handsome; his face was kind of rough, his beard was about eight hours past being a five-o'clock shadow, and his dark hair was too short. But he was one of those men who somehow seemed more *male* than the other men around him, almost as if he had testosterone oozing from his pores, and women definitely noticed that. Plus his body looked totally ripped; the jacket he wore over his black T-shirt disguised that somewhat, but she had grown up around men who made it a point to be in top physical condition, and she knew the way they moved and carried themselves. Unfortunately, he also looked as if his face would break if he smiled. She could appreciate his body, but from what she could see, his personality sucked.

"What's your relationship with Judge Roberts?" he asked, his tone so neutral as to border on uninterested. He glanced up at her, his face delineated by harsh shadows that made it impossible to read his expression.

"He's my employer."

"What do you do?"

"I'm a butler."

"A butler." He said it as if he'd never before heard the word.

"I manage the household," she explained.

"And that involves . . . ?"

"A lot, such as overseeing the rest of the staff; scheduling repairs and services; some cooking; making certain his clothes are clean and his shoes shined, his car serviced and washed regularly, bills are paid, and in general that he isn't bothered by anything that he doesn't want to bother him."

"Other staff?"

"No one full-time. I count as staff the cleaning service, two women who come in twice a week; the gardener, who works three days a week; his office temp, who comes in once a week; and the cook— Monday through Friday, lunch and dinner."

"I see." He consulted his notes, as if rechecking a detail. "Does being a butler also require you to study martial arts?"

Ah. She wondered what had given her away. She had noticed, of course, that beautifully judged kick with which he had taken down the big burglar and known immediately that he did his own share of training.

"No," she said mildly.

"It's an interest you pursue on your own time?"

"Not exactly."

"Can you be more specific?"

"I'm also a trained bodyguard." She kept her voice soft, so it wouldn't carry. "The Judge doesn't like it broadcast, but he's received some death threats in the past and his family insisted he have someone trained in personal security."

He had been totally professional before, but now he looked at her with frank interest, and a little surprise. "Have any of those threats been recent?"

"No. I honestly don't think he's in active danger. I've been with him for almost three years, and in that time he hasn't received any new threats. But when he was on the bench, several people did threaten to kill him, and his daughter in particular was uneasy about his safety."

He glanced at his notes again. "So that wasn't exactly a lucky punch you threw, was it?"

She smiled faintly. "I hope not. Just as your kick wasn't just luck."

"What discipline do you practice?"

"Karate, mainly, to stay in shape."

"What degree?"

"Brown."

He gave a brief nod. "Anything else? You said 'mainly.'"

"I do kick-boxing, too. How does this pertain to the investigation?"

"It doesn't. I was just curious." He closed the little notebook. "And there isn't an investigation; I was getting a preliminary statement. It all goes in the report."

"Why isn't there an investigation?" she asked indignantly.

"They were caught in the act, with Judge Roberts's property loaded in their pickup. There's nothing to investigate. All that's left to do is the paperwork."

For him, maybe; she still had to deal with the insurance company and getting the sliding glass doors in the sunroom repaired, not to mention replacing the broken television. The Judge, typical man, had loved his big screen and had already mentioned that he was thinking about getting a high-definition television this time.

"Does the fact that I'm also the Judge's bodyguard have to go in the report?" she asked.

He had been about to move away; he paused, looking down at her. "Why?"

She lowered her voice even more. "The Judge prefers his friends don't know. I think it embarrasses him that his kids nagged him into hiring a bodyguard. As it is, he's the envy of his crowd because he has a female butler; you can imagine the jokes they make. Plus, if there is any sort of threat to him, it gives me an edge if no one knows I'm trained to guard him."

He tapped the notebook against his palm, his expression still unreadable, but then he shrugged and said, "It isn't relevant to the case. As I said, I was just curious."

He might never smile, but she did; she gave him a big, relieved one. "Thank you."

He nodded and walked away, and Sarah sighed in regret. The packaging was fine, but the contents were blah.

The morning was beyond hectic. Getting any more sleep was impossible, of course, but getting anything accomplished was equally so. Without electricity she couldn't prepare the Judge's preferred breakfast, cinnamon French toast, or do laundry or even iron his morning newspaper so the ink didn't rub off on his fingers. She served him cold cereal, fat-free yogurt, and fresh fruit, which made him grumble about healthy food being the death of him. Nor was there hot coffee, which made them both very unhappy.

An enterprising idea sent her next door to the Cheatwoods' house, where she made a trade with the cook, Martha: the inside skinny on the night's happenings for a thermos of fresh coffee. Armed with caffeine, she returned home and calmed the troubled waters. After her own second cup, she was ready to tackle the day's problems again.

She didn't mind making a pest of herself, if she got the desired results. Two more phone calls to the power company produced a repair truck and a

lanky man who without haste set to work. Half an
hour later, the house hummed to life and he mo-
seyed away.

Harassing the phone company was more trouble; they—the unknown "they" in charge—had so
arranged things that either one could leave a voice
mail message, forgoing the comfort of speaking to
a real human in favor of saving time, or one could
tolerate being put on hold for an obscene amount
of time waiting for said real human to become
available for haranguing. Sarah was stubborn; her
cell phone weighed only a few ounces, and she had
unlimited minutes. She waited; but eventually her
persistence was rewarded, right before noon, by
another repair truck bearing that most precious of
human beings, Someone Who Could Fix Things.

Of course, as soon as the phone line was restored, the phone began ringing off the hook. All
of the Judge's friends had heard about the night's
adventure and they wanted a blow-by-blow description. Some busybody called the Judge's oldest
son, Randall, who called his two siblings, Jon and
Barbara. The Judge didn't mind so much his sons
knowing, but he wrinkled his nose in dismay when
the Caller ID flashed his daughter's number. Not
only did Barbara worry excessively about her father, but she had by far the most forceful personality of his three children. In Sarah's opinion,
Barbara was more forceful than an armored tank.
For all that, Sarah really liked the woman; Barbara
was good-hearted and good-tempered, just relentless.

The insurance agent arrived while the Judge was
still talking to his daughter, so Sarah showed him
the damage and was in the process of giving him

the pertinent information for filing the claim—she even had the Judge's receipt for the purchase of the television, which impressed the hell out of the insurance agent—when Judge Roberts came wandering into Sarah's tiny office, looking pleased with himself.

"Guess who called," he said.

"Barbara," Sarah said.

"After that. The call beeped in, thank God, or I'd still be talking to her. Some television reporter wants to come out and do a feature on us."

"Us?" Sarah asked blankly.

"You, mostly."

She stared at him, startled. "Why?"

"Because you foiled a robbery, you're a young woman, and you're a butler. He wants to know all about butlering. He said it would be a wonderful human-interest piece. Silly phrase, isn't it? 'Human-interest.' As if monkeys or giraffes would be remotely interested."

"That's wonderful," said the insurance agent enthusiastically. "Which station is it?"

The Judge pursed his lips. "I forget," he said after a moment. "Does it matter? But they'll be here tomorrow morning at eight."

Sarah hid her dismay. Her daily routine would be totally destroyed for the second day in a row. The Judge, however, was clearly excited about the prospect of his butler being interviewed. He and his friends were all retired, so they had no outlets for their natural competitiveness other than themselves. They played poker and chess, they swapped tall tales, and they tried to one-up each other. This would be a major coup for him. And even if it wasn't, she could scarcely refuse; as much as she adored him, she never forgot he was her employer.

"I'll be ready," she said, already mentally reshuffling her day so everything would be as perfect as she could make it.

CHAPTER 3

HE ALWAYS WATCHED ONE OF THE LOCAL STATIONS IN THE mornings, while he drank his hot tea and read the financial section of the *Birmingham News*. He liked to keep abreast of community happenings and politics so he could discuss them with his associates. He was actually very interested in what happened in and around Birmingham. This was his home; he had a vested interest in how the area fared.

Mountain Brook was faring very well, indeed. He took immense pride in the fact that the small town just south of Birmingham had one of the highest per capita income levels in the nation. Part of the reason for that was all the doctors who lived there and practiced in and around Birmingham, which had morphed from a steel city into an important medical center, with a disproportionate number of hospitals for its population. People came from all over the country, indeed, from all over the world, to be treated in Birmingham hospitals.

But it wasn't just doctors who lived in Mountain Brook. Professional people of all trades made their homes here. There was old money and there was new money. There were small starter houses, for young couples who wanted to live in Mountain Brook for the prestige and also for the school system for their children. There were mansions, and there were massive estates that made visitors gawk as they drove past.

His own home was his pride and joy, a three-story beauty fashioned of gray stone, lovingly furnished and maintained. It was eighteen thousand square feet, with six bedrooms and eight and a half baths. The four fireplaces were real, the marble was Italian, the two-inch-thick Berber carpeting the best money could buy. The pool was landscaped so it resembled a lovely grotto, with subtle underwater lighting and silver water trickling over stones before gently falling into the pool.

Five acres of land surrounded his home; five acres was a lot in Mountain Brook, with its astronomical land values. His property was completely walled in by a ten-foot gray stone wall. Huge wrought-iron gates guarded the entrance to his domain, and he was protected by the best security system available: motion sensors, cameras, and heat detectors, as well as the standard contact and breaking-glass alarms.

If he wanted to greet the world, he went to it; the world was not allowed to come to him.

A lawn service tended the grounds, and a pool service kept the pool sparkling. He employed a cook who came in at three P.M. and prepared dinner for him, then promptly left. He preferred to be alone in the mornings, with his tea and newspaper, and an English muffin. Muffins were civilized food, unlike the messy bacon, eggs, and biscuits so many people here seemed to prefer. Pop a muffin into the toaster and there was no mess afterward to be cleaned up, nor anyone required to prepare it for him.

All in all, he was very pleased with his world. He always got an extra measure of satisfaction from the secret knowledge of how he had acquired all this. If he had simply let things run their course, none of this would belong to him; but he had been insightful enough to realize that, left unchecked, his father would have made bad decision after bad decision until nothing of the business was left. He had had no choice but to intervene. His mother had grieved at first, but ultimately she had been better off; she had lived in cushioned comfort until heart disease ended her life seven years later.

It was extremely comforting to know that one could do what one must. The only limits he recognized were those he imposed on himself.

The television was background noise while he perused the newspaper. He had the ability to concentrate on several things at once; if anything interesting was reported, he would notice. Every morning the station did a fluff piece, which he usually ignored, but occasionally there was something marginally original on, so he was always aware of what was being said.

"Have you ever wondered what it would be like to have a butler?" droned the morning anchor's smooth voice. "You don't have to be royalty. In fact, there's a butler employed at a home in Mountain Brook, and the butler is . . . a woman. Meet Super Butler, coming up next, after these messages."

His attention caught, he looked up. A butler? Well, that was . . . interesting. He had never considered live-in staff because such intrusions into his privacy were intolerable, but the idea of a female butler was intriguing. People would be certain to be talking about this, so he needed to watch the segment.

The commercials over, the anchor began the lead-in, and the screen changed to a shot of a large, Tudor-style home with lush grounds and an elaborate flower garden. The next shot was of a dark-haired young woman, trim in black trousers, white shirt, and a close-fitting black vest, ironing a . . . *newspaper?* "Her name is Sarah Stevens," said the reporter, "and her day is not your average work-day."

"The heat sets the ink, so it doesn't smudge your fingers or dirty your clothes," she explained in a brisk, low-pitched voice as she smoothed the iron over the paper, sparing a brief glance for the reporter.

He straightened as if stung, his gaze unblinking as he stared at the screen. *Sarah.* Her name was Sarah. It was as perfect as she was, classic instead of flashy or trendy.

Her eyes were very dark, her skin pale and smooth. Her sleek dark hair was pulled back from her face and secured in a neat roll at the back of her neck. Electrified, he couldn't take his eyes from the televised image. She was . . . perfect. He had seldom seen such perfection in his life, and when he did, he made it a point to acquire it. For all the darkness of her hair and eyes, she wasn't Hispanic or any other ethnic group he could recognize. She was simply a little exotic; not flashy, not voluptuous, just . . . perfect.

His heart was beating fast, and he had to swallow the saliva that pooled in his mouth. She was so

neat and trim, her movements brisk and economi-
cal. He doubted anything as inane as a giggle had
ever passed her lips.

The next shot was of her employer, a tall, thin,
elderly man with white hair, glasses, and a narrow,
lively face dominated by a large hooked nose. "I
couldn't function without her," he said cheerfully.
"Sarah handles all the household details. No matter what happens, she has it under control."

"She certainly had things under control earlier
this week when there was a break-in here at the
home," the reporter continued. "By herself, Sarah
thwarted the robbery by tripping one of the thieves
as they carried out a big-screen television."

The shot returned to her. "The television was
very heavy, and they were off-balance," she said
with simple modesty.

Chills of excitement ran down his back as he
watched and listened, waiting for her to speak
again. He wanted to hear more of her voice. The
next shot was of her opening the back door of an
S-Class Mercedes for her elderly employer, then
going around to slide under the steering wheel.

"She is also a trained driver," the reporter in-
toned, "and has taken several defensive-driving
courses."

"She takes care of me," said the old man, smiling from ear to ear. "She even cooks occasionally."

Back to her. "My job is to make my employer's
life as comfortable as possible," she explained. "If
he wants his newspaper at a certain time, then I'll
have it there for him even if I have to get up at
three A.M. and drive somewhere to collect it."

He had never envied anyone before in his life,
but he envied that old man. Why should he have

someone like her looking after him? He would be better off with a live-in nurse named Bruce, or Helga. How could he possibly appreciate the treasure of her, the sheer perfection?

Back to the reporter. "Being a butler is a highly specialized vocation, and there are very few women who enter the field. Topflight butlers train at a school in England, and they don't come cheap. To Judge Lowell Roberts in Mountain Brook, though, price doesn't matter."

"She's a member of the family," said the old man, and the final shot was of Sarah setting down a silver tray loaded with a coffee service.

She should be *here,* he thought violently. She should be serving *him.*

He remembered the old man's name: *Lowell Roberts.* So price didn't matter? Well. They would see. He would have her, one way or another.

Judge Roberts slapped his knees with satisfaction. "That was a good piece, don't you think?"

"It was less painful that I feared," Sarah said dryly as she cleared away his breakfast things. "They certainly took a long time to film about sixty seconds' worth of story."

"Oh, you know how television is: they shoot miles of film, then edit most of it. At least they didn't get any details wrong. When I was on the bench, whenever I gave a statement or an interview, there was always at least one detail that was reported wrong."

"Will this give you bragging rights at your poker game?"

He looked a little embarrassed, but gleeful all

the same. "For at least a couple of weeks," he confessed.

She had to smile. "Then it was worth it."

He turned off the VCR, because of course he had taped the segment. "I'll get copies of this made for the kids," he said.

Sarah glanced up. "I can make copies, if you'd like. My VCR is a twin-head."

"Don't start speaking technical jargon to me," he warned, waving a hand as he ejected the cassette. "Twin-head sounds like something teams of surgeons would have to correct, and one head would die in the attempt. I think I have a blank in the library—"

"I have plenty of blanks." She always kept a supply, just in case he needed one.

He slipped the cassette into the cardboard jacket and carefully wrote, "Sarah's television interview," on the adhesive strip before handing the tape to her.

"I'll get them in the mail today. And don't forget your doctor's appointment at two this afternoon."

He briefly looked mutinous. "I don't see why I need a blood test again. I've been eating better, and my cholesterol should be down."

He had been eating better than he knew; when making his French toast, Sarah substituted Eggbeaters for the eggs in the egg-and-milk mixture, spiced up a little with vanilla flavoring, and she used low-fat, high-fiber bread. She also bought two types of syrup—one was regular, the other fat-free—and mixed just enough of the regular syrup with the fat-free that the taste of the blend didn't make him suspicious. He had agreed to eat a bacon substitute if he could just have his French toast, and she also served him fresh fruit every morning. In collaboration with the cook, she had managed to drastically reduce the amount of fat in his meals without his suspecting a thing.

Of course, he would credit any drop in his cholesterol level to eating the bacon substitute instead of real bacon, and resist any other changes if he knew about them. Outsmarting him was a constant, ongoing struggle.

"Two o'clock," she said again. "And if you cancel the appointment, I'll tell Barbara."

He put his hands on his hips. "Do your parents know what a bully they raised?"

"Of course," she said smugly. "My dad gave me lessons in bullying. I rated expert."

"I knew I shouldn't have hired you," he muttered as he retreated to the safety of his library. "As soon as I saw on your application that you're from a military family, I knew you'd be trouble."

Actually, it was her military family that had tipped his decision in her favor. The Judge was a former Marine; he had fought in the Pacific during World War II. The fact that her father was a retired Marine colonel, forced to leave the service because a car accident had severely damaged his right hip and leg, had weighed heavily with him.

She sighed. While she was making copies of the tape, she would have to make one for her parents, too. They were living in a posh retirement village in Florida, and they would love being able to show this to all their friends. She had no doubt her sister and two brothers would receive copies from their mother; then she would get a phone call from at least one brother, probably both, telling her about this buddy who wanted to go out with her.

The good part of that was that she was in Alabama, while one brother was currently in California and the other was TDY—temporary duty—in Texas. Dating anyone they knew was geographically impossible. But she was thirty years old, and they were all beginning to visibly worry because she hadn't yet shown any inclination to get married and help produce the next generation. Sarah shook her head, smiling to herself. She hoped she would get married, someday, but for now she was working on her Plan.

A butler was well paid; a good butler was very well paid. A butler-bodyguard earned well over a hundred thousand a year. Her own salary was pushing a hundred and thirty thousand. Her living expenses were negligible; she bought her SUV and her clothes, but that was it. Every year she salted away the vast majority of her salary in stocks and bonds, and though the stock market was down right now, she sat tight on her investments. By the time she was ready to put her Plan into effect, the market would be back up.

She would never leave the Judge, but, realistically, she knew he would live only a few more years. All the signs were there: she could get his cholesterol level down, but he had already had one severe heart attack, and his cardiologist, an old friend, was concerned. He was more visibly frail than he had been even six months ago. Though his mind remained sharp, this winter had seen one illness after another, each one taking a toll on his body. He would have maybe two more good years, she thought as tears stung her eyes, unless he had another heart attack.

But after the Judge was gone, Sarah wanted to take a year and travel the world. As a military brat, moving every two years or so, she had developed a real yen to see everything that was out there. Not being a masochist, she wanted to do it in comfort. She wanted to fly first class and stay in good hotels. With a healthy bank account and her investments as a cushion, she could go where she wanted whenever the mood took her. If she wanted to spend a month in Tahiti, she could.

It was a simple ambition, a yearlong treat in the middle of a lifetime of work. She liked her career, she wanted to get married someday and have one child, maybe two, but first she wanted that year just for herself. Since college she had resisted forming any romantic relationships of any depth, because in the back of her mind she was always aware that no man would like his girlfriend, fiancée, or wife heading off to wander the earth for a year—without him.

Her father didn't understand it. Her brothers certainly didn't understand it, because they were constantly being posted TDY all over the world. Her sister thought she was crazy for not getting married while she was still young and had her looks. Only her mother, she thought, understood her youngest child's wanderlust.

But the timing of her Plan depended on Judge Roberts, because for as long as he was alive, she intended to take care of him.

CHAPTER 4

HER FIFTEEN MINUTES OF FAME OVER, ALL THE STATEMENTS MADE and papers signed, Sarah gladly returned to her normal routine. She enjoyed the daily challenges of being in charge of a large home. She didn't have a large staff to oversee, but the house itself was an entity, in constant need of replenishing and small repairs, and she had to be on her toes to spot small problems before they developed into something major.

By the middle of the week, the phone calls from all the Judge's neighbors, friends, and family had dwindled, which was good because Wednesday was her day off. Wednesday was usually the slowest day of the week, the day in which very little happened; on Monday and Tuesday she handled the things that had cropped up over the weekend, and on Thursday and Friday she did whatever was necessary for any weekend plans the Judge had. In addition to Wednesday, she had half a day off on either Saturday or Sunday, depending on the Judge's schedule. She made herself very flexible to adjust to his needs, but in turn he was always mindful of her time off.

On her own time she dated occasionally—very occasionally, since she didn't intend to let a rela-

tionship develop beyond the casual—she shopped
and did "girl things," as her brothers had always
termed it, and she trained.

She had installed a set of free weights in the
basement and hung a punching bag, and she managed to work out for at least half an hour every
day, plus do a half-hour run. Some days she was
pushed to do that much, but if she had to get up
earlier than usual to get it done, she did. She considered staying in top shape part of her job, but she
also loved the way she felt, toned and springy and
full of energy.

In addition to karate and kick-boxing, she also
studied judo and archery, and spent an hour every
week at a local shooting range. She was good, but
she wanted to be better, even if she was in competition only with herself. Okay, she also wanted
to be better than her brothers. Daniel and Noel
were both ranked expert in marksmanship, as had
been their father before them, so if she intended to
handle a weapon, she felt honor-bound to uphold
the family standards. Whenever the entire family
got together, which was usually once a year—at
Christmas—she and her father and brothers would
find themselves on a shooting range taking some
target practice. Whoever won got possession of the
Susan B. Anthony dollar coin with the perfectly
centered bullet hole in it. Noel had threaded a gold
chain through the hole, and if he or Daniel won the
year's marksmanship challenge, they were actually
crass enough to wear the coin around their necks
when they were off duty, and flaunt it whenever
possible. As Sarah had loftily informed them, she
and her father both had more class than that.

She didn't wear it, but she had it. The coin and

chain were in her jewelry box. To her brothers' consternation, she had won it the past two years in a row. Since Daniel was an Army Ranger and Noel was in the Marine Force Recon, they didn't take the competition lightly. Come to think of it, maybe they wouldn't call with a buddy who wanted to meet her after seeing the videotape; they wouldn't like any of their pals learning that their little sister was a better shot than they were.

Sarah was certain that information would somehow slip past her lips in conversation, and neither of her brothers would ever believe it was an accident. Darn.

So on Wednesday, after giving herself a pedicure that morning and painting her toenails a dark iridescent pink, she sallied forth for her usual hour of sparring at a private gym. The guys might not get a thrill getting kicked by a bare foot with iridescent pink toenails, but the sight definitely gave her morning a lift. One could simply kick ass, or one could kick ass with style; she always preferred style.

Afterward, freshly showered and invigorated, she treated herself to lunch at the Summit, did some shopping, then went to an outdoor range for target practice. Only civilians used it; cops had their own range. There was an indoor range, but if you practiced indoors all the time, when you were outside—as she was at Christmas during the matches with the men in her family—then the varying weather and light conditions could throw you.

The day was warm and springlike, though it was only mid-March. The trees were in bloom; the jonquils and forsythia had long since bloomed;

lawns were turning green and growing. Here in the
sunny south, winter was abbreviated, about half as
long as the calendar said it should be. It could get
cold, there could be snow and ice, but for the most
part, winter only lightly touched the south, just
enough for the deciduous trees to lose their leaves
and the lawns to turn brown. After about six
weeks of such nonsense—usually by the middle or
end of January—the jonquils began pushing their
green feelers above ground and the trees began to
blush with swelling buds. The white Bradford pear
trees were now in full bloom, sprinkling lawns and
patches of woodland with explosions of color. All
in all, this wasn't a bad place to live. Sarah could
remember some of her dad's postings where it
seemed as if she hadn't taken a coat off for six
months. That was an exaggeration, of course, but
they had lived through some long, cold winters.

There was a light breeze when she arrived at the
range, but the temperature was in the high seventies and the breeze felt good even though she was
wearing sandals and a short-sleeved knit top. A
cold front was supposed to drop the temperatures
tomorrow and trigger a round of thunderstorms
during the night in advance of it, but for now the
weather was perfect.

She paid her fee and selected her target, then
slipped on her ear protectors and went to her
bench. The range had been dug out of a slope; any
bullets that missed their mark buried themselves in
a twenty-foot high clay bank. Bales of hay had
been stacked around as a further precaution
against any stray shot, though since she had been
coming there, she hadn't seen any accidents; people who practiced their marksmanship were gener-

ally serious about safety and what they were
doing.

She was on her fourth target when someone
walked up behind her and stood just behind her
shoulder. Intent on what she was doing, she finished, ejected the empty clip, and triggered the target return before turning to her visitor.

A little shock hit her in the center of her chest as
she recognized him. She removed her ear protectors. "Detective," she said, then for the life of her
couldn't remember his last name. "I'm sorry, but I
don't remember your name."

"Cahill."

"That's right. I'm sorry," she said again, and
didn't offer an excuse about being distracted that
night. She had been—by him more than the night's
events and all the phone calls she had been making—but she certainly wasn't going to tell him
that.

He was dressed pretty much as he had been
then, minus the jacket but in boots and jeans and
a T-shirt; today's choice was blue. The clingy knit
of the T-shirt clung to broad shoulders, thick bi-
ceps, and the hard slabs of his pectorals. She hadn't
been wrong in her assessment: the man was ripped,
without in any way being muscle-bound.

She was going to have a difficult time looking
him in the eye, because her own gaze didn't want
to go that far north. From the neck down, he was
the definition of eye candy.

The target, on the automatic line, had reached
them. He reached out and pulled it from the clip,
studied the pattern. "I've been watching you since
you got here. You're pretty good."

"Thanks." She began reloading. "What are you doing here? Cops usually use their own range."

"I'm here with a friend. Today's an off day, so I'm just bumming around."

Oh, dear. She didn't want to know that his day off coincided with hers. He seemed a tad friendlier today, though she had yet to see his face relax into anything close to a smile. She glanced at him in quick assessment. Seen in daylight, his face still looked rough, as if he had been hewn with a chain saw instead of the precision chisel of a sculptor. At least he was freshly shaved, but that more clearly revealed the granite lines of chin and jaw. He definitely wasn't a pretty boy. In fact, there wasn't anything the least boyish about him, pretty or otherwise.

"Are you off every Wednesday?" Damn, she wished she hadn't asked that. She didn't need to know.

"No, I swapped with another investigator. He had something special going on."

Thank you, Lord, she thought. She had never yet called a man for a date, but in his case she might give in to temptation and do it, even though he seemed to have the personality of a rock. She knew she wouldn't like it if a man dated her only for her body, so she didn't intend to let herself be guilty of the same offense.

"You could have shot them."

The growled statement was accompanied by a sudden direct look, and she almost blinked in shock. His eyes were blue, and the expression in them was hard and sharp. Cop's eyes, eyes that missed nothing. He was watching her, studying her reaction.

She was so bemused that it took her a minute to realize he was talking about the robbers.

"I could have," she agreed.

"Why didn't you?"

"I didn't think the situation called for lethal force."

"They were both armed with knives."

"I didn't know that, and even if I had, they hadn't threatened the Judge or me; they hadn't even gone upstairs. If the situation had developed into one where I thought our lives were in danger, I would have shot." She paused. "By the way, thank you for not putting anything in the report about my training."

"It wasn't relevant. And I didn't do the report; it wasn't my case."

"Thank you anyway." The reports were a matter of public record; the television reporter would have picked up in a heartbeat on the bodyguard aspect of her employment. But no questions of that type had been asked during the interview, and she and Judge Roberts certainly hadn't brought it up. Being his butler was high-profile enough without the general public knowing she was also a bodyguard. Not only would that knowledge take away her edge, but it would likely attract some of the very attention they both wanted to avoid.

"Your speech," he said, that hard gaze still locked on her face. "Law-enforcement background?"

Was following his conversation always like following a jackrabbit? Still, she knew exactly what he meant. Cops spoke a special language, with certain terms and phrasing, that was similar to the military's. Having grown up a military brat, she still thought of everyone else as civilians, and when she was with them, she automatically adjusted her phrasing to a more informal level. With Detective Cahill, however, she had just as automatically fallen into the old patterns.

She shook her head. "Military."

"You were military?"

"No, my father was. And both my brothers are in service. So if I say anything like 'target acquired,' I picked it up from them."

"What branch?"

"Dad was a Marine, Noel is a Marine, Daniel is Army."

He gave a brief nod. "I was Army."

Not "in the Army," but "was Army." That tiny difference in phrasing seemed to cover a huge difference in attitude. Some guys went in because they wanted the educational opportunity; they did their tours, then they got out. The ones who simply said they were Army were the dedicated ones, the lifers. Detective Cahill was too young though, to have put in his twenty in the military, then attended a law-enforcement academy and worked his way up the ranks to detective.

"How long were you in?"

"Eight years."

She digested that as she placed another target in the clip and sent it on its way. Eight years. Why had he left the service? She knew he had not been booted out, because he wouldn't be on the Mountain Brook force if he had a dishonorable discharge. Could he have received some injury, as her dad had, that made it too difficult to continue? She glanced at him, at that hard, fit body. Nope, she doubted that was the answer.

She didn't know him well enough to ask, nor was she certain she wanted to get to know him that well. No, she was lying to herself; she definitely wanted to get to know him better, find out if there was any humor at all behind that sourpuss face and cop's eyes; but in this case, she would be better off not knowing. Something about him—and not just his body, though that was mouth-watering—elicited too strong a response from her. It was those darn chemicals, or hormones, or something, but she knew this man could get to her. He could suck her into a relationship, against her better judgment, that would interfere with both her job and her plans.

That said, maybe she was a fool not to go after him. Maybe, sour disposition and all, he was a man she could love. Should she stick to her Plan, or go for the hunk?

Decisions, decisions.

She smothered a private laugh. Here she was going through all these mental gymnastics, and for all she knew, he didn't feel the tiniest scintilla of attraction for her. For all she knew, he was married with five kids.

Just leave it alone, she advised herself. If he was single, and if he was interested enough to make a move, then she would decide what to do.

At peace with that, she slipped her ear protectors into place, and he did the same. Taking the pistol in her left hand, she wrapped her right hand around her wrist to brace it, and calmly, methodically emptied the clip at the target. She was accustomed to a critical audience—namely her father and brothers—so Cahill's presence didn't bother her.

He removed the protectors again as the automatic return sailed the target toward them. "You shot left-handed that time."

God, he noticed everything. "I practice left-handed at least half the time."

"Why?"

"Because I take my job seriously. In a crisis, if my right hand is injured, I should still be able to protect my charge."

He waited until the target reached them, and studied the pattern. She was almost as good with her left hand as she was her right. "You train hard for a threat that you don't really think will materialize."

She shrugged. "I'm not paid to play the percentages; I'm paid to be ready. Period."

"Hey, Doc!"

He shifted his gaze down the line of shooters and lifted a hand in acknowledgment. "I think my buddy's ready to leave."

"'*Doc?*'" She was startled by the nickname.

"Long story." And one he didn't seem inclined to relate. "Miss Stevens." He nodded at her in good-bye and walked away before she could reply. He joined a husky guy in jeans, T-shirt, and baseball cap, who showed him a sheaf of paper targets, shaking his head in evident disgust. Detective Cahill examined the pistol, deftly reloaded it, then walked to the line and clipped on a new target.

Sarah didn't let herself watch. She had her own practicing to accomplish, so she burned three more clips left-handed, at different distances, before calling it a day. When she looked around, Detective Cahill and his buddy were gone.

CHAPTER 5

HAVING ESTABLISHED THAT RICK'S NEW PISTOL WAS INDEED A PIECE of shit. Cahill and his pal went to the gun shop where Rick had bought the pistol. Rick harangued the owner for almost an hour with no results: he had bought the pistol, it was registered in his name, the paperwork had been sent in the day he bought it, so his only recourse was with the manufacturer unless he wanted to resell the pistol to some other unsuspecting fool.

They repaired to a bar and grill for an early supper and some liquid comfort. "Order me a beer, will you?" Rick said, and took off for the bathroom. Cahill slid onto a barstool and placed the orders. He was already sipping his coffee when Rick returned.

"That was a sharp-looking woman you were talking to at the range." Rick plopped onto the barstool beside him. "You banging her?"

Cahill slowly turned his head and regarded his friend as coolly as if he had never before seen him. "Who the hell are you, and why the fuck would I care?"

Rick grinned in appreciation. "That was good. Very good. You almost scared me. Mind if I use it sometimes?"

"Feel free."

"So, are you banging her or not?"

"Not."

"Why not? She married or something?"

"Not that I know of."

"Then I repeat: Why not?"

"I haven't tried."

Rick shook his head and reached for his beer. "You gotta get over this, son. So you had a rough divorce; it's over. You're free now and you have to move on to the next flower."

Since Rick was a veteran of two divorces and was now looking for wife number three, Cahill sort of doubted the worth of any advice he gave concerning women. Rick was good at attracting them, but not at keeping them. But because he was also a good friend, Cahill didn't point out any of that. "Give me time," he said mildly.

"Hell, it's been a year!"

"So maybe I need a year and a half. Besides, I date."

Rick snorted. "Yeah, and they go nowhere."

"I don't want them to go anywhere. I just want sex." He stared morosely into his coffee. He definitely wanted sex, but getting it was a problem. The women who offered one-night, no-strings sex weren't the type of women he wanted. Sleaze had never appealed to him. The women who really attracted him were long-term types, and long term was exactly what he didn't need right now.

It wasn't that he hadn't gotten over Shannon; he'd gotten over her the minute he found out she was screwing a doctor from the hospital where she worked. But the divorce had been a bitch, with her fighting for everything she could get, as if she had to punish him for daring to not want her any longer. He didn't understand women, or at least he didn't understand women like Shannon; if she hadn't wanted out, then why screw around? Had she really thought he wouldn't kick her ass out if he found out? He did, he had, and she had reacted with an almost insane sense of vengeance.

He had tried to be fair. That said, he wasn't dumb; the first thing he'd done after finding out about her affair was take out half the money in their joint bank account and open an account in another bank under his name only. He had also removed her name from all his credit card accounts, which wasn't a hardship on her because she had her own credit cards, but damn if she hadn't gone ballistic when she found out. He figured she'd found out when she tried to charge something on one of his cards—after he kicked her out—so he'd made the right call on that.

He'd beat her to the punch in filing for divorce, but she had counterfiled and asked for everything: house, car, furniture, for him to pay all the bills for said house, car, and furniture, even though she made more at her job in hospital administration than he did as a cop, *and* she wanted alimony.

The attorney Shannon hired was a divorce shark known for his scorched-earth tactics. The only thing that had saved Cahill's ass was a sharp attorney and an even sharper female judge who had seen through Shannon like glass. He had thought he was sunk when he heard the judge was a woman, but his attorney had smiled and said, "This is going to be fun."

Cahill wouldn't classify divorce proceedings as *fun,* but in his case the results had been a relief. Since no children were involved, the judge had divided everything in direct proportion to their incomes. Neither of them wanted the house, so she ruled it would be sold, the mortgage paid off, and the profits, if any, split between them. Since Shannon made twice what he did, he would get twice as much of the profit as she because she was better able to afford another house. Cahill had glanced at Shannon when that decree came down, and saw her flush with rage and disbelief. Whatever she had expected, that wasn't it. She had begun whispering furiously to her lawyer, causing the judge to bang her gavel and order her to shut up.

Shannon got her car, Cahill got his truck, and they split the household furnishings. He didn't want the bed, because he suspected her doctor had been in it with her. But when he bought another house and moved into it, at least he'd had chairs to sit in, a table to eat at and dishes to use, a television to watch, and a brand-new bed to sleep in. After the money from the sale of the house came in, he had systematically gotten rid of everything he and Shannon had owned together. Not a single glass remained from his marriage, not a fork or a towel.

He just wished he could get rid of the bad taste in his mouth as easily as he had gotten rid of their possessions.

The worst aftereffect was that Shannon had made him doubt his own judgment. He had loved her and expected to spend the rest of his life with her. They'd had it all mapped out: though he had a good job with the Mountain Brook Police Department—Mountain Brook officers were the highest paid in the state—after she had received her degree in hospital administration and landed a position with a hefty salary, which she had done with astonishing speed, the plan was for him to quit the force and enter medical school. Looking back, he wondered if Shannon just had a thing for doctors. He had received some medical training in the Army and loved the challenge of it, but after a couple of years on the job in Mountain Brook, he had realized he loved being a cop more than he would ever enjoy being a doctor.

Maybe that was when Shannon had started wandering, when he changed ambitions. Maybe she'd had her heart set on big bucks and glittering social events, and when he didn't come through with either one, she felt free to look for them elsewhere. But he'd thought she loved *him*, regardless of which object he held in his hand, a scalpel or a gun. Why hadn't he seen that something was missing? And what if he made that kind of mistake again? He had a knack for sizing up suspects immediately, but when it came to figuring out his own wife, forget it. Now he couldn't trust himself not to pick someone else just like Shannon, and be just as blind to it until he was smacked in the face with infidelity.

"You're brooding again," Rick said.

"I'm good at it," Cahill muttered.

"Well, practice does make perfect. Hell, no wonder; you didn't even order yourself a beer. I'd be brooding, too, if I had to stick to coffee."

"I'll have a beer when we eat. I'm driving, remember?"

"Speaking of eating, I'm hungry." Rick looked around and spotted an empty booth. "Let's move over there and get some food." He grabbed his beer and slid from the barstool. Cahill got his coffee, signaled to the bartender where they were going, and joined Rick in the booth.

"Where did you meet her?" Rick asked.

"Who?"

"*Who?*" he mimicked. "The woman at the range. The one with the pistol and the great ass, which, by the way, nearly stopped my heart the way it was packed in those jeans."

"The house where she works was robbed last week. I took her statement."

"You just met her last week? There's still hope, then. You gonna ask her out?"

"Nope."

"Why the hell not?" Rick demanded, his voice rising. The waitress approached, and he broke off to grab the menu and open it. Cahill ordered a burger, fries, and a beer. After careful deliberation, Rick ordered the same thing. As soon as the waitress left, he leaned over and repeated, "Why the hell not?"

"God, you're like a broken record," Cahill said irritably.

"Don't you think she's hot?"

He sighed. "Yeah, I think she's hot." In fact, he thought she was hotter than hot; she was scorching. The problem was, he'd already suffered third-degree burns in the relationship wars, and he didn't have any skin to spare in another losing round. Not yet, anyway. He knew that, being human, he would eventually grow enough new skin to risk another flame, but not yet.

"Then ask her out! All she can say is no."

"She's not a one-nighter."

"So go for two."

"One night is no-strings-attached. Two is a relationship, and that's exactly what I don't want."

"Maybe not, but it's exactly what you need. When you fall off a horse, you get right back on, you don't brood about it. Get on that horse, pal, and ride."

Cahill groaned. "Give it a rest."

"Okay, okay." Rick drew lines in the condensation on his glass, then glanced up at Cahill. "You mind if I ask her out?"

He wanted to bang his head on the table. "Hell, no, I don't mind." He suspected this was where Rick had been heading all along, trying to make certain the way was clear.

"Okay. I just wanted to be sure. What's her name?"

"Sarah Stevens."

"Is she in the book? You have her number?"

"I don't know, and no."

"You didn't get her number? I thought you had to have that for your files, or something."

"She has private quarters in the house where she works. I don't know if she has a private number as well, but she probably does."

"She works in the house? Whose house? Where? What does she do?"

Sometimes talking with Rick was like conversing with a machine gun, the way he spat out questions. "She's a butler, and she works for a retired federal judge."

"I thought you said her name is 'Stevens,' not 'Butler.' "

"Rick. Pay attention. She's a *butler*, like in an English mansion. With a napkin folded over her arm, and things like that."

"No shit." Rick sat back, amazed. "I didn't know we had butlers in Alabama. Oh, wait, we're talking about Mountain Brook."

"Right."

"A *butler*. Is that cool, or what? I didn't know women could be butlers. Wouldn't she be, like, a butleress?"

Despite himself, Cahill grinned. "I don't think so. I don't think *butler* has a gender, kind of like *pilot*."

Rick's jackrabbit brain had already moved on. "So I could call her at this old judge's number. What's his name?"

"Lowell Roberts."

"Is his number listed?"

"I don't know, and if it isn't, no, I won't get it out of the files for you."

"Some friend you are. Why the hell not?"

"Because if it's unlisted, then it's because he wants his privacy, and I won't get her in trouble by giving the number to men who call her asking for dates."

"Aha!"

"Aha, what?"

"You *are* interested in her!"

Cahill stared at him. "Your brain scans," he said, "must be scary." The waitress slid the beers in front of them and he took a fortifying gulp.

"That's what makes me so good with computers, pal; I think outside the box."

"In this case, there's no box."

"The hell there isn't. You think she's hot, and you won't give me her number. The evidence is in, and the prosecution rests."

"You're not harassing me into getting that number for you. Hell, for all I know, it's in the book. You haven't even looked yet."

"What good is having a friend who's a cop if he won't give me inside information?"

"So you can ask him to look at a piece of shit pistol *after* you've already bought it, and pronounce it a piece of shit."

Rick's quick grin flashed. "Well, there is that, but don't get me sidetracked. I'm on a roll here. You're attracted to this woman. You went over to talk to her, even though, in your own words, you *know* she isn't a one-nighter. My friend, you may not realize it yet, but you're on the road to recovery. Before you know it, you'll be smiling at her across the breakfast table."

"I don't smile," Cahill said, though he was having to fight his amusement.

"So you'll be scowling at her across the breakfast table. That isn't my point."

Cahill gave up on convincing Rick of anything. "Okay, you're right; she's so hot I could walk on three legs every time I see her."

"Now you're talkin'."

"I'll break your back and chop off your legs if you call her."

"That's my boy!"

"Now, what's taking so long on those burgers?" He looked around and, right on cue, there came the waitress carrying two plates almost smothered with spicy fries.

Rick stared at him, then mournfully shook his head. "You're hopeless, Doc. Hopeless."

"So I've heard."

*   *   *

Sarah arrived back at the house feeling both tired and jazzed after a hard workout with her karate instructor. Judge Roberts was having dinner out, as he usually did on Wednesday so she wouldn't feel any need to check on him, as she would if he was anywhere in the house. She did a quick tour of the house to check that all the windows were closed and the doors locked, then headed upstairs to her quarters.

The Judge had put her mail on the small table beside the door to the stairs. She leafed through it as she climbed the stairs: a *Consumer Reports* magazine, a couple of catalogs, and a letter.

She placed the mail on her small two-person kitchen table, put a cup of water in the microwave, then went to the bedroom and stripped off her clothes. She had showered after her workout, but her clothes still felt sticky; she sighed in relief as the ceiling fan sent cool air washing over her naked skin. She'd had two hard workouts today, and tonight she was going to pamper herself. A facial was on her agenda, as was a long, relaxing soak in lavender-scented water.

She turned on the water to fill the tub, dumped in a pack of bath salts, then pulled on a robe and returned to the kitchen to dunk a tea bag of Salada green tea in the cup of hot water. While it was steeping, she flipped through the mail-order catalogs, then dumped them in the trash. The first sip of tea was heavenly; sighing, she sat down and opened the letter.

Dear Miss Stevens:

I would like to offer you a position in my household, in the same capacity you now fill. My estate is large and would benefit from your competent

*management, but I believe the benefit would be
mutual. Whatever your salary is now, I will increase it by ten thousand dollars. Please call me
with your decision.*

Hmm, that was interesting. She wasn't tempted,
but it was interesting all the same. She checked the
return address; it was a street in Mountain Brook.
Judging from the date at the top of the letter, he
must have sent it right after seeing the television
spot.

Somehow she hadn't expected other offers of
employment. It was flattering, but she had no intention of leaving the Judge, no matter how much
money was offered.

The offer deserved immediate attention, though,
so she picked up the phone and dialed the number
on the letter. After two rings an answering machine
picked up and a soft masculine recorded voice
said, *"You've reached 6785. Please leave a message."*

Sarah hesitated. She didn't like leaving a message, but people who had answering machines usually intended them to be used. "This is Sarah
Stevens. Thank you for your offer of employment,
but I'm very happy in my present position and I
don't foresee myself leaving. Again, thank you."

She disconnected and picked up her cup of tea,
then remembered her bathwater. She hurried to the
bathroom to find the water level high and steam-
ing: just right. After turning off the taps, she
turned on her Bose CD player, dropped the robe to
the floor, and stepped into the water, sighing as she
sank down in it to the level of her chin. The hot
water went to work on her tired muscles; she could
almost feel the tension oozing out of them. The

soft strains of the meditation CD filled the bathroom with the sound of slow, relaxing piano and strings. After another sip of tea, she leaned back and closed her eyes, happy and content.

"This is Sarah Stevens." He stopped the recording, hit *replay,* and listened again.

"This is Sarah Stevens."

Her voice sounded just as it had on television, low and warm. He had been standing beside the answering machine, listening, while she left the message.

"This is Sarah Stevens."

He couldn't believe she had turned down his offer. Ten thousand dollars! But that proved her loyalty, and loyalty was a precious commodity. She would be just as loyal to him, once he had her in his house.

"This is Sarah Stevens."

He had a talent for changing people's minds, arranging things to his own satisfaction. So she didn't foresee leaving her current position? He'd see about that.

CHAPTER 6

AS SHE SERVED HIS BREAKFAST THE NEXT MORNING, SARAH TOLD the Judge, "I got a letter yesterday offering me a job. He must have seen the television spot."

For some reason, Judge Roberts was regarding his French toast with definite suspicion. He had put on his glasses and leaned down to peer closely at it. "What are these red specks?" he demanded.

"Cinnamon. That's how you get cinnamon French toast."

"Humph. The doctor says my cholesterol is down twenty points. Switching to fake bacon wouldn't have brought it down that much, so I know you're doing something to my food."

"What can you do to French toast?" she asked rhetorically.

"Maybe it isn't the French toast. Maybe you're doctoring everything else."

She smiled as she placed a bowl of fresh sliced strawberries in front of him. "I'm not doing anything different," she cheerfully lied.

"Humph," he said again. "Does this scum-sucking bottom-feeder who's trying to hire you away from me know he'd be bringing a tyrant into his home?"

She stifled a laugh. "Scum-sucking bottom-feeder?" He was so old-school she wouldn't have been surprised if he had described someone as "dastardly." Hearing slang from him was almost on a par with the idea of the Supreme Court justices doing a rap song on the steps of the Capitol.

"Grandkids."

"Ah." Barbara's two children were fifteen and nineteen; that explained everything. Sarah amused herself for a moment picturing fifteen-year-old Blair, with her pierced eyebrow, teaching the dignified old judge the top-ten teenage insults.

"Next thing I know, you'll be feeding me tofu," he grumbled, returning to his suspicions about his food. He began eating his French toast, red specks and all.

Since the cook had been feeding him skillfully disguised tofu for several months now, Sarah had to hide a grin.

"What exactly *is* tofu?"

"Curds and whey, minus the whey. Soy curds, to be specific."

"That sounds revolting." He studied his fake bacon. "My bacon isn't made from tofu, is it?"

"I don't think so. I think it's just fake meat."

"Well, that's all right, then."

She would have kissed him on top of his white head if that hadn't been totally against all her training. He was such a dear, dutifully eating his fake meat while keeping a sharp eye out for encroaching tofu.

"What did you tell the bottom-feeder?"

"I thanked him for his offer, but told him I'm very happy in my present position."

His bright eyes twinkled through the lenses of his glasses. "You said he saw you on television?"

"He must have, unless one of your friends told him my name."

"It wasn't one of them, was it?" he asked suspiciously.

"No, I didn't recognize the name."

"Maybe he's a handsome young man who fell in love as soon as he saw you."

She barely restrained a snort of disbelief. "People who make job offers to someone without knowing her qualifications or getting references are idiots."

"Don't hold back, Sarah; tell me how you really feel."

This time she did laugh, because that line had to have come from Blair, too.

"You should at least interview," he surprised her by saying.

She stopped in her tracks and stared at him. "Why?"

"Because I'm old and won't be here many more years. This might be a good opportunity for you, and he might offer a higher salary."

"He did, but that doesn't matter. Unless you fire me, I intend to be here as long as you are."

"But more money would help you with your Plan." She had told him of her intentions to take a sabbatical and travel the world, and he had been enthused by the idea, studying the world atlas and researching different countries for things he thought would interest her.

"My Plan is in good shape, and people are more important than plans, anyway."

"Pardon an old man for getting personal, but you're a lovely young woman. What about marriage, a family?"

"I hope to have those, too, just not yet. And if I

never get married, I still enjoy my life and I'm pleased with my career choice. I'm happy with myself, which isn't a bad thing."

"No, it isn't. In fact, it's a rare gift." His smile was gentle as he studied her. "When you do get married—and notice I say *when*, not *if*, because one day you'll meet a man who's too smart to let you get away—he should get down on his knees every day and thank God for his good luck."

She wanted to hug him. Instead she smiled and said, "That's a lovely compliment. Thank you. Do you suppose he'd still feel that way if I fed him tofu?"

"He'll know you're doing it for his own good." Despite that gallant reply, he eyed his empty plate again.

"I promise: no tofu in your French toast."

He sighed in relief and began eating his bowl of strawberries, without pressing for a more extensive promise. He was sharp enough that the omission told her he suspected he had already been tofu-contaminated, and was submitting with good grace so long as his beloved French toast was safe.

After lunch she received the half-expected call from one of her brothers. It was Daniel, calling from Texas. "Hey, sweetie. That was a nice piece of tape; showed you to advantage. None of the guys can believe you're my sister, and they all want me to fix them up with you."

"Fat chance," she said, smiling.

"Why not? Some of them, I admit, I wouldn't set up with a two-bit hooker, but a couple are okay guys."

"Have I mentioned how proud I am of my Susan B. Anthony medallion?" she asked sweetly.

"You wouldn't."

"I believe the subject crops up every time I have a date."

"Moving right along here," he said hastily. "In her note with the tape Mom said you stopped a burglary with a fancy punch."

"It wasn't fancy. Straight to the temple."

"Ouch. Way to go, short stuff."

"Thank you." From an Army Ranger, that was high praise. "I was expecting either you or Noel to call, maybe both, when you saw the tape."

"Noel probably hasn't seen it yet. He isn't in-country."

That was enough said. She had grown up in a military family, and she knew what it meant. Noel was Force Recon; he had been in Afghanistan, then back in California, and only God and the Pentagon knew where he was now. Well, Daniel probably knew; he and Noel had their ways of communicating.

"What about you?" she asked.

"I'm still in Texas."

"I know that." She rolled her eyes, exasperated, and knew he'd heard that tone of voice from her often enough to visualize the eye roll.

"I'll be here until the cows come home. I'm getting rusty from lack of use."

When the cows come home was family code for shipping out that day, since the cows came home every afternoon. She didn't bother asking where he was going, not that he would tell her anyway.

"Have you talked to Mom and Dad?"

"Last night. They're doing fine."

Meaning he had also told them he was shipping out. She sighed, rubbing her forehead. Worry had become a permanent fixture in all military families since September 11, but Daniel and Noel were both lifers, and both good at their jobs. Fighting terrorists wasn't like fighting a regular war, with ground lost and gained by foot soldiers. This particular war required the stealth and skill of the special forces, hitting with quick, devastating force and then vanishing.

"Take care, and don't trip over your own big feet." That was sister code for *I love you, and be careful.*

"You too, Annie."

Despite her worry, as she hung up she smiled at his reference to her shooting skills. They had mercilessly called her Annie Oakley since the first time she won the competition. She couldn't have had two better brothers, even though when they were growing up, both of them had driven her nuts. She had been the tomboy of the family—their sister, Jennifer, had looked on roughhousing with disdain—and even though Sarah had been much smaller, that hadn't stopped her from inserting herself into their football games, sneaking along on their fishing trips, or wading in with her little fists whenever they tried to bully and tease her. In short, she had been a pest, and they loved her anyway.

She heard the little chime that signaled a door had opened, and glanced at the clock: straight up two o'clock. Right on schedule, the Judge was going out for his afternoon walk. On the way back he would stop at the mailbox and collect the mail; then he would want fresh coffee while he sat in his library and went through the day's haul. He loved mail, even junk mail, and leafed through all the catalogs. Retirement was good for one thing, he said: it gave him time to read things that weren't important.

She put on the coffee and readied the tray. The cook, Leona Barksdale, looked up from the tomato aspic she was making. "Is it that time?"

"On the button." She paused. "He asked about tofu today."

"Then he'll be looking for it, won't he? I'll be creative today, and not serve any. Let's see, dinner will be grilled asparagus, roasted baby potatoes and carrots, and a lamb chop. Nothing there even remotely resembling tofu." Leona checked on the rolls she had baking in the oven. "How was his cholesterol?"

"Down twenty points."

They gave each other satisfied smiles. Working in collusion to sneak healthy meals into someone who resisted the very idea was a lot more fun than feeding such food to someone who actually wanted to eat healthfully.

When she heard the door chime signaling his return, Sarah poured the coffee and filled a small four-cup carafe so he could refill his cup if he liked. Also on the tray was a plate with thin slices of Granny Smith apples, a wonderful fat-free caramel dip, and a few whole-wheat crackers, just in case he was feeling peckish. Before Sarah's arrival, his afternoon snack had often been a chocolate snack cake or a couple of Krispy Kreme doughnuts. Getting him to give up the doughnuts had been a battle, and that was one in which she sympathized with him. Giving up Krispy Kreme was truly a hardship.

"Sarah?"

Instead of going into his library, he was coming toward the kitchen. She and Leona exchanged puzzled looks; then she said, "Here, sir," and stepped to the door.

Besides his usual bundle of magazines, catalogs, bills, and letters, he carried a small package. "This came for you."

He usually put her mail, if she had any, on the small table in the hall. "That's odd," she said, picking up the tray. "I haven't ordered anything."

"There's no return address. I don't like this. It could be a letter bomb."

Several years ago, a judge in the Birmingham area had been killed by a letter bomb; that would make any judge cautious around suspicious pack-ages; the anthrax-laced letters in Florida and then New York and Washington areas hadn't helped.

"Why would anyone send me a letter bomb?" she asked as she carried the tray down the hall, him trailing behind her with his mail and the package.

She set the coffee service on his desk where he liked it, but instead of sitting down, he put his own mail on the desk and stood holding the package, staring dubiously at it. Normally she would never open her mail until she was in her quarters for the night, but she sensed he wouldn't relax until he knew the package didn't contain anything lethal.

"Shall we see?" she asked, reaching for it.

To her surprise, he didn't hand the package to her. "Maybe we should call the bomb squad."

She didn't laugh. If he was that worried, then it wasn't a laughing matter. "If it was a bomb, wouldn't it have gone off when you picked it up?"

"No, because if it was motion sensitive, it would

never make it through the mail system. Mail bombs use pressure or friction devices."

"Then let's think this through. Who knows me and would send something to me here?"

"We never should have done that television spot," he said, shaking his head. "It's brought the crazies out."

"First someone trying to hire me, and now someone sending me packages. Should we put it in water?"

Maybe it was that question, and a vision of them dunking the package in the tub and calling out the bomb squad, but he suddenly relaxed and smiled a little. "I'm being paranoid, aren't I? If anyone got a mail bomb, it would be me."

"It pays to be careful these days."

He sighed. "May I open it for you?"

She bit her lip. It was her duty to protect *him,* not the other way around. But he was of the generation that had been taught men protected women, and she could see this was important to him.

"Please," he said.

She nodded, moved more than she could say. "Yes, of course."

He stepped away from her, took a letter opener, and carefully slit the packing tape that sealed the seams of the small box. She found herself holding her breath as he opened the flaps, but nothing happened.

There was some brown wrapping paper concealing the contents. He pulled out the paper and looked inside, a faintly puzzled expression crossing his face.

"What is it?"

"A jewelry store box."

He set down the package and lifted out a small, flat box, about four inches square. It was white, with the store's name stamped on it in gold. He shook it, but there wasn't any noise.

"I think it's safe to say it definitely isn't a bomb," he said, handing the box to her.

She lifted the lid, and peeled back a thin layer of packed cotton. There, lying on another layer of packed cotton, was a gold teardrop pendant, with small diamonds circling a pigeon blood ruby. The gold chain was secured so it wouldn't rattle.

They both stared at the pendant. It was lovely, but disturbing. Who would send her such an exquisite piece of jewelry?

"That looks expensive."

Judge Roberts assessed it. "I'd place it at a couple of thousand dollars. Just a guess, of course, but the ruby is a good one."

"Who on earth would send me expensive jewelry?" Perplexed, she picked up the brown shipping box and pulled out the bottom layer of paper. A small white card fluttered to the floor.

"Aha." She bent and picked up the card, turning it over to read what had been written on one side. She flipped it and looked again at the other side, but it was blank.

"Does it say who sent it?"

She shook her head. "This gives me the willies."

He could see there was something written on the card. "What does it say?"

She looked up, her dark eyes plainly revealing how puzzled and disturbed she was, and handed him the card. "It says, '*A small token of my esteem.*' But who sent it?"

CHAPTER 7

IT HAD REALLY BEEN SO EASY, FINDING OUT HER SCHEDULE. HE could have hired a private detective to watch the house, but he didn't want to involve a third party who might later make inconvenient connections. He drove down the street several times, looking for a place where he could park and watch; the traffic, while not heavy, was still busy enough that he knew he wouldn't be noticed. The problem was that there wasn't any place where he could park. It was a residential street, with houses on both sides, and people coming and going from those houses throughout the day.

But all it took was time, and perseverance. Over the following days, during his hourly drive-bys, he noted when the gardener came, and carefully jotted it down in a little notebook he'd bought especially for this; it had a buttery-soft leather cover, much more tasteful than those brightly colored cardboard covers schoolkids seemed to prefer. An older woman, whom he presumed to be the cook, came every day around ten o'clock and left at five. The arrival and departure of a maid service was also carefully noted.

On Wednesday Sarah had left the house in the morning and hadn't returned until early evening;

he had tried to follow her, but she cut over to Highway 31 and he lost her in the traffic when he was caught by a red light. Rather than drive around fruitlessly, he stopped at a pay phone and called Judge Roberts's house. The number was unlisted, but he had attained the number soon after seeing Sarah on television. He knew people who knew people, and who were always eager to do favors for him. Really, all he had to do was ask, and within a few hours he had the number.

A woman answered the phone, and he asked for "Sarah," thinking that using her first name would imply a familiarity that wasn't there. Or rather, that wasn't there *yet*. He felt as if he knew her already, knew her dedication and loyalty and the utter perfection of how she looked, how she acted, even the way she sounded.

"Sarah isn't in today," the woman said cheerfully.

"Oh, that's right. Wait—I'm confused. Is today her off day?" He deliberately used a more casual tone and speech pattern than normal.

"Yes, it is."

"Is today Wednesday? I've lost track of the days, I've been thinking all day that it's Thursday."

She laughed. "Sorry, but it's Wednesday."

"Okay, I'll call her tonight, then. Thanks." He hung up before she could ask his name and number, and wrote down the information in tiny, precise letters: WEDNESDAY—DAY OFF.

He felt a thrill of excitement. For his purposes she would have to be away from the house. He thought he already had most of the information he needed, but he would continue watching to be certain. That was the key to success: leave nothing to chance.

He would have liked to have followed her around all day and seen what she did, what interests she had or what hobbies she pursued, but perhaps this was better.

He thought of the way she had looked when she drove out of the driveway, her dark hair loose, classic dark sunglasses shielding her eyes. She gave the impression of being aloof, mysterious, and slightly exotic. She drove her SUV with quick competence, as he had known she would; that was another measure of her dedication, that she had taken defensive-driving courses. She had put herself totally at the service of that old man, who had never done anything to deserve such devotion. Why, he hadn't even earned his money, but had inherited it. Which wasn't the same as his own receipt of an inheritance, because he had *saved* it from his father's stupid decisions. Judge Lowell had never done anything but sit on a bench and dispense opinions as if they were Pez.

His Sarah deserved more than that old man.

She deserved . . . everything.

He wanted to give her a gift, something that would make her think of him every time she saw it. And he wanted it to be something she wore, so he could imagine her wearing it every day, touching it, treasuring it. He couldn't give her clothing; that was too crass. Flowers faded and died, then were discarded.

Jewelry, then. Wasn't that what gentlemen had given their special ladies all through history? Special pieces of jewelry had been imbued with mystery, intrigue, even curses, though of course there wouldn't be anything cursed about his gift. He couldn't even make it as special as he wanted, because there wasn't time for him to have a piece made; he would have to buy something commercially produced, but even with that handicap he would find something out of the ordinary.

He would have to buy it from a store he hadn't patronized before, so there wouldn't be a chance of anyone recognizing him. And paying by check or credit card was out of the question; he didn't want anyone to be able to trace the gift back to him. In time, *she* would know, but that knowledge was for the two of them alone.

He drove to his bank and withdrew five thousand dollars, and left annoyed because the drive-through teller had asked to see his driver's license. On reflection, though, he decided she had done the correct thing. He hated to be delayed or questioned, but sometimes one had to accept the burdens of society.

From there he went to the Galleria, where he could be certain he would be merely one face among many, even on a weekday. There were several jewelry stores, and he browsed through all of them before making his selection. Sarah needed something simple and classic; she would be as appalled as he by gaudiness, but anything paltry would be an insult.

He finally settled on a teardrop pendant, a lovely ruby surrounded by diamonds, and suspended from a gossamer chain. The combination of ruby and diamonds captured her essence, he thought, exotic warmth surrounded by perfect coolness.

He paid in cash, to the clerk's astonishment.

With the square, flat box in his pocket he went into another jewelry store and bought a simple chain, secured in a box much like the one that contained the ruby pendant. That chain was a paltry hundred dollars, but it was the box he wanted, not the contents.

Next he had stopped at an office supply store and bought a small shipping box, filler paper to buffer the contents, and a roll of tape. He even remembered to buy scissors to cut the tape. Ordinarily it would have annoyed him no end to be put to so much trouble, but this time he was patient about all the steps he had to take. After all, this was for Sarah.

Once back in his car, he removed the cheap chain from its box and carefully replaced it with the pendant. There. Now if Sarah called the jewelry store whose name was on the box, she would find that no one there remembered selling a ruby-and-diamond pendant, that in fact they had no such item in stock. He pictured her lying in bed, tenderly touching the pendant around her neck and wondering who had sent her such a lovely gift.

He put the jeweler's box inside the shipping box, dropped in a small note to let her know how special she was, packed in the filler paper, and sealed the box. Too late he realized he hadn't bought a cheap pen for addressing the box. Scowling, he took his gold fountain pen back out of his jacket pocket. What would the rough cardboard do to the nib?

He could go to another store and buy a pen, but his patience was abruptly at an end. Unscrewing the cap from the expensive pen, he quickly printed her name and address on the box, in his irritation digging the nib into the cardboard. If necessary, he would buy another pen, but this box was going in the mail without any further delay.

The post office was busy, and despite the security concerns, the rushed postal clerk didn't notice that there wasn't a return address on the box. Besides, he knew his appearance inspired confidence. Mad bombers never looked distinguished and dignified; hairy and disgusting was more like it, from what he had seen. He was prepared even if the postal clerk had noticed the omission, having thought of a fictitious address, but he would rather the package be a total mystery when she received it.

He had noticed that Judge Roberts walked about the neighborhood every day at the same time and retrieved the mail from the mailbox when he returned home. Driving by at precisely the right time was difficult, and in fact he missed it by a few seconds, and short of stopping in the street to watch, he had to be content with what he could see through his rearview mirror. The old man took out the box and stood holding it in his hands, abruptly staring up and down the street.

The street curved and he lost sight of the old bastard. Damn him, why did he just stand there? What was he doing? Was he jealous that someone had sent a package to Sarah?

That was it. Of course he was jealous. He was old, but it had to stroke his ego to have a woman like her living with him, taking care of him. He probably told all of his cronies that he was sleeping with her.

The thought made him clench his hands in rage,

until he was gripping the steering wheel so tightly his knuckles were white. He could almost hear those cronies, cackling and sniggering like filthy-minded teenagers.

He had to free her from all that.

Sarah had placed the box on the kitchen counter, and as she ate dinner, her gaze kept straying to it. The pendant was undeniably lovely, but she didn't want to touch it. A gift was one thing; an anonymous gift was something else entirely. It was somehow . . . ominous, as if someone had sent her a snake in disguise. She thought the Judge was right and the television spot had attracted a weirdo who had fixated on her.

She would certainly never wear the thing. She seldom wore much jewelry anyway, usually just a pair of small gold hoop earrings and her wristwatch. Not only would a lot of jewelry be inappropriate for the job, it wasn't to her personal taste. She didn't like feeling weighted down, and she particularly disliked necklaces.

In addition to that, she had no way of knowing who had sent the pendant. It could have been anyone, someone she would pass in the grocery store or who could be standing beside her in the bookstore. If she only knew who he was, she could avoid him. But, not knowing, if she wore it and he saw her, he might take it as some kind of signal. A signal for what, she didn't want to imagine.

She was trained to spot anyone following her vehicle, and when she was driving the Judge, she was always vigilant. When she was alone was when she was able to relax, and now this bastard had stolen that from her. She would have to be on alert, watchful of everyone who came near her, and she hated that.

But maybe nothing else would happen. Some weirdos backed off when the object of their obsession didn't display the expected reaction. Or, if she spotted someone following her, maybe she wouldn't try to shake him; maybe she would lead him to the pistol range and let him watch her practice. That should cool his ardor.

All things considered, she would have rather he had sent her a death threat; at least she could take that to the police. A diamond-and-ruby pendant and a card saying *A small token of my esteem* couldn't be considered threatening. Weird, but not threatening. He had broken no laws, and, since he had chosen to remain anonymous, she couldn't even return the gift and tell him to leave her alone.

The jewelry store hadn't been any help. The first thing she'd done was call the store whose name was printed on the box. No one there had any recollection of selling the piece of jewelry; none of them remembered even *having* a pendant of that description. She thanked them and hung up, frustrated. He must have had an empty jewelry box lying around and put the pendant in it. That was a dead end; there were a lot of jewelry stores in the Birmingham area, plus pawn shops, where he could have bought it. He could have bought it anywhere. Tuscaloosa was just half an hour down Interstate 59; Montgomery was only about an hour away; even Atlanta could be reached in a couple of hours. Those were just the major towns; small towns had jewelry stores, too.

So there was nothing she could do, no way of finding this guy unless he walked up to her and asked why she wasn't wearing his present. She didn't know if she wanted *that* to happen, even if it would give her a chance to tell him to leave her alone. Since she was dealing with a weirdo, she didn't know what to do. Who knew what would trigger him to greater weirdness?

She didn't consider herself a martial arts expert, but she was better able to take care of herself, and protect her employer, than most people. She was in good physical condition; she was an excellent shot and a pretty good driver. That said, she didn't want to have to use those particular skills. She wanted to run the Judge's household and take care of him, period. But martial arts were useful only to a certain degree, and she was human enough to feel uneasy, even a little frightened, about this development. One episode, without any threat attached, did not mean she was being stalked, but now her mind was open to the possibility and it was all she could think about.

Damn him, for stealing her peace of mind.

There was nothing she could do, other than take precautions and be on guard, and she hated that helplessness more than anything else. She wanted to *do* something, but what? By nature and training, she was geared to go on the offensive, and in this case all her options were defensive.

There was nothing she could do but play with the hand dealt to her, no matter how she disliked it. She had the skills to handle this; she just had to be on her toes. Maybe this was a one-shot deal. Maybe whoever it was would call tomorrow to see if she had received his gift, and she would be able to discourage him. By training she was courteous, but she was the daughter of one military man and the sister of two others, and she knew the art of forceful discouragement. If necessary, she could be nasty.

Okay, essentially this was up to her, unless he did something overtly threatening. She would be stupid, however, not to at least alert the police department and get their input.

Their input? She snorted. *His* input, was more like it.

She had his card, or rather, the Judge had his card. She went down the stairs and wound her way through the house to the library, where the Judge was kicked back in his leather recliner, blissfully watching his new wide-screen, high-definition television. He looked up at her polite knock.

"I'm sorry to bother you, but do you have Detective Cahill's card? I think it would be smart to notify the police about this gift, even if they can't do anything about it."

"Good idea. The card is in the file on my desk." He started to get up, but Sarah waved him back down. Bless his heart, he simply couldn't accustom himself to the idea that he shouldn't do things for her, that she was there to do for him. It was all right for her to serve his meals and take care of his clothes—to people of his generation, that was women's work—but if it involved anything else, she continually had to be on her toes or he would be doing things like opening doors for her.

"I'll get it. Please don't get up." There was only one file on his desk, a manila folder marked ROB-BERY ATTEMPT. She smiled as she opened it. The file contained the police report, the newspaper clipping of the report, some photographs he'd made himself, and a copy of the insurance claim. Detective Cahill's card was paper-clipped to the police report, along with two other cards.

She wrote down his number and closed the file. "Thank you. May I get anything else for you this evening?"

"No, no, I'm fine." He waved her away, engrossed in a police chase on Court TV. It must be a guy thing, she thought, sighing. Her dad liked that show, too.

She returned to her quarters and punched in Cahill's number on her cordless phone, then abruptly disconnected before it could even ring. People with receivers could pick up conversations on cordless phones. She didn't have anything private to say, but the idea that the weirdo might be listening to her calls was revolting.

And the idea that he had so invaded her life with one gesture made her even angrier. She shouldn't have to worry about talking on a cordless phone. She should be able to go about her life as normal, damn it.

She went into her bedroom and picked up the receiver on the land-line phone. While she punched the numbers again, she pulled a pillow out from under the cover, wadded it into a ball, and shoved it behind her back as she made herself comfortable on the bed.

Cahill answered on the third ring, his voice a little surly. "Cahill." Okay, a lot surly.

"Detective Cahill, this is Sarah Stevens."

There was a slight pause, as if he was trying to place the name. "Yeah, what can I do for you?"

She could hear a television in the background, but no other voices. No kids playing, no low murmur of a wife asking, "Who is it?" He sounded alone, which was a relief. Too much of a relief, when she thought about it.

"I know there isn't anything the department can do, but I received an anonymous gift in the mail this afternoon that makes me uneasy."

"Anonymous?"

"There wasn't a return address on the box, or anything inside with a name."

"What was it, a dead cat?"

She was silent, and he sighed. "Sorry. You'd be surprised how many people used to get dead cats in the mail. That stopped when the post offices quit accepting boxes without return addresses."

"Well, they did this time. It's postmarked, but there's no return address."

"What was in the box?"

"An expensive diamond-and-ruby pendant."

"How expensive?"

"Judge Roberts says at least a couple of thousand. The card said, '*A small token of my esteem*,' but it wasn't signed. There was nothing threatening, but . . . it made me uneasy. The Judge was alarmed; he thinks the television spot attracted a crazy guy who's fixated on me."

"That's possible, but are you certain it isn't from your boyfriend?"

"No boyfriend." She could have simply said she was positive it wasn't from a boyfriend, but she didn't. *No boyfriend*. She couldn't be any plainer. If he was at all interested, he would call.

There was another little pause. Then he said, "Look, you're right, there's nothing we can do—"

"I know that. I just want to know what *I* should do, or be doing, in case this turns into something serious."

"Keep everything you get that's relevant. Keep a record of any weird phone calls, such as hang-ups or heavy breathing. Do you have Caller ID?"

"No, not on my private line."

"Then get it. And if you don't already have a cell phone, get one. Don't go anywhere without it, and I mean anywhere."

"I have a cell phone. It's always in my truck."

"Don't leave it in your truck, or in your purse. Have it in your pocket, so you can get to it immediately if you need to. Ordinarily I'd say you probably don't have anything to worry about, but an expensive gift is . . . unusual."

"That's what I thought, too." She sighed and rubbed her forehead. "I hate this. Nothing really has happened, but I feel as if something awful is *about* to happen."

"Don't let it get to you. Use common sense, be careful, and call if anything else happens."

"Okay. Thanks for your advice."

"You're welcome." He hung up, and Sarah gave a little laugh as she disconnected, too. Okay, she had her answer about one thing, at least: Detective Cahill might be single, but he was definitely not interested. His manner couldn't have been less personal, so that was that.

When she went back to the living room, she noticed that her curtains were open. She jerked them together, her heart pounding. Was he out there? Was he watching?

CHAPTER 8

NOTHING ELSE HAPPENED. THERE WERE NO PHONE CALLS, NO more gifts, and if anyone had followed her, she hadn't spotted him. Once she thought someone might be following her, but if he was, he wasn't very good at it, and a white Jaguar wasn't the best car for following anyone, anyway; it was too noticeable. Before long the white Jaguar wasn't anywhere in sight in her rearview mirror, swallowed up by the bumper-to-bumper traffic. Probably it was someone who also lived in Mountain Brook, who just happened to be driving the same route for a while.

She heard from her mom, and Noel had called, so he was okay for the time being. Daniel still hadn't checked in since he left, but they would have heard if anything had happened to him, so everything was fine on the home front. Jennifer was thinking about having another child, her third, but her husband, Farrell, wasn't enthusiastic; he was perfectly happy with their two sons. Knowing Jennifer, Sarah made a mental bet she'd have another nephew—or a niece—within the year.

Just talking to her mom had made her feel better. Everything was normal at home, and that was what she needed to know. Everything seemed to be normal

here, too, except for the existence of that pendant;
whenever she looked at it, she was reminded that
something wasn't right, that there was someone out
there who thought it was okay to send an expensive
gift to a woman he didn't know.

On her half-day off, on Saturday this particular
week, she had her hair trimmed, got a manicure,
then went to a movie. All the while she studied the
people and traffic around her, but there was nothing out of the ordinary. Nothing. The same face
didn't turn up at two different locations, no one
followed her. She thought it was too soon to relax,
but she did feel marginally better when she returned home.

Wednesday, her next off day, was much the
same. No one followed her as she went to her
karate class or kick-boxing workout. She spent a
long time at the pistol range, just because it made
her feel better, then went shopping at the Summit;
that also made her feel better. There was just something about a new outfit that was good for the
soul.

She browsed the bookstore for an hour, ate supper in one of the restaurants, then went to another
movie. She liked movies and saw a new one at least
every couple of weeks, but in the back of her mind
she knew she was making it easy for anyone to approach her if he wanted. If he was still out there,
she wanted to know who he was, what he looked
like. She couldn't go through life worried that
every man she saw might be him; she wanted a face
on him, so he wasn't just a vague, threatening
shape in her mind. Let him sit down next to her; let
him approach her.

But she sat alone in the darkened theater, and no

one spoke or even brushed against her when the movie was over and she made her way out of the theater, or even in the parking lot as she walked to her truck.

Everything looked normal at home when she drove up. The front-porch lights were on, the security lights were on, and she could see a light in the Judge's upstairs bedroom. The digital clock in the dashboard said it was almost ten o'clock, so he was probably getting ready for bed.

She parked in her usual place under the portico, and let herself in through the back door. After locking it, she began a quick tour of the house, as usual, to make certain everything was locked up. As she went toward the front of the house, she heard the television from the Judge's library, and a glance in that direction showed light spilling into the dim hallway. He must still be up, then.

The big double front doors weren't locked, which was unusual. She turned the dead bolt, then headed back to check the doors in the sunroom.

It wasn't like the Judge to leave the lights on upstairs; he automatically turned off the switch every time he left a room, even if he would be returning soon. She paused at the back staircase, a tiny frisson of unease prickling her spine. Maybe he had just gone upstairs for a moment and was coming back down to watch the ten o'clock news. She couldn't hear anything from upstairs, but then she wouldn't with the television in his library on.

She went to the open door of the library and peeked in. One lamp was on, the way he liked it when he watched television. He sat in his leather recliner, as usual, his head tipped to the side. He must have fallen asleep watching television.

But why was the upstairs light on?

Then she noticed the smell. It was difficult to identify, combining what smelled like feces with . . . something else. Her nose wrinkling, all her instincts suddenly on alert—was he ill, had he had a stroke or something?—she stepped farther into the room.

Seeing him from a different angle, she froze.

No. *Oh, no.*

There were dark spots and splotches sprayed across the room, and even in the dimness she could tell that some of the splotches had matter in them. She swallowed hard, standing still and listening for the intruder. She could hear the clock ticking, hear the thumping of her heartbeat, but there was no one else near . . . unless he was upstairs.

She wanted to go to the Judge. She wanted to straighten his neck, wipe the blood from his neck where it had trickled down from the small, neat wound in the side of his head. She wanted to cover . . . cover the gaping hole on the other side of his head where his skull was missing. She wanted to weep, to scream, to fly upstairs and search for his killer—a search-and-destroy mission, because no way would she let him live another minute, if she found him.

She didn't do any of those things. Instead she backed out of the library, careful not to touch anything else in case she smeared a fingerprint, and retraced her steps to the kitchen, where she had left her purse on the island. She had dropped her cell phone in it, not seeing a need to have the phone in her pocket when she was here, at home.

She'd been wrong.

She retrieved her pistol, too, and wedged her

back into a corner so she couldn't be jumped from behind, in case *he* was still in the house. Her hands were shaking as she turned on the phone and waited for the service to connect. It seemed like ages, though probably only the normal few seconds passed, before the phone showed it was in service. She punched 911, and waited for the answer.

"Nine-one-one."

She wanted to close her eyes, but she didn't dare. She tried to speak, but no sound came out.

"Nine-one-one. Hello?"

She swallowed, and managed a thin sound. "This is . . . this is Twenty-seven-thirteen Briarwood. My employer has been shot. He's dead."

Unlike the first time Cahill had been here, the house was blazing with lights. The drive, the street, even the sidewalk was clogged with vehicles, most of them with flashing lights. Crime scene tape kept the neighbors at bay, and this was momentous enough that this time they had forgotten it wasn't genteel to gawk; all the houses on the street were lit, and people gathered beyond the line of tape, whispering to one another. An officer was filming the crowd, because a lot of times a murderer would wait around to watch the show.

The news vans from the city's television stations were pulling up, and Cahill ducked under the line before anyone could grab him.

The front door was closed, guarded by a uniformed officer who nodded at him and opened it to let him inside. The crime scene people were already at work, carefully dusting and cataloging and photographing. The EMT personnel were waiting, because there was obviously nothing they could do now. There was no life to be saved, no injuries to be treated, just a body to be transported.

A murder in Mountain Brook was big news. The last one had been . . . what, five years ago? When the murder victim was a retired federal judge, the news was even bigger. The pressure on this case would be intense.

"Who called it in?" he asked, though of course he knew.

"The butler. She's in that room there." The officer nodded toward a room to the left.

It was a breakfast room, he guessed it was called, with the kitchen connected to it. She sat at the table, a cup of coffee clasped between her hands. She was pale and still, staring at the table-cloth.

She wasn't in her pajamas this time. She wore street clothes, and she still had on lipstick. He said, "Is your car out back?"

She nodded without looking up. "It's parked under the portico." Her voice was thin, toneless.

"What kind is it?"

"A TrailBlazer." There was no interest, no curiosity in her voice.

He went through the kitchen and found the back door in a hallway. The SUV was just outside. He placed his hand on the hood; still warm.

He went back inside and on the way through the kitchen, stopped to pour himself a cup of coffee. The pot was almost full, so she had evidently poured herself a cup, sat down, then forgotten to drink it.

She was still sitting exactly as he'd left her. He took the lukewarm coffee from her unresisting hands, dumped it down the sink in the kitchen, and poured another cup.

He set it in front of her. "Drink it."

She obediently took a sip.

He sat down at the table, to her right, and took out his notebook and pen. "Tell me what happened." That was an open-ended question, not pointing her in any particular direction.

"It's Wednesday," she said, still in that thin tone.

"Yes, it is."

"It's my day off. I did the usual things—"

"Which are?"

"My karate class, kick-boxing, the pistol range."

"What time was this?" She told him; he made a careful note of all the times and asked where she took the classes. He'd check them out, make certain she was where she said she was when she said she was. "What then?"

"I went to the Summit, went shopping."

"Did you buy anything?"

"An outfit at Parisian's, a couple of books."

"Did you notice the time?"

"Between four and five, I think. The time will be on the sales receipts." She still hadn't looked up, though she did take another sip of coffee.

"Did you come home then?"

She gave a tiny shake of her head. "No, I ate dinner out. At the . . . I can't remember the name. There at the Summit. The Italian place. I should have come home then, I usually do, but tonight I went to a movie."

"Why should you have come home?"

"Because then I would have been here. It wouldn't have happened if I'd been here."

"What movie did you see?"

This time she did look up, her eyes blank. "I can't remember." She dug in her jeans pocket and pulled out half of a computer-printed ticket. "This one."

He noted the movie, and the time. "I've thought of seeing that one myself. Was it any good?" He kept his tone casual, easy.

"It was okay. I went so he'd have a chance to approach me, if he was watching."

"What?" She had lost him on that one. "Who?"

"I don't know. The man who sent me the pendant."

"Okay, right." He'd get into that later. "What time did you get home?"

"Almost ten. The Judge's bedroom light was on. He usually goes to bed about ten, though sometimes he'll watch the news first."

"Does he have a television in his bedroom?"

"No." Her lips quivered. "He said bedrooms were for sleeping."

"So he watched TV in . . . ?"

"The library. Where I found him."

"Let's backtrack a little. What did you do when you got home?" He sipped his coffee, and she followed suit.

"I began checking to make sure the doors were locked. I always do, before I go to bed. The front door wasn't," she said. "Locked, that is. That was unusual, for it not to be locked. I could hear the television on, and I wondered why the light was on upstairs when he was still in the library."

"What did you do?"

"I went to the library door and looked in. He was in his recliner, his head tilted as if he'd fallen asleep."

He waited, not wanting to direct her now.

"I noticed the smell," she said faintly. He knew what smell she was talking about. "And I thought he might have had a stroke, or heart attack, and soiled himself. Just one lamp was on, so the light wasn't good; but when I stepped inside, the angle was different and I saw the . . . the blood. And the other side of his head. The splatters . . ." Her voice trailed off.

"I was afraid he was still in the house. Upstairs. That's why the light was on. I thought about going up there . . ." Again she trailed off.

"I hope you didn't."

"No. But I wanted to," she whispered. "I wanted to catch him. Instead I came back to the kitchen and got my pistol and cell phone, and stood in the corner while I called nine-one-one."

"Where's your pistol now?"

"In my purse. I put it there when the first car arrived."

"May I see it?"

"It's on the cooking island."

"Would you get it for me, please?"

She got up and went into the kitchen, moving like a zombie. He followed and watched as she retrieved the pistol. It was holstered, and when he checked the clip he saw that it was full. "I always reload after I've been to the range," she said, rubbing her forehead.

She hadn't cleaned it—not yet, though he bet she did on a regular basis—and the smell of burnt gunpowder still clung to it. The ballistics wouldn't match, he knew; she was too smart to make a mistake like that. He didn't think she had killed the old guy, but he couldn't afford to totally dismiss the possibility. People were most often killed by those closest to them, so until she could be ruled out as a suspect, she was definitely on his short list.

She watched him, her face expressionless, her eyes blank. She was totally closed in on herself; some people handled stress that way, by almost shutting down.

"Let's go sit down again," he suggested, and she obeyed. "Have you had any more gifts in the mail, or strange phone calls?"

"No, just that one gift. Nothing else. I did think someone was following me once, but he wasn't."

"Are you certain?"

"He turned off. And he was in a white Jaguar. You don't follow people in a white Jaguar."

"Not unless that's the only car you have." But if someone could afford a Jaguar, he could almost certainly afford some other kind of car, too. Jaguars were just too noticeable.

So she probably wasn't being stalked. That was the first thing she had thought of, though, when she came inside and found Judge Roberts's body. "You mentioned before that Judge Roberts had received death threats. Do you know anything about them?"

"His family will have the details. I know the basics, but it all happened before I came to work for him. His family—God, I have to call them."

"We'll notify the family," he said, gentling his

voice, because she suddenly looked shattered at the idea. "Do you have their names and numbers?"

"Yes, of course." She rubbed her forehead again. "He has two sons and one daughter." She gave him their names and numbers, then lapsed into silence, staring at the tablecloth again.

"I'll be back in a minute," he said, and got up. He wanted to check out the scene in the library himself and look through the rest of the house.

He was almost to the door when she asked, "Was he upstairs?"

He stopped. "No one else was in the house when the patrolmen checked." He already knew that from the report he'd received in transit.

"He didn't climb out an upstairs window, or something?"

"There wasn't any sign of anyone in the house. No open windows, nothing out of place." He couldn't tell her any more than that.

"I hope he wasn't upstairs," she said, almost to herself. "I hope I didn't let him get away. I should have gone up. I should have checked."

"No, you shouldn't—"

"I'd have killed him," she said flatly.

CHAPTER 9

SARAH WAS TENSE, EXHAUSTED, AND EMOTIONALLY DRAINED when she met Barbara and her family at the Birmingham airport at six the next morning. She waited downstairs in the luggage claim area, a cup of coffee in her hand. She had no idea how much coffee she'd had since finding the Judge's body, but she was absolutely certain caffeine was all that was keeping her going.

She hadn't slept; there hadn't been an opportunity to, even if she had been inclined. Cahill had kept coming back to her with questions, and she'd had so much else to do she hadn't had a spare minute. People had to be notified; the police department had taken care of the family, but she had called Leona and awakened her with the devastating news, rather than let her hear it on the early morning news. Then the calls from the family had started coming in, to such an extent that several times she had been on both the cordless phone and her cell phone.

Arrangements had to be made to house the family. Randall and his wife, Emily, had three children, all of whom were married with children of their own. Since they all lived in the Huntsville area, which was an easy drive, only Randall and Emily were coming down to stay until after the funeral, but everyone—three children and their spouses, plus four grandchildren—would be staying the night before the funeral.

Jon and his wife, Julia, lived in Mobile. They had two children, one married and one single. All of them were coming up to stay for the duration. Barbara and Dwight and their two children lived in Dallas, and they were all staying until it was over. That meant Sarah had to arrange accommodations for eleven people, including herself, in the middle of the night, available for early check-in . . . *very* early check-in. She would worry about the rest of Randall's family after the funeral arrangements were made.

She had booked them all into the Wynfrey. They would probably be eating at odd hours, so they needed somewhere with room service, plus the teenagers would be able to distract themselves in the attached Galleria. She herself had taken a room at the Mountain Brook Inn. It had come as a shock to realize she wouldn't be allowed to stay in the house, or even gather her own clothing. She had given a list of what she needed to Cahill, and he had arranged for someone to collect the items for her.

Her pistol had been taken, as well as the Judge's old service revolver that he kept locked in a display case. Cahill said they would be returned after the investigation was completed, meaning when it was determined whether or not either weapon had been used to commit the murder.

It was obvious she was a suspect, if only because of proximity. She had unlimited access to the house, she had a pistol, and Cahill himself had seen how proficient she was with it. She could ac-

count for her whereabouts, if only by receipts and
tickets, but most of all she had no motive, so she
didn't worry about herself; she couldn't, not with
the constant memory of the Judge's body playing
like a silent movie in her mind.

He had looked so frail in death, as if his spirit had
kept one from realizing how heavily time had laid its
hand on him. She was fiercely glad no one else had
found him, that there'd been one last final moment
between just the two of them, before strangers arrived and his body was taken over by them. The
dead have no dignity, but she knew he would have
hated having lost control of his bowels, hated his
family seeing him like that. He would have hated *her*
seeing him like that, too, but that was the least up-
setting of all the possibilities.

The escalator began spitting out people from the
newly arrived plane; Barbara and her family were
among the first. Barbara was a slim, pretty woman
with attractive gray streaks in her short blond hair;
she was red-eyed and pale, but holding together. She
spotted Sarah while she was still on the escalator,
and when she stepped off, she immediately crossed
to her, and the two women embraced. Tears stung
Sarah's eyes; all through this awful night she had desperately needed someone to hug her so she wouldn't
feel so horribly alone.

"Have you heard from Jon?" Barbara asked,
pulling back and dabbing her eyes with a tattered
tissue.

"They left Mobile about two this morning, so
they should get to the hotel at any time."

"I hope he's careful driving."

"I talked him into letting Julia drive."

"Bless you." Barbara hugged her again. "You're

still on top of things. Have the police found out anything?"

Sarah shook her head. "I don't know. I'm not family, so they won't tell me anything." Not that Cahill would tell her anything anyway, with her a suspect.

"I knew one of those rotten bastards would get out of jail and come after him," Barbara said tensely. "I knew it."

A fresh wave of guilt assailed Sarah. "I should have been there."

"Nonsense." Barbara fiercely turned on her. "It was your off day; there was no reason for you to be there. You couldn't stay with him twenty-four hours a day. Probably the monster watched the house and saw you leave. If it's anyone's fault, it's mine, for not hiring a full-time guard service. It isn't your fault, and I won't let you even think it, do you hear?"

Too late for that. Sarah thought it at least every five minutes. And what if, as she had thought in those first awful, stunned minutes, he'd been killed by the creep who had sent her the pendant? What if he'd actually come looking for her? Killing the Judge wasn't logical, but then people like that weren't logical, so why would their actions be? Knowing a weirdo was out there, she should have been at home instead of out trying to bait him into revealing himself.

It wasn't until Cahill asked about the death threats that she realized that was the most likely answer. Logically she realized it, anyway; emotionally, she hadn't shaken that first impression.

"It isn't your fault, either," she said firmly. "It's the fault of the man who pulled the trigger, no one else. We have to remember that." And she still should have been there. If it hadn't been for that double-damned pendant, she would have been.

Dwight, Barbara's husband, was over at the carousel collecting their luggage, helped by nineteen-year-old Shaw. Blair, fifteen, stood by herself, looking miserable as only teenagers can. Her honey-blond hair had metallic blue streaks in it, and her left eyebrow now sported two gold hoops.

"Wow," Sarah said, moving to reach out and to hug the girl. "Two hoops. When did you get the other one?"

"It's fake," she said. "I wanted to make Granddaddy freak out the next time we saw him, but—but now I won't get the chance!" Her face crumpled, and she hurled herself against Sarah, burying her face in her shoulder. Her slender body shook with sobs.

Barbara took charge of her daughter, taking her into her own arms and cuddling her as if she were still a toddler. Dwight and Shaw approached, loaded down with luggage and looking uncomfortable at the naked emotional display of the women. Barbara got Blair calmed down, and they all trundled out to Sarah's vehicle. Barbara got into the backseat with her kids, and Dwight buckled himself into the front passenger seat.

"What time are Randall and Emily supposed to be here?" he asked.

"Around eleven. He has a copy of the Judge's will in his safe deposit box, and his bank doesn't open until nine. He thought it might be needed."

Barbara rubbed her forehead. "I don't want to think about his will just now."

"There might be instructions for his funeral service," Dwight said gently.

"I still wish——" She sighed. "Never mind. Wishing won't accomplish anything." She took a deep breath as Sarah began winding her way through the parking deck toward the exit. "Sarah, do you know when the police will let us into the house?"

"It will probably be a few days, at least." And she would have to arrange for the library to be cleaned before the family went in; she didn't want them seeing the scene the way it was now, with the blood splatters and smears. She would give anything if she hadn't seen it, if the past twelve hours had never happened. If she could go back, she would do things differently; instead of dawdling at the Summit, she would go home, and whoever the killer was, when he arrived, she would handle it, and the Judge would still be alive.

But she couldn't go back. No one could.

"The detective will be in touch with you at the hotel," she said evenly. "Try to get some sleep, if you can."

"Will you be there? When the detective talks to us?" Barbara's voice wavered a little.

"If you want me to be." As desperately as she had needed to be hugged a little while ago, she just as desperately needed to be alone so she could release the pent-up grief and tears. She had held everything in, mostly from shock, but now the shock was wearing off and the awful reality was setting in.

"Please. I'm so—I can't think clearly."

Sarah didn't know how clearly she was thinking herself, but if Barbara wanted her present, she'd be there. If Cahill gave them a few hours, at least she'd be able to take a shower and change clothes, maybe even grab a nap, have breakfast. As soon as she thought of food, her stomach heaved and her throat tightened. No food, then, not yet. Maybe tomorrow.

Tomorrow. What was she supposed to do tomorrow? Whatever the family needed, she supposed. Whatever they didn't feel they could handle, she would do for them. And when the last service for them had been performed, then what?

She wasn't ready. She had thought she'd have another couple of years, getting things ready to put her Plan in motion. She had thought the Judge would gradually become more frail, or perhaps a heart attack or stroke would take him, but that his death would be natural. She would still have grieved, they all would have, but there wouldn't be this tearing pain at a life cut short. No one had been ready for him to leave, not like that.

She got the family settled in the hotel, and just as she was about to leave Jon and his family arrived. So she stayed, helping them, answering Jon's questions. Finding comfort in numbers, Barbara and Dwight and their kids joined them, and when Sarah finally left, they were all crowded into the suite's parlor, crying a little, but pulling together. Final arrangements would have to wait until Randall arrived, so they could all decide together, but Barbara already had out a sheet of the hotel stationery and was making a list of things that needed to be done.

Barbara would be all right. She was hurting, but she was making a list. That was the way women always coped, by doing what needed to be done.

The day was overcast, and cooler than it had been lately. Sarah welcomed the brisk air on her face as she walked to the TrailBlazer. For the moment she had nothing to do, and it felt odd. Barbara had her cell phone number and her room number at the Mountain Brook Inn, and would call her when it was time to meet with Cahill. Sarah had, probably, a couple of hours to herself. She could take that shower.

When she was finally in her room, the silence was almost overwhelming. For hours now she had been busy, surrounded by people, voices, lights. Even when she had been sitting and answering questions, she had been occupied. Now she was alone, and she had nothing to do for anyone else right now.

Methodically she unpacked the few clothes she had with her, hung the dress in the bathroom to steam out wrinkles while she showered, then finally stepped under the warm, relaxing spray. And there, finally, she cried.

She cried long and hard, crumpled against the side of the tub enclosure with her face buried in her hands and the water beating down on her head. The accumulation of hours of stress and grief tore at her. She wanted to destroy something, she wanted to hit and maim, she wanted . . . she wanted the Judge back, and that wasn't going to happen.

Finally, nature took its course and the violent weeping subsided into dull acceptance. She finished showering, wrapped her wet hair in a thick hotel towel, and fell naked into bed. The room was dim and cool, she was exhausted, and she slept almost immediately.

The phone woke her at ten o'clock. She fumbled for it, fighting to sound alert.

"Hello, this is Sarah."

"Sarah, it's Barbara. Detective Cahill will be here at eleven. Can you make it by then?"

"I'll be there," she promised, already rolling out of bed.

Her hair was a mess, still damp and tangled. She put on the small pot of hotel in-room coffee, then quickly blow-dried her hair and brushed her teeth. The coffee had finished brewing by then, so she grabbed a cup and sipped it while she returned to the bathroom and finished getting ready. There wasn't much to do; she didn't really care how she looked today, so she settled for moisturizer and a sheen of lip gloss, and let the rest go.

She didn't have much choice in the way of clothing. One dress, and two of her everyday butler's outfits. She didn't even have a jacket, and she thought she would need one today. Her normal white shirt, black pants, and black vest would have to do. Maybe Cahill could arrange for someone to get more clothes for her, if she wasn't going to be allowed back in the house by at least tomorrow.

The overcast was beginning to produce a light drizzle, and the chill went right through her on the short walk to her vehicle. The first thing she did after starting the engine was turn on the seat heater; the second was slide on sunglasses to cover her raw, swollen eyes.

Normally the drive to the Wynfrey was a short one, ten to fifteen minutes, but an accident on 280 slowed her and she arrived at the Wynfrey at about five of. As luck would have it, Cahill was entering the lobby at the same time. "Why are you here?" he asked brusquely.

"Because the family wanted me to be." She was a little surprised at how hoarse her voice was.

He nodded, then didn't speak again as they walked to the elevators. She was too tired and empty to say anything pertinent, or even not pertinent. Anything else he had to say to her would probably be more questions, so she was just as glad he refrained. To give him his due, he had to be as tired as she was, maybe more so.

She slanted a quick glance at him. Somewhere along the line he'd showered and shaved, and changed clothes. If he was exhausted, he didn't show it. Maybe he'd grabbed some sleep, too.

He was wearing a jacket and tie. The jacket reminded her that she was cold. "Could you have someone get a coat from the house for me?" she asked. "It doesn't matter which one."

He looked at her, a swift assessment that took in every detail. Maybe he noticed she was shivering. "I'll take care of it."

"Thanks."

The family was all gathered in Barbara's suite. Randall and Emily had arrived, and Sarah felt a moment of sharp guilt. She should have been here when they arrived, helped them get settled. Randall shook her hand, and reserved Emily hugged her, which made her eyes sting with tears again.

Barbara, a hostess to the core, had arranged for a selection of fruit and cheese and pastries to be brought to the suite's parlor. Bottles of water and a fresh pot of coffee stood ready. Sarah asked what everyone wanted to drink, and quietly set about providing them with it. It was a knack she had, re-membering how everyone requested his coffee, honed by the courses she'd taken in the school for butlers. Some butlers could do it in small groups of five or six, some needed to write it down, but for some reason in her brain the information was filed differently. When she was asked to describe Ran-dall, for instance, she would say six feet tall, gray hair, hazel eyes, likes his coffee heavy with cream. Emily was five-seven, dark red hair helped along every two weeks by her hairdresser, brown eyes, two sugars, no cream.

Cahill, she remembered from the endless cups of coffee he drank the night before, was as simple as it could get: black.

When she gave him his requested cup of coffee, he nodded his thanks, then said, "Is it too bright in here for you?"

She had forgotten she was still wearing her sun-glasses. "Sorry," she murmured, removing them. "I forgot." Her red, swollen eyes were par for the course in this room.

"Have you eaten anything?" Barbara asked, coming up to put her hand on Sarah's shoulder.

"Not yet."

"Then sit down and eat. Now. If I can, you can."

At Barbara's insistence, she put some fruit and Danish on a small plate, then looked around for a seat. Barbara had requested the hotel bring in extra chairs to accommodate everyone; the fami-lies were grouped together, of course, leaving the only empty seat beside Cahill. She sat down, and under Barbara's eagle eye forked a small square of fresh pineapple and carried it to her mouth.

She forced herself to chew, and the piece of pineapple began to expand. If she had been alone, she would have spit it out. Briefly she closed her eyes and fought the tightening of her throat. And she chewed.

"Swallow," Cahill said in a low tone that only she could hear.

She tried. On the second try, the pineapple actually went down.

Because eating was only common sense, she tackled that with the same determination she did everything else. While she listened to the family's questions and Cahill's matter-of-fact answers, she broke off tiny pieces of the Danish and concentrated on chewing and swallowing.

Something about Cahill's presence was reassuring. Though she couldn't remember any murders in Mountain Brook in the almost three years she had lived here, he came across as a man who had seen violent death before and knew how to handle it, knew what needed to be done. His matter-of-factness pulled the family away from any highly emotional displays as they unconsciously emulated him. Even Sarah could find a measure of gratitude for his presence; while he was there, he was in charge. All she had to do was chew and swallow.

She listened to his quiet, to-the-point questions about the death threats the Judge had received in the past. Barbara actually had a file on that, reminding Sarah of how much the daughter resembled the father in traits and mannerisms. She handed it over to Cahill, who looked through it, then glanced up. "May I keep this for a while?"

"Yes, of course." Barbara pressed her hands down hard on her knees. "It's so hard to ask this, but . . . where is Daddy? We need to make funeral arrangements."

"The coroner's office took charge of him," Cahill said. "After an autopsy is performed, he'll be released to you."

Heads came up all over the room. "Autopsy?" Randall said. "Why is there an autopsy?"

"It's automatic for a homicide. State law requires it."

"That's ridiculous," Barbara said. "If you don't know why someone is dead, it makes sense, but Daddy was *shot*. The reason why he's dead is obvious." Her voice trembled a bit on the word "dead," but she quickly firmed it again.

"The cause of death *seems* obvious, but sometimes a victim is shot or burned to hide the true cause, such as poison or strangulation."

"Does it really matter, at this point?" Julia asked.

"The manner of death tells us things about the perpetrator. For instance, who would have access to a particular poison? Who was strong enough to strangle a man? I think the cause of death in your father's case is clear-cut, a gunshot wound, but the final decision is the medical examiner's."

"So when will we be able to . . . to get Daddy?"

"I can't say for certain, ma'am, but tomorrow would be my best guess."

"Okay." She pinched the bridge of her nose, then looked at her brothers. "This is Thursday. If he's released tomorrow, we can have the funeral service on either Sunday or Monday. What do you think?"

"Sunday," Randall said immediately. "That will make it easier for people to attend the service."

"I agree," Jon put in.

"Then Sunday it is." She wrote that on her list.

Cahill looked at Randall. "Mr. Roberts, you mentioned you have a copy of your father's will. Do you have it with you?"

"Yes, it's in my briefcase."

"Do you know the contents?"

"No, it's sealed. I mean, we all know the general contents, but not the specifics."

"May I see it, please?"

Randall's eyebrows went up. "May I ask why?"

"Sometimes inheritances play a part in motive."

Barbara sucked in a sharp breath. "Are you suggesting one of us killed our daddy?" All over the room, people were bristling.

"No, ma'am; there's no evidence to suggest that. I'm just covering all bases. I don't want to overlook something that may help me solve the case."

Randall fetched the legal-size envelope. As he'd said, it was firmly sealed. Cahill glanced up for permission, Randall nodded, and with a firm motion he tore the flap open and pulled out the thick document.

He quickly scanned it, flipping the pages. Suddenly he paused, and his head came up, sharp blue eyes fastening on Sarah.

"Miss Stevens, did you know under the terms of this will you inherit a substantial sum of money?"

CHAPTER 10

SARAH BLINKED, MORE BEMUSED THAN STUNNED. SHE WAS A LIT- tle punchy and so tired that she wasn't certain she had heard him correctly. She even looked around, as if there might be another Miss Stevens in the room. Not finding anyone, she looked back at Cahill to find him still focused on her. "Do you mean me?" she asked, still not quite making the connection.

"Judge Roberts's butler, Sarah Stevens. That's you."

She nodded, and in the middle of a nod brought her hand up to rub her forehead. Maybe it was lack of sleep, maybe it was too much caffeine, but she was developing a wall-banger of a headache. "He left something to me?" To her distress, her voice wavered, and she felt her lower lip begin to quiver before she sternly bit down on it. She couldn't do anything, however, to hide the bright sheen of tears in her eyes.

"Of course he did," Barbara said. "He told us he was going to."

"He . . . he never mentioned anything to me."

"He thought you'd argue," Jon explained.

"Excuse me," Sarah said abruptly, and fled to the bathroom before she disgraced herself by breaking down and sobbing like a child. Her face crumpled as soon as she shut the bathroom door, and she grabbed a towel to hold over her mouth to muffle the sound.

By sheer force of will she brought herself back under control, choked back the sobs, and with a tissue blotted her eyes before the tears could fall. A few deep breaths brought a small measure of calm.

She didn't think anything had ever touched her so much as learning the Judge had left a bequest to her. She was well paid, and she had loved taking care of him. She had loved *him,* for his sweetness and humor, his old-fashioned manners, his basic goodness. She hadn't expected any inheritance, and in truth would indeed have argued against it. She had been with him not quite three years; how could that in any way supplant his children, his lifetime friends?

But evidently he hadn't thought the same, and neither did his family. The thought of their generosity brought the tears welling again, and she determinedly blotted them away. She would *not* cry, not here and not now. The family had enough to bear without her adding her own emotional distress to the load.

A cold wet washcloth cooled her cheeks, and felt good to her aching head when she pressed it to her forehead. She would have liked to lie down with an ice pack on her head, but, like crying, that, too, would have to be postponed.

Feeling more in control, she rejoined them in the parlor. "I'm sorry," she murmured, resuming her seat beside Cahill.

"I take it you didn't know."

She shook her head. He either believed her or he

didn't. She couldn't work up enough energy to
care.

"Daddy swore us to secrecy," Barbara said. A
tiny, sad smile wavered on her mouth. "He got a
kick out of sneaking something by you. He said it
was the only thing he ever got by you."

"He said you confiscated his Snickers bars,"
Shaw put in, a real smile breaking over his face and
banishing the sadness and tension. "He always
gorged on them when he came to visit, because he
knew he couldn't have them when he got home."

"And his Twinkies. I'd sneak Twinkies to him
when I came," Blair confessed.

Sarah groaned, looking at a roomful of guilty,
suddenly smiling faces. "No wonder I had such a
time getting his cholesterol level down!"

Barbara patted her knee. "He loved you for taking care of him. We love you for taking care of
him. When he mentioned putting you in his will,
we were all for it."

Cahill cleared his throat, drawing attention back
to him. "Thank you for the information," he said,
getting to his feet. "I know this is a difficult time
for you all, and I appreciate your help. I want you
to know I'm sorry about your father, and we're
doing everything we can to find the perpetrator. I'll
run these names, and with any luck we'll find one
of these guys in the area."

Like lemmings, everyone else stood, and a flurry
of handshakes and thank-yous broke out as Cahill
slowly but inexorably inched his way toward the
door. Somehow he had Sarah by the elbow and was
pulling her with him. "I'll walk you to your truck,"
he said.

Inwardly she sighed. He probably had some

more questions to ask her. Since she was included in the will, in his mind she was probably that much more suspect. But he was doing his job, so she grabbed her bag and sunglasses and managed a quick good-bye to everyone, with instructions to call her if they needed anything, before he had her out the door.

There was a couple in the elevator, so he didn't say anything on the ride down to the lobby. They stepped outside, and the cold, damp wind slapped her in the face, making her shiver. The temperature seemed to be dropping, and the drizzle had progressed to a steady light rain. She hugged her arms and said, "I didn't kill him."

"I'm fairly sure of that myself," he said mildly.

Startled, she looked up at him. "Then why all the suspicious questions?"

"Because it's my job. You'll be checked out, you'll be looked at, and you'll be questioned."

"Cross every *t* and dot every *i*."

"You got it." He took off his jacket and held it over her head. "Come on."

She shivered and hurried her steps as he strode across the parking lot, with her huddled under his jacket like a chick under his wing. The first thing she was going to do when she got into the Trail-Blazer was turn on the seat heater.

"What's your room number?" he asked. "I'll have someone bring a jacket to you. That's if you're going back to the inn now, that is."

She gave him her room number and added wryly, "I hope I make it back there without falling asleep."

His hand abruptly tightened on her elbow, hauling her to a stop. "I'll drive you."

"And then I'd be stranded. Thanks, but I'll make it. I'm punchy and I have a killer headache, but the coffee will keep me awake for a little while."

"You need to eat."

"I ate," she said, startled by all this concern. "You watched me."

"You ate four bites. I counted."

"And it was all I could do to swallow those. Don't push, Cahill."

He had shifted so that he was between her and the truck, the breadth of his shoulders blocking some of the wind from her. The rain was soaking his back, but he ignored it as he stared silently down at her, his expression unreadable. Even through her fatigue, she felt something uneasy begin to stir. "What?" she demanded, moving back half a step.

He shook his head. "Nothing. You're out on your feet. Go get some sleep."

"That sounds like a plan." He moved out of the way, and Sarah hit the remote to unlock the door, hurrying to get out of the wind and rain.

"Sarah," he said as she put the key in the ignition. He still held his jacket, rather than putting it back on.

"Yes?"

"I probably don't have to say this, but don't leave town."

Cahill followed her to the Mountain Brook Inn, just to make certain she got there, and that she didn't endanger herself or any other motorist. When she turned left into the inn's parking lot, he tapped his horn lightly in good-bye, and she lifted one hand in acknowledgment but she didn't turn her head to look.

She was holding up okay, but the stunned, desolate expression in her dark eyes was arousing his protective instincts. Not cop instincts, but man-woman instincts, exactly what he didn't need.

For one thing, he'd been telling the truth when he said he was fairly certain she hadn't killed the Judge. Fairly certain, though, was a long way from completely certain. She hadn't even asked how much money she would inherit, which wasn't normal. Maybe she would have held off in front of the family, but when they were alone, she should have asked . . . unless she already knew. And if she knew she stood to inherit a hundred grand, that could be a motive to off the old guy; God knows a lot of people had been killed for a lot less money.

Balanced against that, her grief and shock seemed genuine. Her eyes were red and swollen from crying; either that, or she had sprayed herself in the eyes with something to make it look as if she'd been crying. She was either a smart killer and a very good actress, or she was grieving.

His gut said she was genuinely grieving. But since his gut was also insisting he try to get her into bed, he had to take into consideration the lust factor, which had clouded his judgment before. Shannon, Sarah. Both names started with *S;* that couldn't be good.

He'd tried to ignore his attraction to Sarah, but it hadn't gone away. Her face had an annoying habit of popping into his mind whenever he tried to relax. He was fine when he was at work, but let him sit down in the evening to watch the news or read the paper and *Bam!*—there she was. He'd see her sitting on the stairs in her thin cotton pajamas, or standing on the pistol range with her concentration totally focused on the target, the sunshine picking out red and gold glints in her hair. A man knew he was in trouble when he noticed the glints in a woman's hair. Boobs, yeah; he was supposed to notice boobs. But hair glints?

When he was lifting weights in his basement, he'd think about lifting Sarah, up and down, astride him, and he'd get a hard-on while he was bench-pressing. Or when he was doing push-ups, he'd think about having Sarah beneath him, with the same result.

The truth was, he couldn't think about much else. It was a miracle he'd managed to keep his distance from her, because he hadn't been this obsessed with sex since he was sixteen. Naw, it wasn't a miracle; it was plain fear. He wanted her *too* much. He didn't think he'd been this desperate to fuck Shannon even in those first falling-in-love days. Of course, he'd already been fucking Shannon, so maybe that wasn't a good comparison.

The investigation was all that kept him from turning the car around and heading back to the Mountain Brook Inn. Until Sarah was cleared, she was off-limits. She had the sales receipts, she had the merchandise to match the sales receipts, the signature on her credit card matched the ones on the charge slips, and she had the movie ticket. A little more verification, some checking into her financial status, and she would be in the clear. Hell, Judge Roberts's kids stood to inherit a hell of a lot more than Sarah did; they all had alibis, too, but killers could be hired.

Cahill didn't have a good feeling about this one.

Most murders were committed by someone close to the victim, a family member, a neighbor, a friend. This felt like the toughest of all cases, a killing by a stranger. What was the link? What had brought the killer to the house? Was it someone Judge Roberts had sentenced? On the surface that made the most sense, except for the fact there was no sign of forced entry or of a struggle. It was as if he had opened the door to the killer, invited him in, and chatted with him in the library.

As if he knew him.

So maybe they were back to the neighbor, family member, or friend scenario.

Cahill tried to mentally walk through it. None of the neighbors had noticed a car in the driveway, but it was dark. Sarah had arrived home just before ten and found the body shortly afterward; she had called 911 at 10:03, the patrol cars had gotten there within five minutes, and he himself had arrived about fifteen minutes after her call. Rigor had just been starting in the body, which roughly placed the time of death, say, between six and eight, maybe eight-thirty. He thought it would be later rather than sooner, because it wasn't dark at six P.M.

Judge Roberts had opened the door to his killer. No shots had been fired right then, which would have been the most likely time and place for the shooting if the killer was someone who had done prison time because of the Judge and was out for vengeance. Instead they had walked into the library and sat down, or at least the Judge sat. He hadn't been alarmed; he'd been relaxed, the footrest of his recliner up.

The killer wasn't a stranger, wasn't someone who had threatened the Judge in the past.

It would be interesting to see what fingerprints the technicians had collected. The Judge's, Sarah's, possibly the cook's, definitely the cleaning ladies': those should be there. Sarah had given her fingerprints in the wee hours, for comparison. The cook, Leona Barksdale, had been scheduled to come in this morning to be printed, though she'd tearfully said she hadn't been inside that room in a few weeks. The cleaning ladies were set for this afternoon. Who else? The house was cleaned regularly, so any prints should be new ones.

The neighborhood would have to be canvassed; anyone could have walked over under cover of darkness, shot Judge Roberts, and calmly walked back home. Again, he ran into the question of motive. From what he'd found out so far, the old judge had been well liked. There weren't any skeletons hanging in his closet, no nastiness that surfaced in private. He didn't cheat, in either cards or business. He didn't gamble, didn't drink to excess, and so far as Cahill had been able to find out, hadn't romanced anyone since his wife died eight years before.

So why would someone who *hadn't* run afoul of him in his court want to kill him?

If the motive wasn't revenge, sex, or money, what was left?

Nothing, that was what was left. So the motive still had to be one of the three. He doubted it was revenge, because the Judge had known his killer, invited him in. Sex? The man was eighty-five, hadn't dated, and from what everyone said, had been completely faithful to his wife while she was alive. That left money.

Somehow, it always came back to money.

And that brought him full circle, back to Sarah.

His kids had grown up rich. They had always known the money was there. So why kill him now? Why not ten years ago, or last year? Why not wait a few years more and let him die of natural causes? Unless one of them was in financial difficulty— which he would find out—there was no reason for any of them to set up his murder. One of the adult grandchildren, perhaps? That bore looking into.

But Sarah was the most likely suspect.

Shit.

Sarah woke at three, disoriented and groggy. She lay there listening to the muted rumble of the air-conditioning, blinking at the thick curtains pulled over the window, and trying to remember where she was. Her head felt as if it were stuffed with cotton; it was an effort to think, much less move.

Then she remembered, and for a long moment the grief clawed at her throat, her chest. She squeezed her eyes shut, but that didn't help. She still saw the Judge sitting so peacefully in his leather recliner, with his blood and parts of his brain splattered across the room. She still smelled the awful, mingled smell of blood and body waste, and with a smothered sound, she opened her eyes.

Slowly, every muscle aching, she sat up. She was naked, pajamas not having been on the list of clothes she'd given Cahill. She had cried herself to sleep, and her eyelids felt gritty and raw. All in all, she thought, she didn't look very much like an ultracapable butler—or even an incompetent one.

The room was cold. Despite the chilly day, she'd turned on the air when she got back to the room, because her nose was stuffy and heat would have made breathing even more difficult. All she had wanted to do was fall into bed, so she had put the DO NOT DISTURB sign on the door and unplugged the phone. She'd placed her cell phone on the table beside the bed, so the family could get in touch with her if she was needed, but other than that, she hadn't want to talk to anyone.

The room was *too* cold. Actually, it was freezing. Sarah darted out of the warm nest of covers, swiftly switched the thermostat over to *Heat*, then dived back into bed and huddled under the covers, shivering.

There was something white on the floor just inside the door. Message slips. Sighing, she retrieved them—there were two—and once more retreated to the bed. This time, though, she switched on the lamp and stuffed the pillow behind her back so she could read the messages.

One was from the front desk. A jacket had been delivered for her, and they were holding it at the desk. The other was from Cahill, and was brief: "*Call me.*" The time was listed as two-thirty.

Sighing, she picked up her cell phone and called the number listed.

He answered almost immediately. "Cahill." His deep voice was alert; he was probably buzzed on caffeine.

"This is Sarah Stevens. I got your message."

"Were you asleep?"

"Mmm. I slept about four hours. By the way, thanks for sending the jacket over."

"You're welcome. Listen, do you by any chance know if anyone owed Judge Roberts some money? Was he worried about any of his investments?"

Sarah rubbed her hand over her face. "He loaned money on a regular basis, but they were more like gifts, because if anyone tried to repay him, he'd just wave it away."

"Did anyone in the neighborhood borrow money from him?"

"Not that I know of. In that neighborhood? Who would need a loan?"

"Depends on whether or not anyone has a gambling problem, or is into drugs. Maybe someone wants to hide the money he spends on his honey. There are all sorts of possibilities. What about his family? Any of them having financial difficulty?"

"He never mentioned it if they were. I don't think there's a bad apple in the bunch." She paused, synapses firing as she followed this line of questioning and saw where it was leading. Coolly she said, "I'll get a copy of my own bank statement to you, and my investment portfolio. Do you want canceled checks, too?"

"Please." His tone remained brisk and professional.

"Actually, you'll have to get them. They're at the house."

"Where?"

"There's a fire safe in the closet. Everything is in there."

"Thank you." He disconnected, and Sarah

growled as she disconnected her own phone. For a while this morning he had seemed a bit warmer, more human, but he was back to his old brusque self. To her dismay, it didn't matter whether he was friendly or not; there was something about him that made her want to lean on him. It didn't even matter that he was checking into her finances, trying to find a motive for her to have killed the Judge; the same process would clear her. He was doing his job. She wouldn't have felt nearly as confident if he'd blown off the possibility that she was guilty. He had to consider everyone, or something crucial might slip through the cracks.

Barbara and the rest of the family were convinced the killer was some ex-con from the Judge's past. After her first panicked assumption that her weirdo had done it, she had gone with logic and agreed with the others. Cahill didn't seem to be on the same page, though; he was concentrating more on her and the family. What had the cops found that he hadn't told?

She knew she was innocent, and she knew the family was innocent. She had observed all of them over the past years, at holidays and on vacation, and one and all they had loved the Judge. He adored his children and grandchildren, and got on well with all of the in-laws. So what did Cahill know that she had missed?

The room was warmer now, and she got out of bed, grimacing when she caught sight of herself in the dresser mirror. Her face was drawn and colorless, her eyes swollen. She felt weak and shaky, the result of almost twenty-four hours without much food. Four tiny bites of Danish and fruit didn't provide a lot of nourishment. She needed to eat something, even if she had to choke it down. Maybe she would go down to the hotel restaurant, later. For now, though, she put on another pot of coffee and turned on the television, then crawled back into bed. She needed to be distracted by something mindless more than she needed food.

She had nothing to do. She was accustomed to there always being *something* to do. Her life was very organized for that reason, so every chore would be accomplished. She should be doing paperwork now, keeping track of the household expenses; she always did that on Thursdays.

She could go buy some pajamas. She was close to three major shopping centers: Brookwood, the Summit, and the Galleria. But it was still raining, she was exhausted and groggy, and frankly she didn't give a damn whether or not she had pajamas to sleep in.

She discovered that the Weather Channel was the most interesting program on at three-thirty in the afternoon. She turned off the television, turned off the bedside light, and pulled up the covers. As soon as she closed her eyes, though, she saw the Judge in his recliner, his head lolled to the side—and she smelled the odor. Hastily she sat up again and turned on the lamp.

What was she thinking? She had just made a pot of coffee. She couldn't believe she'd put on the coffee, then gone back to bed. Nothing drastic would happen, of course, other than the coffee getting old and bitter. Neither she nor the Judge could stand old coffee—

He always came into the kitchen early in the morning, not waiting for her to bring the coffee to him. They would stand there chatting, leisurely sipping and sharing what they both considered one of life's finest little pleasures.

They would never share that first blissful cup of coffee again.

Like a loop of film that never stopped running, she saw him again: his white head tilted to the side, that thin dark streak running down his neck. His hair was a little mussed, but in the dim light that was, at first, the only thing she noted that was different. His hands were relaxed on the arms of the recliner, the footrest was up, as if he had just dozed off.

His hands were relaxed. The footrest was up.

Sarah stared across the room, seeing nothing but the awful scene from the night before. She had the feeling of the ground tilting beneath her, as if she had stepped out of reality into quicksand.

The footrest was up.

He was in his recliner—actually reclining.

The front door wasn't locked.

But the front door was always locked. He locked it himself as soon as he came in from his afternoon walk. In all the time Sarah had worked for him, she couldn't remember him ever leaving the front door unlocked.

What were the odds that the one time he *did* leave it unlocked, his killer walked in? Not very likely. Hell, the odds were astronomical *against* such a thing happening. He was very safety conscious, after the threats against him, and especially after the robbery.

So he hadn't forgotten to lock the door; he had *un*locked it. To let someone in?

Why would he let a stranger come in? The answer was simple: He wouldn't.

There was no sign of a struggle. No sign of forced entry—at least, none that Cahill had mentioned to her or the family, and she was certain he would have told them if there had been.

The bottom dropped out of her stomach. It made sense, in an awful way. The Judge had let someone he knew into the house. They had gone into the library . . . to talk? He'd been sitting in his favorite chair, the big leather recliner; he was relaxed, the footrest in the up position. And this acquaintance had pulled a gun and shot him in the head.

This was what Cahill had figured out, what he hadn't told them. Whoever the killer was, the Judge hadn't felt threatened. He had known his killer, felt comfortable and relaxed in his presence.

She almost vomited, because that meant she likely knew him, too.

CHAPTER 11

HE FELT GOOD. HE'D FORGOTTEN HOW GOOD IT REALLY DID FEEL, to hold all that power in his own hands, to take charge of his own destiny. It had been . . . how long? Seven years? That was proof he was in control, that he wasn't one of those maniacs who were slaves to compulsion. In the almost thirty years since he had taken care of the problem of his father, this was only the third time he'd been forced to act. Four times, total, in almost thirty years.

All in all, he felt justifiably proud of himself. Not many men could control themselves so well, not if they knew the rush, the sheer joy, of the act. Even more important, not many men were intelligent enough to get away with it.

But the old man was out of the way now, and Sarah was free. Nothing stood in her way; she could come to him now.

Cahill sat in his cubicle, slowly leafing through the files and bank statements retrieved from the fireproof safe in Sarah's closet. Finally he dumped everything in an oversized padded bag and sat back in his chair, rubbing his eyes. Holy shit. The woman wasn't hurting for money.

Not that a hundred grand wasn't a lot of money,

but she didn't need it. Must be nice, he thought, to be in a position where you didn't need a hundred grand. Some people would grab for everything they could get, and no amount would ever be enough, but people like that didn't devote themselves to training for a well-paying job, then devote themselves to the job and save like mad. No, people who were just out for the money would steal it, commit fraud, marry old people and then in an effort to kill them, fiddle with the multitude of drugs old people always seemed to take, but they wouldn't work for it.

Sarah had evidently saved the vast majority of her salary from the time she started work. She'd invested it, and from what he could see she'd been smart about it. She hadn't gone heavily into tech stocks, and those she'd had she'd sold just as they started crashing, while she could still make some profit. She had blue-chip stocks, she had mutual funds, she had some workhorse stocks. She'd salted money away in a retirement fund, planning for the future. She had just turned thirty, and with everything added together she was knocking on the door of the millionaires' club.

That was one smart woman.

And being so smart, would she risk everything to add another hundred large to her account? Money was relative. If you were working a minimum-wage job and barely scraping by, with nothing left over for extras, then a hundred thousand was an enormous amount of money. He'd known mothers to kill their kids for a five-thousand-dollar insurance policy. But if you already had way over a hundred thousand, then in comparison it wasn't nearly as impressive. In this case, the risk outweighed the gain.

So there went her possible motive.

Good.

"You got anything?" his lieutenant asked, pausing by his desk.

"The butler didn't do it."

"I thought she was top of your list."

"The motive evaporated."

"Money? How does money evaporate?"

"She has plenty of it. You know how much butlers make?"

The lieutenant scratched his nose. "I gather it's more than we thought."

"She makes more than you and me combined."

"No shit!"

"My thoughts exactly." Cahill shook his head. "She had everything to lose and, comparatively, not that much to gain. Not anything, when you consider that she earned more in a year working for him than she'll get in his will. She'd be better off with him still alive. So there goes the motive. Not only that, she thought the world of the old man."

The lieutenant was a good guy, and he trusted his investigators. "So what else do we have?"

"Not much. The neighbors didn't see anything, and they all have alibis. The family all checks out, so far. Unless forensics turns up a smoking gun, this isn't looking good."

"It's been less than twenty-four hours."

But it was knocking hard on twenty-four hours, and if murders weren't solved quickly, they tended not to be solved at all.

"What about the cons he received death threats from? Anything turned up on them?"

"None of them are known to be in this area. One is currently a ward of the state, in the St. Clair facility, living off taxpayer money. One is in federal lockup. Only two are at large, and one of them is in Eugene, Oregon. The last known location of the last one was Chicago, in January." Cahill flipped a photo onto his desk of a heavyset man with a mustache. "Carl Jarmond. I don't think it's him."

"But he's a possibility."

Cahill shook his head. "Would Judge Roberts have let this man in his house? I don't think so. Every outside door in that house has a peephole, so he didn't open the door blind. He knew whoever it was."

"What numbers were on call return and redial?"

"I checked redial from every phone in the house. Nothing suspicious. The butler called her folks, and the phones the victim would have used showed calls to his banker, and another to an old friend of his—who also has an alibi. Call return was interesting. The phone in the library returned a call from a pay phone in the Galleria."

"Have you found out what time the call was made?"

"We're working on getting a list of all calls, both in and out."

"No way of telling who made it, though."

Cahill shook his head. The time of the call would tell them some things, such as if it was made close to the time of the murder, but that was about it. The Galleria was a busy mall; unless you were green-haired, spike-collared, and wore a Bozo suit—or, alternatively, were naked—the chances were small anyone would pay much attention to you. The chances of getting a viable fingerprint from the phone were somewhere between zero and laughable. Video cameras from nearby stores trained on the store entrances might have caught something, though. That was worth checking. He said as much to the lieutenant.

"Good idea, Doc." He checked his watch. "Get started on that in the morning. For now, go home and get some sleep. You were up all night last night, and you haven't stopped today."

"I grabbed about three hours early this morning. I'm okay." His training in the Army had taught him how to function with a lot less rest than that, and for a longer time. "But I think I will call it a day." He definitely had something else to do, something he didn't think he could put off much longer. He might as well test the waters now.

At eight o'clock that night, the Weather Channel was still on, and Sarah had watched the same weather fronts for almost five hours now. Nothing had changed. She still felt sick, mentally running through all the Judge's acquaintances, the neighbors, anyone whom he wouldn't hesitate to let into the house. The problem was, he knew a lot of people whom she didn't know. She knew his immediate circle of friends, the immediate neighbors and some of the others, but of course he had old school chums, friends in law practice, college buddies, whom she'd never met. But why would any of them want to kill him?

The *why* of it was driving her crazy.

If they only knew why, she thought, they could figure out who. Why would anyone want to kill him, other than someone he'd sentenced to prison? And if it was an ex-con, why would the Judge have let him in the house, sat down, and relaxed? He wouldn't have.

Why?

The phone rang and she grabbed it, glad for the distraction; maybe Barbara needed something done that would occupy her for a couple of hours.

"Have you had supper yet?"

She didn't need him to identify himself; Cahill's deep voice and abrupt tone were identification enough.

"Supper?"

"Or lunch?"

"I slept through lunch, remember."

"Then let's go to Milo's and get a hamburger."

Sarah dragged her hand through her hair. She needed to eat, but her stomach was still tied in knots. She hesitated long enough that he said, "Sarah?"

"I'm here. It's . . . I really don't feel like eating."

"Get ready anyway. I'll be there in ten minutes." He hung up, and she stared at the phone in astonishment.

Ten minutes!

Despite her shakiness, in ten minutes she was dressed, had brushed her teeth and washed her face, and was dragging a brush through her hair when he knocked on the door.

"You look like hell," he said by way of greeting.

"You're pretty, too," she said coolly, stepping back to let him in. Just because she was dressed didn't mean she was going anywhere with him. After all, she hadn't had on any clothes at all when he called.

He looked down at her bare feet. "Get your shoes on. Socks, too. The temperature's in the forties."

"I don't feel like eating," she repeated.

"Then you can watch me eat."

"Your charm is enormous." Despite the sarcasm, despite everything, for the first time that day she found herself smiling. It wasn't much of a smile, but it was real. He was like a Sherman tank, without finesse, but packing a great deal of power.

"Yeah, I know. It's exceeded only by the size of my—" He caught himself, flicking a quick glance at her. "—ego," he finished, and she could have sworn color stained his cheekbones. Evidently cops weren't supposed to make risqué comments to suspects. He bent down and picked up her shoes, extending them to her. She got the impression he'd put them on her if she didn't do it herself.

She sat down on the bed and put on her socks and shoes. "I assume you're hungry and you want to talk to me, so you're killing two birds with one stone."

He shrugged. "You can assume whatever you want."

Well, what on earth did *that* mean? As it happened, she wanted to talk to him, too, about her conclusions on the Judge's murder; she didn't mind watching him eat while they were talking.

They stopped at the front desk for her to get the jacket being held for her there. It was her Berber fleece, and she gratefully pulled it on as they left the hotel. The rain had stopped, but very recently, because the trees were still dripping. The pavement was dark and shiny.

Instead of the car he'd been driving earlier, he led her to a pickup truck, dark blue in color. The truck looked like something he'd drive, being short on fancy extras but with plenty of power. At least it had running boards, so she could get in without help. He opened the door for her and waited until she was settled in the seat before closing it and going around to his side.

Milo's was a hamburger tradition in the Birmingham area, with what most locals swore was the best hamburger in the world, and the best iced tea. The hamburger didn't have all the fancy stuff, like lettuce and tomato and pickles—though you could get cheese on it if you wanted—but it did have a dark sauce that almost defied the taste buds to decipher what was in it. That was it. Double meat, chopped onions, and the sauce. The burgers dripped with sauce. People bought extra containers of the sauce. They dipped their spicy fries in it, they poured more on their burgers, they used it at home on their own grilled burgers.

Needless to say, a Milo's hamburger was a messy affair. Even if her stomach had been cooperating, Sarah wouldn't have felt like dealing with the mess. When Cahill asked if she was sure she didn't want anything, she said, "I'm sure," and went to a table against the wall to wait for him.

When he joined her, he carried a tray with two tall paper cups of iced tea, three hamburgers, and two orders of fries. The tray was also loaded with little paper cups full of ketchup and packets of salt.

She stared at the bounty with disbelieving eyes. "You said you were hungry, but I thought you were talking normal, human hungry, not Koko the gorilla hungry."

He set the tray on the table and took the seat across from her. "Part of it is for you. I hope you like onions, because I do. Eat." He put a cup of tea, a burger, and an order of fries in front of her.

"What does the fact that you like onions have to do with whether or not I like onions?" she murmured, trying to convince her stomach to unknot. She really did need to eat, and normally she liked a Milo's as well as anyone else. She just wasn't certain she could swallow, or that any food would stay down even if she could.

"In case I break down and kiss you, I wouldn't want to gross you out with onion breath." Without looking up, he began salting his fries.

Just like that, the world tilted on its axis. Sarah looked wildly around the restaurant, wondering if she had stepped into some alternate universe. "What did you say?" she asked faintly. Surely she had misheard him.

"You heard me." He glanced up, and snorted. "If you could see your face. You act as if a man's never been attracted to you before."

Okay, she'd risk a stomach in revolt. She had to do something to give herself time to adjust to this sudden shift. She plucked out a fry, dipped it in ketchup, and took a bite. The hot, spicy taste slapped her taste buds awake. She took her time chewing and swallowing, so she was then able to reply in an even tone. "Let's just say few men could have made it plainer than you that you *aren't* attracted."

"When I run scared, I do it right." He unwrapped his first burger, doctored it with salt, and took a big bite.

She took refuge in another french fry. After three or four of them, she decided she needed something bigger, so she unwrapped her burger. Dark sauce coated the waxed paper, dripped from between the two halves of bun. She took a bite—God, *heaven*—while she thought this through. His turnabout was too abrupt; there had to be something behind it. Ah, she had it.

"You think I killed the Judge," she said, "but you don't have any evidence, so you think if you get close to me, I might let something incriminating slip."

"Good try." He looked up at her, his hard cop's gaze very blue, very direct. "Look, my ex-wife would tell you in a heartbeat that I'm an asshole, and, hell, she may be right. *I'll* tell you, up front, that I haven't been fit company since the divorce. It was vicious, and getting over something like that takes a while. I haven't wanted to get involved with anyone, other than—"

He stopped, and she said, "For sex," filling in the blank.

"I wasn't going to be that blunt, but, yeah."

So he was divorced, and the process had been nasty. Healing from a split like that was like healing from any other trauma; it took time, and it wasn't easy. That made him a bad risk right now, not that she was in the market for a relationship, either. "How long has it been?"

"Two years since I caught her cheating on me, a year since the divorce was final."

"Ouch. Very nasty." What kind of idiot would cheat on a man like him? Not that she had any way of judging, but if her feminine instincts had been cats, they'd all have been purring right now in response to the testosterone she could practically smell on him.

"Yeah, it was. But it's over, maybe more over than I realized. I'm attracted to you, I tried to ignore it, and it didn't work. By the way, I've already seen your bank statement and investment portfolio; you don't need Judge Roberts's money."

"So I'm not a suspect now?"

"Let's just say as far as I'm concerned, you're in the clear."

That called for another bite or two of hamburger, chased by a french fry. "Some people might think you're after me because of the money. The timing *is* a tad suspicious."

"A tad," he agreed. "You make almost three times as much money as I do, and Mountain Brook cops are well paid. But I'd say you usually make more than anyone you date, so you're used to it."

"My dates don't usually see my bank statement first," she said dryly.

"Look, money's nice, but I'm not hurting. My ego isn't hurt by a woman making more than I do, either."

"I know, you told me; it's enormous."

There it was again, that flush of color on his cheekbones. Fascinated, she watched it fade as he devoted himself to his second hamburger. Despite the circumstances, she was really beginning to enjoy herself.

He wiped his mouth. "Okay, you've accused me

of trying to get close to you so I can get enough evidence to convict you of murder—a little undercover work, I guess—and of wanting your money. Anything else?"

"I'll let you know if anything comes to mind."

"You do that. In the meantime, on my side of the table is a lot of attraction. How about your side?"

He definitely had the finesse of a tank. On the other hand, that blunt honesty was somehow reassuring. A woman would always know where she stood with this man, for good or ill.

The big question was, what did she want to do about it?

His honesty forced her to be at least as straightforward as he was. "My side looks pretty much like your side. That doesn't mean getting involved would be a good idea."

A very male smile of satisfaction curved his mouth. "Getting involved is what it's all about. Millions of people work hard to get involved, actively search for it. Think of all the hours of hard labor put in in singles' bars."

"I've never been to a singles' bar. That should tell you something."

"That you've never needed to. I figure any time you don't have a man, it's because you don't want one."

She didn't say anything, staring down at the table. She saw that she'd eaten half of the burger, and all of the fries. His method of distracting her had certainly worked. On the other hand, she definitely felt better with some food in her stomach, even fast food. She could almost feel her energy level rising.

"We can take this as slow as you want," he said.
"This isn't a good time for you, and I have a couple of speed bumps in my way, too. I just wanted
you to know I'm interested." He shrugged. "You
don't have to get through this alone, unless that's
the way you want it."

Oh, damn. She'd been doing so well, pushing
her grief to the background for a little while. Just
like that her eyes began swimming, and she
blinked rapidly, trying to hold back the tears.

"Ah, hell, I didn't mean to— Let's get out of
here." He began gathering paper and napkins,
dumping the trash into a bin and placing the tray
on top. Blindly she followed him out of the restaurant, and as they walked to his truck, he put his
arm around her.

"I'm sorry," he said, thrusting a handkerchief
into her hands.

She wiped her eyes, leaning into the strength
and warmth of his body. His arm felt good around
her. She wanted to put her head on his shoulder
and weep; instead she took a deep breath. "He
was a sweet man. I'll cry a lot for him before this
is over."

He unlocked the door and she climbed inside,
reaching for the seat belt. He stopped her, his hand
over hers, and he leaned inside.

She made no move to evade the kiss. She didn't
want to evade it. She wanted to know how he
kissed, how he tasted. His mouth was warm, the
contact light, almost gentle, as if his intent was
more to comfort than arouse.

That lasted about two seconds. Then he slanted
his head, his lips parted, and he deepened the kiss

until his tongue was in her mouth and her arms were around his neck. The bottom dropped out of her stomach and her entire body clenched, and she knew her purring instincts hadn't been wrong. Good Lord, the man could kiss.

He lifted his head, running his tongue along his lower lip as if savoring the taste of her. "That was good." His tone was so low it almost rumbled.

"Yes, it was." Her own tone was a tad . . . breathy. Where had that come from? She had never sounded breathy before in her life.

"Do you want to do it again?"

"We'd better not."

"Okay," he said, and kissed her again.

This man was dangerous. If she wasn't careful, she'd be involved in a full-fledged affair with him before she knew it—maybe even before morning. Now was definitely not the time, and she had to get herself under control while she still could. After giving her the cold shoulder, now he was moving at light speed in the opposite direction, and she was a little shell-shocked.

It took some effort, but she pulled her mouth away, gasping for air. "Red light, Detective. Stop."

He was breathing hard, too, but he stepped back. "Permanently?" The word was raw with disbelief.

"No!" Her answer was embarrassingly forceful. "Just . . . for now." She took a deep breath. "There are more important things to talk about."

"Such as?"

"Such as, I think the Judge knew the killer."

His face went blank. He closed her door and went around to the driver's side, getting behind the wheel and starting the truck. A light drizzle had started again, and he turned on the windshield wipers.

"I know he did," he said. "But what makes *you* think so?"

CHAPTER 12

MAYBE HE WASN'T SO CONVINCED OF HER INNOCENCE, AF-
ter all. The thought cooled her down, gave her a
bit of much needed mental distance from him. "I
know the Judge . . . knew him," she corrected herself. "He never, never left the doors unlocked. I
checked the house every night before going to bed
and not once did he leave any door unsecured. It
was automatic for him; when he came inside, he
locked the door behind him. I guess he got in the
habit after he got the first death threat, when Mrs.
Roberts was still alive. But last night"—God, was
it only last night, it felt like a week—"the front
door was unlocked."

"Could be coincidence."

"That he'd leave the door unlocked on the one
night a killer came looking for him?" She threw
Cahill a derisive glance. "I don't think so. I think
this person came to the door, and the Judge knew
him and let him in. When I found him, the Judge
was sitting in his recliner, with the footrest up. He
was relaxed. He didn't feel he was in any danger.
So he knew the guy."

"Why are you so certain it was a man?"

That question gave her pause. "I suppose I'm
thinking in general terms. It's easier than saying

'the killer' every time. And the cons who made the death threats were all men, so the idea stuck. Plus the weirdo who sent me the pendant is most likely a man, and my first thought was that *he* had done it."

"Hmm." Cahill scratched his jaw, as if considering that possibility. "Has he contacted you again? Sent anything else? Have you had any hang-ups on the phone, or any other kind of strange call?"

"No, nothing else at all. Just the pendant. One incident doesn't establish a pattern, does it?"

"You know the saying. Once in a row doesn't mean shit."

"That's what I figured."

Deftly he steered through the traffic on 280. "Last night, you said you went to the movie so he'd have a chance to approach you, if he was watching."

She'd been in shock the night before, but she thought that was pretty much verbatim what she'd said. Cahill was sharp, very sharp. "That's right."

He glanced at her. "What made you think he'd be watching?"

"Nothing, except the gift made me feel so uneasy. I hadn't been able to put it out of my mind. Something like that is . . . It put me on edge. That's the only way I can describe it." She shuddered. "Just the thought that he might be following me, watching me, gives me the creeps. And not knowing who he is made it worse, so I thought I'd give him the opportunity to introduce himself. At least then I'd know what he looks like."

"But no one approached?"

"No one tried to sit next to me, no one spoke to

me, no one even looked at me a second time that I could tell."

"You know, if someone was fixated on you, and crazy enough to start following you around, giving him an opportunity like that wasn't a great idea."

"Probably not," she agreed. "But if he tried anything, I thought I'd be able to take him by surprise."

"The karate, you mean? What if he'd had training, too?"

"Then I'd be in trouble. I thought the odds were in my favor, though."

He drummed his fingers on the steering wheel. "I don't like the idea of you trying to draw anyone out like that. That's my personal reaction. My reaction as a cop is, don't ask for trouble."

"That's basically the same thing," she said, amused.

"How about that. Look, if anything strange happens, if you think you're being followed, if you get another gift, or a funny phone call, let me know. Immediately. Day or night."

"I don't think you'd be very thrilled if I called you at three A.M. to tell you some drunk had just called the wrong number."

"I said to call me, and I meant it. Who knows? Maybe all you'll need to do will be to roll over and punch me."

She rubbed her forehead. Light speed? He was moving at warp speed now. The biggest problem she had was that it didn't turn her off. No matter how fast he moved, her hormones were keeping pace. For her own sanity, she needed him to again suspect her of murder, so she could pull back. Otherwise . . . she didn't want to think about otherwise.

She had always been cautious about dating, about serious relationships. Part of it was because being tied down didn't fit in with her life plans right now, but another big part of it was something inside herself that was intensely private and self-sufficient. Letting someone in on a romantic level wasn't easy, because that meant letting go of some of her personal control. She could and did make friends easily, she loved the Judge, liked his family, but there had always been another level of intimacy that she hadn't let anyone reach. Cahill, she thought, might reach that level.

It was a case of good chemistry, but bad timing. She wasn't ready to settle down, and Cahill was recovering from a rocky divorce. He might be looking for a relationship, but she seriously doubted he put the word *permanent* in front of it. Rebound romances weren't a good idea at any time. In another year or so . . . maybe he'd be a better risk. As for where she would be in another year or so, that was anyone's guess.

So letting this thing go any further wasn't a good idea.

He waved a hand in front of her face. "Are you in there?"

She batted his hand away. "I'm thinking."

"That's a relief. I was afraid the idea of sleeping with me put you in a catatonic state."

She was surprised into laughing, an actual, honest laugh. "That happens often, does it?"

"I hadn't thought so, but looking back, there

may have been one or two times—" He grinned and shrugged, and Sarah laughed again.

"It must be your enormous charm."

"I thought that was my ego."

"That, too." It was on the tip of her tongue to ask what other enormous qualities he had, but she stopped herself in time. Sexy banter was always fun, but with him she sensed the situation could get out of control before she knew it, as fast as he moved. He could take a quip and move her right into bed with it, if she wasn't on her guard. She was too damned susceptible to him, but at least she knew it.

"Cahill—"

"My name's Thompson. Some people call me Tom, some call me Doc. You can call me sweetheart."

A sound dangerously close to a giggle bubbled in her throat. "Are you always this sure of yourself?"

"Faint hearts, and all that. If you don't like me, you'll slap me down, or just plain slap me. You said the attraction is mutual, so I'm taking you at your word." He turned into the parking lot and slotted the truck into an empty space, turning off the engine and headlights. The drizzle immediately began to dot the windshield, distorting the lights and images.

"I don't rush into any relationship, especially not one with a man who's newly divorced and still carrying around a lot of baggage."

He shifted, angling his upper body toward her, his left arm draped over the steering wheel and the right one stretched out along the back of the seat, inviting her to slide closer. Why couldn't the truck have nice, safe bucket seats, instead of a bench seat? She could have sworn the truck tilted to the left, too, because staying on her own side was more difficult than it should have been.

"Baggage is normal," he said. "It's what makes us who we are. Granted, I'd rather not be an embittered woman-hater, but—"

He stopped, because she was definitely giggling. "Good," he said, his expression softening as he used one finger to tuck a strand of hair behind her ear. "You sounded as if you were convincing yourself of something with that baggage argument. Don't think too much, Sarah. Let's just see where this goes. We may bore each other to tears within a week."

She snorted. "Yeah, right."

"Stranger things have happened." That one finger touched her cheek, lightly stroked. Without thinking she turned her face and nestled it against his hand, and just that simple touch made her nipples harden. He smiled, as if he knew the effect he had on her. "Once you get over this weird hang-up you have about having wild monkey sex with a man you barely know, we can have a lot of fun."

She bailed out of the truck, and was still laughing as she strode into the hotel lobby, sending him off with a backward wave. Laughing felt strange, with everything that had happened in the past twenty-four hours, but it also felt good. Laughter didn't stop the grief, but it made the weight of it a little easier to bear.

In one fell swoop, Cahill had fed her, distracted her, aroused her, and amused her. Not many men were that versatile, she thought as she rode the elevator upward. His sly sense of humor was astonishing when she remembered how dour he'd seemed the night he interviewed her about the robbery.

Which left her . . . where?

She really, really wanted to forget caution and common sense, and have a flaming hot affair with him. The sex would be . . . She couldn't even begin to imagine the sex, because she'd never before had such a strong physical reaction to anyone. And therein was the big problem. Not the sex, but the way she felt. She could get in over her head before she knew it, and letting herself care too much about him was just asking for a heartache.

The smart thing to do would be to start hunting for a job in another state. Florida, maybe, on one of those huge Palm Beach estates. She'd be closer to her parents, too. There was always California, or the Hamptons; she wasn't worried about finding another job. She had to update her résumé anyway; she no longer had a job, or a place to live. She hadn't really absorbed that before, with all her attention focused on what had happened, but the shock had lessened a little and she was beginning to think of all the ramifications.

She probably wouldn't have the option of having a flaming hot affair with him, unless it was a short one—or a long-distance one. Cahill didn't strike her as a long-distance-type man. So all of this angst and indecision was a waste of time; she had to deal with reality, and reality dictated she get a job. She had chosen a very specialized field in which to make her living, so that meant she couldn't find a position just anywhere; she was limited to the moneyed communities, such as Beverly Hills, Buckhead, Mountain Brook.

It was possible she would stay on in Mountain Brook; she'd already had the one job offer, though she doubted it was still open now, after she had so definitely turned it down. That was assuming she would take the position, anyway; the interview process was a two-way street. The employer had to feel comfortable with her, but she also had to feel comfortable with the employer. After all, she would be fitting herself into the home, forming the structure of routine and comfort. If she didn't like the employer, then the level of dedication she demanded of herself would be difficult to maintain, and she would be miserable.

She felt better now that she was focused on the hard facts, rather than the tantalizing possibilities of a relationship with Cahill; the ground beneath her had solidified. She could deal with him, so long as she kept her head. For the next few days, anyway, she had more serious things to consider.

The rain continued the next day, heavier and colder. The medical examiner released Judge Roberts's body to his family and they began the task of making the final arrangements. Sarah handled placing the obituary in the newspapers, and she put herself completely at the disposal of the family.

She drove them to the funeral home they'd chosen, to deal with casket selection and the financial matters. The Judge had wanted to be buried beside his wife, had even bought a double tombstone when she died with his name already chiseled on it, so at least they didn't have to deal with that decision. Selecting a casket, however, shattered them. Randall and Jon held together, but they seemed incapable of making a decision; they kept looking to Barbara, and Barbara began silently crying.

Sarah stepped out of the background and gave Barbara a hug. "I know," she murmured in sympathy. "But it has to be done."

Barbara turned to her, eyes blinded by tears. "Which one do you like?"

The question floored her. Stunned, Sarah looked around at the caskets, and at Randall and Jon. They were both watching her now with a sort of desperate plea in their expressions. It couldn't be plainer that they couldn't handle this.

Sarah took a deep breath. "I like the bronze one." It was expensive, but they could easily afford it, and they would feel better thinking they'd bought the best for their father.

"I like that one best, too," Randall said quickly.

Barbara blotted her eyes. "The bronze?" she asked, her voice quivering. She looked at it. "It's very nice, isn't it?"

"The best," the funeral director put in. After all, business was business.

"I like the color." Barbara took a deep breath and turned to Sarah again. "I think you're right. We'll take the bronze."

From there they visited a florist to order flowers. The service would be at two o'clock on Sunday, at the huge church the Judge had attended. Sarah had already gotten rooms for the rest of Randall's family, who were driving down that day, Friday, after work and school. Visitation for friends would be at the funeral home on Saturday night, and before that, there was shopping to be done.

Sarah had had the presence of mind to request a charcoal suit and black pumps from her closet, but she needed panty hose and a few other small items. Barbara decided the clothes she'd brought wouldn't do at all, and Blair tearfully confided she didn't even *own* any dark clothes. Julia, Jon's wife, also decided she needed something different. Only Emily had come fully prepared.

The most logical thing to do was to begin at the Galleria, since it was attached to the hotel, but Blair had already roamed the mall from end to end, both stories, and wasn't satisfied with anything. Barbara did find some shoes she liked at Parisian, and Sarah quickly picked up the items she needed, including several black umbrellas, since it appeared they would be going back out in the rain after all.

By evening, they had exhausted the contents of the Summit, Brookwood, and Sarah had driven them to all the exclusive boutiques that she knew of in the area. Barbara finally settled on a stylish black suit with a long, slim skirt, which, given the weather forecast, was a good idea. Blair selected a black skirt that ended just above her knees, and a slim-fitting, short jacket in eggplant; she had removed the ring from her eyebrow and washed the colored streaks from her hair. Funerals were serious business, both emotionally and fashionwise. Julia had been much more decisive than the other two, making her selection, a navy blue dress with a matching tunic jacket, at the first department store they visited in the Summit.

Sarah's feet were so tired she was almost limping

by the time she herded her charges back to the hotel. The rain had fallen unceasingly all day long, making shopping even more difficult, as they'd had to juggle umbrellas along with everything else. Her shoes were wet, her pants were damp, and despite the Berber jacket she was cold. All she wanted to do was take a hot shower and sit down with her feet elevated. Her cell phone hadn't rung all day long, and there were no messages waiting for her when she reached the inn. Maybe, she thought, she could rest now.

The room phone rang as she was peeling off her damp socks. She groaned and flopped back on the bed, considering not answering it. But it might be one of the family, so she picked it up on the sixth ring.

"Ms. Stevens, this is Greg Holbrook with the *News*. I'd like to interview you about the tragic murder—"

"I'm not giving interviews," she said firmly. "Good-bye." She disconnected, then immediately rang the front desk and asked for a different room, booked under a false name. The next hour was spent handling that and getting her things switched to a room four doors down. She should have thought of the press before and taken those same precautions.

Her new room was cold, having been empty all day. She turned the heat on full blast, and when the chill was gone, began stripping for that hot shower that she needed desperately now. Right on cue, her cell phone rang.

At least this wasn't likely to be the press. But if it was someone in the Judge's family, then it meant something had come up she needed to handle.

"Where are you?" Cahill demanded irritably. "The front desk said you'd checked out."

"Bless them," she said with deep gratitude. "A reporter called my room, so I changed rooms and booked it under a different name."

"Good. Have you had supper?"

"I've eaten today, if that's what you're asking."

"It isn't. I'm asking specifically about supper."

"Then, no, I haven't, and you couldn't blow me out of this room with dynamite. I took three of the ladies shopping. My feet hurt, I'm cold, and I want a hot shower. Period."

"Poor baby," he said, and she could tell he was smiling. "What's your room number?"

"I'm not telling. I don't want company."

"I give a great foot massage."

The thought of having her feet massaged almost made her moan. She had the presence of mind, though, to say, "I'll take a rain check. I'm exhausted, and dealing with you takes a lot of energy. I'm not up to it tonight."

"That's probably the best kiss-off I've ever had. Okay, I'll see you tomorrow. Sleep tight."

"Tomorrow?" Tomorrow was Saturday. She had . . . nothing to do. The realization was so strange as to be disorienting. Her Saturdays were always busy. If she took her half day on Saturday, then the mornings were spent getting the Judge's day arranged and everything taken care of. If she didn't take her half day on Saturday, that was because something was going on that required her supervision. Either way, Saturdays were busy days.

"I'll be working," Cahill said. "Checking out some things. But I'll see you tomorrow night at the funeral home."

That should be safe enough.

"When will we be able to get into the house?"

"Maybe Sunday. I think we've about done everything we can there."

"Will you let me know ahead of time? I want to have the library cleaned before the family sees it."

"Of course," he said gently, and repeated, "Sleep tight," before hanging up.

The day of the funeral dawned clear and cold, with a wind that sliced through jackets. This was probably winter's last hurrah, Sarah thought—blackberry winter, the cool spell that came right after the blackberry bushes had bloomed. Indeed, the forecast called for a fast warming trend. On Monday the temperature was supposed to reach sixty-two; on Tuesday, seventy-five. By week's end it was forecast to be in the low eighties.

At the family's insistence she sat with them in church. Cahill sat somewhere behind her; he'd said hello when he came in, briefly touched her hand, then pulled back to the fringes to watch. She wasn't certain exactly what he was watching *for*, but no detail escaped his attention.

In her mind, she said good-bye to the Judge. She could almost feel his spirit hovering nearby, perhaps taking leave of his loved ones. Her lips trembled as she remembered all the funny things he'd said, the twinkle in his eyes, the joy he'd had in life. Losing him was like losing a grandfather, and there would always be a tiny gap in her heart, in her life, that only he could fill.

The church was filled to overflowing. His old friends were devastated by his loss, and they all

looked more frail than they had just a few days before, as if some of their spirit was gone, too. The
air was heavy with the scent of flowers, roses and
carnations and mums, and hothouse gardenias
with their hauntingly sweet smell. There couldn't
be many flowers left in Birmingham, Sarah
thought, looking at the huge wall of floral offer-
ings behind the casket.

Southern funerals were maudlin and ultimately
comforting, with their ceremony and tradition. Because the Judge was a war veteran, his VFW chapter posted an honor guard. During the funeral
procession to the cemetery, all traffic they met
stopped, with most people turning on their headlights in sympathy and pulling off the highway if
they could. Police cars blocked intersections for the
procession to go through unimpeded. Sarah had
always been amused by the traffic etiquette for a
funeral, but today, now that she was in the procession, she was grateful for the consideration.

There was an additional brief service at the
grave; then the family pulled back and the somber
work of burial began. After the grave was filled in
and covered with the huge array of flowers, Barbara and Blair each selected a perfect rose from
one of the arrangements for a keepsake. Randall
and Jon looked uncomfortable, as if they, too,
wanted a rose; but they were men, so they stood
back rather than admit to such sentimentality.
Their wives, though, exchanged glances with Barbara and made their own floral selections.

Normally there was food served after a funeral,
at the bereaved's home. With the Judge's house still
off-limits—and having guests there in the house
where he had been murdered didn't seem right,

anyway—one of his friends had offered the hospitality of his house. Many of the funeral attendees trooped off for food, drink, and reminiscing, but Sarah slipped away to her SUV. A couple of reporters were in the crowd, and she wanted to get away before they could buttonhole her.

Cahill caught up with her as she got behind the steering wheel. "You can arrange for those cleaners," he said. "I'll hold the family off until tomorrow, give you time to take care of things."

"Thanks." Now that the funeral was over, she was at a loss. There was nothing else to do, other than handle the cleaning. "Is it okay if I get some of my stuff out?" She was thinking specifically of her laptop, so she could begin updating her résumé.

He looked surprised. "You can stay there, if you want."

She shuddered at the thought. "Not now. Not until the library is cleaned."

He nodded in understanding, and gave her a card. "This firm specializes in hard-to-remove stains." Meaning blood, and brain matter.

She glanced at the name. "Thank you. I'll call them first thing in the morning."

"You can call now; that second number is the guy's home phone. They're geared for emergencies."

That couldn't be a great job, cleaning up after murders. On the other hand, someone had to do it, and in cases like this it was best to hand the chore off to professionals. She knew she couldn't bear tackling the job herself, even though she was trained to handle all types of stain removal.

"Will you be all right?" Cahill asked, blue eyes

very clear and direct as he studied her tired face. He shifted so his shoulders blocked the open door, giving them the illusion of privacy. "I have some things to do, but if you need company, I'll—"

"No." She touched his hand, then swiftly withdrew because just that brief touch was sharp temptation. "Thanks, but I'm okay. I have some things to take care of, too."

"I'll call you tomorrow, then." He leaned into the SUV and kissed her on the cheek. "Keep your cell phone on so I don't have to hunt you down."

"Are you planning to arrest me?"

"We still need to discuss some things, make some decisions. I'll take you into custody if I have to." He walked away, and she stared at his broad back, tiny shivers prickling her spine.

If she intended to run, she needed to do it soon. Very soon.

CHAPTER 13

CAHILL HATED SURVEILLANCE VIDEOTAPES. THE ANGLES WERE weird, the quality was very iffy, and mostly they were boring. They were also invaluable if anything interesting happened within the camera's range. So far, he hadn't found anything interesting.

The pay phones in the Galleria were located all through the mall, some of them close to the parking decks, some of them around the escalators. The one from which Judge Roberts had been called was near one of the escalators. If the gods had been smiling on him, the Galleria would have had surveillance cameras aimed at the huge main concourse; no such luck. He'd had to settle for the stores near that particular pay phone. The security cameras aimed at the store entrances were the only ones that could possibly pick up the traffic at that pay phone.

Most of them were complete washouts. The angle was wrong; one camera had malfunctioned and showed nothing new on the tape for a couple of weeks, which told Cahill how often it was checked. Most surveillance tapes ran on loops; if you didn't get to them before the loop was completed, they would begin taping over whatever was at the beginning. Wait too long, and everything in the desired time period was gone.

The best part about them was that they were timed and dated. He had the exact time of the call made to Judge Roberts, so he didn't have to watch each entire tape. Allowing for discrepancies in the timers, he began fifteen minutes before the targeted time, and watched for fifteen minutes afterward. That was half an hour on each tape, taking note of the people who walked past the store entrances, comparing them to the next tape, and the next one. He finally hit pay dirt: a man in a light-colored suit used that particular phone and the digital time on the tape put it within two minutes of what the telephone company said was the time of the call. Cahill continued watching, and no one else used that phone for at least five minutes. The next user was a young girl in baggy jeans and huge, clunky boots.

Bingo. The man in the light-colored suit was the most likely suspect.

That was the good news. The bad news was that the angle was awful, and showed only the lower two-thirds of the body.

Back to all the other tapes, trying to catch a glimpse of a man wearing a light-colored suit as he walked past the stores on his way to that phone.

Finally he came up with an image, blurred, the face turned away, but at least he had something. When the picture was enhanced, maybe they would be able to pick out something that would lead them to the guy. Maybe Sarah or one of the family would recognize him.

"Sarah, please, stay," Barbara said, leaning over to take both of Sarah's hands in hers. They were in the suite's parlor, alone, amazingly. "The house will have to be closed up and sold, and none of us can spare the time right now. We talked it over, and all of us are strapped for time. There's so much to be done with the legal aspects, Blair is still in school, Randall's granddaughter has to have open-heart surgery—we need you. Your salary will be the same."

Sarah squeezed Barbara's hands. "Of course I'll stay. You don't have to convince me. I'll be here as long as you need me."

"You've been a godsend; you have no idea. If you hadn't been here, I don't think I could have coped." Barbara was tired, her face drawn with grief, but she was dry-eyed.

"Do you have any idea how long—"

"At least a month, maybe more. We have to settle his affairs, his personal effects have to be packed, things put in storage. We don't want the house to sit empty until it sells; houses deteriorate so fast without someone living in them. It may sell immediately, but it may not."

A house on Briarwood, in the old-money section? Some people would be reluctant to buy a house in which a murder had occurred, but the location and the house itself would probably overcome that. Sarah would be surprised if it was on the market for a full month before someone snapped it up. This was a perfect interim situation for her: she could afford to take her time looking for a new position anyway, but this way she wouldn't have to dip into her savings. She wouldn't have to pack in a rush, but could do that gradually, too. Instead of an abrupt uprooting, she could ease into a new job, new quarters, new responsibilities.

"I assume you want the grounds kept up, and the house cleaners in on a regular basis."

"Oh, of course; the house will be much easier to sell if it's looking well kept. It's so difficult to think of selling it," Barbara said, her voice trailing away. "He lived there almost fifty years. I grew up there. It's a wonderful old house, full of memories, and he took such good care of it. Mother designed it, you know. It's her dream house."

"Is there no way you could keep it in the family?"

"I don't think so. None of us want to move back here, and of course the estate taxes are horrendous, even divided three ways. The house will have to be sold to help pay them. None of us can afford to keep the house and pay that much additional tax. I know Daddy would have liked for one of us to have it, but the way things are—" She shrugged helplessly, and moved on to another topic.

"When the police let us into the house tomorrow, Randall and Jon and I are going to select some mementos. Daddy left directions for the main things, of course, but there are some smaller items that we want. Randall and Jon can take their selections home with them, since they're driving, but would you box mine up and ship them to me?"

Sarah got out the small pad that was always in her bag, and made a note. "Do you want me to arrange a meal there tomorrow? Leona will be more than happy to prepare any meal you like."

Barbara hesitated, then shook her head. "I don't know exactly what time we'll be there, or how long it will take us to go through things. I don't even know how many of us will be there."

"I can arrange something," Sarah said. "A big pot of soup, and sandwiches, if nothing else."

"That would be wonderful. Or we could all go to Milo's. Shaw is beginning to complain because he hasn't had a hamburger yet."

Sarah felt a private little zing at the mention of Milo's. Maybe one day she wouldn't associate Cahill's kisses with the hamburgers, but right now the two were closely linked in her mind. She felt a sudden intense craving for a hamburger herself.

Staying in Mountain Brook meant she would be seeing him again. She didn't know if that was good or bad, but she definitely knew the idea was exciting.

Barbara didn't know it, but the cleaners were at the house now. The rate for cleaning on Sunday night was higher than during the week, but Sarah thought it was well worth it for the Judge's family to be able to get into the house as early as possible tomorrow, since Barbara and her brood had a late-afternoon flight back to Dallas. Sarah planned, after leaving the Wynfrey, to go to the house to check that the cleaning job was adequate, but then she was going back to the inn to spend the night. Even though her quarters were totally separate, she wasn't ready yet to be alone there. Going back wouldn't be easy, she thought.

Nor was it. The cleaners were already gone when she got there later that night, and she had to force herself to go inside, to walk down the hall and look into the library. A strong sense of déjà vu seized her just outside the door, and she froze; when she looked inside, would the Judge be sitting there in his recliner, his blood and brains splattered against the far wall, and on the carpet? Would the smell still be there?

No, the smell was gone. She would be able to tell from here if it lingered, wouldn't she? The odor had been pervasive, finding its way down the hall, into the breakfast room, even the kitchen. All she could smell now was something clean and citrusy.

Steeling herself, she entered the library. The cleaners had done a good job with the carpet and wall; they had evidently cleaned the carpet in the entire room, so no one could tell by a clean spot exactly where they had removed a stain. The recliner was gone; she had no idea where it was. Maybe the police had it, though what they would want with the recliner, she couldn't imagine. Or perhaps the cleaners had removed it from the room for some reason; maybe the odor was impossible to remove from leather.

Tomorrow she would ask the whereabouts of the recliner. It might be in the garage, but she wasn't going to look for it tonight. Slowly she backed out of the room, turning out the light and closing the door. She didn't imagine she would ever again enter that room, for any reason.

She hadn't collected the mail since Wednesday, but someone, probably Cahill, had brought it in and put it on the kitchen island. He'd have gone through the mail, of course, to see if there was anything suspicious, any correspondence that bore looking into. She flipped through the stack; if there had been anything unusual, Cahill had taken it with him, because all she saw was the normal bills, catalogs, and magazines.

She left the mail on the island and went upstairs

to her quarters. Everything was subtly wrong, out of place; someone had searched every inch, so she supposed she should be grateful for the relative neatness. At least the contents of drawers hadn't been dumped on the floor and left. She straightened the books in the bookcase, neatly stacked the few magazines, put the potted plants back in place, adjusted the position of a vase, some framed pictures.

In the bedroom, her bed had been stripped. She gathered the discarded sheets to put in the wash, then went into the bathroom and began methodically putting it to rights. She couldn't put her life back the way it was, but she could reconstruct her immediate surroundings.

She put out fresh towels, and arranged all her cosmetics the way she preferred.

Back in the bedroom, she remade the bed, then opened the double closet doors and began rehanging her clothes, arranging them so what she wore most often was close to hand. Her shoes were a jumbled mess; she pulled all of them out of the closet, then sat down on the floor and paired them up, putting them back in the closet in neat rows.

She really hated that someone had gone through her underwear drawer. She was a bit of a fanatic about her underwear, courtesy of two brothers who had loved to tease her by hiding it, or by tying her bra to a forked stick to make a slingshot. Older brothers were a real trial. She wished now she had a video of Noel with her very first pair of lacy panties stuck on his head; she'd love to show it to his Marine buddies. Her brothers had never treated Jennifer like that, but then she would only have cried, and that was no fun. Sarah had chased after them with fury in her eyes and murder in her heart; if she'd ever caught them, blood would have been shed.

Sarah had been forced to hide her underwear for years, stuffing it in unlikely places so Daniel and Noel couldn't find it. Once they were gone, she had reveled in being able to have a real underwear drawer. She always neatly folded each garment, and the lacy, sexy stuff was in its own drawer. She didn't segregate by color—she wasn't that far gone—but it truly annoyed her to see her careful stacks all messed up and mixed together.

Cahill had probably searched her underwear drawer personally. He looked like the type who would enjoy something like that. She could just see him holding up a pair of black lace—

Oh, yes, she could see him. A wave of heat washed over her. She knew she was in real trouble, when the idea of him going through her underwear turned her on instead of making her angry.

Maybe she should forget caution and just go for broke. She'd never devoted herself to a relationship before, but maybe Cahill was someone she could truly love. Maybe there could be something real and permanent between them, and she was in danger of losing it because she couldn't stop listening to her head instead of her heart. Yes, he'd just come through a rough divorce; a year wasn't enough time to emotionally recover; he'd admitted as much himself. Yes, the odds said he was a bad risk right now. But sometimes you lucked out, and won by going against the odds.

So the real question was did she have the guts to give it all she had, to stop holding back? She had always used the Plan as an excuse for walking away before a relationship could really go anywhere; that excuse was real, because she truly wanted to execute the Plan; but the other part of her reason was that loving someone meant giving away some of your personal control, and she had always prized that above any man she was dating.

If she became involved with Cahill, she might eventually walk away from him, but she wouldn't walk away heart-whole. He could do some damage to her. She suspected she could love him as she had never loved anyone before, if she let him get close.

No matter what she decided, there were risks— big ones. She could either risk loving him and losing him, or she could risk missing out on the love of her life because she was afraid.

Sarah didn't like thinking herself cowardly, in anything.

"Do you recognize this man?" Cahill asked the next morning, letting a blurry photograph slide from a big envelope down onto the breakfast table. The photograph had been enhanced and enlarged, and it was still piss-poor. It was, however, all he had.

Sarah looked at the photograph and gave a decisive shake of her head. Randall, Barbara, and Jon all crowded around and stared at it. "I don't think so," Randall said doubtfully. "Not without seeing his face. He doesn't ring any bells, though. Why?"

"He made the last call to your father, from a pay phone in the Galleria."

Barbara jerked back as if stung. "You mean he might be the killer?"

"I can't make that assumption," Cahill said evenly. "I'd like to, but I can't. But your father might have said something to this man about a visitor he was expecting, or any other detail that might help. I'd definitely like to talk to this guy."

They all stared at the photograph again, as if concentration would wrest an elusive memory from their brains. The man in the photograph was trim, wearing a light-colored suit, with neat pale hair, either blond or gray. His head was turned so that the camera caught only the line of his left jaw and cheekbone. Unless you knew the man well, it would be impossible to recognize him from that picture.

Sarah handed Cahill a cup of coffee and tilted her head for another look at the photograph. "He's wearing a suit," she said. "The weather was warm last Wednesday."

Both Randall and Jon looked up, their attention caught. "It was too warm to wear a jacket," Jon said, "unless you were wearing a suit for work."

Barbara looked puzzled. "So what?"

"So he's white-collar," Cahill explained. "Professional."

She sighed. "All of Daddy's friends were white-collar professionals."

"Retired," Sarah put in. "That man isn't retired."

"He's younger than Daddy, then, but that's obvious from the picture. Either that or he's had a face-lift." Barbara pointed to the fairly firm jawline.

"Take what you know," Cahill prompted. "Younger than your father—say, no older than early fifties—professional. The hair is probably gray, or blond that's going gray. He's in good shape, trim, I estimate about six feet tall. No one comes to mind?"

They all shook their heads, regretfully.

"Well, if you think of anything, let me know." Cahill replaced the photograph in the envelope. "Don't concentrate on his close friends, but on someone he would know only casually."

"Sarah would be more help there than any of us," Jon said. "We've all lived away from the area for years, so we don't know anyone he may have met recently." He made a wry face. "By 'recently' I mean the last ten years, at least."

"Longer than that." Barbara sighed. "Dwight and I moved to Dallas before Shaw was born, and he's nineteen. Make that twenty years. I'm afraid we won't be any help there, Detective. Sarah is your only hope."

Everyone looked at Sarah, who shook her head. "He knew so many people. He was forever nodding to someone, then saying he didn't remember his name but he worked with so-and-so. He never really talked about anyone other than his close circle of buddies."

"So unless this guy"—Cahill tapped the envelope—"calls again, he's a dead end."

"I'm afraid so, at least as far as I'm concerned. One of the neighbors might recognize him, or you might try the Judge's friends. They were a pretty close group."

"I'll do that." He looked at the others. "I need to get back to work, but is there anything I can do for you here?"

Barbara gave him a sad, gentle smile. "We're just packing up photographs and personal items that we want to keep. Thank you for all you've done,

the advice you've given. I know you'll do everything possible to find whoever killed Daddy."

"Yes, ma'am, I will." He glanced at Sarah.
"Would you walk out to the car, Miss Stevens?"

The day was warmer than the day before, but
still chilly enough that she grabbed a jacket on the
way out. The sun was bright, picking out the fresh,
bright colors of spring, the pink of the azaleas, the
tender green of new leaves, the white and pink
dogwoods. Sarah squinted at the brightness, lifting
her hand to shade her eyes.

"What is it, Detective Cahill?"

"Nothing much, I just wanted a minute alone
with you. What are your plans for now? They'll be
selling the house, right? What are you going to
do?"

"I'm staying here, for now. They all have to
leave this afternoon, so I'll handle all the packing,
getting things ready for the house to be put on the
market."

"You're staying here? In the house?"

"I can look after things better if I'm here, on-
site."

"Will it bother you to be here alone?"

"It bothers me that the Judge is dead. It bothers me
to go into the library, because I keep seeing his body
there, and smelling . . . smelling things. But it doesn't
bother me to be alone. I think what happened was
targeted specifically at him, though I have no idea
why. So I'm not in any danger." She paused, struck by
a fleeting expression on his tough face. "Am I? Is
there something you haven't told me?"

"No, nothing. I think you're safe. It's just that
you have more guts than most people. A lot of men
I know wouldn't want to stay here by themselves."

"So who says men have more guts than women?"

He grinned at the challenge in her voice. "No one. Men just tend to do stupid things out of pride. Now that I've admitted we're all idiots, will you have dinner with me tonight?"

"What? Go out with an idiot?"

"Think of the entertainment value."

"You have a point." She smiled up at him. "I'd like that, then. What time, and where are we going?"

"Six-thirty, and we'll go someplace casual, if that's all right with you."

"Casual is great."

He winked at her as he got in the car. "See you at six-thirty."

Her heart was lighter as she went back inside the house. She still grieved, but life did go on; the awful thing about clichés was that they were usually right. The terrible pain and depression had lifted, and she was already looking ahead, focusing on the future. She had chores to accomplish, affairs to be put in order, a job to find.

But more immediately, she had a date with Cahill.

CHAPTER 14

"YOU'LL NEVER GUESS," SHE SAID BY WAY OF GREETING WHEN SHE opened the door to him that night, "what came in the mail today."

He tensed. "Another gift?"

"Something almost worse," she grumbled. "Two job offers."

His dark, level brows knotted. "And that's bad, how?"

"They were postmarked Saturday. These people must have written the letters almost immediately after they heard about the Judge."

"I repeat: That's bad, how?"

She gave him an impatient glance. "Vultures. It's like people who read the obituaries and call the surviving spouse for a date immediately after the funeral."

"I think it's smart, if they want you. Get an offer in first, and you might take it before any others come in."

"Too late, since I had one week before last, right after that segment aired."

"But they didn't know that. I'd do the same thing," he said reasonably. "I see you, I want you, I make my move and try to cut out anyone else thinking the same thing."

She snorted as she pulled on her jacket. "Really bad analogy, Cahill. You saw, and you ran."

"Don't I get brownie points for working up enough courage to come back?"

"No. I don't work on the points system."

"Then I guess I'll have to rely on physical coercion." He caught the front of her jacket in his fist and pulled her to him. Sarah lifted her head to meet his kiss; it wasn't until his mouth touched hers that she realized how sharp was her need to feel this again, to have him hold her. Their tongues engaged in slow combat, sliding, probing, twining. He wasn't in any hurry, and neither was she.

He lifted his mouth enough to murmur, "Are you coerced yet?"

"Not yet. Keep trying."

His mouth curled in a smile as he rested his forehead against hers. "I don't want to overstep my bounds. Give me some ground rules, here. If I get rowdy and out of control, at what point do you slap my face? The trick is to stop just short of that point."

Sarah lifted her brows. "I don't slap faces; I kick asses."

"Wow. That sounds interesting. Pants up, or down?"

She buried her face against his jacket, snickering. "I should have guessed you'd be a pervert."

"A boy just wants to have fun." His big, warm hand slid up and down her back in a restless movement that told her he didn't like restraining himself, but was doing it anyway. "And if we don't get going, I may get my ass kicked. I've never been very good at knowing when to stop."

On the contrary, he had wooing down to a fine

art—for wooing her, anyway. He made it very plain he was attracted, but didn't come on too hot and heavy for the early stages of getting to know each other. She was thoroughly charmed by his wry humor, more charmed than she wanted him to know. If he pushed his luck, she thought, she might very well end up in bed with him, and she deeply appreciated that he was restraining himself because she suspected he knew exactly how charmed she was. Cahill was one sharp cookie.

"Did either of the job offers look interesting?" he asked as he opened the door of his truck for her.

"No, they both wanted me to start immediately, and that's out. I'll be here at least another month; when the house is ready to close up, I doubt the family will want to continue paying my salary just to sit in my quarters, so I don't expect it to last much more than a month, but I'm not free until then."

"You don't think they'll hold the position open? It isn't as if butlers are thick on the ground around here."

She shrugged. "They might, they might not. I think they only want me because of the so-called celebrity factor, and I don't like the idea of that."

"Since you're trained as a bodyguard, too, will you consider only jobs with that need?"

"That would be nice," she said wryly. "The pay is a lot higher. But, no, a lot of things come into consideration. How much I like the family, for one thing. Whether or not there are any positions open for both butler and bodyguard, where in the country the job is, things like that."

"You don't like certain parts of the country?"

"It isn't that. I'm a military brat; I'm used to living just about anywhere. But my parents and sister live in Florida, and I like for visiting them to be fairly convenient."

"You're close to your folks?"

"We talk on the phone a lot. I don't get to see them as much as I'd like, maybe three or four times a year, but I'd say we're close. Even though my brothers are both in the military and are sent all over the world, still, we manage phone calls. How about you?"

"Well, we're originally from this area, so I have aunts and uncles and cousins scattered all over central Alabama. My sister, DeeDee, lives in Redneck Riviera—that's Gulf Shores, to outsiders—and my brother, Dudley Do-Right, lives in Montgomery."

"DeeDee and Do-Right?" she asked, amused.

"She was named after the two grandmothers, Devonna and Darnelle. Which one would you like to be called?"

"DeeDee, hands down."

"No joke. Dudley, now—his real name is Thane—is a state cop, so he wears the Do-Right uniform. Between the two of them, they've made me an uncle five times. DeeDee's the oldest, by two years. I'm thirty-six, by the way."

"You don't have any kids?"

"No, thank God. That's the only good thing about my divorce, that we didn't have any kids whose lives we wrecked. The rest of the family always thought I was a slacker for not reproducing, but now they're glad, too."

"What about your parents?"

"They thought I was a slacker, too."

She punched his arm. "Smart aleck."

He grinned, then frowned a little and rubbed his arm. "Ow. You pack a punch."

"I pulled it. You're just a wuss." Yeah, right. His arm was so hard, she could have seriously damaged her knuckles. "Your parents," she prompted.

"They live in Kentucky. They had a reason for moving there, but I don't know what it was."

"What's wrong with Kentucky?"

"It snows there."

"What's wrong with snow?"

"I've been a patrol cop, you know. Have you ever seen what happens down here when it snows?"

She began to laugh, because one inch of snow could and did cause havoc with traffic. Southerners didn't deal well with snow; it was a giant headache for patrol cops, with all the accidents. For someone who had spent one memorable winter in upstate New York, the alarm caused by a snow flurry down here was hilarious.

Abruptly she noticed that they were heading south, away from town. "Where are we going?"

"How do you feel about high school baseball?"

She paused. "Is that a rhetorical question, or are you telling me something?"

"One of my cousins has a game tonight, a doubleheader. We'll miss the first game, but by the time we get something to eat and get to the field, we should be just in time for the second game. JoJo plays shortstop."

JoJo was evidently the cousin. "I like baseball, but this jacket isn't heavy enough for sitting out for hours in the cold."

"I have a blanket behind the seat, a thick wool one. We can cuddle on the bleachers, and with the blanket wrapped around us no one will know if I sneak a feel every now and then."

"*I'll* know."

"God, I hope so. If you don't, then I've either lost my touch or my aim."

Maybe a public place *was* the safest place to be with him. "All right," she said. "I'm willing. We can even grab a hot dog at the game if you want to catch some of the first one."

"I knew you were good folk," he said happily.

Sitting on cold bleachers on a chilly night, surrounded by yelling, laughing, chatting parents and siblings, a few teachers, and clumps of students, turned out to be more fun than she remembered from the days when Daniel and Noel had played baseball. For one thing, Cahill's cousins—there were about ten of them there—were all loony. She had to wonder if the sense of humor was a family trait. For another, cuddling under that blanket with him was . . . more than fun.

The king-size blanket, as he promised, was thick wool. He wrapped it around both of them before they even sat down, so even her legs were protected from the chill. His body heat and the blanket combined to keep her toasty warm, even though the April night was so chilly their breaths fogged. He was pressed all along her left side, his hard thigh rubbing hers, and he kept his right arm around her except for those times when he felt compelled to leap to his feet and yell insults at the home plate umpire who, as it turned out, was yet another cousin.

A few times he even managed to cop a feel, as he

had promised. The caress was subtle, just his thumb rubbing against the side of her right breast, but it was deliberate and she knew it. The first time it happened, she glanced sharply up at him to find him innocently watching the game, a slight smile tugging at the corners of his mouth. She retaliated by trailing her left hand up his thigh, oh, so slowly, stopping just south of the bull's-eye. He tensed, the smile leaving his mouth, and though he kept his gaze on the game, he had that unfocused look that told her he'd lost track of the action on the field.

She felt terribly naughty, doing such things in public, even though they were wrapped like mummies in that wonderful blanket and no one could tell a thing. She wanted to forget about teasing him and go for the gold with a stroke that would make his eyes roll back in his head; she wanted to twist her body a little so his hand was fully cupping her breast.

She didn't have to twist her body. He managed just fine without her help.

She caught her breath at the warm pressure of his hand, at the stroke of his thumb over her nipple. It didn't matter that the triple layers of bra, shirt, and jacket protected her skin from his touch; her breasts tightened, her nipples drawing into hard little peaks, and her entire lower body clenched in response.

"Are you okay?" he asked, his tone casual, as if he were asking if she was cold.

She really, really wanted to grab him, but squeezing a man's genitals on the first date was way out of her league. She settled for burrowing her right hand inside his shirt and pulling his chest hair. Hard. He couldn't control a flinch.

"I'm a little hot," she said, just as casually. "Maybe we can loosen the blanket."

"Good idea," he said, sounding a little strangled now, and they both shrugged the blanket down to their waists. They resorted to coffee to fight the chill for the remainder of the ball game.

Because he had to work the next day, after the game was over he drove her straight home. When he kissed her good night, she was smart enough to hold his hands while he did. He was grinning when he lifted his head. "I haven't had my hands held during a kiss since high school."

"I haven't been groped at a ball game since high school, either."

"It was fun, wasn't it?"

She found herself smiling. "Yeah, it was."

"Do you have plans for tomorrow night? And every night this week?"

"You're asking me out every night?"

"I have to wear you down. How else am I going to get to second base without getting tagged out? Here's the agenda: Tomorrow night we go bowling—"

"*Bowling?*"

"Cosmic bowling. It's a hoot."

She didn't bother asking what cosmic bowling was. "What about Wednesday?"

"Movie."

"Thursday?"

"Symphony."

From the ridiculous to the sublime. She shook her head in amazement; at least she wouldn't be bored. "Friday?"

"I'm hoping by that time we'll have moved on to the wild monkey sex."

She hooted with laughter, and he smiled as he leaned against the doorjamb. "Is it a date?" he asked. "Or dates."

"Up until Friday."

"We'll see," he said, and whistled as he walked back to his truck.

He was positively Machiavellian.

CHAPTER 15

THERE WAS AN ARTICLE IN THE NEWSPAPER TUESDAY MORNING under the headline LACK OF EVIDENCE HAMPERS POLICE IN MOUNTAIN BROOK MURDER. Cahill grunted in disgust as he read the article.

> The Mountain Brook Police Department is offering no information other than "no comment" on their investigation into the murder of retired federal Judge Lowell Roberts. The investigation seems to have stalled, and concerned citizens are wondering if the department, which hasn't investigated a murder in five years, is experienced enough to handle this type of case.

"That's bullshit," he growled, tossing the paper onto his desk. All of the investigators in the detective division were pissed. The lieutenant was pissed. Basically, everyone was pissed. The investigation was stalled, all right, but it had nothing to do with incompetence or lack of experience. If the idiot who wrote that article had done his research, he'd have known that the Mountain Brook department was top-notch, with excellent people and excellent equipment. The head evidence technician

had handled the gathering of evidence, and he'd
done it right. Cahill himself had done a tour of
duty with the Birmingham Police Department,
where murder investigations were much more
commonplace; all of the detectives were experi-
enced. They knew how to run an investigation, but
they couldn't manufacture evidence that wasn't
there.

It came back to lack of motive. When Judge
Roberts had been murdered he hadn't been walking down the street and been a victim of a drive-by
shooting, a for-kicks murder. His murder was deliberate, planned, and executed with precision—an
assassination, in fact. Whoever had killed him had
known it was Sarah's day off and the Judge would
be alone in the house. The mystery phone call by
the mystery man from the pay phone in the Galleria was the only lead they had, but no one so far
had recognized anything about the man in the photograph. They'd talked to friends, neighbors, family, and come up with exactly zilch.

The easy way hadn't panned out. Things would
have been a lot simpler if Judge Roberts had been
gunned down as he opened the door, or walking to
his car; then the revenge scenario would have
played. Instead Cahill kept coming back to the inescapable conclusion that the Judge had known his
killer and willingly let him into the house.

And that brought Cahill right back to the mystery man in the surveillance photo. The timing of
that phone call was right. Someone whom the
Judge knew, from out of town maybe, who had
called and said, *Hey, I'm in the area;* and the Judge
invited him to the house, and the guy killed him.

That was the scenario the circumstances supported. But who, and why? That was the old truism—find out *why,* and you'll know *who.*

Too bad he didn't have any fucking idea.

He scrubbed his hands over his face. His bad feeling about this case hadn't gone away. The answer was out there, but they weren't getting any closer to it and he was afraid they wouldn't. This one was going to be filed under "Unsolved." He hated unsolved crimes of any sort, but a murder really ate at him. Even as a kid puzzles had nagged at him, and he couldn't stop until they were solved. The damned Rubik's Cube had driven him up the wall until he got it figured out. On a scale of one to ten, the Rubik's Cube was like a five, and a murder was like ten zillion. That's how bad it nagged at him. He could easily become obsessed with this case if he wasn't careful.

This one was more personal than it should have been, because it had touched Sarah. If she'd been at home instead of at the movie, she might have been killed, too. She felt guilty because she thought she could have prevented it, but Cahill got a cold feeling in the pit of his stomach every time he thought of her there in the house with a killer. She would have gone to her quarters and left the two . . . friends? acquaintances? talking in the Judge's library; she might not even have heard the shot, if it was silenced. Then, because she had seen him, the killer would have quietly gone up those stairs to her quarters. She wouldn't have been expecting him, she wouldn't have been armed, and he would have killed her. It was that simple, and he broke out in a sweat every time he played it through in his mind.

Going to the movie had saved her life, and she had
gone because she wanted to give the idiot who sent
her the fancy pendant an opportunity to approach
her. Funny how things worked out; by sending her
the pendant and making her so uneasy, the weirdo
had saved her life.

Sarah was . . . he didn't know what Sarah was.
Fascinating. Sexy. Strong and tender at the same
time. He didn't know what would happen between
them; he wasn't even letting himself think about
what might or might not happen. With her, he was
living totally in the present. When he was with her,
he didn't think about the past, and he didn't care
about the future. Hell, that was a lie, because if he
had anything to say about it, the future included
getting her clothes off and having some really hot,
wet, wrecking-the-bed sex. Now that was some
real planning for the future.

It felt good to focus on one woman, rather than
have more of those ships-that-pass-in-the-night en-
counters that took some of the pressure off his
balls but left him still feeling alone the next day.
He enjoyed playing with Sarah, and that was exactly what they were doing: playing. Having fun. It
had been too damn long since he'd had fun, too
long since he'd felt the particular thrill of watching
a woman's face and feeling in sync with her.

Like last night, for instance; she had seriously
thought about grabbing his balls as payback, but
had decided not to ratchet up the intimacy between them to that degree. Her dark eyes had been
cool and challenging, but still he'd *known* what
she was thinking, read it in the slight tensing of her
very toned body. He'd been ready to endure a certain amount of pain—he doubted she'd cripple

him, but she would still have made him hurt—in order to speed things up between them. Too bad she'd thought better of grabbing him, because from the way he looked at it, if she'd hurt him, she would have had to kiss it to make it better. Worked for him.

Getting a hard-on at work wasn't a good idea. Cahill wrenched his thoughts upward.

He had a month to get her, the month she estimated it would take her to get everything packed and to close up the house. She would be taking another job; he hoped she would still be in this area, but nothing was guaranteed. As she had said, if someone needed her combined services of butler and bodyguard, the pay was much better, and how many people around here needed a bodyguard? He figured the odds were at least fifty-fifty she'd be leaving the area, so he had to work fast. Who knows? Maybe if they were having an affair, she'd take a job nearby and they could take their time with each other, see where this thing went.

That thought edged too far into the future, and he pulled back from it. All he could handle right now was *right now*. He would see Sarah every night, and every second in between the murder he had to investigate, plus the other investigations that came up.

The newspaper said the police didn't have a clue in the Roberts murder. What a shame.

He was pleased; once again, he had proven himself more intelligent than others. Of course there were no clues. First he had seen Sarah safely in the movie, then he had driven to the Galleria and made the phone call from a pay phone. Thousands of people were in the Galleria every day; there was no way to pick him out. Judge Roberts, the old fool, had been happy to talk to the friend of a friend about a point of law, and as easy as that he was in the house.

Though his fingerprints weren't in any AFIS data banks for the simple reason that he'd never been fingerprinted, he had still made certain to note everything he touched while he was in the house, and he had carefully wiped those surfaces before leaving. He had refused anything to drink, so there was no cup or glass to be taken care of. He had also picked up the spent cartridge shell from the carpet where the automatic had ejected it, and disposed of it in the trash the next day. The trash had since been picked up, so that was gone.

He was safe. Now he could concentrate on Sarah.

He didn't want to repeat his offer too soon. She wouldn't like that; her sense of propriety would be offended. But neither could he afford to wait too long, because her services would be in demand. He had discovered through his network of acquaintances in the neighborhood—really, one couldn't call them *friends*—that the Roberts family was putting the house up for sale and had arranged for her to stay on to oversee that, for the time being.

Things couldn't have been more perfect. He had time, a grace period as it were, to carefully think through how he would word the next offer. He'd made a mistake the last time, not taking her sense of loyalty into account and reducing her worth to merely that of money. Of course she was worth that amount, she was worth much more, but a woman of her conscientious nature would need something in addition to money: a sense of purpose.

She had to think he needed her. He *did* need her, so much more than she could imagine. Since first seeing her, he had come to realize she was the perfect woman for him, the woman he'd been waiting for his entire life, and he wouldn't be complete without her.

He felt almost dizzy, thinking of her here, in his home. He would give her everything she could possibly want, protect her from a world that couldn't possibly appreciate her sheer perfection. It had to be a trial to her, forced constantly to deal with people who weren't worthy of her. When she was with him, there would be none of that. She wouldn't need other people. Together, they would be perfection.

Tuesday was an incredibly sad and lonely day. It was the first day she had been entirely alone in the house; yesterday the family had been here until the early afternoon; then she had gone out with Cahill, which took her mind off the emptiness. Cahill, she suspected, could take her mind off dying.

Today, however, he wasn't there. The knowledge that she would see him that night was a beacon she kept in the back of her mind, a bit of brightness against the gloom. She kept herself busy. She didn't have to hunt for things to do; there was a huge amount of work to be done.

She began the work of methodically packing up each room, with a master inventory she devised and entered into her laptop, to show what contents were in which box and from which room they were taken. The boxes would be numbered, and on each box she'd tape an envelope containing a packing list for that particular box. The chore was time-consuming and exhausting, but that wasn't enough to keep her mind off the fact that she was alone in this huge house, or to keep her from re-membering every time she passed the library what had happened in there.

The phone rang incessantly. The callers didn't mean any harm, with their questions about the family and what they intended to do, but the con-stant interruptions meant Sarah didn't accomplish as much as she'd planned, and the questions kept the Judge fresh in her mind. She didn't want to for-get him, but she would have liked a little distance from the pain.

Thinking about Cahill provided that distance. Maybe she was thinking about him too much for her own well-being, but . . . well, she'd just have to deal with that.

Far from being the humorless man she'd first thought him, he had a lighthearted streak that made her laugh and kept her on her toes. She sensed that he was being careful with her—not be-cause she was fragile, but rather because she wasn't.

Sarah knew her own worth, her own strength; she was neither a Kleenex to be used and casually tossed away, nor a butterfly who would gaily flit away on her own. Cahill wanted her, but he was wary of anything except a sexual, superficial rela-tionship with anyone, and he wasn't certain ex-actly how serious he wanted to get with her. They had fun together, but on a certain level they were like two heavyweight boxers, circling, each testing the other's strength, not committing until they knew whether or not they were going to get hammered.

She *liked* him more than anyone she had dated before—but then how could she not like someone who would take her to both a bowling alley and a symphony? She had known from the beginning that the physical chemistry was great; *overwhelming* was a better word. Still, she could resist physical attraction if that was all there was. In Cahill's case, the total package was as seductive as a Lorelei, pulling her to him.

Lunch was a sandwich and a glass of water, eaten in her quarters. The silence beat at her, until she thought she could hear her own heartbeat. She washed the knife she had used, and the glass, and put them away. Then she burst into tears.

Half an hour later she found herself sitting on the steps leading from the portico to the flower garden. The bright sunshine beat down on her upturned face, her bare arms, and the air was redolent with the sweet freshness of spring. Birds chirped madly in the trees, their colors flashing as they darted about. Bees zipped from bloom to bloom, drunk on nectar. Inside the house was sadness, but out here was life and warmth.

Footsteps sounded on the stones behind her, and she turned her head to see Cahill. "Hi," he said, dropping down to sit beside her. "You didn't answer the doorbell, so I walked around to see if your truck was here."

"I'm here," she said, unnecessarily. "I'm just . . . taking a break."

He studied her taut face and swollen eyes, then gently eased her into his arms and cradled her head against his shoulder. "Bad day, huh?"

"So far, it sucks." God, being held felt so good. He was solid and strong, and she turned her face against his neck so she could inhale the heated aroma of his body. She put her arms around him, one arm looped around his neck and the other pressed to his back; her fingers dug into the layered muscles there, traced the indentation of his spine.

He tilted her head back and kissed her, and his palm settled warmly over her right breast. She allowed the caress, leaning into him and surrendering to the kiss. Just now she needed cuddling, needed the physical comfort of his presence, so she didn't protest when he unbuttoned her sleeveless blouse and unhooked the front closure of her bra, pushing it aside. Fresh air gently brushed over her bare flesh, puckering her nipples; then they were covered by the hot slide of his callus-roughened palm. "God, you're pretty," he said, his tone low and rough. "Look at this."

She opened her eyes and looked. Her breasts were the color of warm cream, with small, pinkish brown nipples. She wasn't overly endowed, but her breasts plumped in his palm, his hard, tanned fingers in sharp male contrast to the very womanly curves. He stroked his thumb over one nipple and it beaded more tightly, flushing with color.

A sound like far-off thunder rumbled in his throat, and she looked up to see a sheen of sweat on his forehead. "I'm working," he said hoarsely.

"You couldn't prove it by me," she murmured.

She thought she could sit here in the sunshine for hours, letting him fondle her. Except she *wouldn't* be sitting here for hours, she would very shortly find herself on her back, on the stones of the portico; not exactly a comfortable place for lovemaking.

"I just stopped by to check on you. I can't stay." He kissed her again, his hand still working its warm magic on her breasts; then he reluctantly released her. Actually, he released her as if it tore his skin off to separate from her. "Just remember where we were, and we'll pick up there tonight."

Feeling much better, she rehooked her bra and began buttoning her blouse. "Sorry, it doesn't work that way. You'll have to start over."

"Not a problem," he said, smiling.

She snorted. "I didn't think it would be." Then she smiled, too, a little mistily. "Thanks for stopping by. I was feeling blue."

"I noticed. Six-thirty again?"

She nodded. "I'll be ready."

"So will I."

"That wasn't what I meant."

"Well, hell," he said in disgust.

Already she could feel her smile edging into a grin, feel laughter beginning to bubble. "Go back to work, Cahill, and remember: Never take anything for granted."

"Well, hell," he said again.

CHAPTER 16

ON WEDNESDAY, A WEEK AFTER THE MURDER, SARAH FOUND HER-self following her old schedule. She had forgotten to reschedule her karate and kick-boxing sessions anyway, so she worked in the house until it was time for the classes, then devoted herself to the hardest workouts she had put herself through in a long time. It's exactly a week today, she kept thinking. Exactly a week. A week ago, the most important thing in her life had been finding out who'd sent her that pendant. Today, she couldn't remember exactly how the pendant looked. It had been relegated to unimportance by what had happened later that night.

She was supposed to go to a movie with Cahill that night. Remembering that she'd gone to a movie last Wednesday, too, she knew she couldn't do it. She called the number Cahill had given her, and he answered immediately.

"This is Sarah. I'm sorry, but I can't do a movie tonight."

He paused. "Has something come up?"

"No, it's just . . . it was a week ago today, and I went to a movie then, too."

"Okay." His tone was gentle. "We'll do something else."

"No, I—" She wanted to be with him, but maybe after last night a cooling-down period was in order. She had managed to keep things from getting out of hand, or even progressing any further than they already had, but he was making serious inroads in her resolve. The cooling-down period was for her. "Not tonight. We're still on for tomorrow night, but I won't be good company tonight."

"Are you getting cold feet?"

Trust him to bypass sympathy and politeness, and go straight to the heart of the matter! "Trust me," she said wryly. "If my feet are cold, it's the only part of me that is."

He blew out a short, sharp breath. "You just made it impossible for me to sit down."

"I hope no one can overhear you."

He ignored that. "I'll be at home if you change your mind, or if you decide you want company."

"Thanks, Cahill." Her voice was soft. "You're a sweetheart."

"Told you you'd be calling me that," he said smugly.

No matter what, he could lift her spirits. She hung up feeling slightly elated, the way she always felt around him. The fizz saw her through the rest of that difficult day.

On Thursday night, on the way to the symphony, he said, "I have a friend who's dying to meet you. He's lowlife scum who thinks he can charm you away from me, but if you don't mind feeling dirty by association, he really, really wants to do some target practice with you. I have an extra weapon you can use, since we still have yours."

She laughed. "He's a lowlife scum who makes you feel dirty by association? Sure, I'd like to meet him."

"Thought so. How about tomorrow afternoon, about two o'clock, at that range you were at before."

"Two o'clock? Don't you have to work? Or are you sending me out to get dirty by association all on my own?"

"I'm off half a day tomorrow, and all of the weekend." He slanted an appraising glance at her. "Wear that dress."

If that wasn't just like a man. "To target practice? In your dreams."

"You have no idea about my dreams," he said feelingly. In one of those swings of temperature so common to spring, the day had seen the mid-eighties and hadn't cooled down much with sunset. Sarah had dressed accordingly, in a sleeveless aqua sheath that made her warm coloring glow, and brought along a shawl to drape over her arms if she became chilled. The sheath clung in all the right places and skimmed others, and was cut low enough in front to show a hint of cleavage. Cahill had been eyeing that hint since he picked her up.

Prudently she didn't ask him about his dreams, because she was fairly certain he'd tell her. If Cahill had a shy bone in his body, she hadn't found it yet.

The symphony was wonderful; she loved classical music, and Cahill talked knowledgeably about the program, proving that he hadn't picked the symphony just to impress her. "Do you come to the symphony often?" she asked.

"Not as often as I'd like, but a couple of times a year, at least. I have to work it into my schedule."

"I can see how it would be tough making time for the symphony, what with all the ball games and the bowling."

He grinned. "Admit it. You liked cosmic bowling."

"I'd never bowled in the dark before." In fact, she'd had a ball Tuesday night; cosmic bowling *was* a hoot. The balls and pins were painted with glow-in-the-dark paint; the regular lights were turned off and the black lights turned on. Anything white, such as teeth or shoes, or a shirt, had taken on an unearthly glow. It was a little disconcerting to suddenly see teeth flashing at you in the darkness. The next time they went, though, she would make Cahill wear a white shirt so she could keep track of him.

She worked that night after he took her home and got up early the next morning to get in some extra time packing so that she could take off early to meet Cahill's friend. If anything, she was putting in more hours now than she had while the Judge was alive, but she was so wary of short-timing the family that she was doing the opposite. Cahill had a way of consuming time—witness this afternoon—so she wanted to have extra hours built up during the week as a cushion.

It was another warm day, eighty-seven degrees. She wore a pair of tan knit slacks with an elastic waistband for comfort, since she would be sweating on the practice range, a short-sleeved, V-necked T, and sandals, with heavy-duty sunscreen slathered on all exposed skin. "Damn," Cahill said when he picked her up. "I hoped you'd change your mind about the dress."

"Yeah, I could just see me bending over to pick up cartridges in that dress."

"Man, so could I," he said, sighing.

His friend, Rick Mancil, was the stocky man she'd seen him with at the range before. Rick had black hair, pale green eyes, and was as irrepressible as the Energizer Bunny. His opening line to her was, "If you get tired of putting up with this jack-ass, just give me a call and I'll have you at the altar before you can say 'Mrs. Mancil.'"

"Believe him," Cahill drawled. "He's done it twice already."

Sarah blinked. "Married women you've dated?"

"Just married," Rick corrected. "But we won't talk about that."

She sensed that Cahill wanted her to show off her marksmanship for Rick, so she obliged. She and Rick got side-by-side targets; he exclaimed at length about his pistol, how accurate it was, how it had never jammed, and so on; she glanced at Cahill, who was leaning negligently against a post with his ankles crossed, and he shrugged, smiling. "He never runs down," he said.

"That's a good thing in a man," Rick said, winking at her.

Sarah looked back at Cahill. "Aren't you going to shoot?"

He gave a brief shake of his head. Rick said, "We won't bring him into this. He beats me every time, the damn show-off. It's that military training of his, gives him an unfair advantage."

As far as that went, so did her own military training. Hers had been private, courtesy of her father, but training was training.

They began with the targets fairly close, moving them back after every clip. Sarah fired steadily, concentrating as she did when she was competing against her brothers. The buck of the pistol in her hand was as familiar to her as driving a car; she almost didn't have to think about what she was doing, the habit was so ingrained.

"I can't believe this," Rick complained good-naturedly. "Doc said you were good, but *I'm* good, and you're beating me on every target."

"Shoot left-handed," Cahill said to Sarah, and Rick gawked at him.

"Left-handed? She shoots both ways?"

Sarah simply switched hands and proceeded to empty the clip at the target. As usual, you could have covered all the holes in the target with a playing card.

"You son of a bitch," Rick said to Cahill, his tone disbelieving. "You brought in a ringer! She's a professional, isn't she?"

"I'm a butler," Sarah corrected. She had to admit she was enjoying herself, especially the by-play between the two men.

"Pay up," Cahill said, holding out his hand.

Growling, Rick pulled out his wallet and laid five twenties in Cahill's palm.

"Wait a minute," she said indignantly. "You made a side bet and didn't cut me in on the action?"

"What did I tell you?" Rick asked. "He's a jackass."

"*You* didn't cut me in, either," she pointed out, carefully putting down her weapon and crossing her arms, glaring at them.

"Uh . . ."

"Say, 'I'm a jackass, too,'" Cahill prompted in an almost-whisper.

"I'm a jackass, too!" Rick repeated loudly. His pale eyes sparkled with laughter.

"Were you two in high school together?" she asked. "Just wondering."

"God, no. Can you imagine?" Cahill grinned as he put the money in his pocket.

"Not without shuddering, no."

Cahill clapped Rick on the shoulder. "Well, buddy, it's been fun. We'll do this again when I need extra money, okay? We're going to leave you now; I have steaks marinating at home. We'll think of you with every bite."

"You do that," Rick said, managing a forlorn look. He even gave them a sad wave as they left, like a little kid being left behind while the other kids go off to play.

"God, he's exhausting!" Sarah said when they were in the truck. "Fun, but exhausting."

"Two ex-wives said the same thing. If there's such a thing as a manic-depressive who's always manic, that's Rick."

"What does he say about you? Other than that you're a jackass?"

"That I'm sneaky. And stubborn."

"I agree; they're good traits in a cop."

"Mmm. So you think I'm sneaky?"

Sarah looked at him, at ease behind the wheel, long legs encased in boots and tight jeans, a crisp white T-shirt molded to his torso. His lips were slightly curled in amusement, as if he knew where this was going. Oh, yes, he was sneaky.

"What's this about 'steaks marinating at home'?

That's the first I've heard about these steaks, much less their location."

"I have a built-in grill, it's Friday, the weather's warm. What else does a red-blooded southern boy do but cook out? Besides, I know where you live; don't you want to know where I live?"

She did, damn it. She wanted to know if he was a slob, if he had one chair and a huge television, if his refrigerator had nothing but frozen dinners, cheese, and beer in it. She wanted to know if he left whiskers in the sink when he shaved, if he made his bed in the mornings or left the covers tossed on the floor. She definitely had it bad, so bad she wanted to groan.

"Where exactly do you live?" she asked, and he smiled at her capitulation.

"Down 280, in Shelby County."

The Birmingham metro area was spreading fast to the south; Shelby was the fastest-growing county in Alabama, with businesses and subdivisions springing up almost overnight, which was why traffic on 280, the main artery into Birmingham, was such a nightmare. Property values in Shelby were soaring.

"How long have you lived there?"

"Just a year, since the divorce was final. I lucked out finding this house; actually, it belonged to a cousin who was transferred to Tucson. The house Shannon and I lived in sold almost immediately, so I had my split of the money from that as a hefty down payment and that got the mortgage payments down into the reasonable range."

"I suppose I thought you'd have an apartment, or live in a condo."

"I like the privacy of my own house. It's not a

new house; it was built in the late seventies and needed some work done on it. I'm pretty good with my hands, so I've been doing the repairs, fixing it up."

She could see him as a handyman; he had that air of capability that said he could do pretty much whatever interested him. Maybe it was just her, but she thought men with hammers were sexy.

She didn't know what she'd expected, but it wasn't a traditional brick house, with a yard that sloped away at the back, and a neat sidewalk bordered by trimmed hedges. The brick was a soft red, and the shutters were dark blue, the front door painted a shade or two lighter. The driveway curved around to the back of the house. "There's a full basement," he said. "The garage used to be there, but my cousin turned it into a playroom for his kids. Actually, it's a lot of house for just one person, but I like the room."

He parked beside the walkway, and let her in the front door. Either he'd just had in a cleaning service, she thought, or he wasn't a slob. The hardwood in the entry gleamed, and there was a fresh, lemony smell in the air.

His hand was a warm weight in the small of her back. "The living room," he said, gesturing to the left. The room was completely empty, the carpet spotless, and the curtains drawn. "I don't have any use for it, so I haven't bothered with furniture. Same with the dining room. The kitchen has a breakfast nook, and that's where I eat. The den is here."

The den was cozy, with a large fireplace, big windows looking out over the backyard, and an entertainment center with a big television. She felt gratified at that evidence of his guy-ness. He had furniture, though: an overstuffed sofa and two big recliners, plus the requisite number of end tables and lamps. All in all, it looked fairly civilized. The den was separated from the kitchen by a half-wall topped off with a row of white wooden spindles. "The kitchen needed work," he said. "I refinished the cabinets, put in that island." The wood cabinets had a natural finish that glowed with a soft golden color. The island was made of the same wood, with a smooth-surface cooktop surrounded by ceramic tile.

There weren't any dirty dishes in the sink. The counter surface held a block of knives, a microwave, and a coffeemaker, but that was it. The breakfast nook at the other end of the kitchen held a white table with a ceramic tile top in a yellow-and-blue pattern, and the four chairs grouped around the table were painted the same shade of yellow, while the rug underneath was blue.

"Are you sure you weren't in the Navy?" she asked, looking around at the spotless kitchen. Navy people learned to put everything in its assigned place, because there wasn't any spare room aboard a ship.

He grinned. "What did you expect, a pigsty? The laundry may pile up, but I'm fairly neat. I do have someone who comes in every other week and does the basic cleaning, because I don't think of things like dusting. C'mon, I'll show you the rest of the house."

The rest of the house was a half-bath next to the kitchen, two good-size bedrooms at the front of the house, separated by a nice large bathroom, and the master bedroom and bathroom suite at the back. His bed was king-sized, but then she would have put money on that. And it was made up. The room was neat, but it wasn't spotless; one of his shirts hung over the back of a chair, and a coffee cup with an inch of cold coffee in it sat on the dresser. "So that's where I left it," he said, picking up the cup. "I looked all over for the damn thing this morning."

She liked it that he hadn't straightened up the place, not that it needed much. He didn't have to have things perfect, and he wasn't trying to impress her. Perversely, she was impressed anyway, with his confidence and sense of self.

"I don't know about you," he said, "but I'm hungry. Let's fire up the grill and get those steaks on."

The steaks were filets, two inches thick and so tender she almost didn't need a knife. While the steaks were cooking, she microwaved two potatoes, tossed the salad, and heated the rolls. Instead of wine, he produced a jug of iced tea.

If he had put on some soft, gauzy, romantic music, she might have had a chance, but instead he turned on the television to Fox News Channel and had the news playing in the background. Maybe he wasn't trying to seduce her—at least not actively trying—but he was succeeding anyway.

After they had cleaned up the few dishes and put the kitchen to rights, working quickly and easily together, he said, "I want to show you the basement. I think you'll like it."

He led the way down the stairs and turned on the bright overhead lights.

The first thing she noticed was that the walls were very utilitarian, with bare pipes against the brick. The second was that he did some serious workouts down here.

To her left was an impressive set of free weights, and a punching bag hung motionless from a beam. There was a weight machine, the type that converted to accommodate all types of exercises, and a treadmill.

He stayed by the door while she wandered over to the free weights and ran her fingers over the cold metal of the dumbbells, then examined the weight machine and the computerized treadmill. He put a good deal of effort and money into staying in shape, though she bet the treadmill was used only during really nasty weather. A little rain wouldn't keep this man indoors; it probably took a downpour with a lot of lightning to do the trick. Idly she wondered how many miles a day he ran, but what interested her the most was the large exercise mat that covered a full half of the basement floor. There was only one use for a mat like that.

She knew he'd studied karate from the way he had leveled the robber with a kick, but he'd never mentioned it again, and with everything that had happened since then, she'd forgotten about it. She wondered why he hadn't brought up the subject, since he knew she studied karate. His silence couldn't be because he was at a lower level than she; Tom Cahill didn't have a fragile ego. Quite the opposite, in fact.

"You do your karate workouts here?"

He was leaning against the door frame, one ankle hooked over the other, his arms crossed; his eyes were lazy and hooded as he watched her. He lifted one shoulder in a negligent shrug. "It isn't karate so much as a mixture of a lot of stuff."

"What kind of stuff?"

"I've studied karate, judo, dim mak, silat. What works best in the real world, though, is a combination of wrestling and good old dirty street fighting."

He was probably very good at fighting dirty, she thought, her heart kicking into a slightly faster beat. Why on earth would she find that sexy? But, damn it, everything about him was sexy, from the sleek, muscled power of his body to that unnerving stillness he was using to such good effect. It was like being watched by a great cat; his motionlessness only served to underline the sense of tension, as if he was preparing to pounce.

The mood between them while they ate had been light, teasing, but now she could feel that molten attraction throbbing between them. The air was thick and heavy, as if a storm were building—not outside, but in here. She wasn't naive; she knew exactly what kind of storm it was, and if she intended to escape, she needed to move *now*. "Well," she said briskly, swinging toward the door and, unfortunately, toward him, "it's getting late, and I should be—"

"Stay," he said.

Stay. His voice was low, the single word slow and dark, like velvet rubbing against her skin. She froze, held motionless by the promise of his tone, the temptation contained in that single word. There was no teasing now, no lightness.

Sex with him would be good. Better than good—better even than ice cream. It would be mind-emptying. She was very much afraid it would be shattering.

She swung around yet again, facing away from

him. She stared at the punching bag, feeling her heart thumping against her breastbone, sending her blood racing and making her feel hot, jittery . . . excited. Involuntarily her loins clenched as if she already held him inside her. She wanted that, wanted it with an intensity that almost swamped her common sense. Desperately she tried to think of all the reasons why he wasn't a good bet for any kind of relationship *except* a sexual one, but, my God, the sex . . . The physical chemistry between them had grown even stronger, stronger than she had ever imagined it could be, like an electrical field she could sense through every pore of her skin.

She didn't dare turn around, didn't dare look at him or let him look at her. He would know at a glance, if he didn't already, how close to the edge she was. And she didn't want to see the open sexual hunger that was certain to be in his gaze, didn't want to read the signs of arousal in his face and body.

Stay . . . not just for coffee, or for more talk. He meant stay the night, in his bed.

"No," she said, and almost wept at the effort it took to say that one word.

His hand closed lightly, gently over the nape of her neck, his fingers sliding under the thick fall of her hair. She hadn't heard him move, hadn't known he was so close, and her nerves skittered wildly. He wasn't trying to hold her; his touch was more of a caress than a grip. She could move away if she really wanted to. And that was the problem, because what she really wanted was him. Her skin tingled from his warm, hard hand, the slight rasp of his roughened fingers on the sensitive cords of her neck. Involuntarily she imagined how those rough hands would feel on the rest of her body, and a shiver ran down her spine.

He was big, dwarfing her with his size, her head tucked neatly under his chin. His furnacelike heat wrapped around her. He would be heavy, and probably dominating, but she could also imagine him lying back and letting her set the pace—

"Stay," he said again, as if she hadn't refused.

She hung on to her sanity, barely. "That wouldn't be smart."

"Fuck smart." His hot breath stirred over the fine hairs on the back of her neck, making her shiver again. His low voice made the word a weapon to be used, a deeper level of intimacy between them. "It would sure as hell be good." He stroked her neck where his breath had warmed her skin. "If you like it slow, I'll be slow. If you like it hard and fast, then that's the way you'll get it." His mouth replaced his fingers, his tongue slowly licking, and the shiver became a fine tremor that shook her entire body.

"Which is it?" he murmured. "Slow . . . or fast? Slow . . ." He licked the tendons in the curve of her neck and shoulder, then gently bit down. The sensation was electric; she jolted, a moan escaping her as her head, like a daisy too heavy for its stem, fell back to rest against his shoulder. ". . . or fast?"

His hands closed over her breasts, his thumbs rubbing over her nipples. His erection was a rock-hard bulk in his jeans, pushing against her bottom. Her legs threatened to give way beneath her, and she heard her own breathing, shallow and rapid, almost panting.

"Easy?" he whispered in her ear. "Or hard?"

Hard. Dear God, hard.

She pushed away from him and turned, bracing her hands against the wall behind her. He watched her like a patient tiger: hungry, but certain the prey was his. And she was. He knew it; she knew it. The only thing left to negotiate was the degree of difficulty, and pride demanded she make his victory as difficult as possible.

"I have a rule," she said.

Wariness entered his eyes. "Do I want to know?"

She managed a shrug. "Probably not."

He scrubbed a hand over his jaw, five o'clock shadow rasping his rough palm. "Tell me anyway."

She smiled, slow and sure. "I don't sleep with anyone I can beat in a fight."

The wariness slowly edged into disbelief. He stared at her. "Shit! You want me to fight you for it?"

She shrugged again and strolled toward the mat. "I wouldn't put it quite so crudely, but . . . yeah."

He took a deep breath. "Sarah, this isn't a good idea. I don't want to hurt you."

"You won't," she said confidently.

His eyes began to narrow. "You really think you're that good?"

She angled a smile at him over her shoulder, and the smile was almost a smirk. She might be defeated, but she was going to enjoy the process. "I think you'll bend over backward to keep from hurting me."

He got it now, and he didn't like it. "You're that

sure I'll pull my punches and let you turn me into a punching bag? Let you win?"

She heaved a sigh. "If you break my jaw or knock me out, I'll be in too much pain—not to mention a really bad mood—for what you have in mind."

"Yeah, well, if I let you kick the shit out of me, I won't be in any shape to do anything anyway."

She lifted one shoulder in a delicate movement. "What a dilemma."

He scrubbed his hand over his face again. "Fuck."

"Maybe." She paused, and couldn't resist taunting him. "If you're good enough."

He studied her for a moment, then came to a decision, his expression hardening. "Okay, here's how we'll do it: strip wrestling."

Strip wrestling? He was diabolical, she thought. "No fair. I've never studied wrestling, and you outweigh me by seventy-five pounds."

"Closer to a hundred," he said, and she secretly gulped. That meant he was even more muscled than she'd thought. "C'mon, this was your idea. You know we aren't going to stand toe-to-toe and slug it out, so this is the alternative. At least you aren't likely to get hurt. I'll take a handicap, too."

With a handicap, she could probably make it interesting. She had no delusions that she could win, but she could make him put out the effort. "It's a deal."

He put his hands on his hips and studied her. "Here's what we'll do: I have to pin you, but all you have to do is knock me down, and you can use

whatever method you like. The first one completely naked loses."

Her heart was definitely going to jump out of
her chest. The thought of wrestling naked with
him was almost enough to make her dizzy with
sexual hunger.

"*And,*" he continued, "we decide now what
counts as wearing apparel, and we both start out
with the same number of items."

She nodded. "That's fair."

He studied her. "The earrings have to go. The
posts will dig into your head."

Silently she removed the gold studs and laid
them aside.

"Your bracelet and my wristwatch balance each
other out." He glanced at her sandaled feet. "No
socks, so I'm two up on you there."

"Let's both start out barefooted," she said, slipping out of her sandals.

He removed his boots and socks. "Okay, how
many pieces of clothing do you have left?"

"Four, not counting the bracelet." Pants, shirt,
bra, panties.

"I'm only wearing three."

"Put your socks back on and they'll count as
one."

He put his socks on again and stepped onto the
mat. "That makes us even at five. Five throws
won't take long."

He was that certain of victory, the smug bastard.
Well, she was also certain he'd win—she was
counting on it—but if he thought he'd win in five
straight throws, he was seriously underestimating
his woman. Speed was her strength, and she
moved like lightning, whipping her leg behind his

and dumping him on his ass before he could counter the move. She smiled down at him and moved out of reach. "The socks," she said.

Silently he stripped them off and tossed them aside, then climbed to his feet. "You're fast." He was much more alert now.

She smiled. "That's what my *sensei* always said."

Fifteen minutes later he said, "Pin." Breathing raggedly, he crawled off her. His hard gaze swept over her bare breasts, lingered on the tightly puckered nipples. "We're tied again. Take off your panties."

Her stomach tightened with anticipation. Panting, trying to control the rapid gasps, she held up her wrist. "What about my bracelet?"

"I'm saving it for last."

Sarah climbed shakily to her feet. She had been putting every ounce of effort she could into resisting him, and he'd probably been holding back to make certain she wasn't hurt. This match was going on longer than she'd imagined it would, and she didn't know how much longer she could stand the rub of his mostly naked body against hers. But then, looking at him, she didn't know how much longer he could stand it, either. His erection bulged against the front of his shorts, and his skin was covered with sweat. There was a set to his jaw that made her stomach tighten in delight.

She took a few deep breaths, then hooked her fingers in the elastic of her bikini panties and shimmied them down to drop around her ankles. He made a raw, smothered sound, his gaze locked on the triangle of dark pubic curls between her legs.

Without looking away, he pushed his shorts down and stepped out of them.

Now it was her turn to smother the sound that rose in her throat. His penis thrust out, thick and pulsing, so big she couldn't decide whether to worry or celebrate. Wow. She wavered, then caught herself.

"Wait," she said, her voice sounding thick to her own ears. "I haven't won your shorts yet."

"Just pretend they're still on," he said, and pounced.

She was on the mat before she could blink, but at the last second she managed to twist just enough to avoid being pinned. His heavy weight bore her down, overwhelming her, the way it had all the previous times he'd pinned her. While she appreciated his efforts not to hurt her, she was as helpless now against him as she had been the first time he'd pinned her. Her only hope had been to remain on her feet, evade him, and look for her chance, but he'd already taken her down.

Desperately she braced one foot on the mat and pushed, seeking leverage. He shifted to counter her move, and his hips slid between the open V of her legs, the smooth heat of his penis pressing into her labia. He froze, a sound almost like a growl rumbling in his throat. As if he couldn't help himself he pushed, and the thick bulbous head began to enter her.

For just a split second she forgot everything but the burning need in her body to lift, to take. She waited almost too long, but at the last possible moment she twisted frantically, dislodging him, and managed to roll closer to the wall. He gave another growl, this one more like a snarl, and was on her again before she could get to her feet.

That overwhelming weight hit her, smothered her, took her down. His hands were on her shoulders, pushing them down. "Pin," he said hoarsely, and the match was over.

Panting, he lifted his weight off her and climbed to his feet. "Stay there."

She stayed. She was too exhausted to do otherwise, and too turned on to move even if she'd been able. She closed her eyes, gulping in air as she listened to the rustle of his clothing. He was getting a condom, she thought, and opened her mouth to tell him he didn't need one, but he was already back, lifting her arms over her head. Cool, smooth metal clamped around her wrists. There was a snick, and she was caught.

Bemused, she stared at him. Handcuffs? She angled her head back to look. He'd looped the cuffs around a pipe before fastening them to her wrists. Experimentally she moved her hands. He hadn't closed them tightly, but they were tight enough that she couldn't pull her hands out. "Are these necessary?"

"Yeah." His chest heaved as he reached out and slowly rubbed his hand over her breasts. "Just in case you decide to go for two out of three matches."

"I don't renege, Cahill." She arched her torso into that hand, loving the feel of it on her nipples.

"And I don't take chances." He bent his dark head and kissed her. It was a marauding kiss, deep and hard, but she had known when she taunted him into a fight it would arouse all those male, conquering-warrior instincts. She softened beneath him, giving him what he demanded, which was nothing short of unconditional surrender.

He spread her legs and moved over her, and she braced herself for his immediate penetration. She caught her breath, waiting, trembling with need, her hips automatically lifting.

"Not yet," he growled. "I'm too close. I wouldn't last ten seconds."

Neither will I, she thought, but didn't say anything. She wasn't a fool; if he wanted to dawdle, then let him.

Not that there was any *letting* to it; he was in control, and all she could do was lie there and enjoy the dawdling.

God, he was heavy. His body was rock hard, sweaty from exertion. She opened her legs wider to give him a more comfortable cradle, sliding her thighs up his hips and tilting her pelvis, seeking. His erection nudged her again, and instinctively she wiggled, trying to take it in.

He swore and slid down her body, removing temptation from her reach. "Damn, you can't give up, can you?" he muttered. "I said not yet."

"Sadist." She couldn't lie still; desire rode her like an unbearable itch, an implacable hunger. Her body moved under him, dancing its need, calling to him with her open thighs and the hot scent of her body.

"More like a masochist." He kissed his way down her throat, over the slope of her breast, then clamped his mouth over one tight nipple and strongly sucked at it. Electricity arced from breast to loins, bowing her upward; he slipped his left arm around her hips and held her in that position as he moved to her other breast.

He wasn't being gentle with her. The pressure of his mouth verged on pain, but it wasn't quite there, teetering on that exquisite edge between pain and pleasure. Just as it began to tilt over the edge, he moved, sliding down her torso, kissing and nipping. His tongue probed her shallow navel, and a surprised cry burst from her throat, her body arching again. God, he was going to make her come just by kissing her navel. But then he was gone from there, too, his mouth sliding lower as he smoothed his free hand over her hips and abdomen, before slipping it between her legs.

Yes. There. That was what she wanted, almost. She squirmed against his hand, but he just held it there, covering her with his palm, letting her feel the heat and strength. Her hips lifted, riding a wave of painful anticipation. She wanted his fingers inside her, she wanted his mouth on her.

"Do it," she gritted, pushing herself against his hand. "Please!"

He gave a low, raw laugh, his head pressed against her inner thigh and his breath hot on her flesh. With his thumb he probed her, dragging it up the closed folds of her labia and opening them so he could see all of her. She panted, her head tossing back and forth on the mat as he circled her clitoris, teasing it to fullness. Just when she thought she'd scream in frustration, he closed his mouth on her and his tongue began circling and flicking as he dragged his thumb down and pressed it deep inside.

Desperately she grabbed the pipe behind her and held on. Spots swam in front of her eyes and her entire body bucked as she came. She heard her own hoarse cries, but they sounded distant, as if someone else made them. For a long, magic moment nothing existed but her body and the firestorm of sensation as her inner contractions peaked, then slowly began to ebb. Her thighs had been clenched around his head but now her legs fell limply open.

He was licking her.

At first the leisurely caresses were soothing. She made a little humming sound of pleasure as his tongue probed her entrance. But the probing and licking continued, and the glorious lassitude began to fade, replaced by a familiar heat and tension. "What are you waiting for?" she gasped, twisting a little.

"I want you ready again." Gently he blew on her, his breath cool on her overheated flesh.

"I *am* ready!" The need had rebuilt so fast she was breathless.

"Not quite," he murmured, gently catching her clitoris between his teeth, then torturing her with lightning flicks of his tongue. She groaned under the lash of pleasure, but as good as this felt, she wanted more. She wanted him inside her. *Now.*

"Just a little closer," he crooned, slipping his thumb inside her again. Then he replaced his hand with his mouth and he kissed her, deeply, his tongue probing, while his wet thumb moved farther down and pushed into her in a bold, shocking thrust that made stars explode in her head. She came again, convulsing, screaming, trying to fight him because the sensations were too sharp to be borne. He held her down, drawing out the moment, holding her at the peak.

Finally she collapsed, trembling, her ears ringing as she struggled to find some measure of control.

"Damn it," he said, slow and deep, as he moved up her limp body. "There's no way in hell I can wait until you're ready again."

She didn't care. She was beyond caring, beyond even opening her eyes as he positioned himself between her legs and guided his penis to her wet entrance, then began sinking into her.

Oh God oh God. Sarah pressed her head hard against the mat, forcing herself to breathe deeply. He was big enough that his penetration wasn't easy; if she hadn't been so wet from two climaxes, so utterly relaxed, taking him would have been painful. As it was, though, their fit was perfect, so perfect that tears sprang to her eyes. She was tight around him; he was deep within her. He pushed one more time and he was there, touching a place inside her that, impossibly, rekindled the heat of desire. She hadn't thought she could climax again, but as he began to thrust she realized differently. The heat inside her began to grow, became hunger, lifting her body to him.

He held her legs wide and hammered into her, driven now by his own blind urgency. Every inward stroke forced her closer and closer to that moment when the tension would become too much, when the heat was scalding and nerve endings couldn't endure any more. He thrust harder and harder, their loins slapping together, and she was almost there, almost there, almost . . .

He came, his powerful body bowing and bucking, shuddering, pumping. Hoarse, rough cries tore from his throat as he gripped her hips and pulled her groin tight against him. Then, slowly, he collapsed on top of her.

A small, wild sound vibrated in her throat. Almost . . . there.

She needed him to move, needed him deeper. Frantically she tugged at the handcuffs. "Take them off," she panted.

"Wha—" He didn't lift his head. His entire body was shaking, a fine tremor from muscles taxed to the limit.

"The handcuffs." She could barely speak; her voice was guttural. She surged upward, seeking the final touch that would send her over the edge. He was still hard, still inside her, but she needed him deeper, wanted him deeper. "Take them off."

"God," he gasped. "Give me a minute."

"Now!" she shrieked, maddened by the completion that lurked just out of her grasp. She fought the cuffs like a madwoman. *"Take them off!"*

"All right, just hold still!" He subdued her, holding her down as he got the key from under the edge of the mat where he'd stashed it. He stretched higher on her body as he reached for the cuffs, forcing his penis deeper, and something very close to a howl erupted from her throat. Alarmed, afraid he'd injured her, he hastily unlocked the handcuffs and started to draw back from her.

Sarah lunged upward, locking her legs around his in a vise as she grabbed his ass and pulled him in tighter, as deep as she could take him. There, right there—*ah!* Her hips pumped as she pistoned herself on him, and she felt the peak coming closer . . . closer . . . She screamed, caught in an orgasm more intense than the others, so intense she couldn't breathe, couldn't think, couldn't see. She heard him make an inhuman sound; then he was thrusting hard, groaning, his arms locked around her as he began coming again.

She either passed out or slept; she wasn't certain which. Slowly she became aware of the whisper of cool air on her damp skin, of the mat sticking to her naked body, of the man sprawled so heavily on top of her. His heaving breaths had slowed to a more normal pace, telling her that at least a few minutes had passed. The sticky moisture of his semen had seeped out of her to pool uncomfortably beneath her bare bottom.

Was he asleep? She managed to lift her arm and touch his shoulder. He stirred and turned his head so his face pressed into the curve of her neck. "God," he muttered, his voice muffled. "That's the first time I've ever come twice with one hard-on. It damn near killed me."

That was such a guy thing to say that she smiled. She would have laughed if she'd had the energy, but the fact was, she was damn near dead herself.

Slowly, every movement an effort, he levered himself off her and collapsed by her side. He lay on his back with his arm covering his eyes, breathing deeply. After a minute he cursed. "Please tell me you're on the pill."

"I'm on the pill," she parroted obediently.

He groaned, long and heartfelt. "Fuck."

This time she did laugh, though it was a little weak. "No, I really *am* on the pill."

He lifted his arm enough to peer at her with one eye. "You are?"

"I am."

"You wouldn't joke with a poor, crippled wreck of a man?"

"I would, but not about this."

"Thank God." He tried to sit up, wavered, then fell back. "I'll get up in a minute."

Bully for him. Sarah knew for a fact her legs wouldn't support her. "Are you sure about that?"

"No," he admitted, and closed his eyes.

CHAPTER 17

CAHILL LAY HEAVILY ON HER, HIS BIG BODY TREMBLING IN THE aftermath of orgasm. They were in his bed, the room cool and dark around them. Sarah had no idea what time it was; she could have lifted her head to peer at the digital alarm clock on the bedside table, but she didn't have the energy. Nor did the time matter; what mattered was the shattering realization that she was in trouble.

She couldn't say she hadn't known what she was doing. She had walked into the situation with her eyes open, knowing that she was already way too vulnerable to him, too close to falling in love, and that making love with him would only increase her vulnerability.

She had known, and she'd done it anyway.

It wasn't the sex—though God knows the word that best described it was *too*: too hot, too raunchy, too powerful. This wasn't just sex, this was mating . . . at least on her part. And that was the problem.

She hadn't wanted to love him. She'd thought—hoped—that she could keep that core part of herself separate, and inviolate. She'd failed miserably, or maybe spectacularly, because she hadn't been prepared for the inescapable fact that on every level he was her match. Not just physically, but emotionally, even in their personalities, they came together as equals. She might never in her lifetime find another man who matched her as well as Cahill did, and if this didn't work out, it was going to hurt her for a long, long time.

Her arms were still looped around his neck, her legs still hugged him close. Since the moment they had come upstairs and fallen into bed, and that had to be hours ago, she didn't think they had been out of physical contact with each other for more than five minutes, total. They had cuddled and stroked and kissed, dozed in a tangle of legs and arms, and made love with an almost savage hunger. This wasn't just the result of sexual deprivation, though it had been a long time for her; nor was it that first fascination with a new love. This was different. This was more.

As they rested, their heartbeats had slowed, become synchronized. Cahill nuzzled her neck, then gently pulled out of her body and fell on his side. "God, I'm hungry."

Just like that he banished her malaise, and she sputtered with laughter. "You're supposed to say something romantic and loverlike, Cahill. What happened to, at least, *'That was great'*?"

He yawned and stretched. "It fell by the wayside somewhere around the fourth time." Reaching out one long arm, he switched on the bedside lamp and propped up on one elbow, looking down at her with a sleepy, sated gaze. "If you listen hard, I think you'll hear a chocolate chip cookie calling you, too."

"Chocolate chip? Why didn't you say so?" She

scrambled out of bed and headed toward the bathroom. "I'll meet you in the kitchen."

"Do you like 'em hot or cold?" he called as he pulled on a pair of black boxers.

"Gooey."

"Hot it is."

She entered the kitchen just as he was pouring two glasses of milk. The microwave dinged, and he removed a plate piled high with chocolate chip cookies.

"I borrowed a T-shirt," she said as she sat down. "I hope you don't mind." The shirt came almost to mid-thigh, covering all the important parts.

He eyed her. "It looks better on you than it does on me." He sat down across from her, and put the plate between them. "Dig in."

She did. The cookies were warm and soft, the chocolate chips melted just enough to be gooey, the way she preferred. Midway through the second one she asked, "What time is it?"

"Almost four."

She groaned. "It's almost dawn and we haven't had any sleep. Or much, anyway."

"What difference does it make? It's Saturday. We can sleep as long as we like."

"No, I can't. I need to go home."

"Why?"

She stared at the cookie, at the crumbs that fell when she pinched off a bite. "Do you mean other than that's where my birth control pills are?"

He watched her over the rim of the glass as he downed a healthy slug of milk. "Yeah," he said quietly. "Other than that. Not that the pills aren't important."

"You know the saying: Miss one and you're an idiot. Miss two, and you're a mommy." She took a deep breath. She had been honest with herself, and he deserved no less. "And I need to regroup."

"Regroup from what?"

"From this. You. Sex. This is . . . this is—"

"—pretty powerful stuff," he said, completing the sentence. "For me, too. So why is it making you run?"

"I'm not running, just retreating a little." She circled the top of her glass with her finger, then looked up at him, sitting there watching her with his cop's eyes, his jaw darkened with a day's growth of beard. "I think this is more powerful stuff to me than it is to you, and that's a big risk for me to take."

"You aren't in this alone, Sarah. You can't talk degrees of feeling like you're comparing thermometers."

"I can when I'm the one registering the high number."

"You don't know that for certain."

She blinked at him as he continued eating a cookie. "What are you saying?"

"Is this confession time?" He rubbed the back of his neck. "Shit, I'm no good at this kind of talk at any time, much less at four in the morning. Okay, here it is: I don't know exactly what we have, but I know we have something. I know I don't want you to leave. I know I want you in a way I've never wanted anyone else, and I know you're not a woman who plays games. This isn't a game to me, either. You can pull back from me because you're afraid of taking a risk, or we can see where this goes."

She stared at him, feeling the quiet unfurling of happiness inside, like a flower blooming. She had expected him to retreat when she confessed to being emotionally involved. She hadn't said the "L" word, but she might as well have; he couldn't have missed her meaning. Not that the basic situation had changed—he hadn't said the "L" word, either. But he hadn't got that uncomfortable expression guys got when a woman started clinging and all they really wanted was to get the hell away from her.

Cahill had been burned; she, on the other hand, was relatively free of scars. Maybe the fact that this was uncharted territory for her was why she was frightened she'd get hurt. If Cahill could risk it, then so could she.

"All right," she said calmly. "So now what happens?"

"I suggest we finish our milk and cookies, and go back to bed."

"And then what?"

The look he gave her was faintly exasperated. "Are you going to write this down in an appointment book or something?"

"I'm big on organization. Humor me."

"All right. I know you have your job to do. I have mine. Some days I won't have much free time, some days you won't. Unless you want to move in with me—No?" he asked when she shook her head. "I didn't think so. Not yet, anyway. But failing that, then we continue as we have this week, together in our free time. We probably won't get much cosmic bowling done—"

"But I so enjoyed it," she murmured, earning an appreciative grin from him.

"—but I can promise I'll do my best to keep you entertained. How does that sound?"

"Hmm, I don't know. What do you have in mind?"

"Well, for starters I thought I'd fuck your brains out. Then, as an encore, I thought I'd fuck your brains out."

"Just what I like," she said. "Variety."

He set the plate of cookies on the counter and put the empty milk glasses in the sink. "If it's variety you want," he said, turning to pull her to her feet, "what do you think about the table?"

Her heart began hammering at the expression on his face, that heavy-lidded, intent look that meant he was aroused. "It's a very nice table."

"Glad you like it," he said, and lifted her onto it.

They spent the weekend together. She insisted on spending some time at the Judge's house, working on the packing and inventory, so he helped her. Because the house wasn't hers, she didn't feel free to invite him to stay the night, so she packed a few clothes and toiletries and drove herself back to his house with him, where they spent the rest of the day in bed. Sunday was pretty much a rerun of Saturday, to her delight. She put her worries on hold and let things between them develop as they would. What else could she do, other than run? Caution was in her nature, but running wasn't.

Early Monday morning, she drove back home and determinedly set to work. Barbara called at ten, pulling her from the chore of folding and packing more towels and washcloths than a small army could use.

"I've talked to a Realtor," Barbara said. "He'll

be there sometime today to put up a sign, so don't be surprised if you see someone in the front yard. Actually, I've already had a couple of people call me here at home—you know, acquaintances who know someone who's looking for a house in Mountain Brook, so maybe it won't be a problem to sell."

"I don't think it will," Sarah replied, thinking that she might not have a full month here after all.

"I'm flying in this weekend to help you pack up Daddy's clothes and personal things." Her voice wobbled a little. "I'm not looking forward to it, but I need to do it. This still doesn't seem real, and maybe . . . maybe putting his things away will help."

"Do you want me to pick you up at the airport?"

"No, I'll rent a car so I can come and go without bothering you. And would you book a room at the Wynfrey for me? I don't think I can stay in the house."

"I'll be glad to. Do you want a suite?"

"Just a room will do, since I'll be alone. Sarah, you know how long it takes a will to go through probate. I've talked to Randall and Jon about this, and we all agree. If you need the money Daddy left you, we'll go ahead and give it to you now out of our accounts, and take it back out of the estate when everything is settled."

"Oh, no, don't do that," Sarah said, shocked. "I don't need the money, and I really wish you wouldn't—"

"Don't argue," Barbara said firmly. "Daddy left you the money, and that's that."

There was nothing Sarah could do but say,

"Thank you. Truly, though, I don't need the money now."

"All right, but if you change your mind, all you have to do is tell me. Oh, by the way, I've written a letter of recommendation for you, too; I'm bringing it with me, so don't let me forget to give it to you. You've been wonderful; I don't know what we would have done without you."

"It's been my pleasure," Sarah said sadly, because it truly had been a pleasure to serve the Judge and his family.

There was another job offer in the mail that day. She read it and put it with the others. This one didn't require her to start immediately, so it was a possibility. She made a mental note to call later, to set up an appointment for an interview.

To her astonishment, every day there was another job offer in the mail, and a couple of offers were made by phone. She disregarded those immediately, preferring the more formal approach. Still, she was amazed at the number of offers coming in; her salary wasn't cheap, so she hadn't expected what was almost a cornucopia of opportunities.

"It's that television spot," Cahill said when she told him about it Thursday night. They were watching television, sitting together in his big recliner with her in his lap. She was proud they were actually watching television; this was the first night they hadn't gone straight to bed after eating dinner. "You're a celebrity, of sorts, so some people will want to hire you whether they really need you or not."

"That isn't the type of job I want, just to be someone's status symbol. Judge Roberts *needed* someone to organize and run the household for him. He was elderly, he lived alone, he had some health problems, and he simply didn't want to be bothered by the details."

"Plus he needed your bodyguard skills."

Sarah fell silent, because her skills hadn't done any good. When the Judge had needed her, she hadn't been there.

"Hey," Cahill said softly. "It wasn't your fault. You couldn't have stopped it. There would have been no reason for you to be suspicious of this guy, whoever he is, because the Judge knew him, asked him to come in. Would you have stayed in the room with them while they talked?"

"No, of course not."

"Then how could you have stopped it? The guy probably used a silencer; you wouldn't even have heard the shot."

"At least I could have identified him—" She stopped, thinking it through. "He'd have killed me, too."

Cahill's arms tightened around her. "He'd have to, because you'd know his name, what he looked like. Thank God you went to a movie." He kissed her forehead, then tilted her head back and kissed her mouth, lingering until she began to think they wouldn't be watching television much longer.

"When did you say Mrs. Pearson is flying in?" he asked, lifting his head.

"Tomorrow night."

"Does this mean you won't be sleeping here?"

"I can't," she said, regretfully.

"Then why are we wasting time?"

Later, when he'd turned out the light and they

were lying drowsily together, he said, "If you don't mind, let me check out the people who sent you those job offers."

"Why?" she asked, startled into lifting her head. "Do you think something's wrong?" She didn't see how anything could be.

"No, nothing in particular. It's just a precaution. Humor me."

"Okay, if you want."

"I do," he said firmly.

CHAPTER 18

"WE DO A LOT OF ENTERTAINING." MERILYN LANKFORD TOOK A SIP
of coffee from a cup of translucent bone china, the
huge yellow diamond on her hand glittering as it
caught the sunlight. "And we travel, so we need
someone to look after the house while we're
gone." She suddenly smiled, her eyes twinkling.
"I've always told Sonny I need a wife. Miss
Stevens, will you marry me?"

Sarah had to laugh. Mrs. Lankford was a petite,
energetic brunette with artfully done highlights to
hide the growing gray in her hair, bright green eyes
that invited the world to laugh with her, and a
nonstop schedule. Her two daughters were grown,
the older one married and the younger one a sen-
ior in college. She had a job in real estate, an interest in several charities, and a husband who ran
two thriving businesses that depended on contacts
for sales, hence the entertaining. Judge Roberts
had been old money; the Lankfords were un-
abashedly new money, and they were enjoying
every penny.

Two years before, they had built a rambling, ostentatious Spanish-style house, with nooks and
crannies everywhere, arched alcoves, bricked
courtyards, a center fountain, and anything else

they could think of. The pool was Olympic size. Mr. Lankford had what he called a media room, crammed with whatever he could think of in the way of electronics, from computer to stereo, including the big-screen television that all men seemed to need to feel complete—and this was in addition to the home theater, with the drop-down projection screen, the ten reclining theater seats upholstered in lush velvet, and the wraparound stereo sound system. The Lankfords had his-and-her marble bathrooms, closets the size of most people's houses, ten bathrooms, eight bedrooms, and what was obviously more money than they knew what to do with.

The whole setup made Sarah want to laugh, it was so over-the-top. It was also obvious that Merilyn enjoyed everything about her new house, from the silly to the luxurious. She knew it was ostentatious, and she didn't care. She had wanted the sunken marble tub, she could afford it, so she got one; it was that simple.

Sarah liked the Lankfords, Merilyn especially. From her point of view, the setup was good; there were separate quarters for her use, an actual little Spanish-style, fully furnished bungalow set back behind the pool and half-hidden from view by a lush wall of trailing ivy. Merilyn must have paid the earth to have the mature ivy transplanted, but the effect was wonderful.

Even more important, Sarah thought, Merilyn truly needed her. The other prospective employers had, she sensed, wanted her more as a trophy or a status symbol than anything else. She had even received a second offer from the man who had tried to hire her after seeing her on television. People like that didn't really need her. Attitude went a long way in her consideration.

The entire process had become a little weird. She was supposed to be the one being interviewed, not the other way around, but she kept getting the feeling that people were almost auditioning for her. This certainly hadn't been addressed in training, so she pretended not to notice. Regardless of which job she took, after a while things would adjust to their natural state and her employers would become accustomed to treating her as they should.

The Lankfords were the fourth interview she'd had, and she thought they might be the last. Matters had progressed with the Judge's estate faster than the family had anticipated; only a week after listing the house for sale, the Realtor had a serious offer on the table, and the buyers wanted to close immediately. In order to get the house ready for them, on Barbara's instructions, Sarah had brought in extra labor to help with packing and moving. The house was almost empty; all that was left was what was in her own quarters.

The furniture wasn't hers; neither were the dishes or cookware. She did have her own bed linens, because she preferred silky sheets, but for the most part, all she had to move were her personal effects—her clothes and toiletries and books, a music system, and her collection of cassettes and CDs. Cahill had told her she didn't have to rush into a job, she could always move in with him and take her time looking, but she didn't feel right doing that. She wanted a bit more independence than that, regardless of how much time she had been spending at his house.

After she and Merilyn discussed salary, duties,

benefits, and off-days, Merilyn beamed a high-wattage, cheerleader smile at her. "So, when can you start?"

Sarah made the decision right then. "Two days. If you don't mind, I'll move my things into the bungalow tomorrow. I'll need to sit down with you and Mr. Lankford to go over your schedules and needs, and if possible, I'd like a diagram of the house."

"It's awful, isn't it? I'll just give you a set of the blueprints; we have at least ten, fifteen copies left," Merilyn said cheerfully. "We built this house, and I still sometimes get turned around and have to look out a window to see where I am. You know, if it's Tuesday this must be the den, that type of thing. Only in the movies it was Belgium, not the den, but you know what I mean."

"It must be fun," Sarah said, smiling.

"It's more fun than you can imagine. Building the house was like an adventure; we drove the builder crazy, because we'd come up with new ideas for what we wanted almost every day, but we kept paying him bonuses, so he made out okay. This is probably the only house we'll ever build, unless, God forbid, it burns down or something, so we went all out. The first night we lived here, we played hide-and-seek like two kids. I can't wait until we have grandchildren so I can play hide-and-seek with them, there are so many good places to hide." Suddenly she smacked herself in the head. "What am I saying? I'm too young to be a grandmother! I don't know what's wrong with me; comments like that have been popping out of my mouth for the last year or so. Do you think I need estrogen, or something?"

Sarah laughed. "Or grandchildren."

"Bethany, my oldest, is just twenty-four, and that seems so young, too young to start a family, so I hope she'll wait another few years. But I was just twenty when I had her, and I didn't think I was too young."

"We never do," Sarah murmured.

They agreed on the terms of a very simple contract; then Merilyn gave her a set of keys for both the bungalow and the house, the codes for the gate and security systems, and a copy of the blueprints, which was a huge roll consisting of at least thirty pages, and weighed about five pounds. Feeling a bit bemused by the speed with which Merilyn accomplished things, Sarah drove home and called Barbara to let her know that, unless something unforeseen had come up, she was finished clearing and packing and would be moving out tomorrow, clearing the way for the new owners.

"Where will you be?" Barbara asked. "I don't want to lose track of you, Sarah. You've been a part of our family for almost three years, and I can't imagine not knowing where you are or how to get in touch with you."

"I've taken a position with Sonny and Merilyn Lankford, on Brookwood."

"Oh," said Barbara. "New money." Location, location, location; it told everything.

"Very new, and having a lot of fun with it."

"Then God bless them. Do you have their number handy?"

"Actually, I'll have a private line, so let me give you that number." She had already memorized it, so she rattled it off. "And you still have my cell phone number, don't you?"

"In my address book. I'll call the bank and have the balance of this month's salary paid into your account tomorrow. You take care of yourself, you hear?"

"You, too."

After hanging up, Sarah allowed herself a moment to look around the two cozy rooms that had been hers, then shook off the sadness and nostalgia and briskly began packing up her books. As she packed, she called her mom and gave her the details of her new job, as well as the telephone number and address. Dad was well; Jennifer thought she might be pregnant—big surprise there, she'd been trying for, what, a whole month?—and Daniel was back on his home base in Kentucky. Everyone was safe and accounted for.

She worked steadily, her mind already going over what she had seen of the Lankfords' house, working out schedules for having the hundreds of windows washed and cleaning what had to be hundreds of miles of grout. The cleaning itself was the job of the housekeeper, or the cleaning service, but arranging and overseeing was Sarah's job. The house was easily twice as large as Judge Roberts's house, so she'd have her hands full just with domestic responsibilities.

Her cell phone rang, startling her. She grabbed it out of her bag. "Hello."

"Just checking to see when you'll be home," Cahill said, his deep voice easy and relaxed.

Sarah glanced at her watch and grimaced. The time had gotten away from her; it was almost seven o'clock. "I'm sorry; I was packing my things and didn't pay attention to the time. Are you at home?"

"On my way; I'm running late, too. Do you want to meet me somewhere for dinner?"

She looked down at her clothes; she'd changed into jeans before she started packing, and they were stained and dusty. "I'm too dirty to eat out. Do you want me to pick up something on the way home?"

"I can do that. How about a plate from Jimmie's?"

Jimmie's was a mom-and-pop restaurant that served plate lunches—a meat and three vegetables for five-ninety-five, or four veggies for four-eighty-five; your choice of dinner roll or corn bread. The weekly menu never varied. This was Tuesday, but it wasn't Belgium; it was meat loaf day at Jimmie's.

"That sounds good. Just vegetables for me, and corn bread. You know which veggies I like." He should; they had been there something like seven times in the past two weeks.

"How much longer are you going to stay?"

"I'll stop now. I'm almost finished, anyway."

"See you in about half an hour, then. If you get home before I do, leave the things in the truck and I'll take them in for you when I get home."

He hung up, and Sarah made a wry face at the phone. "Damn," she muttered. He thought she would be staying with him, though every time he'd mentioned her moving in, she had resisted the idea.

Maybe it was old-fashioned, even silly of her, but she didn't like the idea of living with him. A sleep-over was one thing; in fact, she had slept over with him almost every night since they became lovers. But the only way she would consider actually living with a man was if they were married or at least engaged. Cahill had asked her to do a lot of things, but marry him wasn't one of them. Until then—

Until then?

She jerked herself up short. Was her subconscious *planning* to marry him? Had it not listened to all her lectures about the dangers of getting involved with a man who had gone through a vicious divorce in his recent past? Despite everything, was she so in love with him that she was already dreaming of happily-ever-after?

Hell, yes, she was.

Her stupidity was surpassed only by her optimism. She closed her eyes, a little amused at herself, a little despairing. Hope sprang eternal, all right, and there was nothing she could do but play out the hand and see what happened.

She loaded some of the boxes in the SUV, then washed her face and hands and locked up, as usual checking all the doors and windows in the house and making certain the alarm was set. That would be her duty only one more time; then she would focus solely on the Lankfords and their comfort, their routine.

Jimmie's must have been busy, because Cahill still wasn't home when she got there. She let herself in with the spare key he'd given her, and jumped into the shower to rinse off the rest of the grime from the boxes. She wrapped herself in the terry-cloth robe she'd left there and walked out of the bedroom just as she heard the back door open.

"Honey, I'm home!" he called, making her grin as she entered the kitchen. He had set the takeout plates on the table and was getting the jug of tea from the fridge. "And I'm starving," he added.

"So am I. Why were you so late?"

"A woman took her three-year-old to his pediatrician, and the doc noticed the kid was covered with bruises. She said he fell down the stairs. The doc was suspicious and called it in, we investigated, and they don't have stairs. Bastards. Plus we were going over some old cases."

Meaning they were still sifting through the evidence taken from the Judge's house, going over it again and again, trying to spot something they'd missed. The case was cold, and getting colder by the minute, but they were still trying. He looked tired, but who wouldn't be after dealing with people who would beat up a three-year-old?

"I had another interview today," she said as they sat down. "Sonny and Merilyn Lankford, on Brookwood; big Spanish-type house."

"Yeah, I know the place. How did it go?"

"I took the job."

He paused with his fork on the way to his mouth, his gaze sharpening as he studied her. "Same setup you had with Judge Roberts? On-site quarters?"

"Yes, a separate little bungalow. I have the weekends off unless they have a party planned, in which case I'll substitute one of the other days."

"When do you start?"

He had on his cop face, and that was his cop voice, cool and dispassionate. He'd been expecting her to move in with him, and he didn't like it that things weren't going his way.

"Day after tomorrow."

"So tomorrow night is the last night you'll be spending here."

Her appetite was fading fast. "Tomorrow is the last night I'll be spending *every* night with you.

Whether or not it's the last night, period, is up to you."

"Meaning?"

"Meaning I have a job to do, and I won't short-time them. But when I'm free, if you want me, I'll be here."

"Oh, yeah," he said softly. "I want you."

"But you're angry because I took the job."

"No, I know you had to find another job. I don't like it because you won't be here. That's two different things."

"I've loved being here with you, Cahill." *Love* being the operative word. "But we both knew it was temporary. My staying here at night, I mean."

"Okay, okay." He looked frustrated. "We'll manage. I just don't like it. And before you stay a single night at this place, I want to check these people out. Remember our agreement?"

"I don't think Merilyn Lankford's a terrorist or a money launderer for the mob," she said, relieved he wasn't trying to talk her out of taking the job.

"You never know. People have all kinds of dirty laundry in their closets. For my peace of mind, okay?" He reached behind him where he'd hung his jacket on the back of the chair and took out his notebook. "Give me their full names again, and address."

Sighing, she did.

"*Sonny's* his real name? Not a nickname?"

"I suppose."

"Never mind, I can find out. If they've ever even had a traffic ticket, I'll know about it." He slipped the notebook back into his pocket and resumed eating.

A disruption in his domestic arrangements

wasn't enough to kill his appetite, she noticed with amusement and made herself begin eating again, too.

Inevitably her mind slipped back to the Judge; how could it not, when what had happened to him was the reason Cahill wanted to check out the Lankfords? Tomorrow would be four weeks since the murder; every Wednesday was a sad anniversary. She didn't know if she would ever be able to live through another Wednesday without remembering.

"There's nothing new on the case, is there?" she asked, though she thought he'd tell her if there was. But maybe not; he kept most things about his work pretty close to his chest.

"No. We're not giving up, though. There had to be a reason, and sooner or later we'll find out what it was. Someone will talk, let something slip, and it'll get back to us. Or someone will get pissed and give us a call, tell what they know. We're still talking to people, showing that picture around, trying to shake some memories. It'll come. Sooner or later, it'll come."

CHAPTER 19

HE COULDN'T BELIEVE IT, WHEN HE HEARD, AND OF COURSE HE did hear; Mountain Brook was a small town, and people knew people; someone always talked. She had gone to work for those nouveau riche Lankfords, with the ghastly house that proved just how nouveau their riches truly were. He received a nice little letter from her, politely telling him she had taken another position, but by the time the letter arrived, he had already heard the news.

He held the letter in his hand, staring at her neat, firm signature. He had read it over dozens of times since receiving it, though the words never changed. He thought he could almost smell her on the paper, a light, fresh scent that hit him with a shaft of pain, because she should be *here*. She should be with *him*. Every day the pain of her absence became more acute, as if something vital in his life was lacking. It was intolerable.

He rubbed the sheet of paper over his face, seeking comfort in knowing that she had touched this, had sent it personally to him.

How could she do this to him? Didn't she know—? No, of course not. She couldn't know, he reminded himself. He mustn't get angry with her, because, after all, she hadn't yet met him. As soon as she did, she would know how perfect their lives would be together. She probably felt sorry for those nasty Lankfords and would try to bring a touch of class to their tacky lives. It was a useless effort, but his Sarah was a valiant creature. She would try, and keep trying, until her heart broke at the futility of it.

He actually knew the Lankfords, because, after all, business was business. He'd never been to their house, though; perhaps it was time he visited. Getting an invitation wouldn't be difficult; they entertained with vaudevillian gusto, as if they had no idea of the pleasure of solitude, or quiet.

What a wonderful idea, visiting the Lankfords; he would be able to see Sarah close at hand, because obviously she would be overseeing everything. Perhaps she would even be introduced to him. One didn't normally introduce the servants to the guests, but Merilyn Lankford was just gauche enough to do it. Not that Sarah was an ordinary servant; in her own way she was queen, but the world she ruled was always behind-the-scenes. She deserved to have *his* world to rule, rather than that monument to tackiness.

For Sarah's own sake, not to mention his, he had to get her out of there. He had to act, the sooner the better. He mustn't be careless, though. This would require planning and thought, and no small degree of skill. He looked forward to the challenge.

People were creatures of habit; they wore their little rut of routine in the fabric of their lives; then they stayed in the rut because it was easier than climbing out. According to psychologists, it was a fact that most people preferred what they knew, even if it was horrible, to the uncertainty of the unknown. Women stayed with abusive husbands, not out of hope, but out of fear of being on their own. It was the great unknown. Only daring souls, or desperate ones, broke out of their ruts.

People tended to follow the same patterns day after day, week after week. The same people would be at the same place at roughly the same time. Cahill didn't expect the man in the photograph to show up and use the same pay phone at the same time of night; but maybe, just maybe, someone would be in the Galleria who was in the habit of being there then and had been there the night Judge Roberts was killed, and had noticed . . . what? Something. Anything.

None of the store clerks had noticed anything, but then they were trained to watch what went on in their stores, not out in the mall concourse. But what about the people sitting on the benches, strolling around, the clutch of teenagers giggling and trying to act cool, the young woman slowly pushing a baby stroller back and forth with her foot while she ate a cinnamon roll? Were they there every night? Every Wednesday night? What was their routine?

At about the same time of night the call had been made, on a hunch Cahill went to the Galleria and stopped every shopper he met in the area of that particular pay phone and showed them the photograph. Did anything about this man ring any bells? Did they know someone who resembled him? Was it possible they'd seen him before, here in the Galleria?

He got a lot of funny looks, *no*'s, and shakes of

the head. Some people merely glanced at the photograph before saying, "Naw," and walking on. Some people took the time to study it before handing it back. No, he didn't look familiar. Sorry.

Cahill kept at it. Nothing was breaking in the case; there were no rumors, no one was dropping a dime to get back at someone—nothing. The wall they'd hit was high and wide. They had the slug that killed the Judge, but not the cartridge. They didn't have any prints that scored a hit on AFIS; they didn't have the murder weapon; they didn't have a witness; they didn't have a motive. They didn't have shit.

He was getting angry. No one should be able to commit murder and walk away. It happened, but it offended him on a deep level, in that part of him that made him a cop.

He stopped a twenty-something guy who had a black-lipsticked girl hanging on him like a window-unit air conditioner. They both had attitude, but they looked at the photograph anyway. "I dunno," the guy said, frowning a little. "He reminds me of somebody, but I can't place him, y'know?"

Cahill kept his own demeanor and voice neutral. He could be a badass when he needed to be, but tonight he'd deliberately been very low-key so if anyone had anything to say, he or she would feel comfortable talking to him. "Is it someone you've seen here in the Galleria before?"

"Naw, it ain't that. Hey, I know! He looks like my banker!"

"Your banker?"

"Yeah—William Teller!"

They walked away laughing. "Cute," Cahill said

under his breath, turning away and not letting himself respond to the smart-ass, but the guy had better hope they never crossed paths if he was doing something he shouldn't—and he looked like the type who would.

Cahill worked the shoppers until the announcement came that the mall was closing. This had been another dead end, but if he kept coming back, kept showing the photograph, maybe sooner or later something would pop.

The house was dark when he got home. He sat in the driveway for a minute staring at the windows. "Shit," he muttered. Coming home to a dark house had never bothered him before, but now he wanted to punch something because he didn't like this worth a damn. In just a couple of weeks he'd gotten so accustomed to having Sarah there that *not* having her there felt almost as bad as when he'd first broken up with Shannon.

Hell, in a way it was worse. He hadn't missed Shannon. Finding out she was screwing around had killed everything he felt for her except anger. He *missed* Sarah, though; it was a constant ache. He could forget about it while he was working, but the knowledge that she wouldn't be there when he got home was always there in the back of his mind, waiting for a moment when he wasn't occupied to punch him in the gut.

He finally got out of the truck and went inside, flipping on lights, turning on the television, getting himself something to drink. It was his normal routine, and it wasn't enough. The emptiness of the house made him furious.

Sarah had spent Saturday night with him, and the sex had been so hot he'd thought his head would explode. He couldn't get enough of her, and that was damn scary. She was openly, honestly sensual, giving freely of herself and delighting in his body as fiercely as he delighted in hers. It almost scared him sometimes, the way they were in such perfect sync, in bed and out.

He was suspicious when something seemed perfect, but the way he and Sarah fit together was . . . perfect. Even when they argued, he knew he didn't intimidate her—hell, he wasn't certain she could *be* intimidated. And that was perfect. He didn't have to handle her with kid gloves. The sex was hot and raunchy: perfect. They made each other laugh: perfect. Maybe it was because she was from a military family, but she seemed to *get* him in a way no other woman had: perfect.

What wasn't perfect was that she wasn't with him.

He hated her living in that damn bungalow. He hated it with a savagery that he tried hard to keep hidden. He'd been reasonable about her career; hell, he'd even been sensitive. When she told him she'd taken the job and would live on-site, he hadn't roared, "Fuck that! Over my dead body!" Which was exactly what he'd felt like saying. Being reasonable was a pain in the ass.

What really pissed him off, though, was he didn't have any right to argue with her about it.

They were lovers, nothing more. He'd never said anything other than something along the lines of, "Let's see where this goes." He hadn't made any commitment, hadn't asked her for one, though he thought it was mutually understood neither of them would see anyone else. That lack of commitment gnawed at him now. He should have said something before, and he didn't know if speaking up now would do any good. She had agreed to terms and signed a contract, and, knowing Sarah, she wouldn't even try to amend the terms—not for just a live-in lover.

That chapped his ass, too. He didn't want to be "just" anything to her. He wanted to be her center.

She was a very easy person to live with, but he'd always been aware that she had an ironclad set of personal standards. That was part of what so attracted him to her. If she said she would do something, she'd either do it or try everything humanly possible to keep her word. If Sarah made a commitment, she kept it. When she married, her husband would never have to worry about Sarah sleeping around. She might kick his ass out and divorce him, but she wouldn't cheat on him—and only a fool would cheat on her.

The two weeks of intense, no-commitment sex had been great, but he'd been a fool to think it would hold her. She had never allowed herself to lose focus on her job with the Roberts family, or on interviewing for another job. He'd just assumed she wasn't in any hurry to find another job, that they'd have more time together.

To what end? The conclusion would have been the same. Whether she was here two weeks or two months, she'd still been looking for another job. He guessed he should be grateful she'd found one fast, because if she'd kept looking, she might have gone farther afield and ended up working in Atlanta or someplace even farther away, which would really suck.

If he'd wanted to keep her here, he should have raised the bar—the commitment bar. But, God, the only thing that would have held her would have been a marriage proposal and just the thought of getting married again made him break out in a cold sweat. Maybe they could have a long engagement.

No, she'd see through that in a heartbeat. And that was assuming she'd say yes to a proposal, anyway. She had her big plan for traveling the world, and she was actively working to achieve that ambition. She really wanted to do it, and she'd structured her life to achieve that goal, keeping herself free and unencumbered. He didn't know how the plan would work within the structure of a marriage, if it could work, if she'd be willing to get married beforehand or if she'd insist on waiting until afterward.

She'd all but told him she loved him. Hell, he *knew* she loved him. But he hadn't done anything about it, hadn't solidified or formalized their relationship; he'd been happily coasting along, seeing "where this thing goes," and it had cost him. Big time.

Sarah wasn't a woman to take lightly, or for granted. He didn't think he'd committed either of those crimes, but neither had he shown her how deeply important to him she'd become.

He could let things rock on as they were now; they'd have the weekends together, which was as much as a lot of couples had. He could talk to her on the phone, maybe even grab lunch together sometimes if their schedules meshed. And he'd have the weekends.

It wasn't enough. He wanted to be with her every night. He wanted to sit at the table and talk about their days while they ate. He wanted to share the morning newspaper with her, and fight over who got the front-page section first. He wanted those sparring sessions they'd had; she wasn't up to his weight, but she was fast enough to almost make up for the difference. And whether it had been karate, kick-boxing—or his favorite, naked wrestling—the session had always ended in grinding, explosive sex. He couldn't work out now without getting a hard-on. The basement gym was permeated with the scent of her, the smell of sex, the memories of what they'd done and how often they'd done it.

Hell, even his breakfast table carried memories. He missed her.

He did a quick check of the time, then picked up the phone and dialed her number.

"Hi," he said when she answered.

"Hi, yourself." He could almost hear the smile in her voice.

"Did I wake you?" Sarah wasn't a night owl; she was often up early, so she was usually in bed by ten at the latest, and sometimes by nine. He'd been taking a chance by calling her.

"No. I'm in bed, but I've been reading."

"What are you wearing?"

She laughed. "Is this one of those heavy-breathing calls?"

"It could be."

"I'm wearing cotton pajamas. You've seen them."

"I have?" He couldn't remember her wearing anything at all to bed, not even one of his T-shirts.

"The first time we met. You may remember the

occasion. I was sitting on the stairs, the electricity was off, two bad guys were lying on the floor."

"Oh, yeah, I vaguely remember that. I thought you were Judge Roberts's bed warmer."

"What?" She sounded outraged.

"Gorgeous young hottie living with an old guy; what else was a cop to think?"

"Umm, maybe that she was a butler just as she said?"

"Cops don't believe anything right off the bat. By the time I talked to you a few minutes, I knew the score."

"It's a good thing you didn't mention this to me at the time."

"I'm smart that way. I miss you, Sarah."

She paused. "I miss you, too. Can't be helped."

"Not right now, no. But there has to be some fine-tuning we can do to this situation, some way of working things out so we have more time together. We'll talk about it this weekend."

"I can't spend Saturday with you; the Lankfords are having a party, so I'll have to be here. I'll be off on Sunday and Monday instead."

He ground his teeth together. That robbed them of a day, because he had to work Monday. But at least he'd get to wake up with her. "Okay, I'll see you Sunday, then—unless you want to come over Saturday night after the party."

"It'll be late. Really late. Early Sunday morning, probably."

"I don't care. Wake me up."

"I'll do that," she said.

CHAPTER 20

THE DRIVEWAY WAS LINED WITH CARS, AND EVERY LIGHT IN THE huge house seemed to be on. Guests milled through the rooms, on the patios, around the pool. Merilyn had a favorite caterer, so Sarah had arranged everything with the owner, a slim, sixtyish woman named Brenda Nelson who handled the behind-the-scenes madness with aplomb. Waiters circulated among the guests, carrying trays of drinks and hors d'oeuvres. A huge buffet table had been set up by the pool, and it groaned under the weight of food; two bars had been set up, one by the pool and one inside.

There were the inevitable spills and splashes. Sarah circulated unobtrusively, trying to spot the accidents as soon as they occurred so they could be wiped up. The real cleaning would have to wait until Monday morning, when she already had a cleaning service set to come in and do the heavy stuff, but liquids and food had to be wiped up immediately before someone slipped in the mess and fell.

Brenda made certain there were plates and glasses aplenty; but there were myriad other details for Sarah to check, such as ashtrays in abundance for the smokers, who didn't number that many and went outside anyway, despite Merilyn's cheery, "Oh, pooh, go ahead and smoke; it doesn't bother me." The ashtrays had to be emptied, cleaned, and put out for reuse. The supply of monogrammed paper hand towels in the bathrooms had to be watched, the guests' personal belongings monitored, a tryst between a drunken lady and her not-so-drunken would-be lover interrupted before it reached an embarrassing stage, lost car keys found—and when, inevitably, a woman tottered on her high heels and fell into the pool, Sarah made certain she had suffered no harm and was dried off, provided with makeup and hair dryer if she wished to repair things and rejoin the party, and found clothes to wear. Luckily the lady was good-natured, normal-sized, and having too much fun to leave.

Merilyn was everywhere, chatting and laughing. She was one of those hostesses who loved a party, and her pleasure was infectious. At one point she was standing with a group of men—flirting, actually—when she spied Sarah and beckoned her over. Sighing inside, because it looked as if she were going to be put on display, Sarah put on her bland, professional expression and approached.

"Sarah, I just found out both of these gentlemen also tried to hire you after the awful thing that happened to Judge Roberts," Merilyn said. "Carl Barnes, Trevor Densmore, this is Sarah Stevens, domestic organization specialist."

"How do you do?" she murmured with a modified bow. She didn't offer to shake hands; that was usually a woman's prerogative, but not a butler's. If someone offered to shake her hand, she would, but she waited on their preference.

Trevor Densmore was a tall, slim man with gray hair and a shy smile; he actually blushed when she gave him a slight smile. Carl Barnes, however, a blond man with harsh features and cold eyes, looked at her with hooded speculation, as if he was wondering if Sonny Lankford found his way out to the little bungalow at night. She recognized both names; Trevor Densmore was the man who had sent her two letters offering employment. Carl Barnes's offer had been so high she'd had to wonder exactly what duties he expected her to perform in addition to running the household. Probably he'd thought his offer was preemptive; instead it had made her suspicious.

"I'm pleased to meet you," Mr. Densmore said in a voice as soft and shy as his smile. He blushed again and looked down at his shoes.

"If I were you, Merilyn, I'd keep an eye on Sonny," Carl Barnes said in a voice that was just a little too loud. "With a woman who looks like this around, a man might get some ideas."

Implying that she herself would go along with any such ideas, Sarah thought, hiding her temper. She shouldn't let herself respond, but when Merilyn looked startled and temporarily speechless, Sarah murmured, "A *gentleman* wouldn't." She could make some implications of her own.

Mr. Barnes flushed, and his cold eyes glared at her. Merilyn recovered enough to slap him on the arm. "Carl, if you're going to be nasty, go stand somewhere alone so you won't bother the other guests. I didn't introduce Sarah just so you could insult her, as well as both Sonny and me." She managed to make her tone just firm enough that he knew she was serious, without being nasty in return.

"I was just joking," he muttered, taking refuge in the classic passive-aggressive response.

"I'm sure you were." This time she patted his arm. "Come on, let's find Georgia; there's something I need to tell her." She towed him away with her, in search of his wife. Watching them go, Sarah had to hide a smile. He thought everything was just fine, glossed over; instead Merilyn was remanding him into his wife's custody.

"I'm sorry," Mr. Densmore said. "Carl can be crude when he's had too much to drink."

"No offense taken," Sarah said, lying without compunction. "It was so nice to meet you, Mr. Densmore. I remember your letters; your offer was very kind."

"Thank you." He smiled shyly. "I wasn't certain if I should . . . I mean, I didn't know how I should contact you. I hope you didn't mind."

Mind a job offer? "I was flattered." She glanced around. "Excuse me, Mr. Densmore, but I have duties I have to attend to."

"I understand. It was nice meeting you, too, Miss Stevens."

She was glad to escape and return to more familiar territory. She made certain to stay away from Carl Barnes, however.

She was beautiful. He'd wondered how she would dress, if she would wear pants, perhaps a feminine version of a tuxedo, though the Lankford party wasn't formal. Her choice was understated and severely elegant: a long, narrow black skirt, slim but not confining, teamed with a tailored white shirt and a short, fitted black jacket. The outfit looked vaguely military, though without the brass buttons or braid. Her thick dark hair was pulled back in a very neat bun, and she wore small gold hoops in her ears. She wasn't wearing the pendant.

At first he'd been a bit insulted, until he realized it would be out of place for the function she was performing. What had the Lankford woman called her? Oh, yes—a domestic organization specialist. She wouldn't be wearing diamonds and rubies in that capacity. The pendant was for when they were alone.

Though perhaps he'd been a bit stingy with the pendant. When compared with the monstrous canary diamond ring Merilyn Lankford wore, the pendant was insignificant. He wasn't in the habit of buying jewelry, so he might have erred. How humiliating, to think that perhaps Sarah wasn't wearing the pendant, not because it was inappropriate, but because it was paltry!

No, she'd never think anything like that. She was too much a lady. Why, look how she had handled that crass boor, Carl Barnes. Not by a flicker of an eyelid had she betrayed any expression, giving only that murmured reply about "a gentleman"—which, obviously, Barnes *wasn't*. He'd been so proud of her.

He had watched her all evening. She was unobtrusive, discreet, and paid excruciating attention to detail. Any mishap, no matter how small, was dealt with immediately and with a minimum amount of fuss and embarrassment. Her dedication to her job was heartwarming in this age when clerks acted as if it was an imposition to help customers.

Could Merilyn Lankford even begin to appreciate the honor Sarah did her by being there? Of course not. Merilyn had no idea what a jewel she had, or how briefly she would have her.

The situation was even more intolerable than he had supposed. His Sarah shouldn't be exposed to crude remarks such as the one Carl Barnes had made. When she was at his house, she would be shielded from that. He would protect her from the world. Things were almost ready to his satisfaction; a few more preparations, and then it would be time to bring Sarah home.

The party broke up around one-thirty, which wasn't all that late. These people were businesspeople, pillars of the community, and most of them were regular churchgoers; they couldn't sleep very late the next morning and still attend services.

Merilyn still looked as fresh as she had when the party started, her green eyes sparkling. "Well, that was a success!" she declared, looking around the wreck of her ballroom-size living room. Nothing was actually destroyed, but nothing seemed to be in the correct place, either. "No one threw up, no one set anything on fire, and no fights were started. That's pretty good, if I do say so myself!"

Sonny regarded his wife with fond, if weary, indulgence. He was a stocky man with graying dark hair and a collection of laugh lines. "You can say it on our way upstairs," he said, spreading his arms and pretending to herd her in the direction of the stairs. "I'm bushed. Let's go to bed."

"But there's still—"

"Nothing that Brenda and I can't handle," Sarah said, smiling. "I'll lock up and set the alarm when I leave."

Merilyn hated to go to bed when anyone else was still awake, afraid she might miss something, even if that something was cleaning and loading a multitude of plates and glassware. "But—"

"But, but, but," Sonny said, no longer pretending to herd her but actually doing it, crowding her with his body and gradually forcing her toward the stairs. "No matter what you think of, there's nothing that won't wait until morning."

She backed up, but she peeked around him like a child being torn away from the playground. When he succeeded in getting her started up the stairs, Sarah waved good night, then joined Brenda and her crew in the kitchen.

Things were well in hand, because Brenda had had someone washing dishes from the very beginning. As they were brought in soiled, they were washed. That way there was always a fresh supply if needed, and when the evening was over, there wasn't an avalanche of dirty dishware to be cleaned before it could be packed in the boxes and taken back to the shop. As a result, the last wave of dirty plates and glasses had already been washed, and the crew was busy packing up the chafing dishes and folding a small mountain of table linens.

With everything going well there, Sarah went on a tour of the house, righting a tipped-over potted plant here, picking up a dropped spoon there, gathering towels and—oops—someone's underwear. Either someone was very forgetful, or a tryst had occurred in the bathroom.

She threw away the underwear, emptied the trash cans, sprayed air freshener all through the rooms, and straightened cushions and chairs. Brenda came in to report they had everything loaded in the vans and were leaving. After seeing them off, Sarah did one more tour of the house, checking windows and doors. Finally, a little after three, she set the alarm, stepped out into the courtyard, locked the door behind her, and traipsed past the pool and down a short path to her little bungalow.

She was so tired she ached all over, but she was wide awake. She took a shower to freshen up; usually a warm shower relaxed her, but tonight she felt even more awake than she had before. She thought of sitting down to read, but Cahill had told her to come over no matter what time the party was over.

She was officially off-duty until Tuesday. She was freshly showered, wide awake, and a naked man whom she happened to be crazy about was just a short drive away.

"Decisions, decisions," she said to herself. Sure. Like there was any doubt. She picked up the phone. She had a key, but only a fool would walk in unannounced on a sleeping man who happened to keep a loaded pistol on the bedside table.

"Cahill."

She knew she'd woken him up, but his voice was clear and cool; since all the detectives were essentially on call twenty-four hours a day, he'd had his share of middle-of-the-night calls.

"The party's over. I'm on my way."

"I'll be waiting."

Humming, she quickly got the small bag she'd

packed earlier, which contained a couple of changes of clothes and her makeup and toiletries, plus a book or two. Not that she had much time to read when she was with Cahill, but it might happen. She secured the bungalow, loaded her things in the TrailBlazer, and in twenty minutes was pulling into his driveway. The kitchen light was on.

She all but danced up the steps to the back door, which opened before she got there. Cahill stood outlined in the light, tall and broad-shouldered, and wearing only a pair of his sexy boxers, which he had put on solely because he knew he'd be opening the door.

"Hubba hubba," she said in a growly tone; then she dropped her purse and overnight bag and hurled herself into his arms. He caught her, lifting her so her legs could curl around his waist, and they sank into a long, deep, hungry kiss.

When they surfaced, he licked his lower lip in that way he had of tasting her. "You didn't plan this right," he said, nibbling at her mouth.

"I didn't?" She pulled back a little, frowning at him. "What did I do wrong?"

"For one thing, you're wearing jeans." He kissed her again as he kicked her bags inside and shut the door, then fumbled with the lock. "If you'd been thinking straight, you'd have on a skirt but no panties."

"Sounds breezy." She went back for another kiss.

Gripping her hips, he moved her against his rock-hard erection as he carried her down the hall to the bedroom. "But if you had," he whispered, "I'd already be inside you."

"You're right; I was incredibly stupid." She

squirmed, rubbing herself up and down on him and making her own breath catch as the familiar hot rush began spreading through her.

"You can make it up to me." He dumped her on the bed and unfastened her jeans, then began stripping them down her legs.

"Really? Got any ideas?"

"Plenty."

"Are they legal in this state?"

"Nope."

"I'm shocked," she said. "Shocked. You're sworn to uphold the law."

"You can make a citizen's arrest afterward." He pulled her knit top off over her head and tossed it aside. Since she wasn't wearing a bra, she was naked. When it came to removing her clothes, he set world speed records.

"A citizen's arrest," she mused. "Does this mean I get to handcuff you?"

"You mean you like the kinky stuff, too?" He shoved down his boxers and stepped out of them, pulled her to the edge of the bed and put his hands behind her thighs, pushing them up and apart. She held her breath as he made the connection and began wedging the broad head of his penis into her, past the tightness of her opening. Then he was in, leaning over her as he pushed slow and deep, and she began breathing again. She arched her hips, taking him in to the hilt.

The hall light was still on, silhouetting him as he leaned over her, his wide shoulders blocking out the light. They fell silent, concentrating on the rhythm and sensations, the heat and moisture, the fullness she felt, the tightness he felt. He wet his thumb and gently rubbed it over her clitoris, bringing her body up to him in a tight arch. Sarah gasped, reaching for him, wanting the heaviness of his weight on her. He gave her what she wanted, coming down on top of her and crushing her into the mattress with the force of his thrusts, his hands under her hips grinding her even harder on him. She came, bowing under him, her heels digging into the backs of his thighs while her nails sank into his shoulders. It was always fast the first time, fast and hard, raw in its intensity. He climaxed right after she did, and as they lay together in the aftermath, she felt herself begin to drift to sleep, so deeply content it went all the way down to a molecular level. This was where she belonged, right here with him. The "here" didn't matter; it could be anywhere, so long as she was with Cahill.

Chapter 21

SARAH AWOKE AT TEN TO THE SMELL OF FRESH COFFEE. SHE rolled over, stretching and yawning. She hadn't been sleeping all that well since moving into the bungalow, but she always slept like a rock at Cahill's . . . for what time he let her sleep, that is.

She'd missed him, both mentally and physically. It wasn't just the sex, though there was no "just" to sex with him; it was too raw and exciting. But more than that, she missed his physical presence beside her in bed, the heat and weight and comfort. As often as not she had slept with her head pillowed on his shoulder, or pressed against his back. If she wasn't touching him, then he was touching her, a subconscious signal even in sleep that they weren't alone.

He came into the bedroom wearing only jeans and carrying a cup of coffee. She sat up and pushed her hair out of her face. "If that's for me, I'll be your sex slave forever."

"It's yours, so I guess we need to talk terms of servitude." He handed her the cup, and she sipped, half closing her eyes in delight at the first taste. The mattress dipped as he sat down beside her.

She took another sip. "For starters, I don't get time off for good behavior."

"Definitely not," he agreed, stroking her arm. "No parole, though I guess you could get . . . special privileges for sucking up to the warden."

"In more ways than one," she murmured, rubbing one finger over the bulge in his jeans. "When do I start?"

The corners of his mouth were kicking up at her boldness. "I think you already have. And if you don't stop that and get your butt out of bed, your breakfast will get cold."

"You have breakfast ready? Great, I'm starving." Dropping the sex-kitten act, she balanced the coffee cup as she climbed out of the nest of covers and headed for the bathroom. "What am I having?"

"Cereal."

"You jerk! That's already cold!" she called after him. She could hear him laughing softly as he went toward the kitchen.

Her reflection in the bathroom mirror wasn't that of a woman who had worked most of the night and was still a few hours short of the recommended eight hours of sleep. Her hair was tousled, her eyelids a little swollen, but she looked rested . . . and glowing. Sex with Cahill could do that for a woman, she thought, smiling as she brushed her hair.

Cahill had brought in her overnight bag and purse. She washed her face, brushed her teeth, and got dressed. Dressed much as he had been, barefoot and in jeans—though she did pull on a shirt—she and her coffee cup made their way to the kitchen.

Breakfast *was* cereal, but he had also sliced some fresh peaches and put a cup of her favorite vanilla yogurt beside the bowl. He'd prepared the same thing for himself, but doubled the amounts. "Yum," she said, sitting down. "But it's so late, you shouldn't have waited for me, you could have already eaten. You must be even hungrier than I am."

"I had a bagel about eight o'clock."

"What time did you get up?"

"Almost seven. I went for a run, ate the bagel, read the paper, twiddled my thumbs."

"Poor baby." She picked up her spoon and dug in. "What else did you do?"

"You still weren't awake, so I had sex with your unconscious body—"

"Did not."

"Did, too."

"Okay, so you dozed off and were dreaming. What time did you wake up?"

"Nine-thirty." He forked a slice of juicy peach into his mouth. "I was tired. My sleep got interrupted last night."

"How are you feeling now?"

"Rarin' to go."

"Good, because I feel great." She stopped eating to stretch, raising her arms high over her head. Cahill's gaze followed the movement of her breasts. "After breakfast settles, I think I'll go for a run, too. Are you up for another one?"

"I'm up for several things. I think I can fit in another run."

She eyed him appreciatively as they finished breakfast. He'd told her he'd started working out a lot when he and his wife split up; physical exercise was a great stress-reliever. He'd been in good shape before, but not like he was now. His abs and pecs were like rocks. He was a big man, but he hadn't bulked up all that much, just hardened and defined. Touching him was a tactile marvel—smooth, warm skin covering muscles so hard there was almost no give to his flesh.

He got up to carry his empty dishes to the sink. Sarah propped her chin on her hand to watch him, her eyes half-closed and a tiny smile on her face. "Your ex-wife has to be the biggest idiot walking the earth."

He gave her a startled look, then shrugged. "Make that a two-timing, vindictive idiot. What made you think of her?"

"You. You're neat, domesticated, intelligent—"

"Keep going," he said.

"—good-looking, sense of humor, sexy—"

"And yours."

She stopped, her stomach suddenly flip-flopping. "Are you?" she whispered.

He put the milk in the refrigerator and gave her a wry smile. "Oh, yeah."

She took a deep breath. "Wow."

"That's kind of the way it takes me, too." He re-filled their coffee cups and sat down. "So that's what we need to talk about. I want more than what we have now. If you do, too, then we need to figure out how to work this."

She nodded.

"Sarah. Let me hear you say it."

"I want more," she managed. She couldn't believe this was happening, so fast, and at the breakfast table on a sunny Sunday morning.

"Okay. Your job—for now—requires you to live on-site. My hours right now are longer than usual. If weekends are all we can manage, then we'll deal with that, but . . . how long are you on duty at night?"

"Until they're ready to go to bed or tell me they won't need me for anything else that night. So far, they usually tell me to call it a day right after dinner. I think they like to have their evenings alone, unless they're entertaining."

"Are you allowed to have visitors? God, this sounds like Victorian England."

She laughed. "Of course I can have visitors during my own time. I wouldn't feel comfortable with you sleeping over—"

He waved that away. "Sex is secondary. Well, almost secondary. The point is we need to see more of each other than we have since you started work there. It's been driving me crazy, not seeing you. Let's just handle this right now, and later on we'll handle your world tour. Somehow. I won't ask you to give it up, because you really want to do it. I'll just whine a lot."

She did really want to have her year of travel, but she really wanted Cahill, too. "I'm a reasonable woman," she said. "I know how to compromise." She had always remained heart-whole and free because she'd never before met anyone who was important enough to her to get in the way of her plans. Cahill was that important. She would travel some, but a whole year away from him? No way. She wasn't willing to do that.

He cleared his throat. "We—uh . . . we'll probably get married."

"Ya think?" she asked, then started laughing. She couldn't help it. If the man got any more unromantic, the people in charge of Valentine's Day would put a bounty on him.

He grabbed her and hauled her into his lap. "Is that a yes or a no?"

"You haven't asked a question. You stated a probability."

"Well, then, do you agree with the probability?"

She might never hear the question, she thought, amused. She'd have to work on him. She intended to be married only once in her life, so she wanted to hear that question. "I agree with the probability." She gave him a serene smile and kissed him on the cheek. "When you're thinking in more black-and-white terms, we'll talk about it again."

He groaned and dropped his head onto her shoulder. "You're going to put me through the wringer, aren't you?"

"Of course, sweetheart. That's what women are for."

He didn't know where Sarah was. When he'd checked early Sunday morning, her SUV was gone, and she hadn't been back to the Lankfords' house since. At the party, casual questions had elicited the information from Merilyn that Sarah's weekends were normally free, but when they entertained on the weekend, she would take a different day off. In this case, when the party ended, she wouldn't be back on duty until Tuesday morning.

Thinking she might go somewhere, he'd gotten up early and driven by the monstrosity; having already checked, he knew her usual parking spot was visible from the street—just the rear quarter panel, but enough to tell the vehicle was hers. But she must have gotten a very early start, because when he drove by right after dawn, she had already left.

Did she have family in the area? He kicked himself for not asking. Of course, her family didn't have to be in the area; she could have flown to visit them, and taken the first flight of the morning.

For a brief moment he entertained the unpleasant idea that she might have a boyfriend—juvenile term—but, no, Sarah had too much class to spend the weekend with some local yokel. The times he'd followed her before, she had shopped and run errands, but never had she met a man anywhere. The problem was, there had been long stretches when he hadn't been able to find her, so he didn't know whom she might know in the area. She was likely visiting family or friends, but he would have liked to have known exactly *where;* he hated not knowing.

After he took care of Roberts, for instance, he hadn't stayed to watch the excitement because he knew criminals often couldn't resist watching the show and police these days routinely filmed the spectators. When he had driven by the next morning, after the hullabaloo had died down, the driveway had been barricaded and the house sealed off with yellow tape. He had no idea where she had gone. A friend's house, a hotel? The Wynfrey was the most likely hotel, so he'd gone straight there but hadn't seen her SUV. It had been raining, anyway, and he disliked driving in the rain, so he'd gone home.

After the funeral, she had gone back to the house. She had then stayed there almost all day, every day, so he had relaxed and stopped driving by so often. According to the grapevine, she was getting the house ready to close, packing everything up for the family. Then one night he happened to check, and she wasn't there; there were no lights on at the house. Where had she gone?

The problem was, there was no place in the neighborhood where he could park and watch for her. If an unfamiliar car stopped, it was immediately noticed. Nor could he continually drive by; he had business to attend to, meetings, phone calls. He had to do all the monitoring himself to avoid the risk of bringing in a stranger who might talk, so he eventually had to accept that he simply wouldn't be able to keep track of her all the time. He didn't like it, but he was a reasonable, patient man; he could wait.

The most important thing was that he knew she wasn't supposed to be back until Tuesday morning.

The other time had worked like a charm, so Sunday night he followed the same routine. He drove to the Galleria in the dark blue Ford he had bought only a little over a month before; after all, the Jaguar was so noticeable. The Ford was so ordinary as to be almost invisible. It didn't compare to the Jaguar, of course, but it was perfect for its purpose. But when he called there was no answer. Frustrated, he tried several more times before giving up in disgust.

The next night, though, he knew the Lankfords were at home, because he'd checked, and there weren't any extra cars in the driveway, either. They were alone. He made the call, and of course Sonny was glad to see him. Sonny was always willing to talk business, and when one owned a bank . . . well, people liked to see him. Sonny was too stupid to see anything unusual in his coming to him, rather than the other way around. The fool was probably flattered.

The silenced pistol was tucked in his waistband at the small of his back, covered by his jacket, when Sonny let him into the house. The man hadn't even bothered to put on a jacket, he saw with contempt. He was dressed in slacks and pullover knit shirt, and he was wearing house slippers, for God's sake. Totally classless.

"Where's Merilyn?" he asked easily. People talked to him, told him things. They trusted him. Why shouldn't they?

"Upstairs. She'll be down in a minute. You said you wanted to talk to both of us?"

"Yes. Thank you for seeing me tonight. I won't take up much of your time." Sonny still didn't see the ludicrousness of that statement.

"Nonsense, it's a pleasure. Would you like something to drink? We have hard, soft, and everything in between." Sonny led the way into the den; thank God he hadn't taken him into that horrible room with the gargantuan television. There was a television in the den, of course, but it was normal-sized.

"A glass of wine would be nice." He had no intention of drinking it, but the pretense of accepting his hospitality would keep Sonny relaxed.

They made small talk, and still Merilyn didn't appear. He began to get a little concerned. He didn't want to spend a lot of time here; the longer he waited, the more likely it was someone would notice the car, as bland as it was, or the phone would ring and Sonny—or Merilyn—would say, *sorry, we can't talk, our banker is visiting.* Wouldn't that be just lovely.

He glanced at his watch, and Sonny said, "I don't know what's keeping Merilyn. I'll go check—"

"No, don't bother," he said, getting to his feet. In a smooth motion he reached behind his back, took out the pistol, and pointed it at Sonny's head. He was so close that Sonny could have reached out and swatted it away—if he'd had time, but he was slow to react. Pity.

Calmly he pulled the trigger.

The bullet entered Sonny's head just above his left eyebrow, angling back and to the right, taking out both hemispheres of his brain. He was always amazed at how small and neat the entry wound was; when the bullet exited, however, it had flattened, and it took a huge chunk of skull and brain with it. Amazing.

The sound of the shot was just a little cough; it wouldn't even have been heard in the next room.

He turned to go in search of Merilyn, and froze. She stood just outside the doorway, her face drained of color, her eyes wide and horrified. He lifted the pistol once more, and she ran.

He didn't have time to get off another shot. Grimly he ran after her; he couldn't afford to let her escape, even briefly. She might run screaming from the house, which would attract attention. But, no, the dear ran into another room and slammed the door; he heard the lock click.

He shook his head and put a bullet in the lock; the door swung uselessly open. Merilyn whirled, the phone in her hand. He shook his head again. "Bad girl," he said softly, and pulled the trigger.

She slumped to the carpet, eyes popped out from the force of the bullet that had entered right between them. He stepped over to her and removed the cordless phone from her hand. He listened, but there was no one on the line; either she hadn't had time to dial 911 or she'd been too flustered to think. He calmly wiped the phone with his handkerchief and replaced it on the charger.

Merilyn's hand lay outstretched, as if she were reaching for him. The canary diamond glittered at him, and he had an idea—a brilliant one, if he did say so himself. If he took the ring, it would look as if a burglary had occurred. The ring had to be worth a small fortune; he had investigated the cost of jewelry more closely today and discovered that a good stone was hideously expensive. This ring, for instance, had probably set Sonny back close to a quarter of a million dollars. Really.

He was embarrassed that he'd given Sarah such a small token in comparison. This was a particularly fine stone, and the color would look wonderful on her, with her warm skin tones. Not in this setting, of course; she wouldn't like such gaudiness. But after a certain amount of time had passed, when the police weren't actively looking for a large yellow diamond ring, he could remove the stone from the setting and take it to a jeweler in, say, Atlanta, and have a wonderful piece fashioned for her, with the canary diamond as the center stone. Yes, he could just see it now.

He leaned down and tugged the ring from Merilyn's finger. It was a tight fit; the dear must have gained a little weight. He'd saved her from having to have the ring resized.

Pleased with himself, he carefully retraced his steps through the house and wiped everything he might have touched. After he let himself out the front door, he wiped the door handle and the doorbell button. As he drove away, he smiled.

That had gone very nicely.

CHAPTER 22

ON MONDAY MORNING AFTER CAHILL WENT TO WORK, SARAH worked out, booked herself a manicure and pedicure for that afternoon, then spent a few blissful hours doing absolutely nothing. After visiting the salon to get her nails done, she bought groceries and cooked a spaghetti supper. Cahill had just eaten his third slice of butter-dripping garlic bread when his phone rang. He squinted at the number in the little window, and sighed.

"Yeah. Cahill." He listened for a minute, then said, "I'm on my way."

He sighed as he got up. He was still wearing his holster, so all he had to do was knot his tie and slip on his jacket. "I gotta go," he said unnecessarily.

"I know." She got up and kissed him. "Is it something that you can finish fast, or will it take a while?"

He sighed again. "I'll probably be a few hours, maybe longer."

"Okay. I'll be here when you get back."

He looked down at her, blue eyes heavy-lidded and sensual. "I like hearing that," he said, bending down to give her a long, slow kiss that made her heart begin pounding. Damn, the man knew how to kiss.

After he left, she cleaned up the kitchen, then watched television for a while. An ad for a fast-food joint showed a picture-perfect banana split, and her saliva buds started working overtime. She didn't need a banana split; it was something like six weeks' worth of calories. She'd have to run a hundred miles to work it off.

She told herself all that. Usually she was very good about resisting cravings, because usually she didn't *have* cravings. She ate a healthy, well-balanced diet, and didn't think about food all that much. It was almost time for her period, though— and when it was that time of the month, she craved ice cream.

She resisted the craving for over an hour, then surrendered.

She got up and looked in the freezer section of the refrigerator. Aha! There was a half-gallon carton of Breyers Natural Vanilla with flecks of real vanilla bean. She reached in to get it, and her heart sank. The carton was way too light. She pried off the top and groaned; there was barely a tablespoon of ice cream left. Why on earth hadn't he eaten that last tablespoon and thrown the carton away? Or better yet, remembered to buy more?

Growling to herself, she got her purse and drove back to the supermarket. If she had known she was going to start craving ice cream, she could have bought it while she was there earlier.

She decided that if she was going to indulge, she might as well do it right and make the mother of all banana splits. Then the craving would be gone, and she could return to eating nice, sensible, healthy foods. Besides, when you added the bananas, that made the ice cream more healthy, right?

She did it right. She picked out the best-looking bananas she could find. She bought maraschino cherries. She bought pineapple sauce. Chocolate syrup. Chopped pecans in caramel sauce, and, while she was at it, caramel sauce. She bought vanilla, strawberry, and chocolate ice cream, because a real banana split had all three flavors. What else? Oh, yeah, whipped cream. And vanilla wafers to hold it all together.

Man, she could hardly wait.

To her surprise, Cahill was home when she got back. She carried in her haul. "What are you doing back so soon? I thought you wouldn't be back until ten or later."

He shrugged. "Things just went faster than I thought. Where have you been?"

"The grocery store. I would have left a note, but I didn't think you'd be here to read it, so there didn't seem much point."

He leaned against the cabinet and watched as she unloaded the bags. "What's going on? Are we having an ice cream party?"

"Banana split. I saw one on television and my mouth started watering. You didn't even have any ice cream," she said accusingly.

"I did, too."

"One spoonful that's almost dehydrated does not count as having ice cream."

He eyed the three cartons. "Well, I certainly have ice cream now."

"You certainly do."

He waited a minute. "May I have some, too?"

"You want in on this banana split lovefest?"

"You betcha. If it's a lovefest, I'm interested. I bet I can think of more things to do with this chocolate syrup than you can."

"You can keep your hands off my chocolate syrup. I have plans for it."

"*All* of it?"

She winked at him. "Maybe not."

She got two shallow bowls from the cabinet, lined up all her ingredients, and set to work peeling and slicing the bananas lengthwise. She put the slices in the bowls, and shored them up with vanilla wafers. Next came the ice cream.

"Just vanilla in mine," Cahill said, watching in fascination. "I don't get fancy with my ice cream."

"You're missing out on a great culinary experience."

"I'll taste you afterward."

Three scoops of vanilla for him, one each of the vanilla, strawberry, and chocolate for her. "Pineapple and pecans?" she asked, holding out the little jars, and he nodded. She added liberal helpings to both bowls. Next came the caramel sauce, then the chocolate syrup. She topped the growing mound with generous globs of whipped cream, and crowned it all with maraschino cherries. She put two cherries on hers, just because she liked them.

"Holy shit," Cahill said when he took the bowl. "This weighs at least two pounds."

"Enjoy," she said, taking hers to the table and digging in.

"My God," he groaned half an hour later. "I can't believe you ate all of that."

"You ate all of yours," she replied, looking pointedly at his empty bowl.

"I'm bigger than you. And I'm stuffed."

"So am I," she admitted. "But it was good, and that took care of my craving." She carried the bowls to the sink and rinsed them out, then put them in the dishwasher. She was so full she thought she might burst, and she didn't want to see ice cream again for another millennium . . . or at least another month.

"Now," he said. "About that chocolate syrup . . ."

"Don't even think it."

He did think it, of course, and say it as well. What's more, after a couple of hours, they ended up trying it. Chocolate syrup on her, chocolate syrup on him . . . It was a shame she'd wasted so much on the banana splits. It boggled her mind, what they could have done with a full bottle.

She was still smiling early the next morning when she drove back to the Lankford house. It was not quite six o'clock, but she wanted to be there bright and early and get started on the day. She stopped at the gate and retrieved the morning newspaper from the box, then keyed in the code, and the gates swung smoothly open. She drove in and parked as usual beside the little bungalow. After carrying in her things, she hurriedly changed clothes and walked across the courtyard to the main house, letting herself in with her key.

She turned to punch in the code on the security panel and stopped when she realized it wasn't beeping the little warning that a door had been opened while the alarm was set. Frowning, she examined the lights. No wonder it hadn't beeped; the alarm wasn't set. Merilyn must have forgotten it.

She and Sonny both were a bit lax about the house's security system, since the property was walled and gated. They figured if the outside property was secure, so was the house.

She went into the kitchen and started the coffee, then carried the newspaper through the tangle of halls and rooms to Sonny's den, where he liked to read it while he caught the morning news. He didn't like to hurry, so he was usually awake and downstairs by six-thirty, giving him plenty of time for the newspaper and breakfast before he left for the office at eight-forty.

The low-level lights were on in the hallway, as were the lamps. Come to think of it, the light over the front door had also been on. Sarah frowned, suddenly uneasy. Something was wrong; maybe one of them had gotten sick during the night, because she thought she smelled—

The smell.

Panic hit her like a tidal wave, sending her reeling back toward the kitchen. That smell! It couldn't mean what she thought; it was just that she associated the scent with something terrible. Anything similar brought back the nightmare. Either Sonny or Merilyn had a digestive virus, that was all. They had her cell phone number, they should have called, and she'd have come back immediately to handle things.

She swallowed the bile in her throat. "Mr. Lankford?" she called. "Hello?"

There wasn't an answer. The house was silent around her, except for the almost inaudible hum of electricity that said the house was wired and everything was working.

"Hello," she called again.

She didn't have her pistol; it still hadn't been returned to her. Since she wasn't performing any bodyguard function for the Lankfords, she hadn't worried about it. The police department would eventually return it to her. Now, with every tiny hair on her body lifting in alarm, she wished she had it.

She should retreat, maybe call Cahill and get him to come check out the house. But the house felt . . . empty, just as the Judge's house had felt— as if there was no life inside it.

She eased down the hallway, then halted, gagging a little.

The smell. That damn smell.

I can't do this again. The thought burned through her mind. This couldn't be happening. Not again. She was imagining things. Maybe not the smell, but she was letting it panic her. She should find out what was wrong, who was sick. She should be calm, and take charge. That was part of her job, handling whatever crisis arose here.

She took two more steps. The door to the den was maybe three more steps away. She forced herself to take those steps, practically throwing herself forward like someone who had finally worked up enough nerve to leap off a tower bungee-jumping. The odor had an almost oily quality to it, sticking to her throat, coating her tongue. She gagged again, and covered her nose and mouth with her hand as she looked inside the den.

He was sprawled on the floor in a half-sitting position, his head and shoulders supported by the heavy coffee table. His head was bent at an unnatural angle, as if he hadn't had room to lie flat. The wound was . . .

She didn't look for Merilyn. As she had done once before, she backed away, slowly, shaking, little mewling sounds coming from her throat. She was vaguely shocked at herself for making such sounds. They sounded so weak, and she was strong. She had always been strong.

She didn't feel strong now. She wanted to run screaming from this house, find someplace safe and dark and cower inside it, until this horror was gone.

She wanted . . . she wanted Cahill. Yes. When he was here, she wouldn't feel so helpless, so shaken. She had to call Cahill.

She kept backing down the hall, and as she had once before, she found herself standing in the kitchen. She was shaking violently now, and she knew she was on the verge of hysteria.

No. She wouldn't give in to it. Couldn't. There were things to be done, that all-important call to make.

Not Cahill. Not first. The first call had to be 911. She had to do things right. Maybe Merilyn was still alive, maybe the medics could get here in time to save her, if she made the 911 call first.

Her hand was shaking so hard she couldn't hit the right numbers on the keypad. She disconnected and tried again, with the same result. Weeping, cursing, she banged the phone against the counter. "Work, damn it! Work!"

The phone came apart in her hand, plastic sections flying. She threw what was left of it against the wall. She needed another phone. She needed . . . another . . . *damn* . . . *phone!*

She tried to think. Phones were all over this house, but where exactly? She hadn't worked here long enough for the knowledge to be automatic, not now when she could barely form a single coherent thought.

And she couldn't hunt for one. She might find Merilyn instead.

She couldn't think about it, couldn't think of that energetic, cheerful, good-hearted woman lying in a pool of blood somewhere. Concentrate. Find a phone.

The bungalow. She *knew* where the phone was in there.

She tried to run, but her legs wobbled beneath her and she staggered, falling to one knee on the courtyard pavers. She didn't notice any pain, but bounded up and staggered the rest of the way to the bungalow door.

There was a phone just inside, in the living room. She grabbed it and started to jab at the buttons, but stopped herself and managed to drag in a few deep, shaky breaths. It was hard won, but she found a small measure of calm. She had to get herself under control; she was no good to anyone if she let herself fall apart.

Her hands were still trembling, but she managed to push 911, and she waited.

Cahill couldn't believe it. He fucking couldn't believe it. At first he thought he'd heard wrong, that the report was a hoax, or that the address was wrong. Something. For one murder to occur in Mountain Brook was unusual enough, but a double murder only a matter of weeks after the first one? And discovered by the same woman who had called in the first one? Un-fucking-believable.

He had an icy feeling in the pit of his stomach, a cold hard knot of dread that had nothing to do with Sarah's safety—she'd called the murder in, so she was okay—and everything to do with being a cop. He was a damn good cop, combining experience, intuition, and a talent for analyzing cold hard facts without letting his emotions cloud the issue. Intuition was telling him now that this stretched coincidence way the hell too far.

When he got to the house, the scene made the one at Judge Roberts's house look organized. Squad cars, unmarked cars, vans, medics, and a fire engine clogged the driveway and street, but at least they belonged. The curious, the sight-seers, the media vans, the print reporters, all formed a crowd that had brought traffic to a grinding halt. Hell, there was even a helicopter overhead.

He clipped his badge to his belt where it could be seen and waded through the clog of onlookers, ducking under the crime scene tape and asking the first uniform he came to, "Have you seen the lieutenant?"

"He's inside."

"Thanks."

Sarah was somewhere inside, or in that little house behind the pool. He didn't search for her, though; he had to see the lieutenant first.

The house was a warren; a big warren, but a warren nevertheless, as if the architect had been both schizophrenic and dyslexic. He finally found the lieutenant standing in a hallway peering inside a room, but not stepping inside and carefully not touching anything. The room would be the crime scene, then, or one of them.

"I need to talk to you," he said to the lieutenant, motioning his head to the side.

"This is a fucking mess," the lieutenant muttered under his breath, still staring inside the room. He looked tired, though the day had just begun. "Yeah, what is it?"

"You may want to keep me clear of this case. Conflict of interest. I'm involved with Sarah Stevens."

"The butler?" Lieutenant Wester said sharply. "Involved, how? You've been out a couple of times?"

"We're practically living together." That was an exaggeration, but not by much.

"I thought she lives in that little house out back."

"That's her quarters when she's on duty. When she isn't, she's at my house."

"Shit." The lieutenant rubbed his hand over his head. He didn't have much hair and what he did have he kept very short, so he wasn't disturbing anything. "How long has this been going on?"

"Since she was dropped from the suspect list in the Roberts murder."

"Shit. I gotta tell you, Doc, I have a bad feeling about this. Maybe we cleared her too soon in the other case. What are the fucking odds, huh?" he asked in a furious whisper. "We don't have a murder here in years; then she comes to town and whoever she goes to work for gets popped in the head, clean shot, professional. The first guy left her a hundred grand in his will. A big diamond worth a quarter of a million is missing now, and, get this:

She's the one who noticed, when she ID'd the woman's body. Coincidence, my ass. Coincidences like this don't happen. My gut says it isn't looking good for your girlfriend."

"Yeah," Cahill said bleakly. "I know."

CHAPTER 23

LIEUTENANT WESTER WAS IN A QUANDARY. HE NEEDED EVERY DE-
tective he had, but he didn't want to jeopardize the
case by muddying the waters with a conflict of interest. The conflict came only if Cahill allowed
emotion to get in the way of his job. He figured
Cahill could do the job; Cahill knew he could. It
would hurt, but he could do it. It was best, though,
if he was assigned to something else.

Cahill knew it was best, but it still pissed him
off. Not that the lieutenant made the decision, but
that there was a decision to be made at all. Cahill
figured he should have been smarter than this; he'd
missed something, somewhere. If Sarah had done
all the killings—or had them done, he couldn't forget that possibility—then he'd screwed up by not
following his initial thought, and two more people
were dead.

And if Sarah was innocent—a possibility that
was looking more remote by the minute—then
there was something colossally wrong. That thing
with the pendant: Had she picked up a stalker, or
had she sent it to herself as a means of deflecting
suspicion, if necessary?

Maybe he wasn't on the case, but his brain was

working anyway, sifting through all the possible scenarios.

He asked permission to see her. Part of him wanted to make certain she was all right, but the cop part of him wanted to see how she looked, how she acted. Body language and physical responses said a lot.

Sarah was in the bungalow, sitting on the sofa in the cozy living room while a medic put a dressing on her right knee and a patrol officer watched from the doorway. Her pants leg was torn, and Cahill could see the bloodstains, like rust, on her leg. Her face was paper white.

"What happened?" he asked, standing back and watching.

"She fell in the courtyard and hurt her knee," the medic said matter-of-factly, taping a bandage over the bluish, oozing wound. "It'll be sore tomorrow," he told Sarah.

She nodded absently.

"When did you fall?" Cahill asked her. "And how?"

"I didn't fall." Sarah's voice was so wispy it was almost transparent, and without inflection. She didn't look at him. "I wobbled and went down on one knee."

"When?" he repeated.

She made a vague gesture. "When I was hunting for a telephone."

"Why were you hunting for a telephone?" From what he'd seen, there were telephones all through the house, including a shattered one in the kitchen.

"To call. About—" She made another vague gesture, this time toward the house.

"There are telephones in the house. Why did you come out here?"

"I didn't know where she was. I didn't . . . want to see her." She paused, and for the first time made eye contact. "But I saw her anyway. They asked me to identify her. I saw her anyway."

The symptoms of mental shock were very good, very convincing. Hell, maybe they were real. Her body language was consistent with shock, too, sitting motionless unless something was required of her, and then her movements were slow, sluggish. She was very pale. Makeup? Her pupils were dilated, too, but eyedrops could produce that effect.

He hated what he was thinking, but he couldn't let himself be blinded. He might not be on the case, but that didn't mean his analysis couldn't be used.

Another thought occurred: Had she developed a relationship with him as a means of deflecting suspicion, maybe, or keeping tabs on any progress with the Roberts killing? If so, she must have been congratulating herself on her success, because the Roberts case was going exactly nowhere.

He wanted to keep questioning her, but it would be better if he backed off now, let the detectives assigned to the case ask the questions. Besides, there was something he needed to check.

He nodded to the patrolman and stepped out of the bungalow, taking a deep breath of the fresh warm air. He sought out Lieutenant Wester again. "Do we have a rough time of death?"

"The ME hasn't made a determination yet, but I saw the bodies myself and rigor is pretty far advanced. I'd say"—he rocked his hand—"twelve hours. In that neighborhood."

Fuck. That fell in the time span when he'd been out on call and she had made that sudden trip to the supermarket, even though she had bought groceries earlier in the day. The trip was nicely explained by a sudden, convenient craving for a banana split. Was she cold-blooded enough that she had come back here, killed two people, then stopped off for ice cream on the way back to his house? Or had she bought the ice cream as an excuse for being out? An alibi, so she could show him the receipt and say, "See? I was here. I couldn't have been there."

This was practically a mirror situation of the Roberts murder. She had no eyewitness alibi to definitely say she was somewhere else at the time of the killing, but she had the receipt from where she'd been shopping.

On the other hand, she couldn't have known he'd be called out last night. She couldn't have planned anything ahead of time. Had she just been waiting, knowing he would eventually be called out at night, and when he did, she'd make her move? She wouldn't have been in any hurry; she could afford to wait for the right moment. After all, she was collecting that hefty salary, and if she had her eye on the missing yellow diamond ring, it wasn't going anywhere.

She hadn't kept the receipt from the supermarket. He clearly remembered her putting the plastic bags and the receipt in the trash. If she was that sharp, that organized a killer, throwing away the receipt was a sloppy thing to do. Or a smart one. She could then say, "If I thought I'd need an alibi, why would I have thrown away the receipt?"

God, this was driving him crazy. No matter what angle he came up with, a tiny shift put an entirely different light on the most significant, or insignificant, actions.

He went home and went through his kitchen trash can. The plastic bags were right there, practically on top, with only the fruit peelings and empty yogurt container from breakfast on top of them. He pulled out the bags—there were two of them—straightened them out, and looked inside. There was the receipt, crumpled but nice and dry, without any smears.

He looked at the time on it. Eight-fifty-seven. That was about the time he'd gotten home. Where had she been for the rest of the time he'd been gone?

The interview room was small, utilitarian, nonthreatening, with a camera attached to the ceiling recording the interview.

The detective, Rusty Ahern, was a good interviewer. He was about five-nine, with sandy hair and freckles and an open expression that invited confessions. Very nonthreatening, very sympathetic. No matter how neutral Cahill made his expression and his voice, he could never be as nonthreatening as Rusty. He was too big, and as Rusty himself had pointed out, "Your eyes always look like a shark's." Rusty was particularly good with women; they trusted that Howdy Doody expression.

Cahill, along with the lieutenant and two other detectives, watched the interview on a monitor as it was recording. Sarah sat practically motionless, for the most part staring at nothing, as if she had shut down emotionally. Cahill remembered she'd acted the same after the first killing. A protective response, maybe? A way of distancing herself? Or a very good act?

"Where were you last night?" Rusty asked gently.

"Cahill's house."

"Detective Cahill?"

"Yes."

"Why were you there?"

"I spent the weekend with him."

"The entire weekend?"

"Not Saturday. There was a party Saturday night. I worked."

"What time did you get to Detective Cahill's house? After the party on Saturday."

"Four o'clock?" she said, making it a question. "I don't remember exactly. Early. Before dawn."

"Why did you go so early in the morning?"

"So we could be together."

Rusty didn't ask any questions about their relationship, thank God. He moved right on with establishing a time line. "Were you together all day Sunday?"

"Yes."

"And you spent Sunday night with Detective Cahill?"

"Yes."

"What about yesterday? Monday. When Detective Cahill went to work, what did you do?"

"Damn, Rusty must think he's a lawyer," Detective Nolan muttered. "Listen to those questions."

The questions were unusually detailed, step-by-step. Usually an interview was less structured, inviting the suspect to just talk. But Sarah wasn't chattering; she was answering only the questions asked, and most of those as briefly as possible. Since she wasn't volunteering information, Rusty was dragging it out of her.

"I worked out. Bought groceries."

"Is that all?"

"I had a manicure."

"Where did you work out?"

"The basement."

"The basement, where?"

"Cahill's house."

On and on, establishing when and where she got the manicure, where she bought groceries, what time she was there. What did she do then? Cooked supper. Spaghetti. Had it ready when Cahill got home. Then he got a call and had to leave. He said he'd be gone for several hours.

Rusty looked down at his notes. He had the exact time of the call to Cahill, as well as what time he'd arrived back home. He had the checkout time of the receipt for the ice cream. If she tried to screw with the timing, he'd know. "What did you do then?"

"I cleaned up the kitchen, and watched television."

"Is that all you did?"

"I went for ice cream."

"What time was this?"

"I don't know. After eight."

"Where did you go?"

She told him the name of the supermarket.

"What time did you leave the supermarket?"

"I don't know."

"Can you estimate how long you were there?"

She lifted one shoulder. "Fifteen minutes."

"Where did you go when you left the supermarket?"

"Back to Cahill's house."

"Was he there?"

"Yes. He got back sooner than he'd expected."

"What time was this?"

"I don't know. I didn't look at the time."

"Did you stop anywhere else between the supermarket and Detective Cahill's house?"

"No."

"You said you bought groceries earlier in the day. Why didn't you buy the ice cream then?"

"I wasn't craving it then."

"You had a sudden craving for ice cream?"

"Yes."

"Do you crave ice cream very often?"

"Once a month."

Rusty looked a little puzzled. "Why just once a month?"

"Right before my menstrual period. I want ice cream then."

"Whoa," Nolan said in Cahill's ear. "TMI." Too much information. He didn't want to hear about menstrual cycles.

Rusty looked a little nonplussed, too, as if he didn't know where to go with that information. Cahill kept his expression impassive as he watched. This was tough enough as it was, having his private life brought into an investigation. What was she thinking? What was going on behind those dark eyes?

Hell, what did he know? When it came to

women, he was evidently both blind and stupid; he was a detective, and it had still taken him over a year to realize Shannon was cheating on him. But it was one thing to be duped by a cheating wife, and another to so totally miss the boat with a killer. He'd had sex with this woman. Slept beside her. Laughed with her. He'd have bet his life that she was one of the straightest arrows he'd ever met, and he was having a tough time reconciling what he knew of her as a woman with the circumstances that said she might be a stone-cold killer.

That was the bitch. Everything was circumstantial. The coincidences stretched beyond credulity, yet they didn't have a shred of physical evidence to tie her to the murders.

"My wife craves chocolate," Lieutenant Wester said. "I always know when she's going to start her period, because she's shoving Hershey's Kisses in her mouth like a squirrel stocking up for the winter."

"God, can't we talk about something else?" Nolan groaned.

Rusty had her up to the time she arrived at the Lankford house. "What did you do then?"

"I went to the main house to start the coffee."

"Did you notice anything unusual?"

"The alarm wasn't set. It didn't beep when I unlocked the kitchen door and went in."

"Was that unusual?"

"When I'm there, I always set the alarm. Mrs. Lankford sometimes forgets, though."

"So it wasn't unusual."

"Not really."

"What did you do then?"

"I started the coffeemaker, then took the newspaper . . . I was taking the newspaper to the den. Mr. Lankford liked to read it there, while he watched the news. The lights were on," she said, and her voice trailed away to nothing.

"The lights?"

"The hallway lights. They were on. And the lamps. They shouldn't have been on that early."

"Why not?"

"I'm the only one up that early, and I had just gotten there."

"What did you think?"

"I thought . . . I thought someone must be sick."

"Why did you think that?"

"The smell. I noticed the smell." She gripped her arms tightly, holding herself, and she began to rock a little, back and forth. The rocking was a sign of distress, the automatic attempt of the body to find comfort. Someone should be holding her, Cahill thought, his stomach knotting even tighter than it already was.

"What smell was that?"

She stared blankly at him, then abruptly stopped rocking and clapped a hand over her mouth. Rusty sprang for the trash can and got it to her just in time. She leaned over the can, retching violently, though nothing but fluid came up. Cahill clenched his teeth. She must not have eaten anything since breakfast, and that was hours ago. She kept retching, straining, even after her stomach was empty, and the sounds she made were painful to hear.

"I'll get you a paper towel," Rusty said, stepping to the door.

Sarah remained bent over the trash can, her body occasionally heaving in spasm. The monitoring room was silent as they watched. Cahill fought

the need to go to her, take care of her. He had to
stay out of this. He had to let Rusty do his job.

Rusty came back with a wet paper towel. Sarah
took it with violently trembling hands, and washed
her face. "I'm sorry," she said in a muffled voice,
then buried her face in her hands and began to
weep in long, shuddering sobs that reminded
Cahill of how she had wept after Judge Roberts
was killed.

God. He couldn't watch this. He got up and
paced around the room, rubbing the back of his
neck to ease the kinks.

If she had done those killings, then she was the
world's best actress, bar none. What he saw on the
screen was a woman in shock and grieving. People
sometimes reacted that way if they had killed in
the heat of the moment, then realized with horror
what they had done. Killers who coldly executed
their victims with well-placed shots to the head
didn't grieve for them afterward. The circumstances were so suspicious they stank to high
heaven, but the details didn't fit. *She* didn't fit.

She didn't fit. No matter what the circumstances
were, she didn't fit. "She didn't do it," he said
softly, suddenly, completely certain. Okay, so he
could be blind when it came to romantic shit, and
he'd taken a hard kick in the chops because of it;
as a cop, he saw very clearly, and she wasn't guilty.

Lieutenant Wester gave him a sympathetic look.
"Doc, you're sleeping with her. Don't let your little head do the thinking for your big head."

"You can mark it down," Cahill said. "I know
her. She *couldn't* have done it."

"You're too involved," Nolan said. "Just let us

do our jobs. If she didn't do it, we'll find out. And if she did do it, we'll find that out, too."

They all looked back at the monitor. Rusty had waited silently as the storm of weeping subsided, and now he asked softly, "Would you like something to drink? Coffee? Water? A Coke?"

"Water," she managed to say, her voice thick. "Thank you."

He got a cup of water for her, and Cahill turned to watch the screen again as she took a couple of sips, cautiously, as if she wasn't certain the water would stay down.

"What happened after you noticed the smell?"

The rocking started again, subtle and heartbreaking. "I . . . I almost ran. I remembered the smell. When the Judge was murdered, the smell was . . . was the same. I couldn't go in there. I wanted to run."

At least she was talking a little more, rather than answering the questions with monosyllables.

"Did you run?"

She shook her head. "I kept telling myself it was just that someone was sick. A stomach virus. It was my job to handle things, clean up any mess . . ." She trailed off again.

"What did you do?"

"I went to the door of the den and looked in. He was . . . lying there. His neck was bent." Unconsciously she cocked her head to show the position Sonny Lankford had been in. Rusty waited to see if she would continue talking, but she lapsed into silence until prodded by another question.

"What did you do then?"

"I b-backed to the kitchen and tried to call nine-one-one. I wanted to call Cahill first. I wanted him there. But nine-one-one . . . the medics . . . maybe they could help. So I tried to call nine-one-one first."

"Tried to call?"

"I couldn't—I was shaking so hard I hit the wrong buttons. The phone wouldn't work. I banged it down on the counter and it broke. The phone broke."

"You banged the phone down on the counter?"

"Yes."

"Why?"

"It wouldn't work. It wouldn't work!"

"Then what?"

"I threw it."

Sarah was the most self-possessed person he knew, Cahill thought. If she had lost control to that extent, she had been hysterical. She was frightened, and hurting, and he hadn't so much as touched her hand when he'd gone to see her in the bungalow. No wonder she was hugging herself; someone needed to do it.

"I needed another phone," she said, for the first time speaking without being prompted by a question. "I couldn't think, couldn't remember where one was. I haven't worked there very long, and the house is complicated. I didn't want to hunt for a phone, because I didn't know where Mrs. Lankford was and I didn't want to find her, I didn't want to see her." New tears streaked down her face. "So I went to my quarters, the bungalow. I know where the phone is in there. I didn't have to hunt for it. I called nine-one-one and they kept me on the line. I wanted to hang up, but they wouldn't let me. They kept me on the line."

"Why did you want to hang up?"

"Cahill," Sarah said, her voice wobbling, her eyes blind with tears. "I wanted to call Cahill. I needed him."

Cahill abruptly left the room. He went into the bathroom, locked the door, then bent over the toilet and vomited.

CHAPTER 24

IT TOOK A WHILE BEFORE SHE BEGAN THINKING COHERENTLY, LOGically, but Sarah had nothing but time on her hands. She sat alone in the interview room for long stretches of time, broken by periods when the detective with sandy hair and freckles would ask her a lot of questions. If she had to go to the bathroom, she was escorted. If she asked for something to drink, it was brought to her.

She wondered if they would let her leave, if she tried. She hadn't been arrested, hadn't been handcuffed, she had come here voluntarily. Besides, she had no place else to go. She couldn't stay in the bungalow, she hadn't been able to think clearly enough to give instructions about gathering her clothes and other needed items so she could stay in a hotel again, and she certainly couldn't go to Cahill's house. When she did begin thinking again, that was the one fact that was glaringly obvious.

He thought she was guilty. He thought she'd committed murder.

He hadn't come near her earlier, at the bungalow, just stood there watching her with cold eyes. This wasn't like when the Judge was murdered; she had been under suspicion then, too, until he'd checked out her story, but it hadn't been personal.

She'd understood. But now . . . he knew her now, as no one else had ever known her. Last night, except for when he'd gone on that call, she had been with him all night. They'd made love, several times. And yet he thought she had left the house soon after he did, driven to the Lankfords' house, shot both of them in the head, then stopped by the grocery store and bought ice cream on the way back to his house.

She would have understood him doing his job. It would have hurt, but she'd have understood. She didn't understand him actually believing she was guilty.

That cut, so deeply and cruelly she wasn't certain the wounds would ever heal. With one slash he'd severed the bonds between them, leaving her adrift. She felt like an astronaut whose safety line has snapped, only no one from the mother ship was making any effort to retrieve her. She was lost, floating farther and farther away, and she didn't much care.

The grief she'd felt when the Judge was killed was nothing compared to this. It wasn't just over the violent death of the Lankfords, those friendly, down-to-earth people whom she'd liked very much; it was for the loss of Cahill as well, of the magic she'd thought they shared. She loved him, but he didn't, couldn't love her, because to really love someone you had to *know* that person, know what made her tick, how she was put together as a human being. Cahill obviously had no clue about her. If he had, he'd have come to her and said, "I know it looks bad, but I believe in you. I'm behind you."

Instead he'd looked at her as if she were dirt, and then he'd walked away.

That wasn't love. He'd wanted to screw her, that was all. And, boy, had he ever.

She understood now why he was so bitter and distrustful after finding out his wife had betrayed him. She didn't know if she'd ever be able to really trust anyone again, either. Her family, yes; she could rely on them through thick and thin, hell and high water, and every other applicable cliché. But anyone else? She didn't think so. The lessons learned hardest were the lessons learned best.

In the meantime, she did something that was foreign to her nature: she endured. She had always been one of those people who, when something wasn't to their liking, didn't rest until they had wrestled, pummeled, and otherwise whipped whatever it was into a shape more to their liking. In this instance, however, there was nothing she could do. She couldn't change the past. Cahill had walked away from her when she needed him most, and no amount of wrestling or pummeling on her part would alter that.

It was a funny type of love that talked marriage one day, and turned its back the next. So why wasn't she laughing?

Instead she sat in the armless chair in the windowless little interview room, and let time wash around her. She was in no hurry. She had nothing to do, and nowhere to go.

Lieutenant Wester rubbed his hand over his nearly bald head. "Okay," he said wearily. "What do we have? Do we hold her, book her, or let her go?"

Everyone was exhausted. The media was in an uproar, the mayor was in an uproar, city hall was in an uproar, and the citizens of Mountain Brook were frightened. Three of their number had been murdered in their homes in the past month, which would have been big news in any community but in Mountain Brook was horrifying. The murder victims had thought they were safe, with their security systems and walled estates, electric gates and floodlights. Instead they had been no safer than a young mother in a drug-ridden neighborhood, cowering with her children in the bathtub at night because the walls were too thin to stop the bullets that regularly whined through the streets.

People paid a high price to live in Mountain Brook, with its crushing property tax. They paid through the nose for the astronomical real estate values, the excellent school system, the illusion of safety. The property taxes bought them a town without slums, and a police department that they expected to keep crime to a minimum, and solve the ones that did occur. When the people in multi-million-dollar homes lost that illusion of safety, they were vocal in their unhappiness. That made the mayor unhappy, which made the captain unhappy, et cetera, et cetera. The pressure was on the investigative division to produce results, or else.

Rusty Ahern consulted the papers before him. "Okay. Here's what I think: We have three spent shell casings, which on preliminary testing appear to match the bullet that killed Judge Roberts. We *don't* have any viable fingerprints, in either case. We have no physical evidence other than the three shell casings, period. We also have no sign of forced entry at either location, indicating the victims knew the perp and opened the door. We have a busted lock on an interior door. Call-back on the Lankfords' phone went to a pay phone in the Galleria, the same pay phone that showed up as the last call to Judge Roberts. I don't know about you guys, but that right there leads me to think Miss Stevens didn't do either murder."

"How so?" Nolan asked. "I'm not following."

"She wouldn't have any reason to call ahead, to make certain the electric gates were open, or the victims were at home, or whatever," Cahill said. "She had full access to both homes. All she had to do was go in, at any time."

"Right. And what would be the motive?" Ahern asked. "That's what's driving me crazy. Nothing was taken in the Roberts killing. Miss Stevens got a hefty chunk in his will, but that's in probate, it isn't as if you're handed a check as soon as the body's planted. And like you pointed out, Doc, she isn't hurting for money."

"That doesn't mean anything," Nolan said. "Some people always want more. And don't forget that big diamond ring that's missing. A rock worth a quarter of a million will get a lot of people's attention. Plus some people are just fucking crazy."

Cahill held on to his temper. "But she isn't. She's as sane and even-tempered as anyone I've ever met, and, Nolan, if you say one more time she has me pussy-whipped, I'm going to feed you your teeth." They'd been in each other's faces a couple of times already today. Both of them were tired and irritable, and Nolan had a habit of carrying teasing too far.

"Let's cool it, guys," Wester said. "Doc, what about that photo you came up with from the pay phone on the Roberts case? Has it been shown around the Lankfords' neighborhood?"

"Not yet. We've been concentrating on Sarah."

"Well, get it out and circulate it. Since the last call to the Lankfords' came from the same pay phone, that guy has to be our man."

"But it still doesn't make sense," Nolan argued. "Why kill Judge Roberts and not take anything, unless it was for the money in the will? So it's in probate; she'll get it eventually. Look at it this way: She works for Roberts and he gets popped. She goes to work for the Lankfords and they get popped. Does anybody else see a pattern here?"

"Then what's your theory on the guy in the picture?" Wester asked.

"It's simple. They're working together. Has to be. She goes inside and gets all the information, the alarm codes, the keys, whatever is needed. I don't know how they'd decide *when*—I mean, she worked for Judge Roberts for almost three years, so why wait so long to off him? Then she's with the Lankfords only a little over a week and they get offed. Maybe it's whenever they need the money. Who knows? But she makes sure she has an alibi, and he waltzes in and does the job. They never even know he's in the house until he walks up on them and pulls the trigger. He has no known connection to the victims, so it's essentially a stranger killing, and they're damn hard to solve."

"Do you have an alarm system in your house?" Cahill asked.

"Yeah, it's called a dog."

"Well, the victims *would* hear the killer come in. In both houses, whenever an outside door or window was opened, an alert is beeped. If you weren't expecting anyone to be there, you'd check it out, right? You wouldn't sit in your recliner and wait."

"Unless they thought it was Stevens."

"In the Lankfords' case, they knew she was gone until Tuesday morning."

Wester frowned. "You're saying in both cases the victims knew the killer."

"Looks like it to me."

"And the killer in both cases is the same guy."

They all looked at one another.

"We're still missing something," Ahern said. "Motive."

"I keep telling you, it's the money," said Nolan.

"And I keep telling *you*," Cahill said impatiently, "the only way money makes sense is if Sarah is doing the killing."

"Or is having it done."

"But the victims knew the killer, who is very probably the man who made the calls from the pay phone. You yourself said her so-called partner wouldn't have any connection to the victims, so it can't be both ways. They either knew him, or they didn't. If they didn't know him, why did they let him in the house? Why did Judge Roberts sit down to talk to him? The killer was an acquaintance of both Roberts and the Lankfords."

"Well, shit." Nolan frowned at the surface of the table, thinking hard.

"So our guy is someone they knew in business, or moved in the same circles. My guess is business," Cahill said. "Judge Roberts was in his mid-eighties, and he didn't do the party circuit. He had his circle of poker-playing cronies, and that was it. But he still had business concerns that he stayed on top of, and Sonny Lankford had more irons in the fire than a blacksmith."

"Looking at it that way, the motive may be money after all," said Ahern. "We need to find out what business ventures or financial concerns they had in common, some deal that went bad but they came out of okay, while someone else lost his shirt."

"But then it would be sheer coincidence that Sarah Stevens happened to be working for both Roberts and the Lankfords when each was murdered," Wester said. "That's bullshit. Coincidences like that don't happen."

"Maybe it's not as far-fetched as you'd think," Ahern said, doodling furiously on his legal pad as he chased his thoughts. "How many people can afford a butler, especially one who makes in the range that Sarah Stevens makes? Not many. It would be a small circle, even in Mountain Brook. Most people here work like hell to pay the property taxes and their mortgages, and keep their kids in school. But these rich folks who can afford her, they probably all know one another, through business if not socially. They had to get rich somehow, didn't they? I say business dealings are the link."

"A lot of companies have had problems this past year. It's possible someone took a soaking and is holding a grudge about it." Wester considered the scenario. So far, it made more sense than any other theory they'd considered. "Okay, I'll take this to the captain. We'll put out some statement that's vague enough it won't spook this guy. He's already killed three people, and he may have started liking it. We don't want any more bodies in this town."

He looked at Ahern. "You can release Miss Stevens, have someone collect some clothes for her and drive her to a motel. And, no, she can't stay at your house," he said pointedly to Cahill. "I want you to stay away from her for the time being. The press is going to be all over us for turning her loose, and if one of those guys follows her and finds out she's living with a Mountain Brook detective, our collective asses will go up in flames. Is that clear?"

Cahill saw the wisdom of Sarah's not living in his house. Staying away from her, though, wasn't in the cards. He had some major bridge repair to do, and he wasn't going to wait until they broke this case to do it. All day it had been burning in his gut, the way she'd cried when she said she needed him. She had walked in on a horror this morning, made all the worse by being a repeat of the scene with Judge Roberts. She'd been a walking basket case, and he hadn't gone to her, hadn't held her. She'd been alone all day, slowly rocking back and forth, hugging herself. Even worse, she knew he'd thought she was the killer.

This wasn't merely doing his job; this was a lack of trust so gargantuan he didn't know if he'd be able to regain his lost ground. He'd die trying, though. If he had to crawl to her on his hands and knees, literally as well as figuratively, to get her forgiveness, then he'd wear out the knees in every pair of pants he owned if that was what it took.

She was in a fragile state right now. He remembered that when the Judge was killed she hadn't been able to eat; today she certainly hadn't had anything since breakfast, which was at least a thousand years ago from the way he felt. They had offered her food, but she had refused it with a silent shake of her head. She was usually the strong one, the go-to person in a crisis, but now she needed someone to take care of her.

The first order of business was to get her things from the bungalow and get her checked into a hotel under an assumed name so she could rest. Ahern would take care of that.

There was no way in hell, though, that Cahill intended to let her leave without apologizing, for whatever good that would do.

He walked down the short hall and opened the door to the interview room. She looked up, then quickly averted her gaze when she recognized him. She was still pale, her face drawn and her dark eyes dull. Coming so soon after the Judge's murder, this had knocked her flat.

He stepped inside and closed the door. The ceiling-mounted camera wasn't on right now; they were private. If she wanted to slap his face, he'd take it. If she wanted to kick him in the balls, he guessed he'd take that, too. He'd take anything from her if she would forgive him afterward. But she didn't move, even when he crouched beside the chair so he could see her face.

"Ahern is going to take you to a hotel so you can rest," he said quietly. "We'll pick up your clothes and bring them to you. Let him check you in; you'll be under an assumed name, so the press can't find you."

"I'm not being arrested?" she asked, her voice thin and colorless.

"Sarah . . . we know you didn't do it."

"Why? Did some evidence turn up today? You thought I was guilty this morning." There was no accusation, no heat in the words, just a statement of fact. He felt as if she had put miles of mental distance between them, between herself and everyone else. It was the only way she could cope.

"I was wrong," he said simply. "I'm sorry. God, I can't tell you how sorry I am. The coincidence slapped me in the face, and all I could think was that you'd gone out last night after I left on the call."

"I understand."

The lack of inflection in her voice made him wince. "Do you forgive, too?"

"No."

"Sarah—" He reached out, and she pulled back, her expression frantic.

"Don't touch me."

He dropped his hand. "All right. For now. I know I fucked up big time, but I won't let you go. We think we're getting this thing figured out, and—"

"It isn't up to you," she interrupted.

"What? What isn't up to me?"

"Letting me go. You don't have a choice."

There was a big black hole yawning at his feet, and he felt as if he were being sucked down into it. If he lost her—well, that wasn't going to happen. He refused to let it. Once she was over the initial shock, she would at least listen to him. Sarah was the most reasonable person he'd ever met. And if she wouldn't listen, then he didn't mind fighting dirty. He'd do whatever it took to keep her.

"We'll talk later," he said, stepping back to give her the space she needed right now.

"There's no point."

"There's every point. I'll give you some room and time now, but don't ever think I've given up. Ever."

"You should," she said, and went back to staring at the wall.

Fifteen minutes later, Ahern hurried her out the back door and across the parking lot to his car. The print and television reporters camped out by the front saw them and the cameramen got some footage, but that was it. One enterprising guy jumped into his car and started to follow, but his way was blocked when a white Jaguar swung in front of him, and by the time he pulled into traffic, both the unmarked cop car and the white Jaguar had vanished from sight.

CHAPTER 25

TREVOR DENSMORE HAD NEVER BEEN MORE SHOCKED IN HIS LIFE than when the news reports made it plain Sarah was being held as a suspect. This was terrible. How could they possibly . . . why, there wasn't a shred of evidence against her. Not a shred. How could there be? He'd been careless last night and left behind the shell casings, causing himself a moment of worry, but they could in no way be linked to Sarah. As for himself, all he had to do next was dispose of the pistol—after first filing off the registration number, of course. He hated taking care of such menial details himself, but he could hardly ask his secretary to handle it, now could he?

The most important thing was to make certain Sarah was all right. She was so pale, in the news footage shown. She had discovered the bodies of both Judge Lowell Roberts, her previous employer, and the Lankfords, which suggested she was like the miscreants who set fires, then called in the report, pretending they had discovered it so they could deflect suspicion from themselves. The police were wise to such tactics, which he supposed explained why she was under suspicion, but, oh, dear . . . he'd done her such a terrible wrong.

Not once had he considered that she would be

the one who found the bodies. Not once. He
should have realized it, because of course she was
the most logical person to do so; she was conscientious, meaning she would be the first one on
duty in the morning. The shocks he'd made her endure had to have been terrible. He couldn't think
how he could have arranged for someone else to
discover the bodies, but he could have thrown a
blanket over them or something. People nowadays
always had those throw things draped everywhere,
like shawls for furniture; he detested such clutter
himself. He could have used them, however, to
spare Sarah a measure of shock.

He was so distressed by his thoughtlessness that
he had his secretary cancel his appointments and
left his office early. What to do, what to do?

The first order of business was to get her released, but how? He could scarcely call the police
department and demand her release, not without
explanations he didn't care to make. Then the brilliant idea occurred. It was risky, but worth the
gamble if it freed Sarah.

Even as efficient as he was, it still took him a few
hours to accomplish the deed. Then, not knowing
what else to do, he drove to city hall and parked in
the parking lot of the nearby bank and waited. He
didn't want to join the jackals who were lingering
with their satellite-dish-equipped vans and video-
cameras, and, really, he had no idea how long it
would be before the effects of his plan were discovered. But when Sarah was released, he intended
to be there to offer his support.

Why, in retrospect, things couldn't have
worked out better. She would be upset, in need of

a safe haven. He could give her that, and more . . . so much more.

He had carefully chosen his vantage point, and when he needed to change the angle of vision to better see what was going on—it was so frustrating not to know exactly; he hated being kept in the dark like this—he would simply walk down the sidewalk as if he were going to the dry cleaners, or whatever.

Luck was on his side, but then, it always was. He became more and more exasperated as he waited; the incompetent yokels, what was taking them so long? Just as he reached his limit and decided to go home—after all, no one would expect him to wait forever—he saw Sarah leave the police department by a side door at the back of the building. She was with a man, probably a detective, since he was escorting her across the narrow drive to the parking lot the police used. The news crews spotted them, of course, as they got into an unmarked city car of common lineage. One reporter ran to his car and jumped in, but Trevor timed things perfectly, smoothly swinging the Jaguar into traffic at just the right moment to block the reporter from pulling out. There was more traffic behind him, inadvertently performing the same blocking maneuver.

Trevor kept his eye on the unmarked car as he followed, keeping at least one car between them. Really, he was getting very good at this.

Where was he taking her? Back to the Lankfords' house? Surely not. But she had no other home. To a friend's home, then, or a hotel. The good news was that she obviously had not been arrested, just detained and questioned, and now they had decided they had no reason to hold her. He wasn't certain exactly how police procedure worked, but he did know that if she had been arrested, she would have been detained until a bond hearing, where bail would either be set or denied.

All he had to do was follow to see where she was being taken; then he would decide how best to approach her. This time she would come to him. He was certain of it.

"Do you have any preferences?" Detective Ahern asked her. "Which hotel, I mean."

"I don't care."

Ahern glanced at her, at a loss. He'd gone into the interview room thinking, like everyone else, that she was guilty. Her reactions during the interview, plus some logical thinking, had convinced him she wasn't. Normally he didn't concern himself much if someone was upset; in his line of work, it was to be expected, and unless they were hysterical and throwing punches or objects, he left them to handle things on their own. This was different, though; because of her connection to Cahill, she was one of theirs. This was more personal.

"The lieutenant told Doc to stay away from you until things settle down. The press would go crazy if they found out you're living with him."

"I'm not," she said flatly.

He was about to step knee-deep in shit, he just knew it, but he plowed on. "So if Doc isn't around much, that's why. He wants to be. By the way, he's been arguing us into the ground all day about your innocence. He believes in you, Sarah. We're working our butts off to get this thing figured out, but he—"

"Detective Ahern," she said.

"What?"

"Shut up." She leaned her head back and closed her eyes.

Now what?

He was saved by a call coming in on his phone. Eyes widening, he listened in disbelief.

"Shit!" he said explosively.

She jerked upright, and he had the impression she had actually dozed off in those few seconds. "What?"

"There's been another killing." He stepped on the gas. "If you don't mind, I'm taking you to the Mountain Brook Inn. It's close by, and I need to get to the scene."

"That's fine."

He was agitated. "It sounds like the same MO, Sarah. We'll know more when we investigate, but if it is, you're totally clear. The press won't bother you."

"Why?" She shook her head. "Who?"

"I don't know; I just have the address. But evidently the kill is recent, just a few hours old. You couldn't have done it." His hands tightened on the steering wheel. "Shit. We have a maniac on our hands."

When they reached the inn, she said, "Just let me out in front. I'll check myself in." She shrugged. "Now it doesn't matter if they know I'm here, does it? I may get some phone calls, but they won't be beating down my door." With this latest development, she had gone from suspect to . . . what? Material witness? Incredibly unlucky?

"Do me a favor," Ahern said. "Use a false name anyway. Use 'Geraldine Ahern,' that's my mother's name. That way we can find you."

"Okay," she agreed. This wasn't something she cared about. Right now, nothing was. She just wanted to be alone, and she wanted to sleep.

She got her purse and got out of the car. Before she closed the door, Ahern leaned over and said, "We'll have your clothes brought to you. Just sit tight."

She'd have to sit tight, she thought as she watched Ahern drive away, unless she called a taxi, because she didn't have a way of going anywhere. The TrailBlazer was still at the Lankfords' house.

She was so exhausted that for long moments she simply stood there in the late afternoon warmth, trying to dissipate the chill that seemed to go all the way through to her bones. What would she do if the staff at the front desk refused to let her stay here? If they had been watching television today, her face and name would have been all over the news. They might even think she had escaped custody, though why she would then try to check into a nearby hotel was more than she could imagine.

The events of the day crashed down on her, sapping what little strength she had left, swaying her on her feet. She closed her eyes, struggling for control.

"Miss Stevens?" asked a softly hesitant voice. "Sarah?"

Dazed, she opened her eyes and found herself staring at a man who looked familiar, though she couldn't quite place him. He stood a few feet from her, watching her with concern. She hadn't heard his footsteps, hadn't realized anyone was near.

"Are you all right?" he asked shyly; and then she placed him. Saturday night. The party.

"Mr. Densmore," she said.

He looked pleased that she remembered him. "Please call me Trevor. My dear, I've been thinking about you all day. This is terrible, what's happened. You must have been so afraid."

Her throat locked, and she stared at him. After the events of the day, this gentle sympathy was almost her undoing.

"The newscasters made it sound as if the police suspect you, but that's ridiculous. You couldn't possibly have done such a thing; the very idea. Are you staying here for the time being?"

"I—" She swallowed. "I haven't checked in yet."

"Then let's go in and get you a room so you can rest. Have you eaten anything today? There's a café here, I believe. I'd be honored if you'd join me for a meal."

He was a virtual stranger, but after only one meeting he had more faith in her than Cahill had. The difference between them slapped her in the face, sent her reeling. She didn't realize she had swayed again until Mr. Densmore reached out to touch her arm. "My dear, you're on the verge of collapse. Come with me. You'll feel better after you've had something to eat, I promise."

It was so easy just to let him take charge. All but the most simple actions seemed beyond her capability now; it was a relief not to make decisions, not even about what she ate. Before she knew it they were in the café and he was quietly ordering hot tea and soup for her, making soft comments that didn't require replies but nevertheless wove a sort of buffer zone around her and gave her something else to concentrate on. All day the same scenes had been replaying in her mind, all day the same horrible thoughts had chased around and around, and he offered surcease from that. She listened to him, and she allowed herself to forget, just for a little while.

He was gentle in his insistence that she eat, but relentless. After a day of feeling battered, it was good to be taken care of. She made herself eat half the bowl of soup, and sip the hot tea. At least she began to feel a little warmer, but her mind was still in a fog and she was surprised when she suddenly focused on what Mr. Densmore was saying.

"You still want to hire me?" she asked in dazed astonishment.

He blushed, and fiddled with his teaspoon, unnecessarily stirring the already stirred tea, then precisely placing the spoon on the rim of the saucer. "I know this is terrible timing," he said. "I'm sorry. This is so embarrassing."

"No, it isn't that," she said quickly. "It's just—I apologize. I'm so tired I can't concentrate. Thank you very much for your offer, but, Mr. Densmore . . . it may not be safe. My employers seem to be—" She stopped, her lips suddenly trembling, unable to go on.

"That can't have anything to do with you," he said firmly. "It's just a horrible coincidence. It's been on the news that there's been another incident, so that proves you aren't involved in any way."

The media was on top of things today if it was

already on the news about this latest killing, she thought tiredly. But they were in a high state of alert, monitoring the police radios and 911 calls, so it was possible they were at this latest scene almost before the cops were.

Another person was dead. She should be horrified for the victim's sake, for the family's sake, but all she could feel was grateful that she wasn't there.

"My offer still stands," he said, his shy smile beginning to form. "I was impressed with your abilities when I saw you on television, and again last Saturday. Please think about it. My estate is extensive; I've been coping with part-time staff, but it would really benefit from permanent, expert supervision. It's very quiet, and I have excellent security."

Her mind felt filled with cotton, but one thought at least was clear: The job offers wouldn't be pouring in this time, the way they had after the Judge was killed. After what happened to the Lankfords, she would at the least be regarded as a jinx, though this last killing would at least prove she wasn't a murderer. Not many people would want someone like her in the house. Probably Mr. Densmore wouldn't have, either, if he hadn't already met her and formed his own opinion about her character.

She should take her time finding another position. She should advertise in the papers in Atlanta and Palm Beach, maybe even New Orleans. She could stay with her parents while she searched, assuming the police would let her leave the area. Right now, even with this newest development, that was a big assumption.

Since this job was falling into her lap, the simplest thing would be to take it. She would have somewhere to live, and something to occupy her mind. When she felt better, when she was more herself, then she could decide what to do on a permanent basis.

"I have to be honest with you, Mr. Densmore. After what's happened, I don't think I want to stay in this area. I'm grateful for your offer, and if you're still interested in hiring me knowing that it may be temporary—"

"I am," he said quickly. "I understand completely how you feel. But after things have settled down and you see the arrangements at my estate, I hope you'll change your mind about leaving."

She took a deep breath. "In that case, I accept your offer."

Chapter 26

THE VICTIM'S NAME WAS JACOB WANETTA, FIFTY-SIX YEARS OLD, the president and CEO of Wanetta Advertising. He lived on Cherokee Road, and he and his wife were golfing enthusiasts. He was working at home that day, and he'd been hale and hearty when his wife was picked up by a friend a little after lunch to play nine holes at the Mountain Brook Country Club, then have cocktails. He'd waved them off from the front door, so it wasn't a matter of the wife *saying* he was alive then, the friend had seen him, too. When the wife arrived home after a fun afternoon of golf and gin, she found her husband sprawled beside the hearth in his den, a bullet through his brain.

The evidence technicians found the shell casing where it had rolled under the sofa, and immediate comparisons were being made to see if it matched the three found at the Lankfords. From the damage done, the bullet looked to be the same caliber as the others, though the ME would have to weigh the slug to be certain. The shot appeared to have been delivered in the same manner as two of the others. Except for Mrs. Lankford, who had been shot between the eyes, the other killing wounds had all entered from the left, indicating the killer had been standing to the left of the victim and was right-handed. That had to be sheer coincidence, where he stood, but maybe not. Maybe, being right-handed, he deliberately maneuvered so he was on the victim's left, giving himself an unencumbered shot. If he stood to the victim's right, shooting would require swiveling his body, and might give the victim time to react.

As it was, none of the victims had stood a chance. They hadn't had time to do more than blink, if that. Except for Merilyn Lankford; she had obviously been trying to call for help.

Jacob Wanetta had been a hefty, athletic guy. If any of them could have fought, he would have been the one. But he'd gone down just like the others, without resistance. There were no overturned chairs, no lamps knocked askew, nothing . . . just that very efficient killing.

He had been killed while Sarah was safely at the police department. There was no question of her innocence, and since by all indications he and the Lankfords had been killed by the same person, that effectively removed the media focus from her. The chief put out a statement that they had been concerned for Miss Stevens's safety, but they had at no time considered her a suspect. That was a flat-out lie, but who cared, if it killed the media's interest in her?

Ahern said he'd left her at the Mountain Brook Inn, with instructions to check in under *Geraldine Ahern,* his mother's name. Cahill wished Ahern had actually gone inside with her and seen to it himself, but he understood the urgency to get to the scene. When Mrs. Wanetta's hysterical phone call had come into 911, there in the police department, everyone had scrambled like fighter pilots racing to meet an oncoming wave of bombers.

They were stretched thin, trying to handle the normal problems that cropped up plus three murders in one day. With this latest development, Lieutenant Wester decided there wasn't any reason to keep Cahill separate from the Lankford case; Wester had only five investigators to begin with, so he needed every one of them concentrating on this. As far as Cahill was concerned, that also lifted the restrictions on him involving Sarah, not that he'd intended to pay much attention to them anyway. Still, it was nice to know his ass wasn't going to get busted for doing it.

It was close to midnight when Wester decided they were all so tired they were losing their effectiveness. They'd have to wait and see if the evidence techs came up with any new physical evidence. They had already interviewed as many friends and neighbors as they could—unless they started dragging people from their beds—and, as Nolan put it, they were starting to get "the stupids."

Sarah hadn't been far from Cahill's mind all day, and abruptly he remembered to ask, "Ahern, did you have anyone take Sarah's clothes to her?"

Ahern gave him a blank look, then groaned. "Shit, I forgot." He glanced at his watch. He had called his wife two hours ago and told her he'd be home soon.

"I'll do it," Cahill said. Wester was listening to them and when he didn't say anything, Cahill knew he was cleared.

"Are you sure about that?" Ahern asked, giving

him a shrewd look. "You might want to stay out of reach for a few days."

"No, that's exactly what I *don't* need to do."

He was as short on sleep as everyone else—probably shorter, considering what he and Sarah had done with the chocolate syrup the night before—but he had no interest in going home without seeing her first. She, on the other hand, probably wouldn't be glad to see him at any time, much less in the wee hours of the morning.

Tough shit.

He picked up her clothes first, figuring she wouldn't refuse to see him if he had her things. He got everything, digging out her suitcases and cleaning out the closet, because he assumed she wouldn't be coming back here to stay anyway. In just the short time she'd been here, though, she had already put her personal touches on the bungalow, with her books and photographs, and her music collection. He thought about packing those up, too, but she wouldn't have room for them in a hotel room, and he didn't want to take the time right now. She needed her clothes; the other things could wait.

He was fast, but thorough, remembering to get all her toiletries and makeup from the tiled bathroom, and her underwear from the built-in drawers in the closet. Packing her things was easy; she was very neat, which made things go faster. Maybe she hadn't been here long enough for her things to have developed a life of their own. He had a stubborn hope that one day her clothes would push his out of the closet, and he'd complain about needing a bigger house just for the closet space. He had a

hope for a lot of things, and they all re-
volved round Sarah.

Finally he had everything packed in his truck,
and as he wound his way over to 280, he called
Sarah's cell phone number, but the recording came
on immediately informing him that the customer
was not in service at this time. He was used to her
keeping it on the entire time she was at his house,
putting it on the charger every night, but now there
was no reason for her to make it easy for anyone
to get in touch with her. Growling, he got the number of the Mountain Brook Inn from Information,
was put through, and asked for Geraldine Ahern.

Sarah was one of those people who woke instantly when disturbed, springing from bed ready
to do battle, thwart burglars, or cook breakfast.
He began to worry when she hadn't answered by
the fourth ring. She did answer on the sixth one,
though, and her voice sounded dull. "Hello."

"I'm bringing your clothes over," he said.
"What's your room number?"

She paused. "Just leave them at the front desk."

"No."

"What?"

There, that was better; there was a little life in
her voice. "If you want your clothes, you'll have to
see me."

"Are you holding my clothes hostage?" More
life. It was outrage, but at least it was life.

"If you don't want them now, I'll take them
home with me and you can pick them up there."

"Damn you, Cahill—" She stopped, and he
could hear her exhaling through her nose in exas-

peration. "All right." She told him her room number and slammed down the phone.

Progress was being made.

He didn't mind arguing. It was not talking at all that drove him crazy. As long as she was talking to him, even if by dint of coercion, then he had a chance.

At the inn, he got a luggage cart and loaded all of her things on it, then wheeled it to the elevator past the watchful eye of the clerk manning the desk. Cahill opened his jacket a little, flashing the tin on his belt, and the clerk became interested in other things.

Sarah must have been standing at the door, because she jerked it open before he could even knock. The squeaking of the luggage cart must have alerted her. She already had a hand extended to take one bag when she registered the load on the luggage cart.

"I brought everything," he said, keeping his voice down because of the other guests sleeping on this floor. It was a wonder he remembered the courtesy, because Sarah was naked, clutching a sheet around her. "I didn't figure you'd be staying there again."

"No," she said, shuddering. "But what about my—"

"You can get the rest of your stuff later." He wasn't above using his size to get what he wanted; he grabbed two of the suitcases and moved forward, and she was forced to step back from the door. He set down the suitcases, planting himself in the doorway, and swiveled to get the other bags. Before she could get the two suitcases hauled to the side, he had the others inside and he stepped forward, closing the door behind him. She had turned on every light in the place, making certain the room was as far from intimate as she could make it, even smoothing the bedspread back over the bed after she'd removed the sheet that was now wrapped around her.

But she hadn't put on her clothes, and she'd had time to do so. Instead she was wrapped in a sheet, and she was naked beneath it. He wondered if she even realized what that revealed about her emotions. Normally he would have said yes, but after the day she'd had, she probably didn't realize.

She clutched the sheet tighter, lifting her chin. "Thank you. Now get out."

"You look like a Victorian maiden protecting her virtue," he said, shifting the suitcases himself.

She had still been pale, her features pinched, but now her eyes narrowed and color washed into her cheeks. She was a good strategist, though; she must have sensed that a good fight to clear the air was just what he wanted, because she bit back whatever she had been about to say and moved several feet away. "Leave."

He moved closer. Maybe he could make her mad enough to swing at him; she'd have to let go of that sheet then. "Make me," he invited.

"I'm not doing this," she said, briefly closing her eyes and shaking her head. "If I have to, I'll call your supervisor and make a harassment charge against you. It's over. We didn't work out. End of story."

"No," he said. Shannon had once said he could give stubborn lessons to a jackass, and he intended to live up to his reputation. "Sarah, I love you."

Her head snapped up, and the expression in her eyes was furious. *"No you don't."*

His eyes narrowed. "The hell I don't."

Then she was advancing on him, holding the sheet with one hand and poking at him with a stiffened finger with the other. "You don't even know who I am," she snapped, breathing fire. "If you did, if you had paid the slightest amount of attention to me other than when you wanted to screw me, you'd never, *not for one damn second,* have thought I murdered anyone, much less someone I liked as much as I did M-Merilyn." Her chin wobbled, and her face began to crumple. "And—and I *loved* the Judge," she said in a trembling voice, trying hard not to cry. "You can't love someone you don't know, and you don't k-know me."

It wasn't just her voice trembling; she was shaking all over. Cahill felt something clench in his chest. Damn it, he hadn't liked it when she said he screwed her. He didn't like the term, didn't like what it implied. *Fucking,* yeah; when they made love, it was earthy and hot and sweaty, and that was fucking. But it had always been making love, too. It had never been just screwing.

She was falling apart in front of him. Cahill breathed a curse and pulled her into his arms, easily subduing the feeble girly-pounding she did on his chest; then she sort of crumpled against him and began to cry as she had earlier, in great, heaving sobs.

He picked her up and sat down on the bed, holding her on his lap and murmuring soft things to her, doing the things he should have done this morning. She wasn't holding the sheet now, her hands were fisted on his jacket, and the sheet began to loosen around her slender body. Ruthlessly he helped it along, pulling his jacket out of her grip and shrugging out of it at the same time as he tugged on the sheet, exposing more and more of her warm skin.

He fell back on the bed, twisting so she was on her back and he was leaning over her as he pulled the sheet completely free. She was still crying and she made a weak grab for the sheet, but he caught her hand and held it as he bent his head to kiss her, at the same time stroking his free hand over her smooth breasts, down her flat belly, then finally to the ultrasoft folds between her legs.

Her mouth was salty from her tears. She whimpered a protest, but she was arching toward him, and when he released her hand, it slid around his neck. He moved fast, opening his pants and shifting on top of her, parting her legs and settling between them. He guided his penis to her, and pushed. She wasn't wet but she was moist enough, though he had to rock several times to get all the way inside her.

She whimpered again, and went still, staring up at him with drenched, heartbreaking eyes.

"Shhh," he murmured, moving gently inside her. Usually she gave as good as she got, standing toe-to-toe with him whether they were sparring or making love, and this vulnerability hurt him deep inside. Maybe this was wrong, loving her now when her defenses were down, but it was the fastest way he knew to reestablish the connection between them. The bonds of the flesh . . . not just sex but the linking of two bodies, the most primitive way of seeking comfort and not feeling alone.

He would have made it last the rest of the

night, if he could have. As it was he stopped whenever he felt his orgasm building, lying still until the urge subsided then slowly stroking again. All the while he was kissing her, caressing her, telling her he loved her as he coaxed her from acceptance to response. He had never concentrated on a woman before as he concentrated now on Sarah, alert for every nuance, every caught breath, every shift of her legs. He'd always been hyperaware of her when they made love, but this was even more so. He felt as if his very survival depended on loving her now, on reforging the link his suspicion had broken.

It was a long time happening, but finally her hips began to move to meet him, and her fingers dug into his shoulders. He kept his pace slow, loving the feel of her tightening around him as if she was trying to hold him inside. The pulse at the base of her throat was hammering, and her nipples were tight, flushed with color. Tension coiled in her finely honed body, lifting her to every inward thrust, her legs sliding around his and locking in that way she had of holding him in, as if she couldn't get enough of him.

Her head tilted back, a groan sounding deep in her throat.

He pushed deep, held there, and felt her begin coming. He was so close, had been on the edge for so long, that he began coming, too, as soon as he felt the first contraction around him. He tried not to thrust, tried to hold himself still and deep for her pleasure, and his own pleasure spread through him like hot melted wax.

She lay beneath him, breathing hard, and tears leaked out of the corners of her eyes to streak into the hair at her temples. "I can't believe I did that," she choked out.

Struggling for breath, he propped on his elbow and wiped his thumb across her wet cheek. "I'd undo the day if I could," he said hoarsely. "God, I'm so sorry. It isn't just that I'm a cop; after I was such a stupid fool trusting Shannon, I—"

"I'm not your ex-wife!" she shouted furiously, and shoved against his shoulders. "I don't give a damn what she did. Get . . . *off* me, damn it; your badge is scratching my stomach!"

Ah, shit. He rolled off her and flopped on his back. He was still wearing his holster, too. He guessed he was lucky she hadn't pulled his pistol and shot him.

She jackknifed to a sitting position and glared down at him, her face still wet with tears. "I'll say this for you," she said bitterly, "you've taught me a lesson. It'll be a cold day in hell before I trust—" She stopped herself, letting her breath out in a long, weary sigh. "Oh, God. I sound just like you."

He got up and went into the bathroom, washing and straightening, tucking his shirt into his pants. Sarah got up and came to stand beside him, unconcerned about her nakedness as she washed her face, then wiped away the results of their lovemaking. Their eyes met in the mirror.

"I love you," he said. "That isn't going to change."

Her shoulders slumped. "The hell of it is, I still love you, too. I just can't get past this right now."

"I can wait." He smoothed her hair back, stroked her cheek. "As long as it takes. But don't throw us away. Don't make any drastic decisions. Give it time, and let's see what happens."

She stared at him in the mirror, and sighed as if in defeat. "All right. For now. I hope I wouldn't have let you make love to me if there was nothing left, so I have to think maybe there is. Just . . . give me some room, okay? Let me get some of myself back."

He took a deep breath. He felt as if he'd won the lottery, or a stay of execution. Something.

She made a wry face. "I don't know if it's drastic, but I've already made a hasty decision. I already have another job."

He felt blank with shock. "What? How? Here?"

"Yes, here. It's someone I'd already met, and he'd offered me the job. He was coming into the hotel this afternoon and saw me, and he made the offer again on the spot. I took it."

"What's his name?"

"Trevor Densmore." Her voice was weary, all her temporary energy fading fast.

He didn't remember the name. "Have I already checked him out?"

"No, his name wasn't on my list of possibles."

"Then why take the job now, if you wouldn't consider it before?"

"It's a place to hide," she said simply.

CHAPTER 27

SARAH WOKE THE NEXT MORNING ACHING FROM HEAD TO TOE. She lay in bed, trying to think of a reason why she should get up today. Though she had slept deeply, she felt as exhausted as she had when she'd gone to bed the night before. The wee-hours visit from Cahill hadn't helped, either.

She'd sent him home, afterward. He hadn't wanted to go, but she supposed he thought he'd won all the victories he was going to win that night. He did take her truck keys so that he could have it picked up and delivered to her. She suspected he'd do it himself; he was in major suck-up mode, and she didn't know if that made her happy or made her want to cry. Maybe both.

She still couldn't believe she'd let him make love to her, not with things the way they were between them. But he'd been achingly gentle, and she had so badly needed to be held. The scent of his body was warm and familiar, excitingly male; she knew all the details of that body so well, from the sandpaper texture of his jaw to the shape of his toes. She'd wanted nothing more than to curl up in his arms and find oblivion, so when he actually did take her in his arms, she caved with embarrassing speed.

He'd never before been so gentle, or so slow. She had gone to sleep with her body still tingling deep inside. But now she ached, her muscles knotting into cramps.

"Damn," she muttered, wanting to roll over and bury her face in the pillow again. Her menstrual period had started; that's why she was cramping, why she felt so achy. It was right on time, so she shouldn't have been caught unawares, but the trauma of the day before had knocked everything else out of her mind.

Groaning, she rolled out of bed. Thank goodness Cahill had brought over all her personal stuff, or else she'd have been in a pickle. She sorted through the bags until she found the one containing the supplies she needed, then she shuffled into the bathroom for a long, hot shower.

She felt as if she should be doing something, but there was nothing to be done. This wasn't the same situation she'd been in with Judge Roberts's family; she had known them, grown close to them, and they'd depended on her. She had never even met the Lankfords' two daughters, Bethany and Merrill. Her heart ached for them, but she was an outsider, and even if they had wanted her to help she didn't know if she was capable of giving it. Not this time. Not now. She was too emotionally battered, too drained.

After she finished showering, she was shaking with exhaustion, but more than sleep, she needed to be with someone who loved her unconditionally, someone who was always there. She dug her cell phone from her purse, turned it on, and called her mother.

"Oh, hi, sweetie," her mother said. She sounded

unusually frazzled. Sarah's mother was normally an oasis of calm, a master of organization. Sarah was instantly alert.

"Mom? What's wrong?"

To her dismay, her mother burst into tears, but she controlled them almost immediately. By that time, though, Sarah was on her feet in alarm. "Mom?"

"I wasn't going to call any of you just yet, but your father had some chest pains last night. We spent the night in the ER; they did some tests and they said he didn't have a heart attack—"

Sarah's breath whooshed out of her, and she sat back down. "Then what's wrong with him?"

"We don't know. He's still hurting a little, though you know him, he still has that Marine mentality that he's going to tough this out. I've made him an appointment with an internist for later this afternoon for a physical and to schedule some more tests." Her mother took a deep breath. "I suppose I wouldn't be so scared if he hadn't always been so healthy. I've never seen him in pain the way he was last night."

"I can be there on an afternoon flight—" Sarah began, then stopped, wondering if she could leave. What had Cahill told her before, after Judge Roberts was murdered? Don't leave town. But she'd been cleared, so there shouldn't be a problem. Then she remembered Mr. Densmore and groaned; she was supposed to begin the job there.

"No, don't be silly," her mother said, her voice more brisk now. "It wasn't a heart attack; all the enzymes or whatever were normal. There's no point in flying down here for what may be nothing more than a severe case of heartburn. If the doctor seems at all concerned this afternoon, I'll call you."

"Are you sure?"

"Of course I'm sure. Now, enough about that. How are things going with your new job?"

Sarah had been aching to cry on her mother's shoulder, figuratively speaking, but no way was she going to add to her mother's worries right now. "It didn't work out," she said. "Actually, I have a new position already, and I wanted you to have the phone number."

"I thought you really liked the new people, the Lankfords."

She had. Her throat tightened, and she had to swallow. "It wasn't that. Something unexpected came up and they had to relocate." She wished she had been able to think of some other lie, because that one was too horribly true; it wasn't a lie at all.

"These things happen." As a military wife, her mother was a past master at relocating. "Okay, I have a pen. What's the new telephone number?"

Sarah had written it down the night before. She got out her little notebook and flipped to the correct page, then read off the number. "And there's always my cell phone, but I wanted to let you know the new developments."

"You concentrate on settling in. I'm sure he'll be okay, he's feeling better and already making growling noises about not needing a doctor. I'll have to twist his arm to get him to the doctor's office this afternoon."

"Call me, okay? If there's the least thing wrong."

"I will."

Sarah hung up and sat there for a long time, trying to come to grips with this added worry. There was nothing she could do, at least not right now; she needed to take care of herself so she would be in shape to act if she *was* needed.

She searched for the aspirin among her scattered effects, found the bottle, and took two. Then she fell back into bed, and was asleep in minutes.

It was almost two o'clock when the phone rang. She rolled over and blinked at the clock in disbelief, then fumbled for the phone.

"I'm bringing your truck over," Cahill said. "I had a patrolman drop me off at the Lankfords to pick it up, so you'll have to take me back to the station."

She blinked sleepily. "Okay." Her voice sounded fuzzy even to herself.

"Did I wake you up?" he asked suspiciously.

"Yeah. I had a rough night," she said, and let him make of that what he wanted.

"I'll be there in ten minutes or so," he said, and hung up.

She hauled herself out of bed and stumbled to the bathroom. All her clothes were packed in suitcases, so they were wrinkled. She herself looked like the Wicked Witch of the West on a bad day. Cahill could just wait until she put herself to rights.

He did, but not patiently. She refused to let him into the room, so he went back down to the lobby. When she was ready and started to leave the room, she discovered why she hadn't been awakened by housekeeping: the DO NOT DISTURB sign was out. Cahill must have put it out when he left. She left the sign where it was and took the elevator down to the lobby.

"Have you found out anything new today?" she asked during the drive to the police station.

"Nothing except the same weapon was used to kill all four people. Have you watched any news today, or read the newspaper?"

"No, why?"

"I wondered if you could remember ever seeing Jacob Wanetta anywhere."

"He's the fourth victim?"

"Yeah."

"The name isn't familiar."

A moment later he stopped at a service station and stuck some change in a newspaper vending machine, pulling out the last remaining copy of the morning paper. Getting back behind the wheel, he tossed the paper onto her lap.

She didn't read the story, didn't let herself focus on the headlines. Instead she focused on the grainy black-and-white photo of a dark-haired, heavy-jawed man who gave the impression of bull-like strength. Nothing about him was familiar. "I've never seen him before that I can remember," she said, laying the paper aside. She couldn't help feeling relieved; at least she had no connection with this killing.

He stopped before they reached city hall and the police department, pulling into a parking lot and turning off the ignition. "Reporters have been hanging around," he said. "I'll walk the rest of the way, so they don't see you." He half turned in the seat, the back of his right hand brushing her cheek. "I'll call you tonight. I'll try to see you, but we're working our asses off and I don't know what time we'll call it a night."

"You don't have to check on me. I'm okay." She

was lying, right now, but she *would* be okay in the future. She needed to regroup, get a lot of sleep, and let time put a little more distance between her and the murders. She needed a little distance between herself and Cahill, too, some time in which she didn't have to deal with him. She didn't want to think things over; she didn't want to think at all.

"It's for my peace of mind, okay?" he muttered. "I know things aren't straight between us, not yet, so I need to see you every so often to make sure you're still here."

"I'm not running, Cahill," she said, stung that he thought she might. "If I leave, you'll know beforehand. And I've already accepted the job with Mr. Densmore, remember?"

He grunted. Even with everything that was going on, he'd made the time to run a check on Trevor Densmore. "For what it's worth, he doesn't have any type of record."

"I didn't think he would have. I might as well call him and arrange a time to move over there."

He gave her a worried glance. "Why don't you give it another day? You still look exhausted."

She knew how she looked: chalky white, with dark circles under her eyes. She *felt* exhausted, even after all the hours of sleep. Physical tiredness wasn't her problem; it was the overload of stress that was doing her in.

"Maybe I'd feel better if I had something to do. It can't hurt."

The move into Mr. Densmore's house was accomplished in little time and with little effort. *House* wasn't the right term, though; it was an estate, a fortress, five acres of prime real estate protected by a high gray stone wall. The entrance was guarded by huge wrought-iron gates that operated automatically and were watched over by cameras positioned at regular intervals.

The house itself was three stories high, made of the same gray stone, which gave it a medieval look. Inside the walls, the grounds were carefully manicured, not a shrub or a leaf out of place, not a blade of grass poking a little higher than the blades around it.

Inside was more of the same. Either shy Mr. Densmore liked a monochromatic color scheme, or his decorator was frigid and lacked imagination. It was more gray, everywhere. The marble in the sleek bathrooms was gray. The plush carpeting was a pale, icy gray. The furniture all seemed to be gray and white, with darker grays thrown in for contrast. The effect was of being in an ice cave.

But he was proud of his home, almost boyish in his eagerness to show it to her, so she had to acquit the decorator. He truly loved the sterile atmosphere that surrounded him. She made appropriate noises of admiration, wondering why he cared what she thought. She was a butler, not a prospective buyer.

She was glad she had been up front with him about it being a temporary position, because she didn't like her accommodations at all. She preferred separate quarters, a small oasis that was hers and gave her a life beyond the job. The room he escorted her to was large and lavishly appointed, like a pricey hotel room. The room was *too* large, making it seem cavernous. There was a king-size four-poster bed and a sitting area, and the furniture didn't begin to fill up the space. She felt cold just looking at the room. The attached bathroom was sleek, dark gray marble, almost black, with polished chrome faucets and handles. Even the thick towels were dark gray. She hated it on sight.

He was almost pink with excitement. "I'll make us some tea," he said, rubbing his hands together as if he couldn't contain himself. "We can have it while we go over your duties."

She hoped there were a lot of duties, something to keep her busy. A place this large should have a staff; the Judge's house hadn't been half this big, but it had seemed to pulse with life. This stone mausoleum felt empty.

She carried in her suitcases, but didn't start unpacking. He instructed her to park her TrailBlazer in the four-car attached garage, in the empty bay next to a surprisingly nondescript dark blue Ford. The white Jaguar that sat in the bay closest to the house seemed much more Mr. Densmore's type, or the white S-Class Mercedes parked beside it. When she came through into the kitchen—more dark gray marble, and stainless steel appliances—he was just pouring hot tea into two cups sitting side by side.

"There," he said, fussing with the sugar bowl and tiny pitcher of cream as if he were an aged spinster entertaining a suitor. It struck her that he might be lonely, here in this huge house by himself, and that made her uneasy.

She was trained to run establishments, not provide emotional or physical companionship. Over time she and the Judge had developed a close, caring relationship, but the circumstances had been entirely different. Mr. Densmore wasn't just a banker, he *owned* a bank, and though she didn't know his age, she guessed him to be no older than his early sixties at the most. He was young enough to be going to an office every day; banking was a complicated business, and even with capable management there would still be a lot to oversee, decisions to be made. She knew he socialized, because she had met him at a party. So this sterile, empty home life was discordant, somehow, as if his business life didn't bleed over into his private life—as if he didn't *have* a private life. During the tour of the house, she hadn't seen a single family photograph or any of the individual touches that marked a home.

She couldn't work here. She hated to leave him in the lurch, but she didn't think she would be; she felt as if there was no real need for her here, or at least not a need she wanted to consider. Exhaustion and desperation had led her to a bad decision, but it wasn't a permanent one.

"There," he said, bringing the tea tray over to the table and setting it down. He placed a cup and saucer before her. "I hope you like it; it's a blend I get from England. The taste is a bit unusual, but I find it's quite addictive."

She sipped the tea; the taste *was* unusual, but not unpleasant. It was slightly more bitter than she was accustomed to, so she added a thin slice of lemon to adjust the taste.

He was watching her with an eager, expectant expression, so she said, "It's very good."

He beamed. "I knew you'd like it." He picked up his own cup, and she sipped again as she tried to think of the right words.

After a few moments, she realized there *were*

no right words, just honest ones. "Mr. Densmore, I've made a mistake."

He set down his cup, blinking at her. "How so, my dear?"

"I should never have accepted your offer. I deeply appreciate it, but the decision was too hasty and there were several factors I didn't take into account. I can't tell you how very sorry I am, but I won't be able to take the position."

He blinked a little faster. "But you brought your luggage."

"I know. I'm sorry," she repeated. "If I've inconvenienced you in any way, if you've made plans based on my presence, of course I'll see that through, and I wouldn't feel right, under these circumstances, accepting any salary for doing so. I haven't been thinking clearly, or I would never have made such a hasty decision."

In silence he drank his tea, his head down. Then he sighed. "You mustn't distress yourself; mistakes happen, and you've handled yourself with dignity. But, yes, I have made plans for the coming weekend, so if you wouldn't mind staying until then?"

"Of course not. Is it a party?"

There was a tiny pause. "Yes, you know the sort, reciprocation for the invitations I've received. Catered, of course. About fifty people."

She could handle that. Since this was already late on Wednesday afternoon, there should be a fair amount of work to keep her busy, getting ready for a party on such short notice. She only hoped he had a regular caterer who would accommodate him, even if it meant bringing in extra staff. If he didn't, she would have to move heaven and earth both to find a caterer at this late date.

"I'll take care of everything," she said.

He sighed. "I really wish things could have worked out differently."

CHAPTER 28

HE WAS VERY DISPLEASED WITH SARAH, THOUGH HE SUPPOSED he should make allowances for the upset she had suffered, part of which was his fault. He simply hadn't expected her to be so . . . flighty, though perhaps that was the wrong word. *Indecisive*. Yes, that was a better description.

He couldn't really be angry with her, because it was so obvious she had suffered over the past day and a half, but he could definitely be displeased. Why, how could she even think of leaving here? Couldn't she see how perfect his house was for her, a fit, wonderful setting for her own crisp perfection? She wouldn't be leaving, of course; he couldn't allow that. He had fantasized about her taking care of him, but it was obvious that, for the time being at least, he would have to take care of her.

Hmm. That must be what was wrong. Sarah wasn't herself. She was very pale, and the serene glow that had first attracted him was gone. He would keep her here and take care of her, and when she felt better, she would be more rational.

Luckily he had planned for all exigencies. No, not luck at all: careful planning and attention to detail. That was the key to success, whether it was in business or in personal matters. He hadn't thought it likely Sarah would be unhappy here, but he had allowed for that remote possibility, and as a result he was now capable of handling it. If he had made any oversight, it was that he hadn't predicted this after seeing yesterday how obviously distraught she was. Soon she would feel much better, and there would be no more foolish talk about leaving.

The printout from the phone company showed three calls to the Lankfords from that pay phone in the Galleria—on Sunday night. There had been a fourth call on Monday night, at roughly the same time as the murders. It was impossible to pinpoint a time of death without a witness; all they could get was a time frame. But it looked as if the killer had intended to go to the Lankfords' house on Sunday night. According to the youngest Lankford daughter, Merrill, who was in college in Tuscaloosa, her parents had driven down to have dinner with her that night and stayed until almost eleven. That had extended their lives by twenty-four hours, and given their daughter one last opportunity to see them.

Cahill wished to hell they'd had this printout on Tuesday, because Sarah couldn't possibly have made those phone calls; she'd been with him every minute Sunday. He wished a lot of things, number one of which was that he'd never met his ex-wife and let her fuck with his mind. That was the final analysis: he'd *let* his experience with her affect him. No more. No matter what happened now, he would focus on the person concerned, and not filter everything through his memory of Shannon.

He'd been emotionally free of her for two years, but for the first time he felt mentally free. She had no influence on him now.

Those multiple phone calls opened up an avenue of opportunity that hadn't existed before. He'd gone back to the shop in the mall that had the camera with the best angle, and got the tape for Sunday and Monday nights. The angles were still piss-poor and none of the images were good, but it was the same man. Same hair, same body build, same style of dress.

That was the bastard. That was the killer. There was no doubt in his mind now, or in anyone else's in the department.

The problem was, no one seemed to recognize him. Granted, the stills taken from the tape and enlarged were poor quality, grainy, and never really showed his face. But you could get an impression of him, and still no one had said, "Hey, he reminds me of so-and-so." The police needed a break, a stroke of fate, a miracle. They needed someone with an artist's eye who would note the line of the jaw, the way the ear was set, and make the connection to a live human being.

Mrs. Wanetta didn't recognize the man, but she was so tranquilized she might not have known her own mother. None of their three grown children found anything familiar about him, so that eliminated the possibility of his being a friend of the family; same thing with the Lankford daughters. It *had* to be a business connection, but again, none of Jacob Wanetta's employees recognized the man in the photos.

Somewhere, someone had to know this bastard.

Leif Strickland, the department's resident electronic genius, stuck his head in the door. His eyes were wide with excitement, his hair sticking up where he'd run his hands through it. "Hey, Doc, come listen. I think I've got the son of a bitch on tape!"

Everyone within hearing distance quickly crammed into his electronic lair. "This is from the Lankford answering machine," Leif said. All answering machine tapes were seized as a matter of course; if the machines were digital, the whole thing was taken.

"Don't tell me he left a message," Cahill said.

"No, not quite. See, the phone Mrs. Lankford was trying to use had one of those buttons for instant record, you know, like if who you're talking to starts threatening to kill you, you can, like, press this little button and bingo, it records on your answering machine. Now, she probably wasn't trying to record anything, she was trying to call for help, but she was nervous, right? She's grabbing at the phone, punching buttons she doesn't mean to punch. I listened to all the messages, but there was this one space with a funny noise on it. Not . . . I don't know, it just sounded funny. So I isolated it and ran it through some enhancement programs, and—"

"For God's sake, we don't need to know how," Cahill interrupted. "Let's listen to it."

Leif gave him the wounded look of a true techie dealing with philistines who didn't appreciate the beauty of electronics. "Okay, here it is. It's not very plain, I need to enhance it some more, eliminate static—" He broke off as Cahill glared at him, and silently punched a button.

Static, fumbling, the harsh rasp of panicked

breathing. Then there was a soft sound, and a tiny whoosh and pop.

"What was that?"

"The sound at the last was the shot being fired," Leif said matter-of-factly. "Silencer. But listen to it again, listen to what comes right before that."

They all listened again, and to Cahill it sounded like a voice.

"He said something. The bastard said something. What was it? Can you isolate it?"

"I'll work on it. Listen again, and you can make out the words."

There wasn't another sound in the room, not even breathing, as he replayed the tape one more time.

How soft the voice was, how gentle. Cahill narrowed his eyes to slits, concentrating. "Something 'girl.'"

"Give the man a prize!" Leif crowed. "It's 'bad girl.'" He played the tape again, and now that they all knew what they were listening for, it was understandable, and chilling.

"*Bad girl.*" Almost an admonishing tone, tenderly scolding. Then the pop of the silenced bullet, and nothing else.

They had an audible record of Merilyn Lankford's murder. If they could get an ID—*when* they got an ID—they'd be able to match voiceprints and put him at the scene.

"Bingo," Leif said cheerfully.

"My dear, if you don't mind my saying so, you look as if you're at the end of your rope," Mr. Densmore said gently. "You've been through an extraordinarily difficult experience. Lightning won't strike if you sit down and have another cup of tea, will it? Tea is a wonderful restorative. I'll brew a fresh pot," he offered.

She needed something to eat more than she needed tea, Sarah realized belatedly, trying to think when she had last eaten anything. It had to have been the soup she'd had with Mr. Densmore late yesterday afternoon, making it more than twenty-four hours since she'd had a meal.

She had just served his dinner. Mr. Densmore's cook came in at three and prepared his evening meal; she had already come and gone by the time Sarah arrived. Obviously she had prepared only for Mr. Densmore, but that didn't matter. As soon as Sarah had Mr. Densmore fed and his dishes cleared away, she would find something to eat.

He had hovered anxiously near her, making her uneasy, but now she realized he was afraid she might collapse. The thought broke through her depression and made her smile. "Mr. Densmore, has anyone ever told you how sweet you are?"

His eyes widened, and he blushed. "Oh . . . my—well, no."

Sweet *and* lonely; she felt sorry for him, but not enough to stay in this ghastly house and provide him the companionship he so obviously needed. Still, maybe the caffeine in the tea would give her a boost, keep her going until she had an opportunity to eat.

"Tea sounds wonderful," she said, and he beamed at her.

"Excellent! I know you'll feel a lot better."

He stood up from the table, and Sarah said

hastily, "Please, finish your dinner first. I'll put on the tea."

"No, I'll do it. I'm very particular about my tea."

Since his tea appeared to be so important to him and his dinner was a cold one anyway, fresh chicken salad with pecans and red grapes—and because even if she didn't intend to take any pay for her stay here, this was his house and he was still the boss—she stopped protesting.

He went into the kitchen and put the water on to heat, then returned to the dining room and sat down at the enormous chrome-and-glass table to finish his meal. With nothing to do until he finished, Sarah retreated to a corner. She had seldom felt so useless as she did here; she got the impression he didn't expect her to do any actual work, just . . . be there. The respite she craved wasn't here; there wasn't any peace, any calm, just boredom and a vague sense of uneasiness.

She was so tired she could barely stand, and she had developed a raging headache, probably from not eating. It could also be caffeine deprivation, since she hadn't had her coffee that morning; if that was the case, the tea was doubly welcome. She might even have two cups.

He finished just as the kettle in the kitchen began whistling. "Ah! The water's ready," he said, just in case she couldn't hear that piercing noise. He strode into the kitchen, and Sarah busied herself collecting his dishes and carrying them through to rinse and put in the dishwasher.

By the time she finished with that and a few other odds and ends, he was pouring the steeped tea into the cups. "There!" he said with satisfaction, carrying the tray through to the dining room. She was forced to follow him and, at his insistence, sit at the table.

"Tell me," he said as she sipped the hot, fragrant brew. "How did you decide to become a butler?"

She could talk about her work, she thought with relief. "My father was a colonel in the Marines," she said. "Growing up, I watched the stewards and how they handled all the functions, and it was fascinating. They knew protocol, they handled the guest lists, emergencies, they smoothed over any embarrassing moments . . . they're a marvel in action. I liked the way they were trained to handle anything."

"But obviously you weren't a steward in the military, were you?"

"Oh, no, there's actually a school where you train as a butler." He asked question after question, and she gratefully focused on answering him. Here at last was something her tired mind could latch on to, something that didn't require a lot of thought.

Maybe it was just the giddiness that comes with extreme fatigue, but she began to feel . . . almost tipsy. Her head swam suddenly, and she clutched at the table. "Wow. Excuse me, Mr. Densmore. I'm dizzy all of a sudden. I haven't eaten today, and I think it's catching up with me."

He looked alarmed. "You haven't eaten? My dear, why didn't you say so? You shouldn't have been standing there waiting on me; you should be taking care of yourself. Here, you sit right there and I'll bring you something. What would you like?"

She blinked at him, owl-like. How could she tell him what she'd like when she didn't know what was available here? Anyway, she wouldn't "like" anything; she would eat because she needed to, but the last thing she had really wanted was—

"Ice cream," she mumbled. The words were alarmingly hard to pronounce.

"Ice cream?" He paused, blinking at her in that way of his. "I don't believe I have any ice cream. Would you like anything else?"

"No," she said, trying to explain. "Not what I want. Last thing I . . ." She lost the thread of what she was saying and stared at him, bewildered. Everything was beginning to slowly rotate around her, and she had the vague, surprising idea that she might be about to faint. She had never fainted before.

He was beginning to move away from her, or seemed as if he was. She couldn't be certain, the way things were whirling. "Wait," she said, trying to stand up, but her legs buckled under her.

He rushed forward and grabbed her before she hit the floor, his grip surprisingly strong. "Don't worry," she heard him say as her vision faded and her ears began to feel as if cotton were stuffed in them. "I'll take care of you."

CHAPTER 29

THE FIRST THING SHE BECAME AWARE OF WAS A HEADACHE, A LIT-
eral throbbing inside her skull. Oh, that's right . . .
she'd gone to bed with a headache. She was in an
uncomfortable position, but she was afraid to
move, afraid the least twitch would set the hammers to pounding even harder than they already
were. She was queasy, too, and she thought she
might vomit. Something was wrong, but the fuzzi-
ness in her brain kept her from figuring out what.

She tried to remember . . . something. Anything.
For a sickening moment there was nothing there,
no sense of place or time, just a horrifying lurch
into the unknown. Then the texture of the fabric
beneath her made sense, and she knew she was in
bed. Yes, that made sense. She had a headache, and
she was in bed. She remembered going . . . no, she
didn't remember going to bed. The last clear memory was . . . but that eluded her, too, and she
stopped fighting for it, letting the darkness and
oblivion claim her again.

When next she woke, she thought she must have
the flu. What else could account for this overwhelming sense of illness? She was seldom ill, even
with the sniffles, but surely only something as serious as the flu could make her feel so sick. For the

first time, she understood what people meant when they said they felt·too sick to go to a doctor. There was no way she could get to a doctor; one would have to come to her.

Something was tugging on her head. It was a gentle, rhythmic tugging, and instead of making her headache worse, it actually soothed it, as if the sensation dulled her perception of the throbbing.

Her arms ached. She tried to move them and found she couldn't.

Alarm pierced through the fogginess in her brain. She tried again to move her arms, with the same lack of result. "My arms," she whimpered, and her voice sounded awful, so hoarse it was unrecognizable.

"Poor dear," a soft voice murmured. "You'll be all right. There, doesn't this feel good?"

The rhythmic tugging continued, slow and easy, and after a moment she realized someone was brushing her hair.

It did feel good, but she didn't want her hair brushed. She wanted to move her arms. Despite the headache, despite her queasy stomach, she shifted uneasily in the bed and found she couldn't move her legs, either.

Panic, hard and bright, made her eyes flare open. Her vision swam with fuzzy images that didn't quite make sense. There was a man . . . but he wasn't Cahill, and that wasn't possible. Why was a man who wasn't Cahill brushing her hair?

"I'll get you some water," the soft voice crooned. "You'd like that, wouldn't you, dear? Nice, cold water will feel so good on your throat. You've been asleep for such a long time I've been worried about you."

A cool hand slipped behind her neck and lifted her head, and a glass was put against her lips. The cold water hit her mouth in a rush, soaking into parched tissues, loosening her tongue from the roof of her mouth. Her stomach heaved as she swallowed, but thank God she didn't vomit. She swallowed again, then again, before the glass was taken away.

"Not too much, dear. You've been very sick."

She was still very sick if she was paralyzed, but maybe this man didn't know she couldn't move. She closed her eyes, fighting for strength, but, dear God, she didn't have any. She was so weak that she felt almost boneless.

"I'll bring you some soup in a little while. You need to eat something. I didn't realize you hadn't eaten, and I'm afraid I accidentally made you ill."

The softness of the voice clicked, and memory crept back. "Mr. Densmore?"

"Yes, dear, I'm right here."

"I feel so sick," she whispered, opening her eyes and blinking. This time she found her vision had cleared a little, and she could plainly see his face, full of concern.

"I know, and I'm sorry for that."

"I can't move."

"Of course not. I couldn't have you hurting yourself, now could I?"

"H-hurting myself?" She was winning the battle against the fog; with every passing second she felt less confused, more aware of her surroundings. She felt as if she were surfacing from anesthesia, which she remembered well from when she broke her left arm when she was six years old, and she'd been put under general anesthesia when it was set.

She'd hated the anesthesia a lot more than she'd hated the cast.

"If you tried to leave," Mr. Densmore explained, but that didn't make any sense.

"I can't. I haven't." Tried to leave? She had tried to get up from the table, and that was the last thing she remembered.

"I know, I know. Don't get upset. Just stay calm, and everything will be all right." The brush moved slowly through her hair. "You have such lovely hair, Sarah. Overall I'm very pleased with you, though your indecisiveness was an unpleasant surprise. Still, you've been through a lot of upset. I'm sure you'll settle down with time."

He wasn't making any sense. Settle down? She frowned, her brow wrinkling, and he smoothed the creases with his fingertip. "Don't frown, you'll wrinkle your pretty skin. I was right about how lovely a ruby would look against your skin. But I've looked all through your things, and I can't find the pendant. Why aren't you wearing it?"

Pendant?

A chill ran through her, and she went very still as an awful suspicion seized her. Her stomach heaved again, but this time with fear.

"Why aren't you wearing the pendant I sent to you?" he asked, sounding a little petulant.

He was the one. He was the stalker, the weirdo whose presence she'd sensed, like a hidden cancer. He'd waited, and seized his chance. She wasn't sick at all, she realized; the bastard had drugged her, and since she hadn't eaten anything in over a day, the drug had hit her hard.

She had to answer him. Don't annoy him, she thought. Don't do anything to make him wary.

Think. She needed an excuse that wasn't her fault. *Think!* "Allergic," she whispered.

The brush paused in its motion. "My dear, I'm so sorry," he said contritely. "I had no idea. Of course you shouldn't wear something that will give you a rash. But where is it? Perhaps you could put it on for just a moment, so I could see you wearing it."

"Jewelry box," she whispered. "Could I have more water?"

"Of course, dear, since the first has stayed down." He lifted her head and held the glass to her lips again, and she gulped as much as she could. "There," he said as he let her head rest on the pillow again. "Where's your jewelry box?"

"At the bungalow. Lankford estate. Crime scene . . . police have it sealed. I can't get in."

He made an exasperated noise. "I should have realized. Don't worry, dear, I'll take care of collecting the rest of your things. You'll feel so much more comfortable with your own possessions around you."

Sarah tried once again to move her arms, and this time she felt something wrapped around her wrists. The truth occurred to her in a sickening rush: she was tied to the bed. She fought the panic that threatened to overwhelm her. She couldn't give in to it, she had to think, she had to concentrate. If she panicked she was helpless, but if she kept her wits, she might outsmart him.

She had one big advantage: She knew he was dangerous, but he didn't know she was.

Cahill. He knew she was here. Sooner or later he would call and want to see her, talk to her. All she had to do was keep things calm and under control until then. She didn't want to do anything to agitate Densmore, prod him into violence. He was a stalker, obsessed with her; he was happy now because she was here, under his control. So long as he believed that, she was safe. She hoped she was safe. But if he thought she was trying to escape from him, he was likely to explode into violence. If that happened, if she couldn't make a clean escape, then she had to make certain she was ready to handle him.

But there was no telling how long it would take Cahill to try to contact her. He knew she was here, but all the cops were working almost around the clock trying to find the killer. He would try her cell phone first, and if she didn't answer, he would try again later. "Later," however, could be days later.

No, Cahill wouldn't wait that long. He was too tenacious.

But in the meantime she had to help herself. The first order of business was to convince Densmore to untie her.

She made her voice weaker than it truly was. If he wanted her sweet and helpless, she'd give him sweet and helpless, at least until she could kick his ass. "Mr. Densmore?"

"Yes, dear?"

"I . . . I'm so embarrassed to say this."

"You don't have to be embarrassed about anything. I'm here to take care of you."

"I need to use the bathroom," she whispered, and she had the benefit of that being so true she was on the verge of really embarrassing herself. Add in the fact that she was having her menstrual period, and the situation was not good.

"Dear me. That does present a problem."

"I—I think I'm paralyzed," she said, and let her voice wobble. It was better that he thought she was more incapacitated than she really was. Not that she would be able to fight or run even if she was untied, at this point, but she wanted him to think she was recovering very slowly.

"Of course you aren't," he exclaimed, his voice warm with sympathy. "I just used restraints to keep you from harming yourself. Now, let me see, how can we work this?"

She squirmed a little; her distress was becoming so acute that it was no problem to let a tear leak out of her eye. She needed to see if she *could* walk, or if too much of the drug he'd given her was still in her system.

"Yes, that will work," he murmured to himself, and folded back the covers. To her immense relief she saw that she was still wearing her clothes; he'd removed her shoes, but that was all. He worked diligently, untying her ankles and then refashioning the thin, woven nylon restraints into a sort of hobble, with an extra length attached to it and held in his hand. If she could walk at all, it would be in very short steps, and if she tried anything, all he had to do was jerk the rope in his hand and she'd fall flat on her face.

She was truly crying by the time he got all that worked out and began releasing her hands.

"I'm sorry, I know you have to be miserable," he crooned. "Just a few more minutes, and I'll help you to the bathroom."

"Please hurry," she croaked, squeezing her eyes shut.

At last he was helping her to sit up, and she saw immediately that even if she were untied, she wouldn't be able to accomplish much. Better to do nothing to arouse his suspicions this time, and wait until she was in better shape. She had to remember that he was stronger than he looked, if he'd managed to get her upstairs all by himself. Unconscious people, since they were totally limp, were a bitch to move.

She was so woozy that she could barely sit up; in fact, she couldn't, not without help, and she leaned heavily into him. It turned her stomach to touch him, but she had to concentrate on allaying his suspicions, and if that meant accepting his help, she'd grit her teeth and do it.

He got her on her feet. Her knees immediately buckled, and he was supporting her entire weight. She clung to him as he half walked, half dragged her, to the big gray marble bathroom that was part of her quarters.

All of her toiletries were set out on the vanity; since he'd unpacked for her, she hoped her personal supplies were in the vanity drawers. Yes, there was the bag she had packed everything in, sitting on a shelf; even if he'd left the tampons in the bag, she could get to them.

He eased her over to the toilet, and stood there a moment looking uncomfortable. "Er . . . do you need any help?"

She braced her hand against the wall, panting. "I think I can manage." He should feel safe leaving her in here; there was a window, but it was glass block; she couldn't see out, no one could see in, and it didn't open. Even if she could break it out, the room he'd given her was on the second floor; the first floor in this house, she'd noticed, had what appeared to be sixteen-foot ceilings, so the drop

would be much higher than from the ordinary sec-
ond-story window.

She'd risk it, though, if that turned out to be her
only chance.

He looked around, and she could see him mentally cataloging the contents of the room to see if
there was anything she could use as a weapon or to
escape. He was very careful, and he didn't trust
her. She leaned heavily against the wall, underscor-
ing her weakness.

"All right," he finally said. "I'll be right outside
if you need me."

"Could you leave the door open a little?" she
asked. "Please? So you can hear me in case I fall."
Talk about reverse psychology, asking him to do
the very thing he intended to do anyway; perhaps
that would convince him she wasn't making a
break for it.

He looked pleased and gave her his shy smile as
he left the bathroom and pulled the door half-
closed. That was all the privacy she was going to
get, but at this point she didn't give a damn.

The relief was almost painful, and those damn
weak tears leaked down her face again. She found
the box of tampons in the bottom vanity drawer
and took care of that problem, too. Feeling much
better and not nearly as desperate, but still very
weak, she hobbled to the sink and leaned against it
while she wet a washcloth and washed her face
and private areas. If he peeped, then he peeped; she
didn't give a damn. She needed to freshen up more
than she needed to worry about her modesty.

She drank more water, greedily gulping it
down, then made her slow and wobbly way to the

door. "Please," she said weakly. "Help me back to bed."

Densmore rushed to her side. "Lean on me," he said tenderly. "Poor dear." He supported her on the trek back to the bed and helped her lie down again. She was trembling, and it wasn't a pretense; her legs felt as if they wouldn't have supported her another minute. He caressed her cheek, smoothed her hair back from her face, then began fastening the restraints around her arms and ankles. She had to bite her lip when he touched her, but she didn't protest, just lay limply, her eyes closed. Cahill did that sometimes, pushing back her hair and stroking her cheek, and she hated that Densmore had so closely mirrored the action. "I'll be right back with some food," he murmured, and left the room, closing the door behind him.

There was nothing she could do, trussed as she was, so she didn't even tug against the nylon restraints. She wouldn't put it past the bastard to have this place wired for both video and audio, and if he was watching her on camera, she didn't intend to do anything that would put him on alert.

That brief excursion had exhausted her small store of strength. She took a deep breath and let herself sink into the waiting darkness. She would use the darkness this time, to get stronger.

"Sarah?"

The voice seemed to come from far away, but she was instantly alert, instantly aware. She lay still, letting herself appear to awake gradually.

"Sarah, wake up. I have soup."

She shifted restlessly and rolled her head to the side. "Wha—?"

"You need to eat. Wake, up, dear."

She opened her eyes as he set a tray on the bed-side table. "Good, good," he said, smiling at her. "Let's see, what would be the best way to do this? I think I should feed you, don't you? I'll put an-other pillow behind you to raise your head more, and here's a towel to catch any spills."

He suited actions to words, lifting her head and stuffing an extra pillow behind her head and shoul-ders, raising her to a more reclining position, then draping a towel over her chest and tucking it under her chin.

"This is a nice chicken soup," he said, and chuckled to himself. "Could I have made a more clichéd choice? But it *is* very good, and hearty. You don't need red meat for a hearty soup or stew, though a lot of people seem to think so. I don't eat red meat, just chicken, turkey, and fish."

In that case, considering how he'd turned out, he should beat a path to Milo's and hope he could be saved, she thought sarcastically as he brought the spoon to her lips and she obediently opened them, like a child. Sarcasm felt good; outwardly she had to be meek, but inside she was still fierce, still her-self.

The soup was good, though, and she forced her-self to eat every bite. She had to concentrate on re-covering as fast as possible; she would need her strength.

After she had finished the soup, she blinked drowsily at him. "Thank you," she murmured. "That was good." She yawned. "Excuse me. I'm still so sleepy."

"Of course." He patted her lips with a napkin and removed the towel from under her chin. "I'll leave you alone and let you rest, but I'll check back

occasionally to see if you need anything. I have a
surprise for you," he said slyly.

"A surprise?"

"It'll be waiting for you when you wake up."

That assurance wasn't conducive to sleep, and
after he left, she carefully examined the ceiling and
walls, looking for anything that could possibly be a
camera. Without looking closer it was impossible
to tell, so she had to go on the assumption that she
was being watched. She didn't overtly tug on her restraints, but she began tensing and releasing her
muscles, starting in her legs and working up. She
had to fight off the lingering effects of whatever
drug he'd given her, and keep her circulation going
and her muscles limber. If an opportunity for escape presented itself, she had to be ready to take it.

Why in hell wasn't Sarah answering her cell
phone? Cahill had called her repeatedly, unwilling
to stay out of touch for very long with matters so
tenuous between them. Yes, they'd made love and
she'd agreed to give him some time, a chance to see
if they could work things out, but the temporary
nature of the agreement nagged at him. He didn't
want temporary; he wanted permanent.

She had gone to Densmore's house late yesterday
afternoon. Okay, he could understand her not answering her cell phone while she was getting settled in, but the phone had been on and when she
checked it, she would see that she'd had some calls.
She should have called him back by now. Today,
the phone hadn't been on; he'd been getting the
"customer not in service" message.

Densmore's phone number was unlisted, but if
you had the right software and search engine, that

didn't matter. Cahill pulled up the information and called the estate, only to get an answering machine that answered in a computerized voice. He left a simple message: Call Detective Cahill at the Mountain Brook Police Department. It wasn't personal, and it was the type of message that people tended to deliver immediately. Still she hadn't called.

A frightened public was calling in tips and leads that led nowhere, but every one of them had to be checked out, and he literally didn't have time to eat. He was frustrated enough in his efforts to contact Sarah, though, that he made time to actually drive by the estate like a lovesick teenager, to see if he could spot her SUV parked there. The wrought-iron gates were securely shut, and he couldn't see any type of vehicle.

The damn place looked like a fortress, anyway, with that high stone wall surrounding it. The wall by itself had to have cost a fortune, and from what he could see, it was wired like Fort Knox. Mr. Densmore evidently valued his privacy.

He called the estate number and left another message, this time letting his impatience show, and leaving the impression that Miss Stevens should get in touch with the department, for her own good. That should get some response, if anyone at all was inside the house.

His phone rang a short time later and he snatched it up. "Cahill."

"Detective Cahill." It was a man's voice, kind of soft, like you'd expect a priest's to be, but full of authority, too. "This is Trevor Densmore. You've left two messages for Miss Stevens and it sounded imperative that she contact you. I'm sorry, but Miss Stevens is ill, and is unable to talk."

"Ill?" Cahill asked sharply, alarm prickling his spine. "In what way?"

"Laryngitis." Densmore chuckled. "I meant it literally that she's unable to talk. Perhaps in a few days she'll be able to call."

The son of a bitch disconnected before Cahill could say anything else. *Damn it!* He wanted to see her, but the estate was walled and gated; he couldn't enter without either an invitation or a search warrant, neither of which was likely to be forthcoming.

Sarah was sick? She'd told him that she almost never even caught a cold, so for her to suddenly catch some bug seemed ironic. She'd been under a lot of stress, and that played hell with the immune system, but . . . that fast? Literally the next day? Bullshit. She might be avoiding him, though.

No, that wasn't Sarah, either. Sarah didn't avoid; she faced things head-on. Even if she did have laryngitis, she'd have gotten on the phone and croaked a reply to him.

He had the feeling that guy Densmore was lying. He didn't know the man and Sarah seemed to like him, or at least appreciate his offer, but Cahill's gut said something was wrong. Why would Densmore lie? There was no reason to, which made Cahill feel even more uneasy. But it wasn't that there was no reason for lying; it was just that Cahill didn't *know* the reason.

Well, one way or another, if Sarah didn't get in touch with him soon, he was going to see her if he had to climb over the damn wall. He'd probably get arrested for trespassing, but at least he'd know whether or not she was okay.

*   *   *

When Sarah woke again, her head was still pounding, worse than it had been when she went to sleep. That awful foggy feeling was back, but this time she didn't have to wonder what was wrong. She knew; Densmore had drugged her again. Whatever it was had to have been in the soup.

But why drug her again? He had her tied, and helpless.

She lay very still, fighting the grogginess, willing herself to throw off the effects of the drug. She mustn't let this happen again.

She couldn't afford to lose any more strength by refusing to eat or drink, but she couldn't escape if she was unconscious all the time, either.

She was too cool, and she shifted uncomfortably but, with her hands tied, was unable to pull the covers up around her shoulders. She could feel air moving on her bare skin—

Her mind seized, paralyzed by the awful realization. Densmore had removed her clothes. She was naked.

CHAPTER 30

"SURPRISE!" HIS VOICE WAS GAY, PRACTICALLY BUBBLING WITH good humor. "I know you're awake, I didn't give you nearly as much this time. Stop playing possum and open those pretty eyes."

Filled with a horror she could barely even begin to comprehend, Sarah opened her eyes and stared at him. Night pressed against the windows, telling her hours had passed, hours in which she'd been unconscious and totally at his mercy. All thoughts of placating him, of pretending to go along with him, had utterly vanished. *"What have you done to me?"* she asked hoarsely.

He was sitting beside her on the bed, fully clothed. He blinked at her. "Done? Why, nothing. Why do you ask?"

"My clothes—"

"Oh, that. They were dirty. My goodness, this was the second day you'd worn them, plus you slept in them. Pulling them off . . . let's just say the logistics were complicated, so I cut them off. They were ruined, anyway."

She held her horror, her gut-wrenching fear, at bay and stared down the length of her naked body. The covers were all thrown back, exposing her. But her legs were still together, still tied so she couldn't move them. She hadn't thought she would ever be grateful she was restrained in such a manner, but in this case . . .

She took several heaving breaths, fighting free of the nightmare that had begun sucking her down. "Ruined?" she managed to gasp.

He made a face, and gestured toward her groin. "You know. You really should have told me you were in the flowers. I wouldn't have allowed myself to become so excited. It was a disappointment to have to wait, but I made do."

In the flowers . . . ? He must mean because she was menstruating. If that had put him off, she had never before been so grateful for her cycle. But that also meant he had looked at her, and she wanted to weep with humiliation. She didn't, she fought off the urge, fiercely reclaiming her control. Then she looked down at herself again; she saw the wet, sticky drops on her stomach, splashed across her thighs, and she almost vomited.

She forgot about control, her mind going blank and her body arching, madly fighting the restraints in her need to get his unspeakable filth off her body. "Get it off!" she shrieked. "How dare you! How *dare* you!"

He actually looked bewildered. "What's wrong? What is it?"

"You jerked off on me, you miserable bastard!" She began to sob, futilely straining to break the nylon cords. "Wash . . . it . . . *off*!" She screamed the last word at him.

"Don't take that tone with me, young lady," he said sharply.

"You *touched* me!" She was roaring in her fury,

her utter outrage. "You *looked* at me! You had no
right!"

"Stop that. Stop it right now. I understand your
modesty, but surely you realize your current state
has only delayed the natural progression of our relationship. I knew the moment I saw you that you
were meant for me. You belong here, with me.
We'll be so happy, my dear. You'll see. I'll give you
anything you want; I'll treat you like a queen.
Look, I've already given you this ring. The stone
needs to be reset, but the color and shape are perfect for you. I knew as soon as I saw it that this
stone was too good for that tacky woman. I'll take
it off in just a minute because I know you're allergic to jewelry, but I wanted you to see it first.
When I have it reset, I'll have the band lined with
something that's hypoallergenic, so you can wear
it." He lifted her left hand as far from the mattress
as he could, given the bonds around her wrists.
"See. Isn't it gorgeous?"

She stared at the ring he'd slipped on her finger,
at the huge yellow diamond surrounded by smaller
white diamonds. She knew that ring. She had mar-
veled at the size of the center stone every time she
had seen it, on Merilyn Lankford's finger.

The bottom dropped out of her stomach in a
sickening rush, as she looked into the smiling face
of a killer.

Cahill checked his watch, scowling. It was getting late, almost time for the mall to close, and he
was damn tired of showing these photographs to
tired shoppers and shop employees. Something
was nagging at him, something he couldn't quite
place. He'd been without sleep more hours than he

cared to count, reminding him of certain missions he'd been on in the Army, and all he wanted was a chance to sit down somewhere quiet and think. There was something Densmore had said that bothered him, but he'd gone over the conversation again and again in his mind, and nothing had clicked. Still, it was there. He knew it—whatever "it" was.

Thursday was ticking to a close. Sarah had been at the Densmore estate only a little more than twenty-four hours—okay, closer to thirty hours, not that he was counting—but it felt as if days had passed since he'd talked to her, and the lack of contact was gnawing at him. Maybe that, rather than anything Densmore had actually said, was what bothered him. He was worried about her, he knew she was there, so he naturally associated his uneasiness with Densmore. Yeah, yeah, he knew the psychology. Too bad he didn't believe it.

He stopped a well-preserved woman, probably in her sixties, with that put-together look that shouted "money." "Excuse me, ma'am, but we're trying to locate this man. Do you recognize him?"

He'd try calling Sarah one more time, he thought. If he didn't get to talk to her, he would present himself at the gate and demand to be let in. He could say he had a warrant for her arrest. Something.

The woman took the photograph and briefly studied it, then handed it back to Cahill. "Why, yes, I do," she said coolly. "I believe it's my banker."

"Thank you," Cahill said automatically, biting back what he really wanted to say. Another

William Teller fan. Ha-ha. He was too tired for this shit—"Wait a minute. What did you say?"

Her eyebrows slightly lifted to suggest she was less than impressed with his attitude in particular and himself in general; she repeated, "I believe that's my banker. He has a certain distinction, a way of carrying himself. And of course there's the hair."

Cahill wasn't tired anymore. Adrenaline was surging through his system. "What's his name?"

"Trevor Densmore. He owns—"

Cahill didn't wait to hear what Trevor Densmore owned. He was running for the exit, his heart pounding in sheer terror as he dialed Wester. He burst into the night air and sprinted across the parking lot to the city Impala he was driving.

"I've got an ID," he barked into the phone when Wester answered. "Trevor Densmore. He's a banker. He has Sarah, God damn it. He has Sarah." He unlocked the car and got in, starting the motor and putting the transmission in drive before he had the door closed. The tires squealed on the asphalt as the car rocketed across the lot toward the exit.

"What do you mean, 'he has Sarah'?" Wester snapped.

"He hired her. She went to the estate yesterday afternoon, and I haven't been able to get in touch with her since. I'm on my way over there now."

"Doc, don't you go off half-cocked, God damn it! We have to do this right. I'll get a search warrant—"

"I talked to him on the phone this afternoon," Cahill snarled. "It's the same voice that's on the Lankford tape. I knew something was wrong, something bothered me about him, but I didn't fucking put it together." When he reached Highway 31, the light was red. He turned on his lights and bulled through the intersection, turning left toward I-459. He hit the on-ramp topping sixty miles an hour.

Wester was still talking when Cahill tossed the phone aside. If he got busted, he got busted. Nothing and no one was keeping him on the outside of that gray wall.

It all made sense now, the *why* that had eluded them and kept all the pieces from falling into place. The killings hadn't been about business, or revenge, or money. They had been about Sarah. He remembered her calling him weeks ago, before the first killing, telling him she'd received an anonymous gift in the mail. That was the bastard's first contact, the first sign of his obsession. Cahill hadn't given it much thought since then because that had been the only contact; there hadn't been any letters or phone calls that would normally signal a stalker's escalating obsession.

But Sarah had known, had sensed something was seriously wrong. She'd been trying to lure her unknown admirer into the open. When Judge Roberts was killed, her first thought was that her so-called stalker had done it.

And she'd been right.

First he'd tried to hire her away from the Judge. When that didn't work, he eliminated the obstacle and once more offered her a job. When she went to work for the Lankfords, he moved swiftly and took them out of the picture, making her once more available. This time there wouldn't be a small rush of job offers, the way there had been before; after all, who wanted to hire someone who appeared to be the kiss of death and was under suspicion herself for the murders? Trevor Densmore did, that's who. He wasn't worried about the murders. He had no reason to be.

All he wanted was Sarah. When the media was running wild after the Lankfords had been killed, saying Sarah had been arrested, Densmore had solved that little problem by immediately going out and killing someone else to prove she couldn't possibly be the killer. As soon as she was released, he made his move, and this time it had worked.

He had Sarah. Son of a bitch, *he had Sarah*.

There was an expression on his face, in his eyes, that made her shudder. He looked at her naked body and reached out, his hand sliding over her breast. Sarah said jerkily, "I can't wear the ring. Please take it off. It's already itching."

He stopped, lifting his hand as he blinked at her. "Of course! I'm so sorry; I merely wanted you to see it. I should have realized how sensitive your skin is." He slipped the ring off her finger and put it in his pocket. His eyes went dreamy again. "You're so perfect," he crooned, reaching out to touch her breast again, and Sarah cringed.

She had to stop him. She couldn't bear it if he kept touching her. She would rather he killed her than touch her.

Stalkers did that, when the object of their obsession didn't measure up to the fantasy they had built up in their minds. The obsession turned to rage and they struck out, destroying the person who had so painfully failed them by not adhering to the fiction.

She would drive him to that rage before she'd let him rape her. But he wasn't at that stage yet; because of her menses, she had a little time. She had no idea how long she could hold him off, but she would do it as long as possible. She knew Cahill; he would be knocking on the gate before long. It might be tomorrow morning, it might be tomorrow night, but he *would* be there. If she couldn't escape, then all she had to do was hold out, and keep Densmore at bay.

"I don't like to be touched," she said, shrinking away from his fingers as they tweaked her nipple. She made her voice innocent and distressed, the way he seemed to like.

He did that blinking thing again, really fast several times in a row, as if he were connecting with reality. He looked confused. "But . . . it's all right when I touch you. We're supposed to be together."

"I don't like being touched," she repeated. "It hurts. It hurts my skin."

He drew back, staring at her in consternation. "Oh, dear. I hadn't realized your skin is so sensitive. That's a problem I hadn't considered. But you aren't *allergic* to being touched; it's more of an acute sensitivity to being touched. Am I right? I'll be very gentle, my dear, and you'll gradually become accustomed to—"

Oh, *God*. She clenched her teeth. "No," she said, keeping her voice soft. "I'm sorry. It's a medical condition; it won't go away."

"A medical condition?" He had been reaching out to her again, but he paused, the dreaminess in his eyes morphing into something hard and ugly. "I've never heard of such a thing."

"You're right, it's an acute sensitivity. My nerve endings are permanently inflamed. I can tolerate clothing, if it's made from certain material, but I have to take pain medication even for that—" She was babbling and she didn't care if it made sense or not, so long as he believed it enough not to touch her again. "—and anti-inflammatories. I'm out of my anti-inflammatory medication. With everything that happened I was so upset I forgot to get my prescription refilled. Every time you touch me it feels as if you're burning me with a hot iron."

"Well, my word." That seemed to have stymied him. If he'd had a firmer grip on reality, it would never have worked, but he was so caught up in his fantasy world that he couldn't concentrate on anything else. "I certainly don't want to do anything that causes you pain." He smiled at her. "Unless you need to be punished, of course. But you'll never do anything to make me angry, will you? You'll iron my newspaper and prepare my breakfast for me, just the way you did for that old goat, Lowell Roberts."

"If you like," she managed, hurting inside at the thought of the poor Judge, of the Lankfords, and that other man this lunatic had killed.

"You'll take care of me," he crooned. "And I'll take care of you." He leaned down and pressed his mouth to her forehead.

Sarah gagged, and her control broke. "Don't touch me!" she screamed.

Like lightning his hand was on her throat, pressing hard, and he bent over so his face was close to hers. He was livid with rage. "Do not *ever* speak to me that way again," he ground out.

He was cutting off her air. She gagged again,

choking, frantically trying to think what to do. She'd pushed him too far; she had to hold him off but keep him as calm as possible until Cahill could get here. Surely he would be here soon. She could make it to morning. "I'm . . . sorry!" she managed to gasp. "Hurts."

His face was still red as he released her throat and stood. Desperately she sucked in deep breaths, fighting the darkness that had begun to edge her vision.

"You have to learn," he hissed, dragging his belt from his pant loops. "You must be disciplined until you learn proper behavior. You . . . do . . . *not* . . . speak to me . . . that way."

Sarah choked back another scream and tried to roll away as the belt whistled down.

Those fucking gates had to be twelve feet high; the wall was at least ten. He thought about ramming the gates with the car, but that would set off an alarm and warn the bastard he was coming. Cahill pulled the car as close to the wall as he could get it, then climbed on top of it. Standing on the roof of the car, he jumped and caught the top of the wall.

Pain seared his hands. The top of the wall was embedded with glass, or barbed wire. Something. He dropped back, took off his jacket, and tossed it so it draped over the wall. He jumped again, hoping the jacket would snag and stay in place instead of sliding to the ground. It did. He braced his bleeding hands on the jacket and hoisted himself the rest of the way up and over, landing on the grass and rolling. He came to his feet with coiled balance, and took his pistol from its holster. Then he set out across the wide expanse of lawn, toward the gray stone mansion that loomed in the night like a hulking beast.

A shrill beeping split the air. Densmore halted the belt in mid-swing, his head coming up. "I do believe we have company," he said mildly. "I wonder who it could possibly be. Excuse me, my dear."

Sarah choked, sobbing, as the door closed behind him. He'd wielded the belt with savage fury, raising bloody, stinging welts all along her back and sides. She'd managed to roll over, to protect her breasts and belly, but not before he'd hit her across the stomach at least twice. She was crying so hard she couldn't catch her breath, but as soon as the door closed she flipped onto her back.

One of the restraints holding her hands had come loose. She would never have been able to roll over if it hadn't, but her panicked lunge had pulled it free from the bed frame where he'd secured it. In his rage, Densmore hadn't noticed.

Her right hand was free, but the way the restraints were looped and crossed to restrict movement, she needed to reach under the bed to free her left hand—and with her legs bound she didn't have enough range of movement to do so. Ignoring the searing pain in her back, she jerked frantically against the nylon cord, hoping the one around her left hand would give, too.

It didn't.

There was a glass of water sitting on the bedside table. She grabbed the glass and slammed it against the edge of the table. Water splashed the bed, her bare flesh, and the fine crystal shattered, sending shards of glass flying. She was left clutching most of the base of the glass, her hand bleeding from a dozen tiny cuts. Frantically she began slicing at the nylon cords, not caring if she sliced skin, too. Her left hand jerked free, and she turned her attention to the cords binding her ankles.

When she was free, she bounded to her feet; her knees promptly gave way and she sprawled on the carpet. Cursing, sobbing, she stood again, and staggered toward the door. By the time she reached the hall, she was running.

That's when the first shot was fired. Then another.

Cahill.

Cahill was beyond caring about his job, about his own possible stay behind bars; by the time he reached the house, his only thought was of getting to Sarah. He didn't politely ring the doorbell, he put two forty-caliber bullets in the dead-bolt lock, then kicked the door open. He went in low, rolling across the floor, but the bastard was waiting for him, hidden in the darkness of the hallway.

The first shot barely missed Cahill's head. He fired at the muzzle flash, then the second shot caught him high on the chest, with a kick like a mule. He was wearing his body armor, but the impact knocked his breath out and he sprawled across the floor, unconscious.

"Cahill," she whispered, standing at the top of the stairs and staring down at the wide expanse of the foyer, and Cahill's body lying limp and unmoving on the granite floor.

She went numb. This wasn't happening. Not

Cahill. The bastard couldn't have taken Cahill from her, too.

She swayed, reaching out, and half stumbled against a gray metal floor lamp standing sentry beside a black enameled table.

Not Cahill.

The rage was a red tidal wave, rising in one massive surge and seizing her in its grip. She wasn't aware of pulling the floor lamp free from the plug. She wasn't aware of moving. She went down the stairs with a steady, purposeful stride, gaining speed as she went.

"*Densmore.*" That wasn't her voice. It sounded like something from *The Exorcist,* deep and raw. She reached the bottom of the stairs. "*You bastard, where are you?*"

There was movement to her right, in the shadows. She swung in that direction and saw Densmore materializing from the darkness into the dim light, like a phantom, a demon. His face was twisted with fury. "I told you not to speak to me that way," he hissed, his hand rising.

She didn't care. The rage suffusing her made the heavy floor lamp feel like nothing in her hands as she stepped forward, into the pistol, into the bullet, swinging the lamp like a baseball bat. If Cahill was dead, she simply didn't care anymore what happened. The explosion of the shot was deafening in the cavernous foyer, a blast of hot wind along her left side just as she slammed the base of the floor lamp into Densmore's skull. He crashed backward into the wall, a fine spray of blood flying from his head, his chest, and she swung the lamp again, and again, screaming wordlessly.

"Sarah! *Sarah!*"

The bellow finally pierced her consciousness. The lamp was suddenly too heavy to hold, and dropped from her nerveless fingers. Slowly, numbly, she turned as Cahill struggled to stand. He was holding a hand to his chest and wheezing, but she didn't see any blood.

"Easy, sweetheart," he said. "The son of a bitch can't die more than once."

EPILOGUE

CAHILL SLUNG HIS JACKET OVER HIS SHOULDER AS HE ENTERED the house. He was in a good mood; the review board had ruled the shooting a righteous one, and he was no longer on administrative leave. He'd missed doing his job, though for the first week he'd been glad enough to take it easy; even through body armor, a slug gave the body a beating and left a hell of a bruise. At first he thought it had cracked a couple of ribs, too, but they were just bruised—as if there were any "just" to it. He'd felt as if the mule had not only kicked him, it had then turned around and stomped on him.

He and Sarah had recuperated together. He was fine, and Sarah's mother had called to let her know that her father had indeed had a bad case of heart-burn, so she didn't have that to worry about. And physically Sarah was fine. She'd been living with him since they were released from the hospital early the next morning, after he'd been X-rayed and poked, and the cuts on his hands sutured. His wounds were simple in nature. Sarah though—

On the surface, she wasn't badly hurt. Some cuts on her hand, one requiring four stitches, but the others had been minor. The welts that striped her smooth skin and left raw, bleeding patches had been treated the way you'd treat a skinned knee, with cleaning and an antibiotic ointment over the worst patches. No matter how long he lived, he'd never forget the sight of her coming down those stairs, steady and unstoppable, naked and so covered with blood his heartbeat had faltered, but her eyes had glittered like black fire in her white face. She'd been carrying that heavy floor lamp in one hand, roaring for Densmore, and when the bastard started to shoot her, she hadn't paused, just waded in with that lamp like she was DiMaggio going for the long one. Cahill, struggling for breath, still woozy, was amazed he'd been able to make the shot. He'd barely missed Sarah, and the bullet had exploded Densmore's heart. Densmore had been dead before the lamp ever hit his skull, not that a little thing like that had stopped Sarah.

By the time Cahill could get to her, he could hear sirens as squad cars converged on the house. He'd have to open the gates for them, he thought, but right now he needed to take care of Sarah. He'd taken off his shirt and put it on her, and she'd just stood there staring down at Densmore and the hole in his chest. She'd turned then, her expression already growing remote as she said, "Damn you, Cahill; *I* wanted to kill him."

He'd wanted to hold her, but there wasn't any way he could put his arms around her without causing her pain. Instead he'd held her left hand, the one that wasn't cut, getting blood all over her from his own cuts. He'd moved the lamp aside, and been astonished at its weight. Most people would have needed two hands to lift it, much less swing it.

After he opened the gates, he and Sarah were carted off to the hospital, and since then he'd been on administrative leave, so he hadn't been involved in any of the investigation or mop-up. The other guys, though, had kept him informed.

Densmore had planned that Sarah wouldn't ever leave that room. They'd found tiny cameras everywhere, even in the bathroom. She'd have had no privacy at all. The room, like the house, was a fortress. Its windows were unbreakable, and didn't open. The door had been reinforced steel. The only reason Sarah had been able to escape that night was that, in his hurry to see about the intruder, Densmore had left the door unlocked.

Who knew what made a sick bastard like that tick? Everyone who knew him said he seemed like such a nice man—yeah, they always were—on the quiet side, a little shy, but a shark when it came to business. He did tend to become obsessed with little things, though, and could turn nasty if everything wasn't done to his satisfaction. According to his secretary, he'd gotten more obsessive over the years, to the point that she had to have her chair sitting in one precise spot or he went into a rant.

His personal papers had been more revealing. Evidently sweet, shy Trevor Densmore had killed his own father over a business disagreement. Why he'd document a thing like that was anyone's guess, since if he hadn't already been dead, it would have been one more nail in his coffin—Alabama was a death penalty state, and this would have been a death penalty case—but the department psychologist read the papers and said the contents were an almost perfect example of how the mind of an egomaniac worked. Trevor Densmore thought he was smarter than everyone else, better than everyone else, and deserved only the best. That was it in a simplistic nutshell: Densmore thought he should have whatever he wanted, and he had no internal brakes when it came to getting it. If there was an obstacle, he either moved it, or he destroyed it.

Evidently, when he'd seen Sarah on television, he'd developed an instant obsession with her—Cahill could kind of understand that, given his own feelings about her—and had set out to obtain her. When she refused his first offer out of loyalty to the Judge, he'd removed that obstacle by killing Judge Roberts. But she still hadn't accepted his offer; she'd gone to work for the Lankfords, which had enraged him because he thought the Lankfords were so far beneath him. Killing people meant no more to him than stepping on a bug; they were unimportant, nothing. What mattered was getting what he wanted.

Cahill wished he could kill the son of a bitch again. What he'd done to Sarah . . .

She'd been withdrawn since then, and he couldn't reach her, even though it had been over three weeks; the bruises and welts had faded and healed, the sutures had been removed, and they'd lived together under the same roof the entire time, but he couldn't reach her. She'd retreated to some-place inside herself where he couldn't go, and it was driving him crazy.

When he'd first seen her, naked and bloody, he'd taken a second kick to the chest, thinking Densmore had raped her. He'd asked her if that was so, before the first patrolman came in with weapon drawn, and she'd shaken her head. But the assault she'd suffered had bruised her inside, in her mind, and that hadn't healed.

It wasn't just the brutality of the beating, or coming face-to-face with death; it was everything, the accumulation of shock and grief and horror. She'd been helpless, in the control of a madman, and she couldn't forget it or get past it.

They hadn't slept together since then; she slept in one of the other bedrooms. At first he hadn't minded. They'd both been sore and wounded, and she hadn't been able to bear the slightest touch for several days. But now after three weeks, he definitely minded. He wanted her, he needed her, and he wanted to put their lives back together. Sarah had simply ignored everything he said.

"Sarah?" he called now, wanting to tell her the news about the inquest.

There was no answer, but the door to the basement stood open. He went down the stairs; the solid *thunk* of fists hitting the punching bag telling him she was working out some major hostility.

She was wearing gray sweatpants and a black sports bra, and she'd evidently been beating the hell out of the punching bag for quite a while, because her shoulders gleamed with sweat and the waistband of the sweatpants was dark. The expression on her face was grimly intent.

He leaned against the wall and watched her. There was still some pink discoloration showing the location of the newly healed stripes, but in a few months they would be completely gone. She'd lost some weight, a few pounds, making her sleek muscles a little more pronounced. She looked lean and fit, kind of like Linda Hamilton in *T2*, and he felt a serious hard-on growing.

She glanced over at him. "How did it go?"

"I'm off administrative leave. They ruled it a righteous shooting. I go back to work tomorrow."

"Good." She threw a flurry of punches that impressed him with their fury. He was glad she was taking it out on the punching bag and not on him.

He took a chance and said, "What about you?"

"When am I going back to work, do you mean?"

"Yeah."

"I don't know that I will, at least not for a while. And I don't know if I can find a position in this area again; I sort of have a bad rep with employers right now."

"Are you going to look for a job somewhere else?" he asked, as casually as possible, though his lungs felt as if they were decompressing.

"That depends."

"On what?"

She stopped punching the bag and mopped off her face and arms with a towel. "He took something from me," she said quietly. "He didn't have to rape me to do his damage. Every time I think of sex, I think of being helpless, and hating, and being so disgusted and repulsed I can barely breathe. I think of all the time I've put into my training, and when it came down to crunch time, it was totally useless. I was helpless against him."

"Not quite," he said. "You bashed his head in."

"That doesn't count. He was already dead." She gave him a feral smile. "But it felt good anyway."

"It damn sure did." He hadn't said it out loud

before, but the thought was there. "I enjoyed killing him."

The look in her eyes said she understood, and envied him the privilege.

"So where does this leave us?" he asked. With everything that had happened, that was still the most important question.

She walked up to him with a prowling, danger-ous, totally feminine rhythm that set his heart to racing. "That depends."

He felt like a broken record. "On what?" She was close enough now that he could smell her, sweaty and hot and all female. He was so hard he was hurting.

She slid her hands around his waist, and he felt the tug as she pulled his handcuffs free. "On you," she said, and for the first time in three weeks, she smiled. "Let's see if we still fit."

He lay on the exercise mat, his arms stretched over his head and handcuffed to a pipe. He was naked, and sweating, and so desperate he was beg-ging. The woman was killing him.

She was in no hurry. She sat astride him, but she wasn't riding him. She had tucked him in, slid down to the hilt, then just sat there. At first he wondered what she was doing, and then he'd known; he'd felt her internal muscles clenching him, releasing, clenching, milking him while she sat virtually motionless. The sensation had been electric, and maddening, taking him to the edge of orgasm without pushing him over.

She'd already come twice. The first time had seemed to take her by surprise as she convulsed around him, but she'd determinedly chased the second one. By then he'd been begging, dying to thrust, but every time his hips moved she stopped.

God, she was something. Just looking at her made his heart feel like bursting. She was magnificent, naked and totally given over to what she was doing, her head thrown back and her eyes half-closed, her nipples red and tight. Surely by now she had all the bad memories replaced with good ones, but if she hadn't, Lord, he'd die happy.

She leaned over and kissed him, her mouth hot, her tongue promising wild things. "We still fit," she murmured.

"I never doubted it," he managed to say, but the words ended in a groan.

"I did, but I couldn't let him win. You're too important to me, Cahill. I had to make certain I could push him away."

"Did you? Is he gone?"

She rotated her hips. "Oh, yeah."

"Then for God's sake," he whimpered, "put me out of my misery."

To his everlasting relief, she did. When he could think and hear and speak again, she was lying propped on her elbow beside him, leisurely stroking his chest.

"I love you, Cahill," she said seriously.

"I love you, too, and don't you think it's about time you started calling me Tom?"

"I'll think about it. Maybe on our fifth anniversary."

Now, that sounded good. "When's our first one going to be?" he asked as casually as possible.

"Hmm, let me see. What do you think about July of next year?"

Since they were now in the last week of May, it sounded fine.

She stretched above him, unlocking the cuffs; as soon as he was free, he rolled, tucking her beneath him. She tensed for just a moment, then relaxed beneath his weight, her hands sliding up his back. "I thought he'd killed you," she whispered fiercely, burying her face in his shoulder. "I hate him for what he's done to our lives, for the damage he did to so many lives."

"He wins only if we let him, sweetheart." He kissed her, slowly, lingering. "Did you mean it, or was I reading more into your answer than I should? Are you going to marry me?"

"Oh, yeah," she said, grinning. "At least he clarified that issue for me. When I thought you were dead, I knew that nothing was more important than loving you: not traveling the world, not even if he shot me, too. I got over being mad at you in a hurry."

"I'm not going to make a practice of getting shot every time you get mad at me," he muttered.

"You won't have to, sweetheart." She kissed his shoulder and snuggled against him. "You won't have to."

Read on for a taste of

CRY NO MORE
by Linda Howard

Available in hardcover
from Ballantine Books
in November 2003

Mexico, 1993

Milla had fallen asleep while the baby was nursing. David Boone stood over his wife and child and watched them, aware of the silly grin on his face, of the fullness in his chest. His wife. His child.

God, his world.

The old fascination, the obsession, with medicine remained, but it was tempered now by something equally fascinating. He'd never suspected that the process of pregnancy and childbirth, of the rapid development of the infant, could be so engrossing. He'd chosen the field of surgery because of the sheer challenge of it; obstetrics, in comparison, had seemed kind of like watching grass grow. Well, sometimes things went wrong and the doctor had to be on top of things, but for the most part babies grew and were born, and that was that.

He'd thought that until it came to his own child. Clinically he'd known every detail of the fetal growth, but he hadn't been prepared for the sheer emotion of watching Milla round out, of feeling the small kicks and flutters of the baby grow into stronger, more demanding ones. And if the sheer emotionalism had blind-sided him, how had Milla felt? Sometimes, even during the physical misery of the last month of pregnancy, he'd caught an expression on her face, a rapt, absorbed look as she unconsciously stroked her belly, that told him she was lost in a world inhabited only by herself and the baby.

And then Justin had arrived, squalling and healthy, and David had felt light-headed with relief and euphoria. In the six weeks since, each day seemed to bring some small change as the infant grew: the dark fuzz on his head had become blond; his eyes were more blue and alert. He was noticing things, recognizing voices, waving his arms and legs in a jerky, uncoordinated rhythm as his little muscles grew in strength. He loved his bath. He had an angry cry, a hungry cry, an uncomfortable cry, and a cranky cry. Milla had been able to tell the difference within days.

The changes in his wife were fascinating, too. Milla had always had a way of holding herself apart from the world, as if she were more of an observer than a participant. She'd been a challenge from the moment he'd first seen her, but he had stubbornly courted her until she couldn't help but notice him as a person rather than moving scenery. He could remember perfectly the exact moment when he'd won: they had been at a New Year's Eve party and in the middle of all the laughter and drinking and general silliness, Milla had looked at him and blinked, a faintly startled expression crossing her face as if he had suddenly come into focus. That was it; no hot kiss, no heartfelt exchanges in the night, just a sudden clarity in her gaze as she finally, truly saw him. Then she smiled and took his hand, and with that simple touch they were linked.

Amazing.

Okay, it was also amazing that he'd surfaced from his studies and work long enough to notice her at one of the deadly dull staff parties his professor parents often hosted, but once he had, he couldn't get her face out of his mind. She wasn't beautiful; maybe she barely qualified as pretty. But there was something about her, in the strong, clean lines of her face and the way she walked, an almost gliding stride that made him think maybe her feet didn't quite touch the ground, that had kept consciousness of her nagging at him like a persistent mosquito.

Learning about her had fascinated him. He liked knowing

that her favorite color was green, that she didn't want pep-peroni on her pizza, that she enjoyed action movies and, thank God, yawned at the idea of chick flicks, which was surprising because she was so essentially feminine. As she explained it, she already knew about woman stuff so why would she want to watch more of the same? Trivial stuff, mostly. But he was beguiled by her serenity; if she had a temper, he'd never seen it. She was the most evenly balanced person he'd ever met, and even after two years of marriage he still couldn't quite believe his luck.

She yawned and stretched, the move popping her nipple out of the baby's slack mouth. The baby grunted and made a few sucking motions, then was still. Fascinated, David reached out and stroked one gentle finger over the plump mound of her bare breast. He admitted it; he was delighted with the new size of her breasts. Prepregnancy, Milla's shape had been lean, like a long-distance runner. Now she was rounder, softer, and the postbirth moratorium on sex was driving him crazy. He couldn't wait until tomorrow, when she had her six-week checkup from Susanna Kosper, the team's ob-gyn. Actually, because of a couple of emergencies that played havoc with Susanna's schedule, it was almost seven weeks now and he was close to howling at the moon. Jerking off relieved the tension but was a long way from being as satisfying as making love to his wife.

She opened her eyes and drowsily smiled at him. "Hey, Doogie," she murmured. "Thinking about tomorrow night?"

He laughed, both at the nickname and how she'd read his mind—not that reading his mind was any great feat. He'd had little else besides sex on the brain for two months now. "Nothing else."

"Maybe Doogie Jr. will sleep all night." She stroked a gentle hand over the baby's fuzzy head, and he responded by making more sucking motions with his mouth. Si-multaneously they both said, "I doubt it," and David laughed again. Justin had a voracious appetite; he wanted feeding at least every two hours. Milla had been concerned that her breast milk wasn't rich enough, or that she didn't have enough, but Justin was clearly thriving and Susanna said there was nothing to worry about, the baby was just a pig.

Milla yawned again, and, concerned, David touched her cheek. "Just because Susanna will give you the all-clear tomorrow doesn't mean we have to make love. If you're too tired, we can wait." Susanna had made damn certain he understood how exhausted a new mother was, especially if she was breast-feeding.

Interrupted in midyawn, Milla glared at him. "Oh, yes, we do," she said fiercely. "If you think I'm going to wait another minute—Justin will be lucky if I don't leave him with Susanna while I hunt you down at the clinic."

"Gonna hold a scalpel on me and make me strip?" he asked, grinning.

"It's a thought." She caught his hand and pulled it to her breast again, rubbing her nipple against his fingers. "It's been over six weeks. We don't have to wait for Susanna's official okay."

He wanted to go with that idea. It had, in fact, occurred to him before, but he hadn't wanted Milla to think that all he cared about was sex. He was relieved she had brought up the idea first, and temptation gnawed at him. He glanced at his wristwatch and the time made him groan. "I have to be at the clinic in ten minutes." Already people would be lining up outside the clinic doors, patiently waiting hours to see a doctor. He was the team surgeon, and in fact had a surgery scheduled in half an hour. He barely had enough time to get to the clinic, change, and get scrubbed. Not that he'd need more than ten seconds to climax, the way he felt, but Milla definitely needed more time than that.

"Tonight, then," Milla said, turning on her side and smiling at him. "I'll keep Justin awake as much as possible so he'll sleep."

"Good plan." He stood and reached for his keys. "What are you doing today?"

"Nothing much. I'm going to the market this morning before it gets so hot."

"Get some oranges." He'd been on an orange kick lately, as if his body craved the vitamin C. He'd been spending long hours in surgery, so maybe he did. He leaned down and kissed Milla, then brushed his lips against Justin's satiny cheek. "Take good care of Mommy," he told his sleeping son, and hurried out the door.

Milla stayed in bed a few more minutes, luxuriating in the peace and quiet. Right this moment, no one was wanting anything of her. She thought she'd been prepared to care for a baby, but somehow she hadn't realized it was practically nonstop. When Justin wasn't needing to be fed or changed, she was rushing around trying to stay abreast of all the other chores, and she was so tired that every step was like slogging through water. She hadn't had a good night's sleep in what felt like months. No, it had been months; about four of them, since the growing baby had gotten large enough to press on her bladder and she'd had to pee practically every half hour. She had carried him low, which Susanna said made it easier to breathe, but the trade-off was peeing a lot. Being a mother was anything but glamorous; rewarding, but definitely not glamorous.

She knew she was beaming as she examined her sleeping son. He was so gorgeous; everyone said so, exclaiming at his blond hair and blue eyes and the sweetness of his mouth. He looked like the Gerber baby, that idealized, big-eyed infant whose image graced millions of baby care items. Milla was entranced by everything about him, from the tiny fingernails to the dimples that were forming as he gained weight. She could just sit and watch him all day long . . . if she didn't have so much else to do.

Immediately her mind switched into work mode as she remembered everything that needed to be done today, such as laundry, cleaning, cooking, and, whenever she had a spare moment to sit down, catching up on the clinic's paperwork. And some time today she needed to take care of girly things like washing her hair and shaving her legs, because she had a hot date with her husband tonight. She would never get tired of being a mother, but she was definitely ready to be something else, too, like a sexually desirable woman. She missed sex; David made love with the same total concentration he gave to everything that interested him, which was very nice when one was the recipient of said concentration. Actually, it was better than nice. It was pretty damn wonderful.

First, though, she would go to the market, before the day got too hot.

Only two more months here, she thought. She would miss Mexico: the people, the sunshine, the slowness of time. The year David and his colleagues had donated to the free-care clinic was almost over; then it would be back to the rat race of practicing medicine in the States. Not that she wouldn't be glad to be home, back with family and friends and such niceties as an air-conditioned supermarket. She wanted to do things like take Justin for walks in the park, or visit with her mom during the day. She had missed her mother a lot during the long months of her pregnancy, and sporadic phone calls plus one quick visit home just hadn't filled the need.

She had almost decided not to come to Mexico with David; she found out she was pregnant just before they were scheduled to leave. But she hadn't wanted to spend such a long time away from him, especially while she was carrying their first child. After meeting Susanna, the ob-gyn part of the medical team, she had decided to stick to their original plan. Her mother had been horrified—her grandchild would be born in another country!—but the pregnancy had gone by the book, without any medical problems arising. Justin had arrived almost on time, just two days past her due date, and since then Milla felt as if she had existed in a fog composed of equal parts love and fatigue.

This was such a polar opposite to how she had imagined her life would be that she couldn't help but feel amused. Armed with her grand liberal arts degree, she had planned to change the world, one person at a time. She would be the kind of teacher people remembered when they themselves were grandparents, the kind of teacher who made a real difference in her students' lives. She was comfortable in academia, even the highly political side of it; she had planned to continue her education until she received her doctorate, then teach at a university. Marriage—yes, after a while. Maybe when she was thirty or thirty-five. Children—maybe.

Instead she had met David, a wunderkind of medicine. He was the son of her history professor, and when she became the professor's student assistant, she learned all about him. David's IQ was way above genius level; he'd finished high school at fourteen, college at seventeen, blew through medical school, and was already a practicing surgeon at the age of twenty-five when she met him. She'd expected him to be either an arrogant know-it-all —with some justification—or a total egghead.

He was neither. Instead he was a good-looking young man whose face was often lined with exhaustion from long hours in surgery, added to a bottomless need for more knowledge that kept him poring over medical books long after he should have been asleep. His smile was sweet and sexy, his blue eyes full of good humor, his blond hair usually shaggy and disordered. He was tall, which she liked, since she was five-seven and liked to wear high heels. Actually, she liked everything about him, and when he asked her out she hadn't hesitated at all.

Still, she'd been surprised, at a New Year's Eve party, to catch him staring at her with dark, potent desire in his eyes. Realization had hit her like a blow to the stomach, as if Joshua had blown his horn and all the walls had come tumbling down. David loved her, and she loved him. It was that simple.

She had become his wife at twenty-one, as soon as she got her degree, and now at twenty-three she was a mother. She didn't regret a minute of it. She still planned to teach, when they returned to the States, and she still planned to further her education, but she wouldn't undo a single decision that had led to the small miracle that was her son. From the moment she'd realized she was pregnant, she'd been consumed by the process, and so in love with the baby that she felt as if she were lit from the inside with a powerful, incandescent glow. That feeling was even stronger now, to the point that she felt the tug between her and Justin if he were just in the next room sleeping. No matter how tired she was, she reveled in that connection.

She got out of bed and carefully placed the pillows around the baby, even though he couldn't yet roll over. He didn't move while she quickly washed and dragged a brush through her short, curly hair, then dressed in one of the loose sundresses she had brought specifically to wear after giving birth. She was still fifteen pounds heavier than she'd been before getting pregnant, but the extra weight didn't bother her . . . much. She kind of liked the motherly softness, and David certainly liked the way her breasts had expanded from a B cup to a D.

She thought of the coming night and shivered with anticipation. A week ago David had brought home a box of condoms from the clinic, and the mere presence of the box had made them both a little crazy. They had used condoms for a short while when they first became lovers, then she had been on birth control pills until they had decided to have a baby. Having to use the condoms again made her feel as if it was the first time all over again, when they were in a frenzy to have each other and everything was so new and intense and scary.

Justin began squirming a little, his mouth pursing as if searching for her breast. His blue eyes opened, his tiny fists began waving, and he made the grunting sound that preceded his "I'm wet, change me" cry. Pulled from a daydream about making love with his daddy, Milla got a clean diaper and bent over him, cooing as she changed him. He managed to focus his gaze on her face, and he stared at her as if nothing else existed in his universe, his mouth open with delight, his arms and legs pumping.

"There's mommy's baby," she crooned as she lifted him. As soon as she settled him in the crook of her arm he began rooting at her breast. "Make that mommy's pig," she amended, sitting down and unbuttoning the front of her dress. Her breasts tingled in response, and she sighed with pure pleasure as the baby latched on to her nipple and began sucking. Gently she rocked back and forth, playing with his fingers and toes as he nursed. Her eyes closed dreamily, and she hummed a lullaby, drifting in the moment. She could do without the dirty diapers and loss of sleep, but she loved this part of being a mother. When she held him like this, nothing else mattered.

He finished nursing, and she put him down again while she grabbed a quick bite of breakfast. After brushing her teeth, she draped a blue denim sling over her head and put the baby in it. He settled down with his head resting where he could hear her heartbeat, his blue eyes already drooping shut as he dozed. Grabbing a hat and a basket, with money in her pocket, she set out for the market.

The walk was only about half a mile. The bright morning sun promised to deliver scorching heat by midday, but for now the air was cool and dry, and the small village open-air market was busy with early shoppers. There were oranges and brightly colored peppers, bananas and melons, yellow onions on strings. Milla browsed, occasionally chatting with some of the village women as they stopped to admire the baby, taking her time in picking out the produce she wanted.

Justin was curled in the ball shape of the very young, his legs still automatically drawing up in his prebirth position. She held her hat so it shielded him from the sun. A soft, pleasant breeze played in her short, light brown curls and lifted the baby's wispy blond fuzz. He stirred, his rosebud mouth making sucking motions. Milla set down her basket and patted his tiny back, and he lapsed back into sleep.

She stopped at a display of fruit and began carrying on an

animated, if fractured, conversation with the old woman behind the stacks of oranges and melons. Her understanding was better than her speech, but she managed to make herself understood. She used her free hand to point to the oranges she wanted.

She didn't see them coming. Suddenly two men were bracketing her, their body heat and odor assailing her. Instinctively she started to step back, only to find herself blocked by their bodies closing in on her. The one on the right pulled a knife from the sheath at his waist and grasped the straps of the sling, hastily slicing through them before Milla could do more than give a startled cry. Time seemed to stutter, giving her freeze-frame impressions of the next few seconds. The old woman fell back, her expression alarmed. Milla felt the sling that held Justin to her begin to drop, and in panic she grabbed for her baby. The man on her left snatched the baby from her with one hand, and shoved at her with the other.

Somehow she kept her balance, terror twisting in her chest as she leaped at the man, screaming, fighting to wrest her baby from him. Her clawing nails scratched down his face, leaving bloody furrows, and he reeled back from the assault.

The baby, startled awake, was wailing. The milling crowd scattered, alarmed by the sudden violence. "Help!" she shrieked over and over as she tried to grab Justin, but everyone seemed to be running away from her rather than to her. The man tried to shove her away again, his hand on her face. Milla bit him, sinking her teeth into his hand and grinding down until she felt blood in her mouth and he was yelling in pain. She clawed for his eyes, her nails sinking into spongy softness. His yells turned into shocked bellows, and his grip on Justin loosened. Desperately she grabbed at the baby, managing to catch one tiny, flailing arm, and for one heart-bursting moment she thought she had him. Then she felt the other man moving in close behind her, and a searing, paralyzing pain shot through her back.

Her body convulsed and she dropped like a rock to the ground, her fingers scrabbling helplessly in the grit. The two men raced away, one carrying the baby like a football under the arm and holding a bloody hand over his face, screaming curses as he fled. Milla lay sprawled in the dirt as she tried to fight through the agony that gripped her body, fight for breath to scream. Her lungs pumped wildly but didn't seem to be dragging in any air. She tried to get up; her body didn't respond. A black veil began closing over her vision, and she managed to whimper, over and over, "My baby! My baby! Someone get my baby!"

No one did.

David had already repaired a hernia and was washing up while Rip Kosper, Susanna's husband and the team anaesthesiologist, did a final check of the patient's blood pressure and heart rate to make sure he was okay before turning him over to Anneli Lansky, the nurse, for monitoring. They had a good group working here; he'd miss them when the year was up and they all returned to regular practice in the States. He wouldn't miss the cramped, one-story concrete-block clinic, with its cracked tile floors and barely adequate equipment, but he'd definitely miss the group as well as his patients—and he'd miss Mexico itself.

He was thinking about the next case, a gall bladder, when he heard a commotion in the hallway just outside the door. There was shouting and cursing, some scuffling sounds, and high-pitched wails. He dried his hands and started for the door just as Juana Mendoza, another nurse, began yelling for him.

He hit the door, already running, and skidded to a halt in the hallway before he rammed into a knot of people that included Juana, Susanna Kosper, and two men and a woman who were clumsily carrying another woman. The crush of bodies hid the wounded woman's face, but David could see that her dress was drenched with blood and he immediately switched into emergency mode. "What happened?"

he asked as he kicked a box out of the way and dragged over a gurney.

"David." Susanna's voice was tight and sharp. "It's Milla."

For a moment the words didn't make sense, and he looked around, expecting to see his wife behind him. Then Susanna's meaning kicked in, and he saw the wounded woman's unconscious, paper-white face, saw the froth of soft brown curls around her face, and everything tilted out of kilter. Milla? This couldn't be Milla. She was at home with Justin, safe and sound. This woman who looked as if she'd bled out just resembled his wife, that was all. It wasn't really Milla.

"David!" This time Susanna's tone was even sharper. "Snap out of it! Help us get her on the gurney."

Only his training enabled him to function, to step in and lift the woman who looked like Milla onto the gurney. Her dress was bloody, her arms and hands were bloody, her legs and feet and even her shoes were bloody. No—just one shoe, a sandal that looked just like a pair Milla often wore. He saw the pink nail polish on her toenails and the delicate gold chain around her right ankle, and he felt as if all his insides caved in.

"What happened?" he asked, his voice hoarse and far away and not his own, even as his body moved into action and they rapidly wheeled Milla into the surgical bay he had just left.

"Knife wound to the lower back," Juana said, listening to the babble of voices around them before they closed the door and shut out most of the noise. "Two men attacked her at the market." She caught a shuddering breath. "They took Justin. Milla fought them, and one of the men stabbed her."

Rip, alerted by the hubbub, burst back into the room. "My God," he blurted when he saw Milla, then he fell silent and began readying his equipment.

Justin! David reeled from the second shock, and he half-turned toward the door. Two bastards had stolen his son! He actually took a step away from the gurney, toward the door, to race out and search for his baby. Then he hesitated, and looked back at his wife.

They didn't have time to clean the operating room or restock the supplies. Anneli ran in and began grabbing what they'd need. Juana wrapped a blood pressure cuff around Milla's limp arm and swiftly pumped it up, while Susanna used the shears to cut away Milla's clothing. "Blood type O positive," Susanna was saying. How did she know? Oh, yeah, she'd typed Milla's blood before Justin's delivery.

"Sixty over forty," Juana reported. Moving so fast her actions were a blur, she started an IV line in Milla's arm and hooked up a bag of blood plasma.

He was losing her, David thought. Milla was dying right in front of him, unless he snapped out of his shock and acted. From the position of the wound, the knife had probably hit her left kidney, and God knows what other damage had been done. She was bleeding out; she had only a few minutes left before her internal organs began shutting down —

He pushed everything else out of his mind and shoved his hands into the fresh pair of gloves Anneli held out for him. He didn't have time to scrub up, he didn't have time to search for Justin; all he had time to do was reach for the scalpel that was promptly slapped into his palm and call on every ounce of skill he had. He prayed, he cursed, and he fought time as he cut into his wife's body. As he'd suspected, the knife blade had hit her left kidney. Hit it, hell, it had all but sliced the organ in half. There was no saving the kidney, and if he didn't get it out and the blood vessels tied off in record time, there would be no saving Milla, either.

It was a race, savage and merciless. If he made one misstep, if he hesitated, if anything was dropped or even fumbled, then he lost, and Milla lost. It wasn't surgery as he was accustomed to doing it; it was battlefield surgery, fast and brutal, with her life hanging on every split-second decision and action. While they poured all of their available blood into her, he fought to keep it from pouring out of her just as fast as it went in. Moment by moment he stemmed the bleeding, searched out every severed vessel, and slowly he began to win the race. He didn't know how long it took; he never asked, never found out. How long didn't matter. All that mattered was winning, because the alternative was more than he could bear.